OSCAR DIGGS
The Wizard of Oz

Scott B. Blanke

Black Rose Writing | Texas

©2021 by Scott B. Blanke
All rights reserved. No part of this book may be reproduced, stored in a retrieval system or transmitted in any form or by any means without the prior written permission of the publishers, except by a reviewer who may quote brief passages in a review to be printed in a newspaper, magazine or journal.

The author grants the final approval for this literary material.

First printing

This is a work of fiction. Names, characters, businesses, places, events, and incidents are either the products of the author's imagination or used in a fictitious manner. Any resemblance to actual persons, living or dead, or actual events is purely coincidental.

ISBN: 978-1-68433-844-3
PUBLISHED BY BLACK ROSE WRITING
www.blackrosewriting.com

Printed in the United States of America
Suggested Retail Price (SRP) $19.95

Oscar Diggs, The Wizard of Oz is printed in Baskerville

*As a planet-friendly publisher, Black Rose Writing does its best to eliminate unnecessary waste to reduce paper usage and energy costs, while never compromising the reading experience. As a result, the final word count vs. page count may not meet common expectations.

Oz Acknowledgments

To paraphrase Robert Frost, two yellow brick roads diverged in a classic L. Frank Baum novel, and I took the less traveled one. After the original 28 Oz classics were written, dozens of similar novels followed from amazing writers such as Roger Baum, Donald Abbotts, Rachel Cosgrove Payes, Eric Shanower, and others. Then an unfamiliar look at Oz came from Gregory Maguire with '*Wicked*' and Danielle Paige's '*Dorothy Must Die*' series. Standing on the shoulders of these brilliant authors, I am taking a fresh, somewhat humorous, look at the classic origin of the *Wonderful Wizard of Oz*.

    Many people helped with the writing of this novel. First there were my two great writing groups, Mississippi Valley Writers Guild and La Crosse Area Writers Guild. They listened week after week to each chapter and gave corrections and support. They encouraged me to keep going. Another support group was my Facebook Oz groups. So many Oz collectors and readers. Special thanks to a great Oz author, Marcus Mebes, my first beta editor. A gentleman who really knows his Oz. Of course, I would like to give thanks to my Black Rose Writing family and Mr. Reagan Rothe, he helped walk a beginning author through the editing process. Finally, foremost, I wish to give special thanks to my wonderful author wife, Heidi, who put up with my constant spelling, grammar, and just plain what do I do now questions. She not only supported me but didn't kill me after a thousand stupid computer questions.

Chapter One

"Keep your eye on the lady. Find her and win one dollar," pitched Oscar Diggs as he showed the crowd the Queen of Hearts and the two black aces. "Only a three-cent piece to play. Win more in '64. Use your winnings to help beat those damn Rebs." He swiftly mixed the tattered, creased, and dirty cards, put them face down next to one another on a large old handkerchief. The bandana, held down by four rocks on the corners, covered a splintery, wobbly, wooden table.

Diggs lifted the center card and showed the Queen. "See? It's easy. Come one come all and win." He smiled at the group, his face etched with multiple laugh lines. The rotund, short man exposed the other two cards and revealed that they were the two black aces. He quickly reshuffled the three cards and put them face down again.

A thin yellow-skinned man stepped forward and plunked down a three-cent piece. He was a full head taller and several years younger than most of the crowd. As he bent down to look at the cards, his long black braid swung forward and brushed the legs of the rickety small card table. "Ah, so, I want to win. It must be that card." He pointed to the right-hand one with a long nicotine-stained finger, the pointed fingernail encrusted with dirt. The man tugged at his black tunic, straightened up, and smiled.

Diggs turned over the right card and revealed the Queen of Hearts. "A winner!" he bellowed. "See how easy it is?" Diggs quickly handed over an old, worn silver dollar to the winner. As he straightened up, he winked at the Chinese man.

The rail-thin man melted back into the crowd as multiple workers surged forward with their three-cent pieces. The group appeared to be coming from their jobs, carrying lunchpails, pickaxes, and shovels. They were filthy and coarsely dressed, while an occasional one wore a hard hat. The younger men usually suffered war wounds, missing arms, or limped. There were no further winners. After one hour, the crowd started muttering about the lack of payouts.

A police officer rushed up, displaying his badge. His hat slipped over his eyes as he came running up. "Be off with you all before I run everyone in. Diggs, you'll be coming with me. You know the streets of New York don't allow three-card Monte. Tis a night in jail and you'll stand before the judge in the morning."

The cop pushed his headpiece back, adjusted the strap, and then walked up to Diggs. The officer pinned his badge back onto his chest, took his nightstick off his belt, and swung the stick back and forth. He then tapped it into his left hand and glared at the group.

The crowd disappeared faster than blocks of Hudson River winter ice put in boiling water. The cop faced Diggs, shoved his baton back through his belt, and pulled out a pair of rusty handcuffs from a large front pocket of his coat. "I'll be taking you in now, Diggs." He reached for the short, chubby card dealer with his other hand.

"Sure you will, Patrick. And if you do, how will you get your daily gratuity for letting me work?" Diggs reached into his now-bulging pocket and he poured ten coins in the police officer's outstretched hand. The removal didn't make a dent in how much the front pocket sagged.

"You must have had a good day, Oscar. This is more than usual." The cop carefully counted the coins before putting them and the handcuffs into his huge front coat pocket. Patrick pushed his nightstick into the side of his belt, where it rattled against one of the big brass buttons of his coat. The buttons strained to close his heavy coat over the enormous belly.

"Yes, the count really picked up," said Diggs. "It usually does after Woe works the marks with our initial performance." He smiled at the bustling crowds of the upper West Side. "This was a good place to set up. Most of the men had jobs and were already back from the war. This early, cold, fall weather, luckily didn't keep people away. It's too bad we won't be able to use this location again for months. We'll have to move soon." He frowned and shook his head. "Unfortunately, I am getting too well known in this part of Manhattan and I've already been run out of the Bronx and Brooklyn by honest cops."

"You be watching your mouth, or I'll run you out too. A man has to survive on his pitiful police salary. These small gifts help." Patrick jingled the coins in his pocket.

"You seem to be surviving fairly well." Diggs glanced at the cop's belly.

"Moving to a new spot is a good idea. The men would probably have strung ye up in another couple of minutes." Patrick looked around for any irate stragglers. "Where's your partner, Chang Wang Woe?"

"He'll be back soon," said Diggs. "I don't know how he does it, but he always senses when the game is finished." He peered around for Woe with near-sighted eyes. "Then he comes to help me clean up, and more importantly, give me back our only dollar. Best associate I ever had."

"True, but I still don't kin how these marks fall for your con each time," said Patrick. "Tell me, how do you get away with it?" The cop gestured at the three cards.

Diggs picked up the center card and showed the cop the Queen of Hearts. "Want to bet your take against the rest of my daily winnings, you can find the lady?" He raised his eyebrows.

"Do you take me for a fool? I'm not a mog and even if I were drunk, I wouldn't play against you." The cop mockingly shook his fist at Diggs. "But I'll be asking, how do you win?"

"Calm down, Patrick, I don't think you are stupid or tipsy. Just this once, I'll show you the trick. You can't find the Queen if she was never there." Diggs picked all three cards and showed two aces of spades and one ace of clubs. He then shook his sleeve and the Queen of Hearts slid out into his hand. "See, the hand is quicker than the eye. Someday, I am going to try something with a rabbit or maybe several guinea pigs to make them disappear."

Diggs picked up the cards, flattened them out to get rid of the multiple creases and folds, and placed them into the pocket in his coat. The threadbare, oversized, long coat was grimy and loose on his short, pudgy body. He tipped his battered top hat towards the officer and said, "It's been a pleasure doing business with you, as always. See you tomorrow?" A gust of wind blew his sparse, mousy brown hairs around on his bald head. "Glad we had no puffs like this before, or my cards would have blown away. That's why I always use the rocks to hold down my handkerchief." He quickly put his hat back on and shivered.

"Yes, I'll find you. But it be the Lord's Day, and should you be working? I'll be at Mass myself and won't be around 'til afternoon. Where will you be setting up to work your tools?" The cop stroked his handlebar mustache.

"I'm not partaking in religious practices myself tomorrow, and Woe certainly won't. I'm going to set up on the east side of Central Park. Hopefully, any rich society personages going to the new zoo will wish to partake in my game. I'll be there bright and early if I don't freeze first." Diggs shivered again and clapped his hands together. "This wind is picking up, and it's now so frigid, I can barely feel my fingers."

"I'll look for you since it is my day off. You won't be on my beat, so I might have to split the sweetener with my friend Clancy."

"I hope I make enough honey in my new location. This cold weather might keep people away." Diggs wrapped his arms around himself.

"Yep, just beginning November and already freezing my arse off. I hope this cold doesn't hurt our boys in the War. I'm surprised you aren't fighting for the union. Myself, I am too old and slightly out of shape." Patrick patted his beer gut. Then he pretended to wheeze dramatically. "I hope it's not tuberculosis."

"No, probably all those stogeys you smoke. Now don't tell anyone, but I'm actually a southerner. Born in Selma, Alabama. Had to work for years to get rid of my southern drawl." Diggs bowed deeply and removed his hat with a flourish. "Honored sir, you all." He straightened up and grinned. "I moved here to New York in '58. I've always hated slavery. Also, I couldn't make a living with my prestidigitation in Selma. My marks couldn't even try to follow the cards. Confused them too much."

"Prestidigi what shune? Begora, you really don't have any strong southern accent. You sound just like me."

"Sure, I sound just like an Irishman. Prestidigitation is magic, my good man. It is known as sleight of hand." Diggs pulled ten knotted scarves from out of the cop's huge front pocket and handed him back his baton.

Patrick first checked that his handcuffs, underdrawers, and compensation were still present and then asked, "How did you do that?"

"A magician rarely reveals his tricks." Diggs stuffed the scarves into a second inside pocket and patted all his other pockets to make sure they still accounted for all his supplies. He quickly cleared his rocks and handkerchief off his small, rickety table. He bent down and put the items into a worn carpet bag, previously stowed under the table.

"Yep, a good trick," said the copper. "I'll see you late tomorrow. Make sure you have something more to give me than scarves and my nightstick back. Now I be going home to my gaff. Are you off?"

"Yes, as soon as Woe returns," said Diggs. "We'll be heading home to our gaff, err, house." He picked up the small table. The wind tried to tear it from his hands.

The cop ambled off and Diggs thought about his long walk home. Not a home, just a run-down rear tenement house. He looked up and saw Woe in the distance.

Woe ran from around a row of tenement buildings up to Diggs and anxiously said, "If you have any brains, head for the proverbial hills, Master Diggs. Your less than satisfied customers are coming this way. They do not look happy." Woe pointed, and his hand shook. "Most of them are carrying pick-axes or clubs, but one even has a musket."

"Retreat!" yelled Diggs.

Chapter Two

Chang Woe grabbed Diggs' heavy satchel and ran through the streets. Diggs followed behind, carefully carrying the small wooden table just above his black top hat. Even with the tall hat, Diggs only came up to Woe's nose. Diggs stumbled over the cobblestones as he ran. Woe ran effortlessly but often had to stop, look back, and encourage Diggs to move quicker.

They wove through the streets, dodging horses, hansom cabs, and heavy four-wheeled wagons. Accumulations of manure from horses filled deep cracks in the street. The two men weaved around dead dogs, rats, and piles of refuse. They ran through pools of stagnant water and urine from clogged sewer drains. The odor was horrendous.

"Chang," panted Diggs, "stop for a minute." He ran up to his carpetbag and pulled out the large handkerchief. He tied it over his nose. "Somewhat better, I can almost breathe. Now, let's go down Broadway."

Woe leaped easily over the pools of yellow water, areas of thick mud, and the hundreds of road apples. Diggs had to stop and haltingly step over the obstacles, slowing down the escape. Angry cries from their pursuers mingled with the creaking of wagons, equine neighs and brays, and teamsters yelling.

The icy wind blew from the east, carrying the smell of smoke, cooking fires, fresh dung, and garbage. The pale setting sun did little to add warmth to the New York City November day.

Diggs removed his handkerchief and tucked his bandana into his pocket. "It won't stay in place and I can't lose it." He shivered, pulled his coat more firmly around himself, and clenched it tightly. His hold on the table became very precarious since he was using only one hand.

"Oscar, please ambulate faster." Woe effortlessly breathed. "The men are catching up. They do not look any less irate at having to pursue us through this quagmire of streets."

"I need a… breather," puffed Diggs. He bent over and now his hold on the table became even dicier.

"I wish some of them would go visit some of these many brothels or taverns we are passing," said Woe. He tried to reach back, grab Diggs, and get him to move faster.

"I need… a dram shop for a drink myself," gulped Diggs. He looked back over his shoulder and flinched.

The musket user was easily in range but didn't fire. He aimed several times at the two fleeing men.

"That man must know that discharging a firearm in the middle of the city necessitates punishment," said Woe. "Unfortunately, the more fit club and pick-ax wielders are hot on our heels. I observe that luckily some of the horde probably must be war veterans. They are lagging far behind, limping badly, I assume due to battle injuries. Please ambulate more rapidly, Oscar."

"I'm running as fast as I can," panted Diggs. "Most of my exercising comprises lifting heavy draughts of beer to my mouth."

"Abandon the table, Oscar. It is slowing you down," said Woe. "If we do not move more quickly, I do not wish to consider the outcome."

"No, Chang," gasped Diggs. "We can't leave Betsy." Diggs shook his head. His battered top hat wobbled but stayed on. "Could… never afford… another stand."

Woe looked behind them. "Master Diggs, either you jettison the performance pulpit, or we will certainly abandon our lives."

Diggs reluctantly placed the table behind them and turned it on its side. "I hope it will slow them… down. Maybe they'll think we're hunkered down behind it with muskets. I'll call it the famous Civil War Battle of Manhattan."

"I think your old table will impede them less than the fecal landmines and carcasses," said Woe. "Now please hurry. We must decide how to avoid and lose these ruffians."

Diggs wiped his brow with the back of his hand and then pointed with a shaky hand. "I do have an idea. We'll go that way."

"Why?" Woe was not even sweating.

"Three blocks south and two avenues east is a possible sanctuary. The Astor House wouldn't allow thugs like those in the lobby. I hope my regalia is impressive enough to earn a room." Diggs brushed off his dusty long-coat, groaned, and began running at a mildly increased pace. "And, I hope I have enough money to pay for lodging."

Diggs now led the way, weaving around horse-drawn vehicles. Woe easily kept up with him, even while lugging the huge satchel. Soon, they entered the main foyer of the Astor House. The doorman gave an alarmed glance at Woe and tried to stop him. Woe slipped easily past.

The elderly doorman hobbled, but caught up to the men. "Sir, can I hep you?" He looked only at Diggs, completely ignoring Woe. He surreptitiously held out his hand for a tip. The man looked hopeful.

Smoke from kerosene lamps and cigars filled the hotel's main entrance hall. Huge palm plants wilted in the corners of the room. Dingy silk tapestries adorned all the walls. In the front of the lobby, sat a dusty oriental screen. Two strapping bell-hops stood at attention next to the desk, looking exceptionally bored. They perked up when they saw the potential customers. Several elderly patrons sitting in the lobby didn't even glance up from their newspapers when Diggs and Woe barged into the hotel.

The two men now ran up to the hotel receptionist. "I would like a room for myself and my man-servant, my good man," bellowed Diggs. He tipped his battered hat at the clerk.

The receptionist frowned at Woe. "I'm sorry sir, your domestic will have to stay in our servants' quarter and enter through the appropriate door. Astor House doesn't allow Chinamen or coloreds to inhabit these premises." The clerk turned a haughty stare towards Diggs. "Now, do you have a reservation?"

Woe drew himself to his full six-foot four-inch height. "Sir, I will have you know I am a visiting dignitary from China. A relative of the emperor himself. I am not just a Chinaman, and I resent your tone. I now would not allow my royal feet to perambulate the floor of this second-rate abode. Please recommend a different suitable residence for a member of my royal presence."

"Yes, your highness," said the clerk in a sarcastic tone, "I am sure all of New York high society seeks after your body. On the lower east side, there might be a tenement house that will put you up for the evening. The Opera House doesn't take Chinamen either, even imperial ones."

"Now sir," said the receptionist, turning back to Diggs, "How many nights will you be staying with us? Twelve dollars includes breakfast and of course we are one of the few establishments in New York with indoor plumbing." The clerk pushed the large register towards Diggs with his right hand. His empty left sleeve was pinned up at the shoulder. "Sign here. I'll have our bell-hop take your luggage up. Where are those lazy boys?" He slapped his hand on the desk.

"Not so fast, sonny, I'll never stay at an establishment that turns away the youngest grandson of the Emperor of China." Diggs haughtily pushed the register back at the clerk. "Ahem, where is your back door?"

The man pointed down the hall with his middle finger. "Probably can't afford us anyways. We don't want your kind."

Diggs turned to leave. Woe picked up the satchel and joined him. They strode past the wilting palms plants and entered the corridor to the rear of the building.

"So now I am the grandson of the Emperor of China?" said Woe, while laughing.

"That fact is just as believable as us being able to afford twelve dollars for a room," replied Diggs. He looked behind him to see if the clerk or bell-hop were following them.

"I cannot believe that this hotel might have men of draft age working and not fighting," said Woe. "The city just recovered from the Lincoln Draft Act Riots. Why were those couple of bell-hops not in a Yankee union uniform?"

"I saw two that could even lift a gun," said Diggs. "The only way this high-falutin' hotel still has healthy help is if some palms were greased. High society would be upset if patrons had to bring their own luggage upstairs to their room." Diggs laughed, "I've been looking over my shoulder avoiding recruiters myself for weeks. I don't want to be in this war. I hate the sight of blood, especially my own."

The men exited the hotel through the back door and carefully looked around. "Things appear quiet for now," said Woe. "Let us ambulate for home."

They walked up the back street for several blocks. Piles of garbage filled the alleyways. Rats ran in front of them, chased by large cats. A familiar-looking, gasping, irate group of men confronted them as they turned back to Broadway.

"Dash it all. What bad luck. How did they find us? How can one be so upset about losing a crummy coin?" Diggs bolted.

After one block, the horde was almost on their heels again. They sped up, ducked into an alley, and ran around a corner. The street they came upon had a large storefront with a welcoming open door. They rushed through the opening.

"Welcome, men," said a large, older man dressed in blue. "Here to enlist?"

Chapter Three

"Wonderful Master Diggs," said Woe. "We have gone from the axiomatic cooking implement to the conflagration." He stared around the room while holding onto the satchel.

In a small drab room, illuminated only with a scant amount of sunshine coming through the open door, sat a union soldier. The room had peeling whitewash on the walls. Muddy footprints adorned the floor. Despite the large storefront, the space inside was small. There was only one tiny window covered with black tar paper.

The soldier slowly rose from behind a small, ancient desk piled high with disheveled papers. Next to the chair was an antiquated rifle with a fixed bayonet. The union man gave a haphazard mock salute. Unfortunately, the hand saluting the two men held a huge ham sandwich. The yellow-tinged meat smashed into his forehead and pushed aside his union cap.

"Sergeant Timothy Whitman, here to greet ya," said the soldier. "Glad you came to see me today. Close the door behind you, Chinaman." Dull yellow mustard smeared his forehead. Almost as much old mustard stained the front of his shirt as was in his unruly beard.

Woe put down the carpet bag and turned to close the door. Then Woe rotated back, and both Diggs and he shuffled forward three steps.

The soldier moved forward and reached out to give Diggs a handshake. Whitman noticed that his hand still held his sandwich in it.

He instead turned his hand around and took a large bite out of the homemade bread. The soldier sighed, and tossed the rest of the ham sandwich on top of the crumpled papers on the desk, next to a huge mug of beer. He held out his now empty, greasy hand. "As I said before," he mumbled through a mouthful of food, "are you here to enlist?"

Diggs drew himself up to his full height. "Good afternoon, Sergeant. My friend and I have wandered into the wrong establishment by accident. I assume this isn't Mrs. Peabody's Emporium and Flea Market? Just looking for a rabbit to pull out of my hat and a hairpiece to keep my dome warm while doing it. I am the famous magician, OZ the Great." Diggs took off his wrinkled top hat and groped inside it. His hand came out with a dozen scarves, and he pretended to make them hop. His nearly bald head sweated profusely. Diggs' stomach rumbled loudly.

"Huh, what?" said the soldier. "Hold on, boyos, you're in my arena now. Mister Lincoln's draft law gives me power over any able-bodied man who walks through my door. You're not the greatest dat I've ever seen, but we need experienced fighters, like me." The union man held himself fully erect and tried to pull in his stomach. Whitman tugged at his wrinkled and stained uniform. He gazed fondly down at his sergeant stripes sewn crookedly onto his sleeve. Then he scowled at Woe, and said, "Hey Chinaman, you a fighter? You speaka da English? Do… you… understand me?" he roared.

Woe immediately took one more step forward and threw up his arms. He glared at the soldier. "I perceive your attempt at communication entirely. And I dare say, no, I am a lover, not a fighter. I will try even harder to elucidate. My grasp of the King's English is doubtless more notable than yours. Plus, I am not hard of hearing, sir."

"Dem's some three-bit words," said Whitman. "How comes you talk so good, Chinaman?" The soldier took several steps backward and carefully reached behind himself for the beer. While still facing Woe, he dragged the beer mug forward, lifted it, and took a huge gulp. With his other hand, Whitman wiped the foam off his face, and then replaced the beer on the desk behind his back, without turning around. The mug just made it to the very edge of the desk. Papers fluttered to the floor. The beer mug tottered, but did not fall.

"I was born in China," said Woe. "My father always claimed to be an illegitimate son of the Empress Dowager Cixi. We moved to Hong Kong because my old man worried that his brother, Tongzhi, would try to kill him. Too bad we left China, for today I might have been the next Qing Dynasty Emperor." Woe stood tall and tried to look imperial. "Then as Britain tightened its claws into Hong Kong, my parents made me learn fluent English."

"Is dat where you learned such good talking?" Whitman's hand inched backward for his beer glass. He shook his head and stopped reaching for his drink. "Continue."

"Yes, but I left when the British completely moved in," said Woe. "Randomly, I picked the southern portion of the United States to move to. Poor decision, as that portion held extremely unrefined personages." Woe squatted down and sat on the carpet bag. He rotated around to face Diggs. "There is no use running still, Master Diggs. I presume those ruffians are continuing to congregate outside?"

"I agree, your highness," Diggs bowed deeply, straightened, and smiled. "We certainly are in the frying pan now."

"How'd ja get here?" said the soldier. "Don't see many Chinamen in these parts. 'Scuse me for a minute—parched." The sergeant turned, grabbed his mug, and drained it in a single gulp. After a tremendous belch, he said, "Ah, much better. So?"

"In Alabama," continued Woe, "the only job I could get was in a circus. They hired me as a servant. Soon I found I could do more than serve. I could be a star. I was a contortionist. They called me 'The Strawman.'" He hopped up, bent over, did a handstand, and slowly lifted his legs into the air, and then placed his feet on the floor. Woe quickly leaped upright again. "I am 'The Strawman.'" He lifted his right leg and put it around his neck.

"And a great sideshow act he was." Diggs pulled up his leg and could barely get it knee-high. He sighed. "Must be arthritis."

"No, you never stretch or practice yoga." Woe leaned over, did a forward roll, and ended up in a lotus position. "I met Master Diggs in the circus and became his friend. I pretend to be his servant, but actually am the brains of our performances. We have traveled together for over ten years."

The soldier looked at Diggs right in the eye. "You certainly ain't a controtion whateverist." He then scratched his beard and crumbs fell out.

"No," said Diggs. "I was a ventriloquist in the sideshow. Trouble was, I was terrible. Everyone could always see my lips move."

The union man turned from Diggs and Woe and put down his mug. He let out a second burp. The soldier turned back to face them. "What the hell is a ventriloquist?"

"It is someone who can throw their voice." Diggs inhaled deeply.

The soldier's rifle suddenly exclaimed, "Let's shoot dos Rebs."

Then Whitman's ham sandwich screamed, "Don't eat me! I'm too young to die."

Both the soldier and Woe laughed. "His lips definitely moved," they said at the same time.

"I'm sure you want to hear the rest of our tale," said Diggs. "I became a hot-air balloon pilot, taking people up for rides for ten cents a head. The circus owner made quite a profit 'til the balloon's cloth envelope got too near a tall tree and ripped to shreds. I was lucky not to crash and die, or worse, fired. At the same time, our stage magician wanted to retire. He liked me and taught me some simple sleight-of-hand tricks." Diggs took a step forward and suddenly handed the soldier a bouquet of very dingy paper flowers. "We traveled all over the US with several circuses. But after many years, Woe and I finally got bored and struck off for the north together and ended up in New York City. We've worked here ever since."

The soldier nodded. "Well gents, I'm not sure what the army will do with bendy man here, but the northern bosses are again looking for pilots. Earlier in da war, balloons were a large part of our success. Colonel Thaddeus Lowe used the flyers in his Union Army Balloon Corps. But da use of balloons finally stopped." Whitman took a step back, turned around, and picked up a piece of paper from the messy desk.

"Why?" asked Diggs. He gestured with his thumb to get out of the door.

"Two reasons," said the union man as he turned back again. "One: da head aeronaut had seven gas bags but only two remaining pilots. Most of da damn fools kept falling out of da baskets. And two: after Fredericksburg, things got too costly. Dey got rid of Lowe and closed down the program. But Mister Lincoln figures we can end the war now by using all of our military toys. Yep, 1865 will be the end of the war when we throw everything at those damn Rebs. You, short stuff, will do fine as a pilot recruit." He smiled and picked up a piece of paper and quill.

Diggs turned and ran for the door. He yelled over his shoulder. "No, sorry! I have a sudden fear of heights." Woe picked up the carpetbag and followed. He yanked on the door to open it. The door screeched open.

The soldier dropped the parchment application and quill and picked up his rifle. "Halt men or I'll shoot!" The sergeant pulled back the bolt, turned, and pointed it at the fleeing cowards. "Welcome to the Union Army."

Chapter Four

Woe emptied the officers' chamber pots into the small, torpid stream. "Well, Master Diggs, this is another fine mess you have gotten us into." He held his nose with both hands, carefully planted his right foot, and used his big toe and second toe to lift and dump each pot. Showing no strain, he poured carefully, trying to get as little of the brown stream on his naked feet as possible.

The two men stood next to a tiny, meandering tributary of the Alabama River. The day was sweltering hot, and an occasional storm cloud filled the sky. Many flies swarmed around Diggs' and Woe's heads and the chamber pot containers.

Diggs took a step back from the foul, smelly mixture. "I can't believe how long and nimble those monkey toes are of yours. Now, why are you putting this blame on my noggin? Either we joined the union army immediately or those thugs would've strung us up. And I seem to remember you were a contortionist performing on sawdust, not a high wire specialist. They did not train you to do well with a rope around your neck." He leaned on the shovel he was using to deposit any night soil, not making it to the stream. Diggs had the old handkerchief tied over his nose and mouth. "This is not what I thought I was signing up for with the Union forces."

"Yes, I indubitably agree," said Woe. "Of course, the New York sergeant was told to recruit for General James Wilson forces. Did Wilson especially want a balloonist? No, he only wanted cavalrymen. I can ride, but you do not know which end of the animal to mount." He carefully dumped another pot into the water with his foot. This time, he rinsed his toes thoroughly. "And worse, you had to tease the recruiter at the get-go."

"What are you referring to, my friend?"

"The soldier picked up a quill pen and asked for your complete name to record. You had to give him the entire ridiculous name your father blessed you with. Oscar Zoroaster Phadrig Isaac Norman Henkel Emmanuel Ambrose Diggs. The poor man not only did not know how to spell half those names but probably would have run out of ink recording the mouthful."

Diggs straightened up and strutted. "That is my name."

"But you never use that tongue twister. You go by Oscar Diggs, or sometimes the stage name, OZ the Great. No one ever heard of the word Zoroaster, but you love it. Teasing the soldier with your unusual name is probably why he assigned us to Wilson's forces, not somewhere behind the lines in a nice safe supply chain." After dumping the last chamber pot, he took his fingers off his nose, rinsed each foot and gathered up the receptacles.

"Well, we're not exactly involved with riding the mounts yet. I'm tired of being specialists in taking care of the nags' other end." Diggs put all his weight on his shovel while leaning. "I wish there were something more interesting than just shoveling manure from all sources. So far, this job really stinks. And we've slaved away with Wilson's troops for months. At least we're not freezing in New York anymore."

"Yes, we are just boiling in Alabama. Still, at least our lives are intact. We are not exactly on the front lines, and there is talk of needing more observation information in the future." Woe shook his toes carefully to get the last of the water off his feet. "So, you will get to be a pilot soon, and hopefully they will let me be your assistant in the basket."

"It's lucky they don't have a Chinese brigade. Or in this here army, you wouldn't be able to be my assistant in our balloon." Diggs placed his shovel carefully over his shoulder in order to not smudge his clothes.

Woe shook his head. "Not enough of us Orientals in all the services. Just a handful of individuals. I have heard that at least some of my countrymen are playing the role of skilled warriors. However, some are serving on the wrong side." He slowly climbed up the embankment.

"Come Chang," said Diggs. "We have to pack up the carts. Colonel Lewis says we'll be attacking Franklin tomorrow. I remember that city was one of the most enjoyable to play in Alabama with our circus, years ago." Diggs trudged back to camp, shovel over his shoulder.

Numerous two-man tents nestled amongst small rolling hills. All the canvases were filthy, and many torn. The tents surrounded a large central area, occupied by a hundred skittish horses. Campfires giving off thin amounts of pine tar smoke ringed the outskirts. Union soldiers lazed around the fires smoking corncob pipes or headed into their respective bivouacs.

The next morning, Woe woke up in their tiny two-man pup tent to thundering booms. Diggs and two unknown soldiers piled in with him continued to snore loudly and didn't rouse. Woe got up and carefully tried to walk past the men's prone bodies. He had to walk significantly hunched over. Woe trod several times on one soldier or the other, but finally made it to the opening and peered out. He didn't see a cloud in the sky, but noticed the explosive sounds continued.

The opening was closed and Woe reached over and shook the sleeping magician. "Oscar, get up. A battle has begun. Get dressed! You do not want to die attired only in your long johns."

Diggs slowly woke up and pushed off his moth-eaten blanket. "What's that noise, Chang? Good God, what's that smell?"

"The sound is the beginning of warfare," said Woe. "I assume the smell is from one or both of our two new roommates. Some regiment must have gotten in last night, and it appears our two-man tent has suddenly necessitated the boarding of two more occupants. It is so crowded I could barely breathe last night, let alone sleep. It did not affect your slumbers, however."

Diggs jumped up, his bald head easily clearing the roof of the tent, and grabbed his pants. "Wake up, men!" he screamed. "We're under attack." Diggs nudged the unknown sleeping soldiers by kicking them in their ribs.

"Huh, what?" muttered one soldier. "What's going on? Our regiment only got in here at four in the morning. We grabbed this here tent to sleep. Much obliged, the name is Henry Johnson, from Chi-town. My partner is Floyd Griminger from Peoria. We're both third cavalry, from Illinois, here to join General Wilson." He rubbed his eyes and then stood up. "Ouch," he cried as his head smashed into the tent ceiling. "Forgot how short these dang things were."

Diggs fanned the air in front of him. "Well Harry, happy to make your acquaintance. But why does it smell like you brought your horse into the tent with you?"

"Well, my buddy and I are kind of superstitious," said Henry. "We haven't washed our long johns since we both survived Gettysburg." He shrugged and then beamed, "Real good luck."

"Gettysburg? That was a year and a half ago," said Diggs. "Now man, I've heard of people not changing socks once in a while for good luck, but long johns? You reek." He stepped into his boots and pants and carried his shirt and top hat out to the opening of the tent. Diggs took a huge breath of air.

"Don't smell much different to us," said Henry. "We haven't washed arenselves since Gettysburg either." He scratched his armpit and then sniffed his hand. "Hey since we are new in these parts, anything to do in Franklin after the battle?"

Diggs began pulling on his clothes. While dressing, he turned to stare at the man. Diggs stumbled as he pulled on his pants. "If, of course, you or Franklin survive."

"Been lucky so far in war, not lovin'." Henry reached down for his pants. "How have you been doing with the ladies?"

"I don't believe it, man," exclaimed Diggs. "We're about to get our heads blown off and you're thinking about sex?" He shook his head.

"He sounds like you," laughed Woe, "Especially when we were with the Mount Pitt circus. You are always chasing after women. Nevertheless, you even caught that one in Omaha."

Diggs put his hand over his heart. He smiled, a silly grin on his face. "No, that was genuine love. Ah, Martha Gale, my one and only."

Woe smirked. "Until the next one."

"Whatever happened to your sweetie?" said Henry. His pants were so rigid with mud and sweat that he was having trouble pulling them on.

"Got a letter later from her," explained Diggs. "Received it right before Chang and I quit Mount Pitt. It was months after I last seen her. She was with child and was moving to Liberal, Kansas." Diggs pretended to wipe a tear from his eye. "She was trying to escape the shame and going to live with her sister Emma and brother-in-law Henry. Martha was even going to name the child after me."

"So, there is an Oscar junior," said Henry. "Or a girl named Olivia up north?" He began to yank and tug at his pants, but they barely budged.

"No, the name would be Donald or Dorothy," said Diggs. "Her family's tradition is to use the first initial of the last name from the father. I wonder if I have any other little ones running around?" Diggs frowned and looked up at the ceiling of the tent.

"So, di'ja track her down and make an honest woman of Martha?" Henry plopped to the ground to forcibly yanked up his trousers. While down there, he pulled on his boots.

"No. By this time, Chang and I were traveling eastward. To me, Kansas was on the other side of the world."

A bugle sounded the call to arms. Diggs finished dressing and rushed out to saddle up the horses. The number of equines had multiplied significantly since the previous day. Woe followed and began putting bits into the skittish horses' mouths. The nimble man moved so quickly he wasn't nipped even once.

Explosive booms, screams, and yells filled the air. But none echoed nearby. Harry and Floyd finally emerged from the tent, grumbling something about no breakfast again. They ran to mount their steeds, jumped on, and rode towards the yells. From out of many other tents, streamed union troops heading for the horses. After one-half hour, Diggs and Woe were standing by themselves.

"Now what chores should we undertake?" said Woe. "All the horses have left, and I doubt there is much new manure that has to be processed."

"There are no balloons ready or needed," said Diggs. "I'd rather stay away from the front lines, anyway. I seem to remember the captain telling me we should report to the surgeon's tent if we are not occupied with any other chores. We are to get rid of all the cut off arms and legs, and just help the doctors. I wish the doc knew something to help our boys besides hacking off their limbs."

Woe sighed. "I despise this miserable war. It is an absolute abomination. I do not look forward to partaking in that necessary chore in the hospital tent."

Diggs lifted his palms upward. "It's too bad that I'm not a real magician and could make all this horror disappear."

Chapter Five

Diggs shuddered. "There are more Rebs being brought in than our own boys. The surgeon can't even keep up." He and Woe ran from the entrance of the huge hospital tent, bringing wounded soldiers and occasionally dying ones to the surgeons for their assessment. The doctor made the same statement over and over, "we have to cut the limb off if we want to save this man's life." Troops filled the hospital tent, and more were being brought in every minute. Blood coated the canvas walls and screams resonated through the air.

"I never saw such misery," said Woe. "Even during warfare in China." He put down a stretcher which had a man dressed in confederate gray with both legs mangled from the knees down. "It is my assessment that his injury results from cannon fire." Woe turned to go when the surgeon grabbed him with a bloody hand. In the dim, smoky light in the tent, Woe looked a paler white than his usual yellow skin tone.

"I need you to hold him down," said the doctor. "My other assistant fainted dead away, again. When the idiot first started, he bragged he was sure that castrating his farm bulls would be harder than being my helper. Boy, was he wrong. I think this little bit of blood bothers him." The surgeon's leather apron dripped, and he had a hacksaw in his hand.

Woe turned back to help. He carefully tried to step over soldiers lying on the dirt of the tent to get to the patient. The ground was so crowded;

he trod on many writhing people or in pools of blood. Vomit and ichor covered his bare feet.

"Oscar, this is terrible," said Woe. "I am not confident that I can tolerate these atrocities. This is the first battle they have involved us in with such horrors. I think I should desert and go back to Hong Kong." Woe shook his foot, but clotted blood continued to cling to it.

"Quiet Chang, don't use the 'D' word," said Diggs. "It's a shooting offense. Although you might pull it off. The officers think all people from China look the same and you might blend into the civilian population. Your height might be aginst you. But I certainly look distinctive and would stand out." He stood erect, straightened his top hat, and smoothed the blue shirt of his wrinkled union uniform. Diggs then reached into a pocket and pulled out a dozen scarves, and draped them around his neck. He turned and went toward the tent opening for another patient.

"Chinaman, help me lift the man onto the table," said the doctor. "I can't get the correct angle to amputate while he is on the ground." The surgeon pointed to a filthy cloth-covered bench that was sagging precariously.

Woe looked at the operating table. "Are you sure this rickety table will support his weight?" The old blood-entrenched table was listing badly. "And he is wiggling so severely, he probably will fall off."

"The table held up my last twenty amputations," said the surgeon. "And it has to last for the next twenty. I wish we had more help. I'm exhausted. Who knows when this battle will be over?"

Woe lifted the Reb onto the table. It creaked precipitously but held. "Do you need me to help hold, or should I try to find the next victim, no, I mean to say, patient?"

"Yep, just hold," said the doctor. The surgeon picked up an old leather belt with his left hand. "Open your mouth, Reb, we're out of whiskey and this will save your teeth. What there are of them."

"No, please," screamed the Rebel soldier. "Not my leg." The man tried to bat at the surgeon's hacksaw.

"Open wide," intoned the doctor. He shoved the leather between the Reb's rotten teeth amidst screams. "Sorry, I ain't going to say this won't hurt a bit." The surgeon began the operation.

Woe continued to hold him as firmly as he could. He had to look away from the terrible sight. His hands trembled, and he tried to take a deep cleansing breath to calm down, but coughed instead from the stink. Woe shook and talked to himself in Mandarin. "*Kěpà, Kěpà*, So Terrible, so terrible," but he stayed at his post.

When the surgeon hit the femur bone, the patient fainted dead away. "Damn," said the doctor. "This hacksaw is so dull, it's almost worthless. I could do better with my teeth." He continued sawing. The physician finished the amputation, dropped the hacksaw on the ground, reached over, and grabbed the branding iron. He cauterized the stump. The smell of burning flesh filled the air.

Woe tossed the leg onto a growing pile of limbs. He then muttered, "Sorry," raced to the tent opening, and vomited on the ground. "I cannot get used to this!" He screamed into the air. Woe wiped his mouth on his sleeve and turned back to assist some more.

Diggs and another helper came through the opening with a Confederate soldier, adorned with many medals, thick gold braid on his shoulders, and a wide silk sash around his waist, on a stretcher. "Colonel said this high up muckety muck goes next."

Diggs and the union soldier placed the stretcher on the table. The surgeon peered down at the figure and said, "Nope, nothing I can do. Deader than a stuck pig." Diggs looked down and noticed a black bullet hole right between his eyes.

A well-dressed union soldier rushed into the tent. "Did you save him?" said the man. "That there is General John Adams. We could get some important information from him." Diggs, Woe, and everyone still standing in the tent, but the surgeon straightened and saluted the man.

"Colonel Ericson, it's hard to talk to a dead man. But I can try." Diggs bent down and lifted the torso of the general.

"Boy, that really smarted," came a voice out of the general's mouth.

"Shit," said Colonel Ericson, "you sure he's dead?" His eyes were as big as silver dollars.

"Oscar, now is not the time to play tricks," said Woe. "Do not try to fool our fellow combatants. Plus, your lips moved as usual." He shook his head, his long braid swinging widely. Woe did not smile.

"Soldier," said the Colonel. "You're an idjit. I should court-marshal you for that. Just get rid of the body." He turned and strode out of the tent.

Diggs bent over the body and lifted it up. "Hey doc, what should I do with this guy's amazing possessions?"

The surgeon waved a bloody hand. "I don't give a damn."

Diggs and Woe carried the general's body out of the tent. They placed him to the side of the hospital tent, on matted down grass. Woe stopped with his barefoot the body which was attempting to roll down the significant embankment. Since the sun was setting, the reflection off the general's chest medals shone into Diggs and Woe's faces.

Diggs rifled through the man's pockets and pulled out a large leather purse. "Woe, we struck it rich. There are at least ten gold Eagles in here." He took two matching pearl-handled dueling pistols from the general's belt and a beautiful saber. "Too bad. The general's fancy hat probably flew off when he got shot in the head. My chapeau is getting very worn."

Woe bent down and pulled off the general's boots. "I will appropriate this footgear for myself. I have not been happy stepping in things with my naked feet." He stood on one leg and slipped the boot onto the other foot. Effortlessly, he did a small hop, changed stances, and repeated the maneuver. "Oscar, it feels wonderful to be wearing footwear again. A little large, but acceptable." Woe didn't hold out his arms to keep his balance, and despite the slope of the ground, didn't fall over.

Diggs smiled and shook his head. "I'm always impressed at how you can do something like that. Now take our loot and stash it into my carpet bag in our tent. I'm sure the weapons will come in handy at a future date." Diggs pulled a small penknife out of his pocket and cut the ornamental braid off the general's shoulders. "Never know when some rope might also come in handy." He handed everything but his knife to Woe.

Diggs walked back into the surgeon's tent. He pulled off his sweat-soaked union tunic while entering.

Woe headed for their tent, calling over his shoulder, "Private Diggs, I will be back in a moment, I have to use the latrine." He hurried towards their tent.

Soon, Woe returned, accompanied by a sergeant. "The sergeant has indicated he has some paramount communications." Woe looked concerned.

"Attention men," said the soldier. "Infantry Master Sergeant Brown, from the Illini regiment, reporting. Captain Huxtable says that the damn Reb General Hood has led a cavalry and infantry charge on our flank. They completely took us unawares. Our fortification should hold, but expect many more casualties, and…" he stood up even straighter at attention, "if Hood's troops breakthrough, he's headed right for this position. The colored eighth battalion is all that stands in his way." He turned to stare at Woe, "Who is you? Why ain't you fighting with them brave negroes? Hiding back here?"

Woe held up his pale hand. "Sergeant, I am neither colored nor a fighter. I support the cause in the medical fields." He pointed to his blood-soaked black hemp pants and shirt. "No union uniform embellishments adorn my personage."

"Well shoot," said Brown. "Chinaman, you better hope our boys hold. Oh yeah, is there a Private Diggs here?" He peered through the smoky interior.

"Yes, sergeant," said Diggs. "How can I be of help?" Diggs grimaced, then frowned, and hesitantly stuck his head out from behind the surgeon's body.

"General Wilson needs more information," said Brown. "Hood's charge completely took us by surprise. He wants you to get your arse to one of those observation 'loons, go up, and then report. Bring your signal flags. On the double soldier."

"Wonderful," said Diggs. "In the middle of a battle, I get to ascend in a hydrogen-filled death trap to get information on a skirmish, which I assume we will win handily. At least, with this sunny day, I assume no lightning will hit my balloon." He hopped over the growing pile of amputated limbs, pools of blood, and vomit. Diggs headed slowly for his balloon. "We go to ascend Chang."

Chapter Six

Diggs brought his carpet bag over to his gondola. "I can't believe that there bloody battle of Franklin was already months ago. It seemed like yesterday. I'm glad I didn't have to go up in my balloon after all. I sure hope I don't have to go up in Columbus." He opened up his bag and took out his pistols and telescope. Diggs verified the loading of the pistols and then put them back. He extended his telescope and held it up. "There will be an awful lot of shrapnel flying. I hope we don't stop any."

"It was a fortitudinous that we won that altercation outside of Franklin," said Woe. "I am glad the Reb General Hood will not be facing us in Columbus. His attack was brilliant and almost devastated us." He laid out the cloth envelope of one of the balloons.

"Well, if it wasn't for General Opdycke's brigade," said Diggs. "We'd all be whistling Dixie now. I didn't even have time to fill up my balloon to go up and observe when Hood broke through our middle." He held his cheap spyglass up to his eye and looked at Woe. "Nope, still ugly as sin."

"You fill up your own envelope. Today, I had to charge up all the generator wagons. The fumes from the dilute sulfuric acid almost asphyxiated me." Woe took deep breaths of the fresh Columbus air. He then coughed as the smell of cannon and rifle fire smoke still lingered in the atmosphere. "Plus, it was difficult finding our stash of iron filings. I do not know what use anyone could need them for. Both items are necessary to generate hydrogen for the balloon."

"Although I didn't get to go up in Franklin, we certainly have gotten lots of practice ascending during all these minor skirmishes throughout Alabama. I'm all right going up when no one is shooting at me. But tomorrow, ascending during a tremendous battle, will be scary. Now, since it is quiet before the coming battle, I'm going to take a nap." Diggs turned and trudged towards their tent.

Woe held up his hands. "Wait, Oscar, there is a lot of work to perform still. Do not leave it all for me. Just because someone designated me your assistant and gondola engineer, you should not assign the tedious tasks to me."

"Poor baby, but I'm chief pilot of this rig." Diggs yawned. "But I'm glad General Wilson was smart enough to allow you to be my chief engineer. We make a great team. Now, nighty-night."

"Wait, there is just too much work," said Woe. "I do have to agree, Wilson certainly appreciates an intelligent fellow engineer. He is truly an exceptional leader, and so young. I understand he is only twenty-four? About a third of your age, right Oscar?" Woe smiled.

Diggs looked back, patted his chubby tummy, and smiled. "I resent that statement. I am barely forty. And my svelte body doesn't even look that old."

"Indubitably. Able to button your pants lately? I am sure Wilson's engineering background made him resurrect the balloon corps. If he really is going to continue to use observation balloons, then I better pack up the gas generation wagons. I hope no one keeps stealing the sulfuric acid. I think some of the backwoods boys think it is just strong moonshine." Woe glared at Diggs. "You would not be selling it to those marks, would you?"

Diggs put one hand on his change purse and placed his other hand behind his back with crossed fingers. "I would do nothing like that." He suddenly looked into the distance and pointed. "Oh crap, Chang, there's an open flame over there again."

"Amazing! It does not stop," said Woe. "I have told those idiot pilots and ground crew not to smoke. It is exceedingly dangerous to indulge in that habit near the balloons." He ran over and slapped a lit pipe out of a pilot's hand. "Do you not know how flammable hydrogen is? One spark could blow us all the way back to Franklin."

Diggs panted as he came running up. "What a great way to celebrate Easter tomorrow. Something tells me the Easter bunny might have trouble finding us here in Columbus. Last time we were here, it was with the circus. It seemed a lot more peaceful."

"If I remember correctly, Columbus was the location where you had the slight mishap with the cloth of the balloon and the large tree. And the circus owner was not peaceful as he lambasted you over the incident." Woe trooped around the basket, looking for anyone else, who were smoking.

"I hope I don't run into any trees here. I would hate to ruin my new balloon envelope."

"Where in the world does the general find so many pilots who are smoking idiots?"

"The general needs observation reports. Our men won't give up their refreshing tobacco. I myself don't indulge in smoking the weed, just an occasional chew." Diggs spat a gob of brown liquid onto and next to Woe's new boots. "Whoops, sorry."

Woe hopped back from the tobacco-induced puddle and wiped the top of his soaked boot on the back of his leg. "Sure, you are sorry. Since Franklin, we have ascended weekly for the past several months. Our regiment has lost three pilots during maneuvers. Three men panic, one jumps out, and two fall. How could so many men be afraid of heights?"

Diggs walked over to a supply cart and took out a pail of whitewash and a brush. "Yes, a tough way to rise up the ranks." He brought the paint near to the cloth envelope of his balloon and put it on the ground. "That explosive situation, just now from the lit pipe, woke me up. No nap today. I think I'll paint my envelope."

"But now, you are chief aeronaut," said Woe. "It was sure nice of Major Fredriksson to allow you to individualize your union balloon. Are you going to paint clouds on the blue fabric?" He pointed at the limp envelope lying on the ground.

Diggs squirted another mouthful of juices onto the dry ground. The liquid sank in quickly. "No, just my initials."

"How in the world do you expect to fit all the letters on the fabric envelope? I know we have the largest envelope and gondola in the entire union army, but that is some mouthful. Plus, have you ever noticed what your initials spell out? Do you want the world to call you that?"

"Yes, that's a problem. I'll probably just go with 'OZ' in white. I won't even include 'the great.' That's a given." Diggs reached down to jut out some suspenders and strut, but realized that the union uniform didn't have any braces. He frowned as he remembered how he missed his normal clothes. Diggs patted his unique top hat. "I'm sure glad they let me at least keep my own long coat and topper. My coat sure keeps me warm when I ascend above. The top hat is just because I'm unique."

"Maybe we should convince General Wilson and the rest of the aeronaut pilots to convert over to hot air. The burner system will keep us warmer on these cool Alabama nights, and hot air will be much safer than explosive hydrogen." Woe picked up a stick and drew engineering diagrams in the dirt.

"I can't believe it is almost Easter, and the air up high is still this freezing. Now I'll name my balloon." Diggs removed his long coat and put it into his basket. He picked up the whitewash brush, dipped it in the pail, and carefully painted a twenty-foot 'OZ' on the deflated blue fabric of the envelope. "That and a thirty-five-foot inflated balloon should get everyone's attention."

Woe loaded the large carpet bag into the basket. "I hope it does not attract the attention of any rebel sharpshooters. I would like my hair and head intact for the rest of the war." He walked to the generator and carefully mixed the sulfuric acid and iron filings together into the gas generator. Slowly the envelope of the balloon filled and rose in the air. Woe attached the drop ropes to sandbags, tethering the balloon in place, even when the envelope was completely filled.

"Today is just another practice run, right?" said Diggs. "The major doesn't seem to want to talk to me after I took him for four dollars during our last poker game. Just need to build up our nest egg for after the war." He reached into the basket, pulled out his new heavier purse, and jingled it. Diggs smiled and put it back.

"Oscar, you are playing with fire," said Woe. "You should not play poker with our officers. When you win so often, I am sure you are cheating. It is in your nature." He disconnected the hose from the gas generator and stepped back from the balloon envelope. The inflated fabric was now a good thirty-five feet tall, with a huge 'OZ' painted on it in white letters.

A sergeant came meandering up, smoking a stub of a cigar. "Men, begorrah, quit your lollygagging. Major Burns wants a rapid ascent up to about 100 feet. It should be easy with this cloudless day. Get a good practice in. Tomorrow, we enter Columbus. No Easter bunnies for those rebels, just good union steel." He tapped the lit stogie and flicked the ash off the cigar on the basket.

Both Woe and Diggs, turned pale. "Sergeant O'Sullivan," Woe yelled. "Hydrogen blows up easily. Stop it!"

"What men?" said O'Sullivan. "I smoke where I wish. Now, get your practice in. The troops will need your observation help."

Woe saluted the sergeant, then placed his hands on O'Sullivan's shoulders and turned his body and lit cigar so they were facing away from the gondola. "No offense sir, but I would rather you did not blow us all up today."

Diggs shuddered. "I agree with my esteemed colleague. Perhaps we should retire. It feels like it could storm tomorrow, even though it seems pleasant now. My bunions are killing me, and that is always a sure sign of a coming storm." He tilted his boot up on its heel. Diggs looked down at the toe area of his heavy clodhopper. "Going up in a thundercloud is not safe."

"If it's an order, soldiers," said Sergeant O'Sullivan, "you'll ascend to the heavens come rain or shine." He tossed down his smoldering cigar and strode away.

Diggs ran over and ground the smoldering cigar into the dirt. "I have a terrible feeling about this."

Chapter Seven

Booms from cannon fire and thunderous crashes from Mother Nature awakened Diggs and Woe the next morning. After Woe stuck his head out of the tent, pouring rain immediately drenched him. The raindrops pounded on the canvas of the tent, the noise only barely drowned out by the roar of cannon fire. The area near the tent opening was a quagmire.

"Not a great day," said Woe. "I am not thrilled to have to ascend in our hydrogen balloon." He pulled his soaked head back in, swinging his braid back and forth. Drops flew all over from it, like water off a dog's body when it shook. "It sounds like we have begun the assault on Columbus. I wonder if they will require our observation assistance."

"Sounds like it." Diggs looked at his saturated friend and grinned. "You should add some lye soap and call this your monthly bath. You're wet enough."

Woe grabbed his long braid, leaned forward, and carefully squeezed the moisture onto Diggs' head. "With all the lightning strikes, and bullets flying, I would rather not expose my naked body to the elements."

Diggs sputtered and got up. He sank back down and wiped his face. "Refreshing."

Sergeant O'Sullivan burst into the tent and pulled his rifle out from under his long coat. He pointed the bayonet at Diggs, then Woe. "Men, get your arses in gear and saddle up that there balloon. General Upton was waltzing towards Columbus, about to enter the city on the southern bridge, when those damn Rebs pulled up part of the planks and set fire to the rest of the bridge. The way it's burning in the rain, they must have soaked it in turpentine."

"Were many men killed?" said Woe. He bent down and pulled on his black pants over his long johns. The garments slid on easily. When he again rose, his head smashed against the canvas of the tent's top.

"Not this time, no," said O'Sullivan. "The troops got off the bridge before it went up in flames. But the north bridge is now the only way to get into the city."

Diggs slowly crawled out from under his moth-eaten blanket. "Why does the staff request my help?" He yawned, reached down into his long johns, and scratched his groin.

A voice came from the vicinity of his stomach. "I'm hungry. Is it time for breakfast?"

O'Sullivan peered down at Digg's belly. "What the hell was that? Good God man, are you with child?"

"No sergeant," said Woe. "Oscar is just as rotund as a pregnant lady. The idiot is throwing his voice again, but poorly." He hopped into both of his boots at the same time. Then Woe leaned forward, did a handstand, balanced on one arm, and picked up his black blouse with the other. He had to bend his legs significantly because of the low ceiling in the tent. Woe did a forward roll, stood upright, and drew on his top.

"Damn," said the sergeant. "You two are strange. Now listen up. General wants you to go up in your balloon and report via semaphore the following important facts. Is the upper bridge still intact? Are the ironclad and the huge Reb gunboat still moored in the naval yards? General heard rumors the Rebs were going to use them to attack Washington." O'Sullivan stared suspiciously at Digg's belly.

"When does the staff want the aeronauts to go up?" said Diggs. He pulled on his pants. Once his drawers were in place, he groaned, bent over stiffly, and tugged on his boots. "This weather is terrible for my lumbago."

"The other four balloons are being inflated as we speak," said O'Sullivan. "With this rain, we're having trouble with the generators, but the envelopes are distending slowly. Get moving." The sergeant turned, started to walk out, stopped, gave one more backward glance down at Digg's stomach, shrugged, and shook his head.

Diggs continued to dress. "Chang, you fill-up the envelope, and I'll pack up the carpetbag with all our possessions. If we come down and get captured, I'll want to defend ourselves with my new revolvers and sword. Now git."

Woe ran out in the rain and headed for the OZ envelope. His mission was always to make sure he tied securely all the sandbags to the lines attached to the basket and then inflate the envelope. "Hey, ground crew! Where is the other half of my acid?" Chang complained to the winds, "I'm going to have to take the extra from the Intrepid's allotment." The rain came down in sheets, but the balloon slowly inflated.

Diggs came out of the tent, lugging his heavy carpet bag. The very top of his hat filled with rain, becoming concave. He ran over to check on the sandbag ties, bent over, and a deluge of water poured off his head, soaking his boots.

"A nasty day for us to go up," said Woe. He shielded his eyes from the rain and looked toward the heavens. Woe added the last of the iron fillings to the tank of acid.

"Yes, unfortunately, orders are orders," said Diggs. "I can think of more pleasant things I'd rather be doing." He took off his hat and wiped his face with his hand. It didn't change the amount of rainwater streaming down into his mouth.

One of the smaller aeronaut's envelopes finished inflating, and the two-man crew climbed in the tiny basket. The ground crew disconnected the gas generator hose and untied the sandbags. The balloon ascended and drifted towards the north.

Diggs glared at the distant balloon. "We should be in the lead. I'm chief pilot." He loaded the carpetbag into the basket of his OZ balloon.

"If you did not sleep so soundly," said Woe, "we would have been the first on the lines. At least we do not have to wait to gas up until the Intrepid fills completely. That five-man crew uses one huge envelope and has an oversized gondola. Ours is even bigger." He looked over at the limp envelope of the Intrepid, barely filling with hydrogen. "Our gondola is the largest in the Union army. I am still amazed you could manipulate your way into obtaining this gargantuan of a basket, larger than the dinky townhouse we lived in during our sojourn in New York."

The warm rain continued to pour down. The sound of cannon fire was barely louder than the crash of thunder.

Diggs straightened up and sputtered as the rain ran into his mouth. "I deserve the best since I have so much piloting experience. Since we have the largest basket, we need the largest balloon. We convinced the brass we could observe and attack with troops in the basket. Too bad no one else will ship with us."

Woe checked the valve fitting. "Whoever heard of an both an attack and observation balloon? They wanted to put two small cannons into the basket. Just what we need near the hydrogen gas, an open flame vent port. They wanted one cannon soldier and five sharpshooters. We stalled long enough that they never placed the cannons, and all the soldiers quit. They could not follow orders fast enough in the gondola to your satisfaction."

Diggs began to climb into the gondola. "I'm going to drown, with all this water. If the rain didn't run from out under the slats, we'd be swimming laps in here."

"The troops really left because they could not stand your sense of humor. There was the fact you constantly made voices come out of your rear end, and always cheated them in poker."

Woe and Diggs could faintly hear the men in the first basket cheering as the lead balloon reached the designated height. Suddenly a bolt of lightning struck a tall tree far underneath the soaring balloon. At the same instant, a branch bolt of lightning went sideways from the main chain and struck the envelope of the first balloon. Diggs jumped at the tremendous explosion. He looked up and saw a flaming ball plummeting to the earth.

Burning remnants of the envelope fabric and a blazing basket crashed to the ground. Slumped in the flames was the partially destroyed body of one of the crewmen. There was no sign of the other.

"*Wǒde tiān na*," screamed Woe. "Oh my God, Oh my God! Where is Jones? Is Freemont alive? The horror!" He sprinted over and beat at the flames on the basket with a saturated horse blanket.

"Deader than a doornail," said a union private from the ground crew. "I think? They were good men, and this was a terrible way to die. At least it was quick." The soldier hugged himself and slumped over.

Diggs screamed, "This is senseless. An absolutely horrible way to die." He pulled Woe back from the futility of fighting the flames, "Maybe this is a sign we shouldn't go up." Diggs trembled.

Woe fought with Diggs, trying to continue dousing the fire. Finally, he dropped his hands onto his knees. Woe stared hopelessly at the corpse with tears in his eyes. "I hate to say it, but we still have to go up. These two should not have died in vain. Our fellow soldiers will need the information, or many more will die."

"Let someone else risk their lives," said Diggs. "I have too much to live for." He shook his fist and turned away from his expanding balloon. "Besides, we didn't ask to be in this damn war."

Sergeant O'Sullivan rushed up. "Damn, *uafáis dho-inste an chogaidh*." He stared down at the burned corpse.

"Ufa — what, Sergeant?" said Diggs. "I'm going to get the doctor, then please excuse me, but I have a very important telegram to send." He began to bolt.

O'Sullivan pointed his bayonet at Diggs. "Halt, soldier. You ain't leaving. Uafáis, means 'this is one of the unmentionable horrors of war' but one has to accept them. We still need those reports. Cannon fire is pinning our troops down, and we must take the upper bridge to get into the city."

"Let someone else get them," said Diggs. "I'm not going up." He crossed his arms and pushed his boots into the mud.

O'Sullivan stepped forward and stabbed Diggs greatcoat with his rifle. "We need you, pilot. You are the chief aeronaut of this unit. You must go up now." He took one hand off his gun and pointed. "Make sure you drift to exactly over the north bridge. That's where we desperately need the information."

Diggs shook his head. "I ain't going." He gingerly tried to disengage from the bayonet while shaking.

"I volunteer," said Woe. "I will ascend even if Oscar does not." He gently pushed the rifle away from Diggs and then gave a salute to the sergeant.

"Why are you so patriotic?" said Diggs. "You don't even belong in this war." He looked down at his chest and checked for puncture wounds.

Woe resolutely looked Diggs in the eye. "Oscar my friend, your Lincoln was right. Slavery is wrong and every man should be equal. Plus, if we do not relay important observations, many of our troops, our friends, will die." He began walking towards the balloon. "I am going up with or without you."

Diggs took a step and grabbed Woe by the arm. "Chang, you're an idiot, but a loyal one." His entire body trembled, and he pulled Woe closer. "I can't let you die alone. We are partners to the end. I would never let you go up by yourself. But to tell you the truth, I'm scared out of my wits." He turned and faced the sergeant directly. "Now how in the world do we control the direction of drift in this crazy, blustery weather?"

"General Wilson said something to me about side venting the hydrogen once you get the right height," said O'Sullivan. "He said they learned about that in engineering school. Not exactly sure what this means. But it should allow you to control your direction of the drift."

"Works better with a hot-air balloon," said Diggs. "But we can try. Do you understand the general, Chang?" Diggs shuddered as he looked at the charred, dead man. The smell of burnt flesh permeated the air. "Chang, talk me out of this. I can't believe I have to follow your principles to a certain death."

"I have never heard of that balloon maneuver," said Woe. "But it sounds logical and we can do it together. But remember, you are the pilot, I am only the engineer." Woe walked over to their balloon to check on the progress of inflation.

Once the envelope fully distended, Diggs watched Woe disconnect the gas generator hose from the manufacturing machine. Woe carefully left the hose connected to the envelope of the balloon and pinched it off. The OZ engineer coiled the other end of the hose into the basket and he climbed aboard. "I am as ready as I ever will be, my friend."

Diggs climbed in and motioned to the ground crew to cast off. The OZ slowly ascended to about one hundred feet, and Woe opened the hose slightly. With the balloon side vent facing southward, the escaping gas propelled the balloon quickly to the north. The men headed for the upper bridge into Columbus.

Immediately, Confederate sharpshooters fired at the envelope, but the bullets missed the balloon. A cannonball hurtled past the two men.

Woe partially pinched off the hose, slowing down the escape of hydrogen gas. Now the balloon was just slowly rotating in place. The rain plummeted onto the balloon envelope.

Another Reb cannon boomed. The two men saw the ball ascending towards them. Suddenly, a bolt of lightning came out of the sky. The bolt struck the cannonball.

A hiss of hydrogen could be heard.

A flash of intense light.

An enormous explosion.

The OZ balloon vanished.

Chapter Eight

Woe slowly lifted his head and looked around. "Where in the world are we? What happened?" He peered out through slats in the basket and saw a good distance beneath him continuous hills of pure white sand. Billowing waves of heat radiated off the desert. There was a lack of any discernible odors of any sort in the air. No creatures stirred on the sands below.

He swayed with dizziness as he grabbed onto the railing. "Am I still alive?" he muttered. He ran his hands up and down his body. "I seem to be in one piece? Where's Oscar? Did he get blown up?"

The air over Columbus, Alabama, on Easter had been bitterly cold. This locale was quite warm, nay hot. Woe sweated, while even dressed in his light clothes. He felt his pulse racing, either from the heat or fear, or both.

There were no clouds at all in the intense blue sky. The sunlight glared down on the balloon.

Woe saw the body of his friend Diggs at the far end of the gondola. The explosion must have blown him the entire length of the basket—a good fifteen feet. Was Oscar dead? Woe hesitantly walked over to Diggs and stumbled twice. He threw himself down next to Diggs and cradled him in his arms. Then he detected that the man appeared to be breathing. "*Xiè tiān xiè dì.*" Woe stopped holding him and raised his arms to the heavens instead. He bent over and felt for the pulse in Diggs's neck and said in English, "Thank goodness." Woe felt a firm but slow heartbeat. Diggs' head lay next to the carpetbag. The bag must have protected his cranium from any severe trauma, thought Woe. Not even any injuries worse than some minor lacerations and abrasions. He eased his friend's head away from the bag, opened it, and rummaged through it to see if any medical supplies remained. Woe took out a partially full bottle of whiskey and uncorked it. He waved the fumes under Diggs' nose. Woe paused, looked at the bottle in his hand, raised it up to his lips and he took a long swallow. His hand trembled as he lowered it down to Oscar's mouth and poured a trickle into Diggs' mouth. He smiled, raised it up, and then took another swallow himself. Finally, he recorked it and put it back in the bag.

Woe shook Diggs. Gently at first, then with increasing urgency. "Wake up, friend. Where are we? I do not remember the Sahara Desert being in Alabama. How did we get here?"

Woe stopped shaking Diggs and shook his own head to clear it. "This had to be a dream, or is it a nightmare? I had better check to see if we are floating normally?" He walked on wobbly legs back toward the central gas hose and vent. It was intact. "I assume the balloon is still in the air?" Woe peered over the rail and estimated that they were fifty feet up in the air, about half their previous altitude.

In the basket's corner was a pile of dirty rags, coiled rope, and stacked up sandbags. A soft scurrying sound emerged from the accumulation of trash. Diggs remained unconscious, so Woe walked over to the pile in order to investigate the noise, and cautiously nudged it with the toe of his boot. Exploding from the rags were a dozen mice. They scattered to the four corners of the basket. Two of the mice scampered under the bottom slat of the basket and fell down through the sky. The remaining ten cowered up against the wooden slats. They froze, quivering in fear.

Woe walked to the edge of the basket and looked over the rail. As far as the eye could see were only pure white hills of sands. Even at fifty feet, he could feel intense waves of heat reflecting from the ground. Woe muttered to himself. "I doubt I could observe anything that small at this elevation. I do not see any little mouse corpses littering the sands." He yelled over his shoulder. "Oscar, I will vent some more hydrogen gas, partially to decrease explosive risks, partly because we will be safer flying lower." Woe looked up at the sky. "I hope I am not talking to a dying person."

Woe walked back to the main clamped-off hose in the center of the envelope. As he went past Diggs, a quiet moan escaped from the man's lips.

Diggs stirred. "Oh, my head, how much did I drink last night? Did I at least win at poker?" He opened only one eye, screwing his other tighter against the glare of the sun. Diggs rolled over to his belly and attempted to push himself up. He collapsed back down. "What the hell happened? Why is it so blooming hot? Are we in Hell?"

"Oscar, calm down," said Woe. "Take a deep breath. It will help."

"That's the problem Chang, I don't think it will help." Diggs looked up at his friend and inhaled. "I can't smell any odors in the air at all. Where are we? What kind of place has no scent?"

Woe contemplated and then looked concerned. "A void? Maybe we are in your Christian purgatory?"

"Yes, complete lack of scent. What makes this place so different? How can we be alive? What happened?"

Woe looked down at Diggs. "Well, I am extremely relieved you are back with me. Since you smell so atrocious from sweat, I assume we are in the land of the living. As to what happened, I do not know. It is so hot because we are not high in the cold air above Alabama anymore. Maybe we got blown all the way to Africa or westward to the Mojave?" Woe walked over and unclamped the hydrogen hose. He vented some of the gas, causing the envelope to deflate slightly. The balloon dropped rapidly. Woe counted out loud and when he felt enough gas escaped, pinched the hose again. He walked over to the slats and looked down. "Perfect. I estimate we are hovering only twenty-five feet above terra firma and still drifting somewhere. I only see sand everywhere."

Diggs slowly rose to his feet and put one hand to his head. "All I remember is seeing a flash of light and then experiencing an explosion. My head sure is killing me, but at least I have my top hat. Is anyone still shooting at us? Where did the sand come from?"

Woe looked down at the desert and frowned. "Yes, where in the world are we? I am not religious, but if we died, this is a terrible afterlife. At least no personages are shooting at us anymore."

Diggs stamped his foot on the floor of the gondola. "At least our basket is still intact."

At the stomping sound, the ten mice scurried all over the floor of the basket. They settled down in the four corners again and mainly just traded places.

Diggs peered at one group of mice. "I see vermin have infested us. I told Sergeant Brown something was nibbling on the drop ropes."

"I agree," one of the mice seemed to say. "Where are we? How did we get here?"

Woe frowned and shook his head. "Oscar, you are not amusing, and your lips are moving again."

"I have to continue to practice," said Diggs. "Maybe a sheik of this Arabian Desert might need a ventriloquist." He removed his top hat and used it to fan himself. Then Diggs took off his long coat, folded it, and placed it into his carpetbag. "But as our rodent friend said, how in the hell did we get here, wherever 'here' is?"

"I think I actually saw a bolt of lightning," said Woe. "Just before the explosion. Perhaps there was a second flash, but I cannot be positive. I started to black out at that time." He rubbed the few wispy hairs on his chin as he ruminated. "It happened so fast."

Diggs shuffled over to the slats of the gondola and looked down. "During our circus days, we traveled all over the states. No matter where we traveled, I never exactly saw a landscape such as this. These desolate hills look a little like the arid areas of the lower Midwest. But I never saw this much sand. And it sure is a hell of a lot hotter than Oklahoma or even Alabama in the summertime."

Diggs slowly walked towards one group of mice. "Here mousey, mousey."

Woe used his hand to fan himself. "Why in the world do you want a mouse? I think there were about a dozen before two jumped overboard."

"I can't pull a rabbit out of my hat," said Diggs. "But wouldn't pulling ten rodents out be amazing?" The mouse tried to escape but was chased by Diggs. The mouse ran under the bottom slat of the basket and fell. "Oops, nine, I guess."

Both Diggs and Woe ran to watch it hit the sands. Immediately upon contact, the mouse melted faster than a piece of ice in the scorching sun.

"I assumed the sand is warm," said Diggs. "But what in the world just happened?" He shielded his eyes with his hand. "Where did the mouse disappear to? Even at this height, shouldn't we be able to see it?"

"I know neither," said Woe. "But I think we should stay up here. I recommend we not try to ambulate on the desert. It looks deadly." He ran over to make sure someone tightly clamped the hose. "We should not try to go any lower." Woe then walked back to the railings of the gondola.

"This adventure is getting stranger and stranger," said Diggs. "And something tells me that Corporal Beekman will never pay me the sixty-five cents he owes me from the poker game three nights ago." He stalked the mice again.

Woe looked over the side. "Land ho. No more sand, about one-half mile ahead. The wind is blowing us towards the non-sandy terrain. I think I even see some buildings."

Diggs went to his carpetbag and removed his spyglass. He extended the telescope and raised it to his eye. "Beautiful countryside, but strange? It's all red. I've seen nothing quite like it. I want to go home, mommy."

"What is so strange about this?" said Woe. "We had red maples in Selma." He reached for the telescope.

Diggs refused to give up the spyglass and pushed Woe away from him. "Everything is that shade of color, not just the trees, the grass, the foliage, the buildings, and even the cows. I see nothing that resembles Alabama here. What in the hell is going on?" He began to rub his forehead.

The two men continued to stare downward as the balloon finally drifted over the red countryside. After a few minutes, they looked down and saw extremely short people wearing strictly red garb strolling from building to building in a small village.

Nine rodents stood on their hind limbs, shoulder to shoulder, front paws clenched, and pleaded with the men. "Can we see also, please?"

Woe rapidly turned his head back and forth between staring at Diggs's mouth and the mice. "Oscar, this is no time for foolish tricks."

Diggs put his hand on his heart. "I swear, Chang my friend. This time I didn't throw my voice. I wasn't doing the talking."

Chapter Nine

Woe leaned over the basket's edge. "Oscar, where in the world are we? How can we explain living through an explosion which should have killed us, the red miniature cows, the talking mice? Can this day get any more impossible?"

Diggs walked slowly to the edge of the balloon basket near Woe, being careful to skirt farther around the gaggle of gossiping mice. "That is the problem. I don't think we are in our own world."

Woe pointed with a shaky finger at a man exiting a house in the tiny village below. "Good grief, Oscar, that man is terribly shorter and fatter than you are. He is dressed ostentatiously and completely in red."

"Hello from Glinterville," yelled the man in red upward. "Are you coming to liberate us, oh great OZ?" He waved upwards at the low-flying balloon. "Come out, come out, fellow Quadlings, and rejoice, a wizard has arrived."

Even twenty-five feet in the air, Diggs and Woe could see a very short man jumping up and down. A tall, peaked crimson hat with dozens of bells on the rim tinkled merrily as he excitedly leaped. He wore maroon boots with long toes that curled at the tips, puffy mid-calf pantaloons, and a burgundy jacket over a blood-red striped shirt. The man's beaming face was a pale ivory color, but everything else about him was red.

The wind from the South died down, as the balloon now drifted slowly over the village. Red tree leaves covered the dome-shaped roofs of the buildings. The leaves barely moved off the roofs.

Dozens of short, round people streamed out from cardinal-colored houses. Small children scurried out. All the populace congregated around the central well in the middle of the tiny village, waved and cheered.

"What is going on?" said Woe. "I wonder if we were we slipped opium during the battle? Did we suffer a concussion from the explosion and are hallucinating? Where is Columbus? How can mice speak English? For that matter, how can we understand these strange foreign, little people so well?" Woe leaned over and tried to yell a greeting in Mandarin to the crowd. No matter how many times he attempted his native tongue, the words came out in English.

"Come down, oh Great OZ," yelled one of the crowd. The man nearest the well pulled up a bucket of liquid and poured a libation on the ground. "For you, Great OZ! Red wine. Please be our ruler."

The wind picked up and the balloon finally drifted past the tiny village. Both men stood frozen in a state of shock. From under the rag pile, small voices called out, "We're hungry! When do we eat around this place?"

"Chang, please pinch me," said Diggs. "Perhaps I'm sleeping, and this is all a dream." He took off his hat, wiped his brow, and then plopped down on the floor of the basket.

Woe came over and pinched Diggs on the arm. "There."

Diggs furiously rubbed his sore arm and whimpered, "I didn't really mean for you to do it."

"I cannot believe this situation either, Oscar," said Woe. "And, to add to the mystery, how did they know your name is OZ?" Woe pointed up to the huge white letters on the envelope of the balloon. "Just because they all spoke English, how could they all read English writing? I doubt the mice signaled them with semaphore, and I did not hear you call out your stage name." Woe frowned and shook his head.

Diggs inhaled deeply. "Chang, smell that difference from the air over the desert. Now it smells of cinnamon, strawberries, and life? I think I like this part of this strange land a lot better than the sand."

The wind picked up, and the balloon continued to drift over the red countryside. Majestic miniature redwoods almost brushed the bottom of the gondola.

Woe shook his head. "When I first arrived from Hong Kong, I went through the Redwood forest, in California." Woe smiled. "These trees, as well as the people of this land, are rather on the small side."

Five of the mice climbed up the slats of the gondola basket and described the scenery to the other four. The leader started a running commentary. "Nothing to eat. Nope, still nothing, Darn! Still nothing. Nope, nope."

A second fat male mouse, even larger than the leader, stared down. "You all ain't looking in the right places. There's got to be grub somewhere in this here countryside. Nope, you all are right, there's nada."

A young mouse peeped, "What kind of food is nada? Why is Slim talking so funny, Frederick?"

"Slim came to Alabama," said the first mouse, Frederick. "During a cattle drive. He hid in a chuck wagon. He's originally from somewhere called Texas." The mouse suddenly pointed up, not down, and began yelling. "Look, look! Something's coming towards us. Maybe it will be lots of yummies to eat?"

Woe ran over and stared upwards. "Oscar, now I think I am dreaming. There is a flying carriage coming towards us. And it is not being pulled by flying horses, but by giant red swans."

Diggs slowly uncurled from his sitting position and rose. He walked over to his carpetbag, rummaged inside, and pulled out his spyglass. He turned toward the flying birds and placed the telescope to his eye. "Twenty swans are pulling a woman in a chariot. She is controlling them with long reins. It appears the lead swan keeps turning his head around and saying something to the woman. Maybe just quacking? Do swans quack?"

"Could this day get any stranger?" said Woe. He ran over to borrow the spyglass, but Diggs would not give up his turn. "I cannot see the impending situation adequately. Oscar, give me an equal opportunity at the telescope."

"The woman is wearing a silvery-white tiara," said Diggs. "Maybe we are going to be visited by royalty?" He shoved the telescope up against his eye. "Wait, she just picked up a… wand?" Diggs twisted the focusing ring of the spyglass over and over. "My eye must be deceiving me."

The remaining four mice climbed up to join their brethren. All nine rodents chattered among themselves and waved at the approaching vehicle. The chariot swiftly drew closer and finally stopped, the swans hovering just in front of the balloon.

Diggs gaped at the chariot. "Holy smokes. That thing is just floating in the air. And she's driving something that's as long as our oversized gondola basket."

As the OZ balloon continued to drift with the wind, the swans had to back up slowly in time with the balloon's movements. Their wings flapping in unison made a "whu, whu" sound in the air.

Embossed on the chariot was a filigree of gold lacquer and red enamel designs, with white trim around the edges. It had no wheels. The woman in the vehicle was so short she barely could see over the front rim at the swans.

"I am Glinda the Good," stated the woman in the chariot. "Who are you two? Do you mean to claim the throne of Oz, wizard?" Glinda pointed her wand first at the "OZ" on the envelope and then at the two men.

"How is that thing staying up?" said Diggs. He stared at the woman. "What is a Glinda the Good? What is the throne of Oz?" Diggs backed up slightly and handed the spyglass to Woe.

The twenty swans easily maintained pace with the drifting balloon, only occasionally flapping their wings. The lead swan snapped at the rodents and then gave an explosive snort. One of the mice then blew a raspberry at the swan, and the other mice booed loudly. Slim held up his middle part of his paw.

"Your flying machine displays the white royal emblem of Oz," said the woman. "White is only to be used by the most powerful witches and wizards." Glinda touched her white tiara as she spoke.

The lead swan leaned his long red neck towards the chattering mice. "I'm hungry. Can I eat those rodents, Your Majesty?" The bird's beak and eyes were black, the rest of his body a ruby red. He opened his mouth widely and meowed. "Sorry, old habits. I should have hissed."

Diggs' eyebrows rose up, and he frowned. "Do my senses deceive me? Talking swans, mice, witches, and wizards? None of this can be real. There's no such thing as witches. Talking animals proves nothing. I can make anything seem to talk. I'm a great ventriloquist." Diggs took a deep breath and even then, his lips moved.

Woe rolled his eyes. "That is debatable."

"Not now, Chang." Diggs turned towards the chariot. "Where are we? And you mice, keep quiet or I might let you be eaten."

"You are in the Quadling Country," said Glinda. "In the Land of Oz." She raised both hands and gestured at the countryside. "And as for your assuming that there is no such thing as witches or magic… I assume you call yourself a wizard and are the owner of this flying machine?" Glinda pointed her wand towards the basket and waved it. Diggs's union clothes and boots turned pure white. She waved the wand again and the nine filthy, grayish-white mice changed into miniature reddish piglets. "Mice, since you were so rude and acted like pigs, you are now piglets. And wizard, you should wear white. Show that you deserve to wear the royal white wizard garb, or I will destroy you. Show me true magic."

Diggs stepped to the edge of the basket. "Um, pick a card, any card?"

Chapter Ten

Diggs saw the swans pull the magnificent chariot to within ten feet of the balloon. He hopped down from the railing into the gondola.

The lead swan said to the woman, "Please Mistress, can I just eat one of the transformed piglets? You changed them into such a nice bite-size, still just as tiny as mice. But I enjoy pork even more than rodents."

"Salvador, I never should have used my magic to change you from a cat, into a bird." said Glinda. "You still think like a hungry feline rather than a majestic swan." She stepped off the chariot onto the air itself. Glinda floated across the gap, up over the railing, and walked as though using steps down into the gondola.

Diggs stared at the woman in amazement. "How do you walk or float on air? What is going on? Where is your flying carpet? I'm confused!" Diggs rubbed his eyes.

"For short distances, I don't even need a broom or buoyant bubble to convey me," said Glinda. "It's simple to use magic to walk on air." She cavalierly waved her hand.

The witch wore a red taffeta dress, cardinal-colored shoes, and a white tiara with a giant ruby stone in the center. Around her neck, she had a string of the same stones, each the size of goose eggs. Diggs was surprised that she could even lift her hand to pat her hair or wave, since Glinda had gaudy, massive, jeweled rings on each finger and thumb, and a solid gold bracelet inlaid with more giant rubies on each wrist. Diggs thought she appeared svelte, but it was hard to be sure. He estimated she was wrapped in about fifteen yards of fabric. The woman appeared to be approximately Chang's age—late twenties. She barely came up to Digg's chest.

"If I knew I was going to have to entertain a fellow magic user, I would have dressed up," said the witch. Glinda waved her wand, and a small hand mirror materialized and floated in front of her. She first smoothed her hair back in place with her free hand. Then she snapped her fingers, and a lipstick appeared. Glinda applied another thick coat of ruby red to her already brightly colored mouth, waved again, and the lipstick vanished. "Now impress me or suffer the consequences."

"They grow them small here in Quadling county," said Woe. "I need to put the spyglass away." He waved the telescope over his shoulder as he began to walk away. Then he turned around and peered back at the woman. Woe tried to estimate the worth of the precious stones. Could he and Diggs borrow a few, he wondered? Turning once more, he dropped the scope into the carpetbag.

"Quadling country is just one of four countries in the marvelous Land of Oz." Glinda walked the length of the gondola and stared up at Woe's back. "We don't have many giants in our land like you gentlemen."

Glinda tapped Woe's back with a regal, appearing crimson wand. "This is my symbol of power." She then turned and walked back to the railing and looked up at Diggs. She held her wand up to his nose. "Don't make me use this."

Woe back flipped in place and turned to face the witch. He stretched and then did two cartwheels over to her. He rose to his full height and held out his hand. She looked confused, but then transferred the wand to her other hand and reciprocated. Woe grasped her hand with both of his and gave it a quick, firm shake. As he disengaged, he had three of her rings in his palm. He transferred them up his sleeve when Glinda waved her wand, and he froze in place.

The witch daintily took the rings back and replaced them on her digits. "Naughty, naughty. That was not a smart thing to do. Don't you have any brains at all? I should leave you enchanted forever. But I do enjoy scoundrels."

Diggs ran over and shook Woe. Woe didn't respond or even blink his eyes. "Chang, are you dead? You are my best friend and you still owe me two dollars from our last poker game!" Diggs stood up on his toes and whispered, "You should never try to fill an inside straight."

"Just frozen," said Glinda. She transferred the wand back to her other hand and waved it.

Woe blinked, took a huge breath, and shuddered. "I could not move, it was horrible. I could still see and hear." He laughed. "And it is you who are beholden to me for two dollars for the last game. I realize it is illogical to go for inside straights." Woe rolled his shoulders and twisted his neck. "Much better. That situation was exceedingly frightening."

Glinda pointed her wand at Diggs. "Now, if you both don't want to end up as permanent statues in my red rose garden, prove you should be allowed to be called a wizard."

"Lovely lady, can't we negotiate?" said Diggs. "It's too pretty of a day to turn people into pigs or statues." Out of the corner of his mouth, he asked Woe, "How do we get out of this?"

"If you want your flying conveyance to carry the royal emblem of a white OZ, then you have to earn it," said Glinda. "Prove to me you are a wizard." The witch ignored Woe and glared at Diggs.

"Wonderful, now notice there is nothing up my sleeves." Diggs pushed up the sleeves of his long coat and shook his hands briskly. Suddenly in one hand appeared a filthy bouquet of wilted paper flowers.

Glinda frowned.

Diggs stepped closer and pulled a dozen dirty scarves out of Woe's nose.

The witch grimaced.

He stepped up to the railing and picked up two of the red piglets. Diggs held one in each hand and pushed the piglets together. The two swine appeared to mold into just one pig. He continued to do this with each pair until only a single piglet remained. Diggs snapped his fingers and the last pig disappeared.

With this last magic trick, Glinda appeared somewhat impressed, until from inside Digg's coat pocket came tiny voices. "It's dark in here! We're hungry. Let us out."

"Sir, you are nothing more than a humbug." Glinda looked up at his face. "A cute scallywag, but certainly not a true wizard." She shook her head and lifted her wand.

"Wait, madam, one more attempt to prove I am worthy. It necessitates the sacrifice of one of your swans, though. It involves a mighty spell, with the use of one of my powerful... err... thunder sticks."

"I can't allow the loss of Salvador. Let me protect him." Glinda walked over and grasped the lead swan gently by its long neck. She pulled his head towards her and she planted a red kiss on its forehead. The bird squawked and looked startled. The lipstick mark glowed brightly, then vanished. "There, perform your spell."

Diggs walked over to his carpetbag, reached in, and removed his two pearl-handled single shot dueling pistols. He marched over to the edge of the basket, yelled, "Abracadabra" and discharged them both into the lead swan's breast. There were two loud bangs, the swan jerked backwards by one foot, and two black soot marks appeared on its crimson breast. It flinched, but appeared unharmed.

"Pretty toys, but we have gun trees all over Oz," explained the witch. "They produce all sizes of pop pistols. The ones in north Gillikin country are much bigger and make a louder noise. They are an ugly purple though, not a pretty red, like the ones from my Quadling trees." Glinda frowned, then smiled at Diggs' confused expression.

"Why didn't anything happen to the fowl?" murmured Diggs. "Why didn't it die?" He held up the empty guns and continued to gape at the bird.

"The special kiss of Glinda the Good protects him," said the woman. "Nothing can harm anyone so blessed. I'm not sure the insolent fowl really deserves it, but he is a faithful servant."

Salvador tugged at the chariot's reins. "Wow, that smarted. I want to leave."

"Halt, bird. We leave when I say so." Glinda frowned at the swan and gestured for it to stop. She turned, smiled at Woe, and winked at Diggs. "You both are scoundrels and the short one is a true fraud."

"Madam, wrong use of the vernacular," said Woe. "I consider myself someone who is picaresque. Diggs is quite the charlatan indeed."

"What does that mean?" said Glinda. "In plain Ozian?"

Chang made an extremely low, sweeping bow to the witch. While bending over, he did a one-handed handstand and pointed to himself with the other. "The expressions mean that I am a daring rascal and Oscar is a humbug."

"I resent that remark," said Diggs. He also bowed but didn't get anywhere as low. Diggs stumbled and almost fell over.

"I enjoy your language, nimble man," said the witch. "Perhaps I won't enchant you both. You did amuse me for an afternoon. It's so boring here for me. Nothing to do, and no one interesting to talk to. No good gossip in my Magic Book of Records." She yawned. "I will let you leave Quadling country and let the other witches take care of you. I will follow your progress in my Book. Do not come back to my realm if you don't want to be severely dealt with." Glinda turned to go.

"Wait Glinda," said Diggs. "That kiss was real magic, wasn't it?" He turned one pistol up to his eye and looked down the barrel. Diggs saw Woe flinch at this maneuver. "Can you teach me some tricks so we can survive? I will pay you with gold."

"Bah. A pretty, but common metal. In Oz, we use it to line our toilet bowls," said Glinda. "It is lying around everywhere. We have so much of it. You might bribe the Gnome King, to obtain magic—a greedy creature who constantly adores all gold and gems. Or work a trade by bringing something of huge importance to one of the evil witches, like Mombi, the Wicked Witch of the North. Either might teach you magic, but I'm not interested in a transaction."

"Where do I find this Gnome King or Mombi?" Diggs put his revolvers back into his carpetbag.

Salvador glared at him, hissed, and spat.

Glinda began to walk up steps of air until she was at the basket railing. Then she turned and looked down into the eyes of Diggs. "You won't be able to find the Gnome King. He lives in another land and underground. Mombi will probably try to eat or enchant you the minute you cross her doorway. But she lives that-a-ways." She pointed north.

"Can you at least tell me what I can do, so Mombi won't try to enchant us immediately?" said Diggs. As he pleaded, he gave her a hangdog look and clasped his hands together.

"She is a powerful witch and very evil," said Glinda. "She loves to be flattered, but is she uglyyyy." Glinda lifted one hand and shook her head. "She doesn't have a lot of friends. All of us fellow witches never visit her, and she must be lonely. Try to get on her good side, if she has one, or maybe even charm her, like you have me. That might work. She lives up in Gillikin country, way past the village of Jinxville."

"Where is this Jinxville? We'll need to buy supplies." Diggs reached over to the railing and took up Glinda's hand. He bent over it and planted a huge kiss on the back of it. "And I would be forever in your debt if you could think of some way to help us." He straightened up and stared deeply into her eyes.

Glinda blushed. "You might be a humbug, but you are somewhat lovable. Jinxville is north, past the Great Chasm." She waved her wand, and the wind began to blow briskly from the south. Huge black storm clouds came with the winds. The balloon drifted rapidly north.

"Darn the spell didn't work exactly as I planned… again," said Glinda. She turned her wand and looked at its end. "Well, practice makes perfect. Sorry, gentlemen. I think you're going to run into some rain."

The rag nest blew into absolute chaos. "Look like we need to batten down the hatches, mateys," yelled a tiny voice.

Woe faced the nest. "Now we have a mouse—no, a tiny swine—that is nautical in nature?"

"Thank you, oh great sorceress, for the wonderful assist." Diggs held her hand a moment longer than necessary and gave it a squeeze. He winked at her.

"Oh, I know I am going to regret this," said Glinda. She smiled and stared into Diggs' twinkling eyes. The witch pulled her hand away, then floated over and up to Woe. Glinda raised up on her tippy-toes on the air and planted a kiss on his forehead. She floated back and repeated the maneuver with Diggs. The ruby-red mark of her lips glowed brightly on their faces, then quickly magically faded. "I'll even leave your clothes white, humbug. Let people think you are a true wizard. I love a good joke."

"Wow, does that tingle," said Woe. He quizzically touched his forehead. "I assume that this mark will somehow protect us?"

"I see why the duck, I mean swan startled," said Diggs. "It felt a little like a branding iron."

"As if you ever were near a cattle range," laughed Woe.

"Perhaps not," said Diggs. "That is one occupation I never partook of. So now Glinda, we are safe? Nothing to worry about?"

"You'll do fine, much harder to kill," said Glinda. "Good luck. Oh yes, in that direction, watch out for the Great Chasm Dragon." She looked towards the north and applied her lipstick. "It will probably try to either battle, eat, or just plain destroy you. The beast loves a good fight."

"Mommy," whimpered Diggs.

Chapter Eleven

The balloon drifted lower and lower as the hydrogen gas in the envelope slowly leaked out of the hose nozzle. The canvas of the envelope looked as wrinkled as a prune.

The black clouds continued to gather, and the wind picked up. Suddenly, large rain droplets pelted the envelope. The squall drenched the gondola and puddles formed on the floor. As quickly as the rain started, it ended. A brilliant sun came out and the northerly wind died down to more sedate gusts. During the rainstorm, the temperature dropped by twenty degrees. The air rose back to a sweltering level.

Diggs looked up at the envelope, peered anxiously down over the railing, took off his hat, and scratched his head. "I hope that drop in temp didn't cause an even greater gas loss. This leak is worrisome. If there are any mountains, then we'll never elevate over them." He shook his hat and tried to get as many droplets of water off as possible. "And I hope we don't drop into the chasm. I didn't sign up to be a USS Alligator submarine captain; just a balloon pilot."

The balloon sank lower and lower over a group of exotic fern-like plants that stretched their branches towards the gondola. The two men stared down at the strange foliage.

"Chang," said Diggs, "I think those weird plants have a gigantic mouth. The orifices have long, sharp teeth, keep opening widely and appear to be drooling more than these piglets. They scare the wits out of me." He shuddered and crossed himself. Diggs stopped when he couldn't remember the proper sequence.

Because of the heat, the wood of the gondola dried. Some drips continued to rain down from the envelope.

They now floated over a yawning slit in the ground. The chasm had suddenly appeared, pitch black with a freezing cold mist came forth.

Diggs bent over the railing. He reached into his pocket and took out his money purse. After opening the bag, he reached in and pulled out a Golden Eagle coin. Diggs leaned further over and was about to drop it, but he shook his head. "Something smaller." He replaced the gold piece and pulled out a three-cent coin. Diggs tossed it over and watched it fall. "Chang, I can't see or hear it hit bottom. How deep is that ravine?"

"I do not know," said Woe. "I cannot process the information. Also, I wonder if it is the cold vapors or the situation itself that is making me shiver?" He wrapped his arms around himself.

The nine piglets came out of their nest and frolicked in the puddles. "Yo ho ho and a bottle of rum," sang one piglet. He started giving navigation advice.

"Quiet Benno," said Frederick. "You can't see a thing down here. We're too low on the floor."

Benno climbed up the railing, slipped once, and got to the edge. "Mister Diggs, you need to build us a crow's nest."

Five flying monkeys came up out of the ravine and hovered around the balloon. The creatures were gray and silver, furred, and their pelts were moth eaten.

"What in the Sam Hill are those?" said a filthy piglet, looking through the bottom slat.

"I have the heard the expression, 'when pigs fly,' but never monkeys!" said Diggs.

"Indubitably," said Woe. "And speaking of such, little piglet, what is a 'Sam Hill'?"

"I came to Alabama with the Vermont regulars," said the dirty piglet. "Before that, I was in a copper mining camp. Liam is my name, mining my game. 'Sam Hill' is the newest way of swearing."

Hundreds of giant ants, the size of dogs and enormous lizards, as big as Clydesdale horses, crawled up the sides of the chasm. The reptiles looked up at the balloon and stuck out their tongues, which almost reached the basket. Drops of drool dripped off the tongues. When the liquid hit the ground, it sizzled and smoked. The reptiles slithered back into the crevasse. The ants scurried around in aimless circles at the top of the chasm, then went back down.

The monkeys stared into the gondola. The beasts had muscular shoulders sprouting huge leathery wings with large holes in them. Their faces had many scars and deep wrinkles. One closest to the balloon wore a battered, tarnished crown, and the other four wore bowlers. The monkeys chattered among themselves. The leader monkey pointed at the OZ on the envelope and gave a thumb down to the others. They all dove back into the chasm.

The nine piglets looked out from the railing. They all jumped down, sniffed, and scurried back under the rags. "Call us," one said, "when there is something to eat, rather than everything looking like it wants to eat us."

"I have a terrible feeling about this area," said Woe. "Huge reptiles, giant ants, and flying primates." He trembled. "I fear this, locale. We need to dissect the situation more clearly. I will see if there is anything in our bag to make me feel safer." Woe rummaged through the carpetbag. "Is there nothing normal in this entire land? Very confusing. Perhaps we should somehow try to get back to Columbus?"

Diggs wrinkled his forehead and threw up his hands. "We won't make it. I haven't any idea how to get there, plus we're running out of hydrogen!"

"Once we get to Jinxville, I will convert to hot air," said Woe. "We are going to continue to fall lower." He stretched and then bent over. The nimble man did a handstand and walked on his hands over to the hose. Balancing on one hand, he shook the other, and rainwater droplets flew off from it. He repeated the maneuver with the other one. "I do not want to get my boots all wet." Woe flipped upright again and squeezed the connection tighter by hand. The gas leak slowed slightly.

"We probably can get a fire going to produce hot air in Jinxville." Diggs stared out over the railing, his hand shielding his eyes. "We just have to be sure to vent all the hydrogen gas away from any open flames or we might get blown back to Columbus. We are luckily that rainstorm didn't involve lightning. We'll empty this volatile substance fully and then fill up with the safe stuff."

The ravine seemed wider than most rivers. When the balloon was about halfway across, a gigantic entity flew up from the bottom. It appeared larger than the envelope and basket of the balloon combined. The vague red shape soon revealed a massive head, body, and two wings. The now-distinct creature lifted its head, opened its mouth, and a flame shot out.

The creature's wings beat lazily as it rose. With each flap, the men heard a thunderous whoosh. The balloon swayed and then moved back from the force of the beast's beating wings.

"Oh damn! It must be that dragon." Diggs ran over to his carpetbag and pushed Woe to the side. "Who knew that they were real? We must prepare, I'm too young to die." He reached into the bag and pulled out his dueling pistols and saber. He kept the guns in one hand and stabbed the saber into the wood of the deck. The sword quivered back and forth. Diggs transferred one pistol to each hand. His hands were trembling so much he dropped one pistol. He bent over and picked it back up again. "With these, at least we'll go down fighting."

The flame burst, stopped just short of the gondola of the balloon. The fire dissipated quickly, leaving a brimstone smell behind. No damage occurred to the basket, but it heated the air hotter than the atmosphere of the desert they had originally arrived over. The dragon continued to rise.

"We are doomed," said Woe. "If the slats of the wooden basket do not burn, then the bottom might. We will fall out or fall through. I have not learned the art of levitating or flying. Worse, the leaking hydrogen could explode and destroy us all." He moved away from the carpetbag and dropped in a lotus position. Woe put two fingers to his forehead. "Let me think, let me think. I must use my brains and solve this."

"Don't just sit there man," said Diggs., "Find a gun and shoot." He ran to the edge of the basket, aimed both revolvers, and pulled the triggers. Loud clicks occurred. "Damn, I forgot to reload after shooting the swan."

The dragon belched fire again and just missed the basket. The beast rose to the level of the gondola and faced the occupants. "Why do you invade my domain?" the dragon bellowed. "I am the Great Chasm Dragon, ruler of this ravine. Who dares come here uninvited?" The dragon's head was as large as the entire basket of the balloon. His massive eyes were the size of dinner plates, the teeth as long as stalactites. Smoke came out of its cavernous nostrils. The beast inhaled, preparing to flame anew.

Woe jumped to his feet and ran over to the saber. He slipped once on the mildly damp wood. Woe yanked it from the wooden floor and waved it in the air. "Surrender, lizard," he squeaked.

One of the giant dragon's eyes squinted almost shut. "Is an insect speaking to me?"

"What do you want?" yelped both Diggs and Woe at the same time. Woe charged toward the railing, waving his sword in the air.

Diggs retreated to the carpetbag to rummage for ammunition. He threw items out of the bag helter-skelter until he found a handful of bullets.

"No one dares to invade my realm," said the beast. "I am going to cook you and eat you white-dressed man, and your stick-waving companion." The gigantic dragon took another deep inhalation.

Diggs straightened up and turned towards the creature. He transferred both pistols into his left hand and shoved a bullet towards each pistol. His hands trembled, and not one bullet went into his guns. The pellets scattered and bounced all over the floor of the baskets. Diggs switched one pistol to his right hand and raced towards the railing.

"Wait, oh great Lizard," said Woe. He ran away from the railing, towards the rag nest. He plucked up some rags with the tip of the saber, reached down, and grabbed one piglet with his left hand. Woe lifted it to the sky and yelled, "Something to appease your royal hunger?"

The beast yawned, and a little smoke dribbled out of its mouth. "Bah! That wouldn't fill my back tooth."

"Help," squealed the little pig. "Put me down! I wet myself."

"Then will I do?" said Woe. He flung down the piglet and leaped up on the railing. He balanced on the thin edge and bent his knees. Woe clasped the saber in one hand and lifted it above his head. He stared at the mouth of the creature. "One, two, three, four," Woe said out loud.

"Chang, why are you counting?" said Diggs. "Don't do what I think you're stupidly planning." He swerved toward Woe, threw down one pistol, clutched at Woe's pant leg, but missed.

The dragon flamed. Timing it perfectly, Woe leaped over the fire. Diggs' fingers got singed.

Woe landed on the dragon's neck, just behind the head. He could barely straddle the broad neck. A huge neck spur just missed impaling him. Woe faced the beast's tail.

"Amazing how hot the skin is!" yelled Woe. "I can barely hang on!"

"Woe, what the hell are you doing?" said Diggs. "Come back or I'll jump over as well." Diggs stared as Woe clung on. Diggs raised the one empty pistol.

Woe now flung himself backward, landing flat on his back. He looked towards the dragon's tail, but his head pointed towards the dragon's head. Woe grasped the saber with both hands, raised the weapon skyward, blindly reached over his head, and plunged the blade down into the beast's eye.

The dragon screamed, belched more flame, and its globe exploded. The beast writhed in the air and tried to scrape at the weapon in its punctured eye. Its limbs were too short. The creature could not dislodge the saber from its orb. The Giant Chasm Dragon plummeted back into the chasm. Blood and ichor poured from the giant dragon's eyeball.

Diggs screamed as Woe barely hung onto the neck with his legs.

Woe plummeted into the ravine. "Farewell Oscar… my friend… *Au revoir*, until we meet again."

Diggs rushed to the gondola railing. "Changgg…!"

Chapter Twelve

"No," yelled Diggs. "Noooooooo."

Diggs hung over the basket railing and repeatedly pulled the triggers on his empty dueling pistol. He peered down into the chasm and furiously pounded on the wood. There were only patches of flames on the damp wooden sides of the gondola.

"What can I do?" he screamed. As Diggs bent over the railing, his top hat wobbled but didn't fall off. He watched his friend and the creature plunge down into the deep trench. Diggs ignored the fire, slowly creeping up the side of the gondola.

"Perhaps I should follow him?" cried Diggs to the air. He ran back to the gas escape valve, dropped his gun, and opened the valve to let some hydrogen out. His hands shook. The balloon deflated slightly, despite the valve being opened for a good five minutes. "Damn, this will take too long," he muttered.

One piglet ran out of the messed-up nest. "Dadgum it, Mister Diggs," squeaked Slim, "unless y'all fixin' to have us all burn to death, the basket is on fire. The damp wood from the rainstorm is slowing it down, but it's still so hot that any hens here be laying hard-boiled eggs. Do something."

Diggs ran back to the railing and looked down. "Oh my God! Leaking hydrogen and exposed flames." He rushed back to the release valve and relocked it. Diggs ran back to the railing and peered helplessly for his friend. He turned in a circle, threw his hands up in the air, and turned in another circle. Diggs stopped, took a deep breath, and hurried over to a sandbag. He pulled a penknife out of his coat and slit the bag open. Diggs grunted as he hoisted the heavy bag to the railing and poured the sand on the patches of flames. Then he used the now-empty bag to beat out the rest of the fire.

Diggs threw the empty bag to the floor. Staring forlornly down into the ravine, he attempted to project his voice into the ravine. "Pip, pip, I am perfectly all right, Oscar, my good man. Don't worry." His ventriloquial attempt at Woe's voice sounded false, even to his biased ears. Diggs' entire face trembled. "Chang, please come back and tell me my lips moved again." He flopped down on the wooden floor of the basket and burst into tears.

Eight little heads peeked out from the mess of rags. "Big wizard man," squealed one piglet. "Is everything safe now? Can we come out? Is there anything to eat?"

Diggs looked up as tears ran down his face. "Quiet rodents! My friend is gone. Eaten by a magical talking dragon. I don't know what to do." Diggs slowly stood up and looked over the edge. He stood at the railing and wept. He didn't say another word.

The balloon drifted over grasslands and foliage for hours. A small village came into view. The balloon was only ten feet above the top of tiny red houses.

Short personages, dressed completely in red, poured from the houses. All the townsfolk looked upward, pointed, jumped up and down, and screamed "OZ!"

In the center of the village, was a well. Diggs side-vented hydrogen to direct the balloon towards a large vacant space near the well. The crowds flocked around it and continued to look upward and yell excitedly among themselves. Next to the central structure was a building labeled "Bar". The people streaming out of this building wobbled, carrying mugs of liquid. Next to this building was one labeled "Town Hall". The members coming from there also staggered and carried even larger mugs.

When Diggs maneuvered over to the space, he opened the gas nozzle as wide as possible. The balloon now deflated. Diggs threw a sandbag, tied on to a drop line, down to the crowd. One man grabbed the line and was pulled upward off the ground.

Quickly, a few townspeople grabbed onto his legs. One child leaped as high as she could and grabbed on, but only pulled off one of the man's crimson pointy shoes. The townsfolk's combined weight slowed the ascent of the red man, and they dragged the balloon downwards. The Bar and Town Hall faction cheered mightily and waved their mugs about. Many of them yelled, "This calls for another drink!"

Diggs threw down two more sand-bags tied to drop lines, to completely tether the balloon. The nine piglets scurried up the slats of the baskets and peered at the crowd.

A rotund, elegantly dressed man with a larger mug than the others stepped forward. He was wearing clothes in various shades of red, a short jacket, knickerbockers, shoes with long curled toes, and a wide hat with little silver bells on the rim. "Welcome, oh great Oz, from all these Jinxians," he slurred. "You coming was predicted. But" he paused and took a large gulp of liquid, "we've been awaiting you for four hundred years. Somewhat late, oh great one ain't you?"

"Can you help me?" sobbed Diggs. He yelled down to the crowd. "A giant talking dragon ate my friend." He leaned over the railing and trembled. His hand shook as he pointed back in the direction he came from.

"You must be a powerful wizard indeed," projected the well-dressed man. "Few have ever survived the Chasm Dragon before." The man nodded his head briskly. Then he grabbed his forehead. "Oh, shouldn't have done that."

"Is there no one in this damn country that will help me?" Diggs bawled from over his shoulder as he walked back to the central hose. He checked on the progress of the escaping hydrogen.

"Hey! Where did he go?" said the elegantly dressed man. He tilted his head back, looked up at the gondola, staggered about, and took a few steps backwards.

After pinching off the gas hose, Diggs turned and came back to the railing. "Are you sure there is no one who can help me? Where exactly am I?"

"Oh, hooooo, so there you are," said the red man. "This here is Jinxville, inhabited by us Jinxians."

"And what the hell is a Jinxian?"

The short man saluted Diggs with his mug. "We are. The inhabitants of this wonderful village of Jinxville, where we drink all day and play all night. And as mayor of this fair village, it is my solemn duty to make sure I strictly enforce this rule. Reminds me, elections are coming up, I have to kiss some babes." The red man grabbed two women standing next to him and planted huge kisses on their cheeks.

One woman pushed him away. "Now Horace, quit that! You are running unopposed for your three hundred and thirty-third term. No one else wants the job. Besides, it should be babies, not babes." The other woman just frowned and swiped at her cheek.

"Jinxville? So we aren't in Oz anymore?" Diggs started to climb over the slats of the gondola. He saw he still was several feet from the ground and stopped. Although only a small distance above the ground, he hesitated, turned pale, and muttered to himself. "Now I develop a fear of heights? Chang would have laughed at me."

"Of course you are! Jinxville is the best village in all of Quadling country," said the mayor. "Here in the merry old Land of Oz. Fairly isolated in the north." Now the mayor tried to point in the other direction, but stumbled as he turned. "I assume, you floated in from the south. Those mountains to the north, are soooo high." The man twirled around to gesture, turned green and sat down. While sitting, he scooted around on his rear and pointed southwards. "Over there is the Deadly Desert, which you already passed over. You must indeed be a powerful wizard to best the Chasm Dragon, and to successfully pass over those burning sands. One touch of those grains and you dissolve." The mayor fell backwards.

"Ah yes, I am indeed a powerful wizard," said Diggs. "But I need a slight more magical help to defeat the dragon. We just fought to a standstill. Any ideas on which of you could help me?" He pointed his finger at one of the closer men and made a get over here motion.

"We are not as powerful as you are, oh Great One," said one man. "We Jinxians would not win in a fight against the beast."

The entire crowd nodded in agreement and muttered amongst themselves. Everyone took two steps backwards.

"I know I'm only five hundred years old," said the mayor. "But I haven't heard of anyone who dared fight the dragon. Even the four witches wouldn't oppose the beast." He appeared very nervous and continued to back away slowly.

"Oh yeah, witches. I'll get that Glinda to help me." Diggs looked back the way he had come.

The nine piglets jumped off the basket railing and burrowed under the rags. A muffled, tiny voice squeaked, "Don't go back! We hate that foul fowl."

"You know Glinda the Good?" said the mayor. "She's powerful, but still learning her magic."

"I'll say," said Diggs. "One wave of her wand and she blew me all the way here. And those pink piglets used to be mangy rodents."

"We're not mangy," peeped a tiny voice.

"We have heard many stories," said the mayor. "That Glinda just sits in her castle all day and reads from her Book of Records. Her book tells her everything that goes on in the world concurrently." He tried to raise his head to look up at the gondola, moaned, and settled back down again.

Diggs held up his white top hat and held out his arms. "She came out yesterday, to consult with me. We had major magic matters to discuss."

The Jinxians oohed and aahed and stepped back.

"Usually, she only goes up against beings or magic users weaker than herself," said the mayor. "She might try to protect you in your fight, but she won't assist you. Glinda supposedly guards all of Quadling country, but we haven't seen her for hundreds of years."

"Great, so who do I get to help me?" Diggs walked away from the basket railing and put his dueling pistols away. The balloon finally settled. Diggs jumped out of the basket before the envelope collapsed and covered him totally. "I can't fight the dragon all by myself."

Several voices cheeped from inside the basket. "Hey, who turned out the lights?"

The mayor got up, staggered over to Diggs, and bowed. "A drink in your honor." He snapped his fingers and motioned for another mug. "Ever since Pastoria gave up being king, some of the evil witches would love an alliance to take over and rule the entire Land of Oz. They only rule one country each. We need a strong wizard to control them." He took a huge swallow, and some liquid ran down his chin. The foam from the beer speckled his handle-bar mustache. "Perhaps, you could convince one of them to help you against the dragon. Then you, mighty wizard, could rule the entire Land of Oz with one of them. They could be your ass—, assocsh—, asscoshiates—, err, helpers. We haven't had one—hic-hic—central ruler since Pasterororia."

"Oh yeah, who is this, Pastoria? When and why did he abdicate?" Diggs had to look down to talk to the mayor. The man barely came to Diggs's chest, even when occasionally standing fully upright.

"He left the ruling of his kingdom around the time of one of my first terms in office. About three or four hundred years ago. Pastoria and his wife refused to talk about it. He was an okay king, but only had weak magic powers. Finally, he left with his wife and settled down in Jinxville. They finally had a baby just one year ago. Must not have had sex verrrry often. Somehow, Pastoria's wife died in childbirth. Strange?" The mayor stroked his chin and looked confused. "Few people ever die in Oz."

Diggs reached into the gondola, dragged out the collapsed envelope, and laid out the cloth. "Where do I find one of these powerful, evil witches?"

"The strongest evil witch is Mombi the Mad. She is on the other side of the mountains, past Winkie country. Go through that yellow land and you will find her in the purple Gillikin country."

"Each country is a different color? Why? And how does one persuade the witch to help me?"

"Each country in Oz has always been its own color. By the way, Mombi either assists you or eats you."

Diggs put his hand up to his forehead and rolled his eyes. "Wonderful."

Chapter Thirteen

Diggs laid the cloth balloon envelope onto the red grass and folded it as small as possible. He carefully pushed on any bulges as he folded to make sure no pockets of hydrogen remained. He left the deflated cloth on the ground, removed the long end of the balloon from the nozzle, carried it to the railing, and heaved it on top of the rest of the envelope. Then he walked to the gas nozzle, checked that there was not any residual hydrogen gas left, and tightened the valve one more time. When finished, he climbed over the slats of the basket and walked back to the crowd.

"This is a powerful magic flying machine," said Diggs. "Much better than brooms or swan-pulled chariots. But I need to make it even better to rescue my friend from the Giant Chasm Dragon. Who do I talk to about converting this into a hot-air balloon? I of course could do this myself, but I don't want to waste my energy. It needs to be done as soon as possible."

"A what?" slurred the mayor. "Never heard of this kind of magic? You should talk to the most famous engineers in Oz Smith and Tinker. We usually find them at their workshop in Evna, but the last I heard, they were hanging out on the moon." He took another drink from his mug.

"A little far for me to go to consult them. Any engineers closer than Luna I can use?" A small boy chimed up, "My next-door neighbor calls himself a tinker. Maybe he could help you?"

"Thank you, my lad," said Diggs. He reached into his pocket, pulled out a coin and flipped the boy a one-cent piece. "Please go fetch him for me."

"Thank you, oh Great Oz," said the lad. "Wow, Gee whiz." He looked at the Indian Head one-cent piece. "What's this lady got on her head? I'm sure this must be strong magic and will bring me good luck." The boy reached into his pocket and pulled out a small leather bag. He opened it and poured out a dozen huge rubies. "I am the Jinxville marble champion. These are my shooters." The lad put the coin into the pouch and closed it. "I can always get more marbles, they are everywhere on the ground." The boy ran off.

Diggs stirred the pile of discarded rubies with his foot. "These are everywhere? Just pebbles? Amazing." He climbed back into the basket and carried out the gas valve and empty tank. Diggs put them into the central square of the village, next to the well. "Don't let any flames get near this magic equipment. It would cause a terrible explosion. Another example of my powerful magic."

The mayor staggered as he headed back to the bar. He was careful to bring his empty mug with him. "I'll be back as soon as I get a refill."

After one-half hour, the Jinxville lad came back, accompanied by an extremely thin Quadling man. Tall by Oz standards, he came up to Diggs' neck. He carried a kit overflowing with work tools. The man bowed to Diggs while turning his head and looking down towards the short mayor's face. A crowd of men, women and children had followed to gawk at the wizard.

"Sorry it took so long, your honor," said the thin man. "I had trouble finding anyone to watch over my baby daughter." The Quadling man straightened and smiled. "I didn't think I should bring little Ozma to work, and I certainly didn't want the mayor to kiss her."

"Huh, what?" The mayor squinted up at the tall man, then he swayed side to side. "I know you! You fixed my shoes once."

"I am called Pastoria," said the man. "How can I be of help, oh Great Oz? My neighbor, Marvin the Marble Maven, told me you needed a tinker. So, I came." Pastoria turned to the lad. "Thanks for bringing me here. Now, run off son."

Diggs held out his hand to shake the tall man's hand. "So, you are a tinker?" He turned back to the lad. "Wait, Marvin, you can stay. How are you at getting rid of mice, err… piglets?"

Pastoria put his gear on the ground and hesitantly extended his hand. "What are you doing with your hand, some kind of spell?"

"A magic spell of greeting," said Diggs. He enthusiastically pumped Pastoria's hand up and down. "Pastoria? I heard that name before. Are you the same Pastoria who once was the king of the entire Land of Oz? What are you doing being just a tinker here in this little town?"

"Yep, that's me. Unfortunately, I always had to fake my magic powers," said Pastoria. "Once I lost control of the powerful flying monkey clan after using up my three wishes, I figured I couldn't win a battle with the evil witches."

"Wait, what the hell do you mean, flying monkey clan? I saw some in the Great Chasm. But there sure weren't a lot of them, and they didn't look strong. And what do you mean by three wishes?"

"The flying monkeys are a tribe of primates controlled by a magic gold cap. Whoever wears the headpiece gets to control the beasts three times. They will do anything the owner commands."

Diggs grabbed Pastoria's shirt. "Anything? Oh God, I could save Chang."

"Yes, the cap does anything. I escaped with my wife from our castle, the Emerald Citadel. Mombi the Mad stole the used-up golden cap from my castle, and her first wish was to raze the citadel. Her second was to have the monkeys conquer the Gillikins, and her third wish was to find me. She wanted to make sure I would never come back and try to regain my throne. But Mombi wasted the wish cause she couldn't locate me. Mombi is now a sworn enemy, furious that I still exist."

Diggs nodded. "I must get that cap. I'll use it to fight the dragon and save my friend."

"You just keep talking," said the mayor. "I'm gonna lay down and take a little nappy-poo." Falling to the ground, he closed his eyes and immediately began to snore loudly.

"I came here to Jinxville and lived with my wife for many years." Pastoria teared up as he spoke. "My beloved wife, Lorelei, and I, finally had a child after years of trying. Despite her being part fairy, my wife died during childbirth. I have lived in Jinxville, being disguised for years. My wife's last spell was hiding me, and Mombi never located me. I'm happy being a simple tinker here. I never wanted to be a king again."

The mayor stopped snoring and opened one eye. "Who the hell would want to be king? Even being mayor of this dinky town is too much work." He closed his lid and snored again.

Pastoria frowned at the sleeping mayor and tisked disapprovingly. "In Jinxville, I have tried to be a cobbler, a tailor, and now a tinker. None of my occupations have ever been successful. But enough of me. How can I be of help?"

Diggs pointed to his deflated balloon envelope. "I'll tell you what I want. This is my magic flying machine."

"Ah, a simple, but large hot-air balloon."

"It's not hot air yet." Diggs instructed Pastoria that he needed a firebox in the center of the wooden balloon basket to generate the hot air. The box had to produce enough to lift the huge gondola.

Pastoria pondered the problem and then pointed out two dilemmas. The first was any firebox could probably ignite the wooden basket. The second question was how to direct hot air into the balloon's envelope only. "I'm sure you already thought of this, Oz, but we can easily solve both problems. We could place the entire structure on a sheet of thin, cheap metal and the firebox should have long thin legs. The vent of the box will flow directly up into a chimney. Then the smoke will rise through the chimney and into the opening of the cloth envelope. We will lose some of the smoke, but not much." Pastoria climbed into the basket while lugging his work kit. He measured the central area with a cloth tape ruler. "Wow, this is a massive basket."

Diggs spread his arms widely. "It is the largest gondola in all the union army. I had to whine for days to get it. They wanted me to have a crew of ten and cannons. But," Diggs sniffed, "it holds only Chang and myself."

"Where is this Chang?"

"That's why I need some powerful magic. He's gone and I'm going back to save him, or die trying. I need a better working balloon."

Pastoria put his fingers to his mouth and blew a harsh whistle. Then he called, "Hey boys! One of you run back to my house and bring me one sheet of scrap metal from my closet. Fifteen by thirty inches should suffice." He held up his hands to show the approximate size. Pastoria motioned for the two young men to hurry.

Both lads rushed off, arguing between them as to who would have the honor of bringing the sheet. A short time later, they both brought back identical thin sheets of solid gold.

"This is the cheap metal?" said Diggs.

"It should work perfectly," murmured Pastoria. "Now I can build a fire box to sit on the metal. We can use pyrite coal to burn. It is extremely lightweight, stores easily and burns intensely, giving off significant amounts of hot air." He continued to draw out diagrams in the air with his finger.

"Now I need to plan how I'm going to get this Mombi to lend me that golden cap," said Diggs.

The mayor lifted his head. "Oh, my aching sinuses. What did I miss? Any lightning bolts, oh Great Oz? I love lightning bolts." He squinted up at Diggs.

"I am not sure oh Oz, that Mombi still has the cap," said Pastoria. "It's worthless after three wishes. I've heard through the Ozvine that she used the third wish years ago." He hesitantly held out his hand to help the mayor to his feet. "She might have sold the cap to one of the other witches, or she might have traded it for some magic potion or elixir."

The mayor's face turned red green, and he immediately sank down again. "I think I'm going to puke. Maybe some more to drink, to take the edge off? Great Oz, you can stay in our guest house and help me govern. It involves a significant amount of drinking."

Over the next four days, Pastoria built fireboxes. Daily, the nine piglets staggered around the central square. "Please Mister wizard, less decision making. Which red beer should everyone drink today, how many lunch box pails to eat for dinner? Our little tummies are going to burst."

Diggs saluted the piglets and Pastoria with his mug. "Governing is a heavy responsibility. Now friend, how is it going?"

Pastoria looked at Diggs with a frown on his face. "We have a problem. The first box made of iron was too heavy once placed in the gondola. The second attempt, out of solid gold couldn't take the heat and melted."

Diggs hiccupped. "I'm sure you'll figure out something."

"Can't you use a spell to make the iron one lighter oh Great Oz?" Pastoria looked down at his daughter crawling on the floor of the basket. "Sorry about Ozma being underfoot. No babysitting available today."

"That spell is not in my current repertoire," said Diggs. "Keep trying or I'll have to enchant you." Diggs sat in the shade of a tiny red maple tree, which barely protected him from the blazing sun. Diggs held his glass tankard up against his forehead. "Ahh, nice and cool." Condensation ran down his face.

Pastoria gestured at the mug. "Oz, you are brilliant. That's how to make the firebox."

Diggs peered up at Pastoria. "What are you talking about?" He took another gulp of beer.

"We have a master glass blower here in Jinxville. Sven Myxtomackelson will first blow us a large hollow box out of flame-resistant glass. He will then create four sturdy long legs. I will cut out a door on the main body with a diamond saw and attach glass hinges to it. He will blow separately the chimney and keep it hollow. Sven has the best annealing oven in all of Oz and will use it to fuse the chimney and legs to the main fire box. It is genius."

Diggs slowly got to his feet. He put his hand on his chin and rubbed it. "Sounds simple. Now all I have to do is figure out where the magic cap is, determine how I can steal, err… borrow the golden cap, how to use the damn thing, survive an evil witch, and finally can save my best friend in the entire world."

Chapter Fourteen

Myxtomackeson and Pastoria worked diligently for an entire week on the firebox. The master glassblower created a box by blowing the glass inside a large, square iron mold. They carefully cut away the mold and fused separately blown legs onto the main body. But it took three days for the box to cool enough for Pastoria to cut a door into it. Sven created two intricate hinges and attached them to the door. Finally, he formed a latch above the door and fused it to the main body.

Diggs contributed his share of working on the firebox by supervising the assembly and drinking amber-red beer with the mayor. He did work on the main basket of the balloon by commandeering a broom and sweeping the floor.

"Hey! Quit making so much dust," squeaked Slim, the piglet. "We're all just getting comfortable in here."

"I have a use for you piglets," said Diggs. "And I don't just mean miniature pork chops." He put down the broom and uncovered the rag nest. Diggs picked up one of the nine tiny pigs and placed him inside an inner pocket in his long coat. "I had one of the Jinxville seamstresses design and sew this for me. Snug? The lady also made me twelve new scarves. Unfortunately, they are all shades of red. I have improved on the piglet vanishing trick that almost convinced Glinda that I wasn't a humbug wizard. You swine are going to be my best trick yet. Just don't complain out loud this time."

"So, what's this new *meshuggeneh*-oops! I mean, crazy-trick?" peeped the piglet from Diggs' pocket. "Us New York Jewish mice are hard to fool. By the way, please turn me back into a mouse. If my rabbi mouse knew I was a piglet, he would just *plotz*. Sorry that's a wrong term for those who don't speak Yiddish. He would just die."

"Now one of my mice's clan is from New York?" said Diggs. "What are you called and how in the world did you end up in Alabama?"

"My name given to me by my mother is Abraham. Unfortunately, there aren't a lot of Jewish cheeses, even in New York. My clan lived in the Bronx and survived on herring. One day, they assigned me to get some fish for my little group. I went down to the harbor and smuggled myself aboard a boat that I knew would have a large herring shipment. I planned to bring some home to my family. *Oy veh*, what a mistake. The *meshugina*-sorry, crazy-boat sailed, and I found myself shipped to the union troops fighting in Alabama. I abandoned ship, traveled inland, and found this group of mice. We made a gracious home in your gondola and the rest is history."

"Welcome to the group fella," said Diggs. "Just remember, you are not to squeak once inside my pocket. Please pass the instruction to your fellows, especially that loudmouth from Texas."

Pastoria shouted up to the gondola, "Great Oz, we are finished. Sven did a wonderful job. My assistants will carry the gold sheets onto your balloon."

"Are you sure that you don't have a couple extra sheets of gold?" said Diggs. "It's so shiny."

"Sven and I will bring the glass fire box, loaded already with the pyrite coal. All the Jinxville people are bringing you their personal supplies of our super lightweight coal to store for future use. Even Marvin is here with his pockets stuffed full of coal for you. The mayor is asleep again. He was to bring a torch."

Diggs lifted some coal and stared at it. "So how do we light this stuff?"

Pastoria pointed at one piece. "Can't you just use a spell, oh Great Oz?"

Diggs felt incredibly nervous about being asked to do real magic. "Can't you do it for me? I feel a might peaked today."

"I don't think I can," said Pastoria. "The fact I only had weak magic was my downfall." Pastoria waved his hands and said an incantation over the coal. Absolutely nothing happened. "See? Nothing? It's not good to be so weak in a land of witches and wizards. The evil witches found out how limited my powers were and ran me out of the Emerald Citadel."

"Ah, wait! I do remember a spell." Diggs went to his carpetbag and rummaged through it. He pulled out a small rectangular metal container. After opening it, he pulled out a short wooden stick and scraped it on a piece of coal. "Inflamo!" The match burst into flame and lit the side of the coal. Diggs shook his hand to put out the match. Still, it singed his finger.

Marvin emptied his pockets and dropped the coal onto the growing pile. "Boring! We have match trees all over Quadling country, right next to our fireworks trees. Taking advantage of the combination of these trees is one of my favorite ways to get in trouble." He peered at Diggs' burnt finger. "Ouch. Our matches are more reliable."

Diggs gave Marvin a lopsided grin. "I tried." He tossed the burning coal into the filled firebox. The entire load quickly ignited. Hot air rose through the glass vent and slowly filled the cloth envelope of the balloon. After several hours, the balloon fully inflated.

"As a present, we have brought you food supplies," said one of the Quadling ladies. "Rare roast beef sandwiches, mashed red potatoes, strawberries, apples, and a red leaf salad. Finally, a small keg of beer was donated by the mayor. And for your adorable piglets, lots of red popcorn."

The piglets came out of their nest and volunteered to sample the popcorn to make sure it was fresh. Diggs shooed them back and thanked the woman. "It all smells wonderful."

Diggs instructed which order the remaining sandbags were to be tossed into the basket and to be stored for future use. While he watched Pastoria do all the work, he had a Jinxville seamstress sew the fourth bag back up and had Marvin's friends fill the slit bag with fresh sand.

They now tossed all the sandbags into the gondola. The fire box continued to blow out hot air. As the balloon slowly rose into the air, Diggs yelled thanks and goodbyes to the Jinxians.

"Oh, Great Oz," yelled the mayor. "Where do you head?" He stumbled up to stand under the rising balloon. The mayor shielded his eyes, bent his head back, and looked up. "Sorry I was late. It was time for my third nap of the day."

"I'm going to visit Mombi the Mad," replied Diggs.

"A word of advice!" screamed the mayor.

"What...?" Diggs could barely hear the man as he floated away.

"Don't call her --"

As Diggs floated towards the north, he pulled a crudely drawn map from his carpetbag, supplied to him by Perto the Hobbleman, the only Jinxian explorer. When Diggs asked Perto how he got his name, the man removed his left wooden leg, showed an empty eye patch, and took off his left-hand hook. Perto opened his mouth and pointed to a partially amputated tongue. "I goooot these, explorinining nea da eevil weicht."

Perto told him that Mombi the Mad theoretically lived in the northernmost country of the land, the Gillikin country. According to the map, Diggs calculated that if he hugged a due north direction, he would float over a narrow strip of Winkie country and then be in Gillikin country. A rapidly flowing river divided the two countries. Plus, he remembered, he would recognize where he was by color. Everything in Winkie country was yellow and Gillikin country purple. A pure red cow was hard to take, he thought, but a purple one would be amazing.

It took several boring several days, to float over the mountain range between Jinxville and Winkie country. Diggs looked down and saw huge red boulders on the south slopes of the mountain chain. He threw more coal into the firebox to make sure his balloon had enough elevation. Diggs walked over to his carpetbag, pulled out his spyglass, and peered down at the mountain slopes.

"Good God! The boulders are giant rubies." Diggs realized they were so large that a couple would fill his balloon basket.

Leaping from boulder to boulder were crimson-colored mountain goats. As Diggs watched, he saw a cardinal colored lion attack one goat and tear out its throat. The lion looked up at the balloon and grinned. The beast licked its lips as blood dripped down its muzzle. Then the lion waved at Diggs.

"I'm sure glad I'm up here," said Diggs to the air. "This sure is a dog-eat-dog land."

Frederick, the leader, came out of their rag nest and whined. "We're all hungry. When are you going to feed us? My group is bugging me to ask you." He put both trotters on his stomach.

Diggs tossed him a fourth helping of popcorn. "Take it back and share it. Don't eat it all yourself. I can't believe how much the group eats. You all are just pigs. I think Chang would have loved this popcorn. God, I miss him so much."

The balloon drifted over the apex of the mountains, and Diggs saw that the north slope was yellow. There were many golden rocks and huge yellow boulders on these slopes. Diggs scanned with his telescope. "Of course. They're giant gold nuggets." Here the mountain goats were yellow. He saw no lions.

The air over the yellow countryside had a bright, clean smell. The temperature was significantly warmer than on the other side of the mountains. "Piglets, this air smells of sunflowers, a bright summer day and just-out-of-the-oven baked goods. Now it's making me hungry." He reached into his carpetbag and pulled out one of his last large sandwiches. "Not bad roast beef. Those Jinxian women sure are superb cooks." Diggs gorged it, but did scatter bits of bread for the nine piglets. "Boy, it's warm." He took off his greatcoat and put it in the carpetbag.

Soon he came to a wide, rapidly moving river. The trees on the south bank were yellow birches, but the ones on the far bank were a strange purple hue. While traversing the waters, an enormous snake lifted its head out of the liquid. The creature stuck out its tongue.

"Come down," yelled the snake. "I love fruit. What kind are you?" The long tongue stretched skyward.

Diggs pitched more coal into the firebox to get more elevation. "What manner of snake are you? Are you friend or foe?" he yelled.

"Snake?" replied the creature. "How dare you! I am not a simple water snake. I'm the famous Winkie River Serpent. Come down and play."

"I think I'll skip your invitation. I'm just passing through." Diggs added extra fuel.

As the balloon elevated, the serpent lifted its head as high as possible out of the river. Its tongue darted out once again, just missing the bottom of the gondola. "Rats," screamed the serpent.

It took a full day before the balloon drifted over now purple countryside. The temperature shifted once again. Diggs shivered. "Now it's so cold, I need my coat, piglets." He took a deep breath of the cool air and detected the stench of rotten vegetation and dead beasts. "It reminds me of pure despair." Diggs peered down at the ground and saw an extensive area of purple grasses. Gigantic birds huddled on stunted trees. Suddenly, from the depths of the forest came a loud roar. The birds took off, their shapes obliterating the sun for a full minute. He never saw the source of the thunderous growl.

Diggs pulled out Petro's map and studied it. He realized he should be close to Mombi's castle. He opened the firebox door and put a sheet of gold between the chimney flue and the balloon opening, causing the air to dissipate out. Losing hot air caused the OZ balloon to drift lower to the ground. After cresting a small hill, before him appeared a tiny, but stoutly constructed stone fortress. A multitude of armed guards stood around the structure. They dressed all in filthy purple furs, wore tall hats, and carried ferocious looking spears. Several of the guards looked up and at the same time yelled, "Oz."

The air surrounding Mombi's castle was frigid. "Now I know why Gillikins wear fur," said Diggs. He pulled his coat tighter around himself.

Diggs quickly vented the hot air, and the balloon descended. He tossed one sandbag over, first tied to a drop-rope. The bag just missed one guard as it struck the ground. The man shook his fist up at the balloon, but still picked up the bag and rope and secured them to a misshapen purple tree. Several of the guards came over and tugged on the line. The balloon settled to the ground.

The guards cheered and yelled "Oz" over and over.

From the front door of the castle rushed a woman who was even shorter than Glinda, dressed in the dark shade of purple. She had on a large, torn, peaked hat. Her skin was a dark shade of green. Even from ten feet in the air, Diggs saw the largest wart he had ever seen on the side of her nose.

Glinda was correct. She sure is ugly, Diggs thought. "Do I have the extreme honor of addressing the famous Mombi the Mad?" Diggs boomed out his voice and raised his hand in greeting as he leaned over the railing.

"What the hell did you call me?" screeched the woman. She raised a twisted tree branch wand and began chanting an incantation.

Diggs ducked down below the rail. "Oops."

Chapter Fifteen

While squatting, Diggs tossed the rest of his sandbags over the railings. He anchored the drop lines to the bag with elaborate knots. As the balloon settled slowly, Diggs scooted on his butt towards the firebox, and bled off more hot air in order to hurry the descending process. He looked through the slats and saw that the guard was composed of many short, emaciated men, dressed in moth-eaten purple furs. Diggs also observed that several of the guards were not moving, frozen in mid-stride. Covering the area around the small castle were rocks, trampled grasses, foliage of different purple hues, and large pieces of broken glass. In a corner, there was also a strange, twisted tree with huge metal rectangular containers nestled among its lilac colored leaves.

The gondola hit the ground and bounced once. Some guards grabbed onto the drop lines, while others just waved their spears at Diggs. He noted that many of the guards' spears were broken, or had no tips. A soldier wearing cleaner furs and a chest full of medals rushed towards the basket. He bumped into one of the nearly transparent guards. The glass-like figure fell over and shattered, producing a loud crash, causing shards to fly all over the dirt.

"You idiot," screeched Mombi. She turned away from facing the gondola and waved her wand at the lead soldier. He immediately froze in place and turned transparent with a violet hue. Mombi put her sleeve up to her mouth. She bit the cloth, tore off a piece, chewed, grimaced, and then spat it onto the ground. "Bah, tastes terrible."

Diggs stood and did a deep bow. "I'm sorry, fair lady, did you mishear? I called out a welcome to 'Mombi the Bad.' Everyone in Oz knows you are the wisest and most evil witch in the land." He bent down, blindly groped in his carpetbag, straightened up, and surreptitiously held a revolver below the level of the basket slats. "I'm so glad to meet you."

Mombi started to wave her wand at Diggs, but then pulled it down. She coughed out an enormous ball of phlegm and it dribbled down her chin, onto the ground. "Who are you flying man and why do you wear wizard white?"

Diggs attempted to vault over the top slat of his basket, but stubbed his heel on the wood. He fell out, landed on his face, and came up with a mouthful of purple grass. The pistol flew out of his hand. Diggs crawled on his hands and knees to the gun and picked it up. He leaped to his feet, staggered slightly, and held out his hand. Noticing that there was a revolver in it, he shoved the gun into the front pocket of his coat. "Oz, the Great, at your service, fair maiden," he blurted, as he tried to spit out vegetation at the same time.

"What was in your hand man?" said Mombi. "Do you mean to harm or rob me? Do ya think something like that could work against someone as powerful as me?" She cackled, "Never."

Diggs startled at the strange laugh. He gave the witch a half-smile. "I would never consider doing anything like that, beautiful one! It's strictly for protection against wild beasts of the forest." Diggs bowed deeply, straightened, and held out his hand again.

Mombi stared at the outstretched hand. She frowned at Diggs with a face showing wrinkles as deep as ravines, incredibly long eyelashes, and a thin pointed nose that appeared as sharp as Diggs' saber. On closer look, three purple hairs sprouted from the wart on her nose. Mombi wore a tattered, filthy, long-sleeved paper-thin purple dress, which was extremely low cut. Frayed cuffs on the gown, with many chew marks, were on both sides. Draped over her shoulders was a moth-eaten fur cloak. The nose on the animal head of the fur cape was nestled deep into her cleavage. On her head she wore a towering, dented, blackish-purple hat, the tip of which had fallen over at a right angle. The hat kept sliding from one side of her head to the other. Greasy, stringy wisps of hair escaped from under both sides of the headwear, and fell down over her crossed red eyes.

Diggs stepped forward, spit out the last of the grass, and bent over. "No one cautioned me about how elegant you are, magnificent Mombi." He grasped her lime-colored hand and kissed the back of it. He wrinkled his nose at the smell, and frowned upon seeing her black, broken fingernails.

Mombi jerked her hand away, but actually looked pleased. "Ha. What do you want?"

The fur piece on her shoulders lifted its head and said "Ha" as well. The head had purple glass eyes and yellow sharp teeth. As its eyelids slowly opened and closed, its long ears slowly rose and tickled under Mombi's chin.

"Oh, do you do ventriloquism also?" said Diggs. "Your cape is an impressive puppet with just a body and flat, empty fur." He gestured at the fur piece.

"WHAT! Are you accusing me of faking?" screamed Mombi. "No, flying man, I killed, skinned and reanimated the Jackalope myself." Mombi reached her hand up and patted the fur cape on its head. "The meat tasted good in a stew. Now it keeps me warm. My Perry is a delightful companion to talk to, and he makes me look so spiffy, don't you think?"

The Jackalope purred. It then turned towards Diggs, growled, and bared its teeth. The fur piece's ears now caressed both of Mombi's cheeks.

Diggs jumped back from the skin. "How the hell is it alive?"

"Don't you own or ever create any Powder of Life, wizard?" said Mombi. She made a sprinkling motion over the Jackalope. "I got mine from a minor local wizard, Dr. Pipt. Guards," she suddenly screeched, "get rid of this broken glass and put my newest statue by the front door." Mombi reached down and picked up a shard of glass. She put it in her mouth, chewed, and then spit it out, along with some purple blood. "Bah, another thing that tastes terrible."

Diggs flinched. "I have no Powder of Life, I'm all out. Where do I find this Dr. Pipt? I'll get some from him."

"Bah," screamed Mombi. "He only trades the most powerful spells in exchange for the powder. It is precious, since it takes the Crooked Magician seven years to make each batch. What will you give him? I traded him my far-seeing spectacles and never-ending loaf of bread for my last small amount. Perhaps one of the other witches in the land would be stupid enough to give you some powder. Both the Witch of the West and East have traded for it."

"Who are they?" said Diggs. "Did they have to give up a powerful spell for this powder? I really need some to save a friend."

"The Witch of the West is Theodora, who gave him an Elixir of Forever Love for a batch," said Mombi. She appeared lost in thought. "The magician wasted the amulet on his fat wife. Theodora's witch sister, Evanora, cheated the magician by giving him a counterfeit Amulet of Ultimate Beauty spell. She used the real one on herself. Still," Mombi paused, "Evanora is not as gorgeous as myself." She primped as she pushed some of her hair from off her forehead.

Diggs bent over to kiss her hand again, gagged, and backed away from the smell. "There is no way she could be as magnificent as you. Such a rare beauty."

"Some of our most powerful spells for only three measly draughts of the powder, each. But it is amazing. I hope you have something special to trade for it with the Crooked Magician."

"I do have magic, but it's of a limited nature. I consider myself strong instead." Diggs held up his arm, flexed, and tried to make a muscle. Nothing happened. "Only, I left my wand in my other coat. Perhaps you have a small extra pinch of the powder?" He held his hand up and put thumb and forefinger an inch apart.

"You are crazy, flying man," Mombi yelled. "Few can afford Pipt's price. Even Glinda the Good has nothing powerful enough to trade with him. She won't give up her only wonderful power, her Book of Records. Why should I give you even one dose? Pipt at first asked for the Golden Cap that controls the Flying Monkeys, but I refused. Heh, heh, heh," she chortled. "I even used up my three wishes with the cap, but I wouldn't give it up. To me, the cap is worthless to use, but it is an extremely powerful trade item."

Diggs took a step toward the witch. "Is that the magic cap that Pastoria once used? That might help save my companion even better than the Powder of Life."

"What! How do you know of my enemy?" Mombi screeched.

"I am a wise wizard. I know a lot of things. Plus, I met him in the past." Diggs nodded his head, took a deep breath to push out his chest, and reached for his suspender struts. He stopped when he realized they didn't exist. Diggs just pinched and pulled out the front of his greatcoat to mimic his quirk.

"Tell me, wizard: where is Pastoria? I need another statue." Mombi reached up and grabbed Diggs' coat with one hand and waved her wand under his chin with the other.

Diggs gently pushed away the wand and then patted her hand. "Calm down, my beautiful one. I'm sure a trade for the Magic Golden Cap can be worked out to our mutual benefit."

Chapter Sixteen

Mombi gestured towards the massive stone castle and began walking. "Come, let's go inside and talk." Her guards were scurrying around, trying to move any glass statues from her path. One guard brushed against her filthy dress.

"You idiot," screamed Mombi. "You're getting me all dirty." She pointed her tree branch wand at him and yelled, "MRZZABUB." The soldier immediately transformed into a crystalline statue. His features froze in an expression of horror and despair.

Diggs backed two steps away and bowed. He then made a huge sweeping gesture with his hand and pointed to the doorway. "Madam, please, you go first." Diggs was extremely careful not to brush her. "Geez, she turns everyone into glass," he muttered under his breath.

They crossed a moat on a wooden drawbridge. In the water, massive snakes with wings undulated. One creature lifted its head out of the water and hissed, "Mombi, is that my dinner? I can fly up to get it if necessary."

Mombi ignored the request and trudged to the stonework door. She pulled on the iron ring door knob and tugged it open. Diggs scurried up to enter while looking over his shoulder at the moat. He stayed close behind the witch. Once Diggs came through the doorway, he abruptly halted.

"What in the world!" Diggs exclaimed as he looked around. "I entered what I thought was a castle and now there is only a small one-room hut?"

The room comprised a muddy floor, piecemeal thatched roof with holes in it, moldy walls, and a dense soot which clung to various portions of the walls and ceiling. In the entire room there were only two pieces of furniture; a huge dusty cabinet with many drawers in one nook and a lumpy bed with a threadbare sheet and a rock for a pillow in the corner. A putrid aroma of a hundred rotting animals filled the hut. In the center of the hovel was a collapsed fireplace. Dense soot covered the walls and ceiling of the hut. Despite a roaring fire going in the fireplace, an ominous chill filled the hovel.

A high-pitched voice came from the fireplace. "It's about time you came in. I've been slaving all day on this dinner."

"What is that horrible smell and what the hell happened to your colossal castle?" Diggs stepped back towards the door, but it swung shut by itself.

"My dinner, stinky skunk cabbage and tattle-tale turnip stew," cackled Mombi. "Want some?" She walked over to the central fireplace and breathed in the sulfuric odor of the huge bubbling kettle. She reached for the stirring ladle when it reprimanded her. Mombi opened her arms wide. "This is my castle. Um, what exactly was your question?"

"It's not ready yet," said the ladle. "It needs a touch of arsenic." The ladle opened its one eye and stirred the viscous liquid in the pot by itself. The ladle blinked. "Mombi, use less poisonwood for your fire next time. The smoke is irritating my eyeball."

Diggs rubbed his stomach and smiled, but really tried not to retch. "Sorry, I'm not starving. I just ate before I descended in my balloon. How can that ladle talk and stir your soup by itself?" He pinched his nose and peered intently at the huge spoon.

Mombi ignored Diggs, grabbed the ladle, skimmed some liquid, and slurped it up. "No, Ladle, it don't need no arsenic. Your taster must be off. I might have to transform another of my soldiers to replace you."

The ladle stirred rapidly. "Will you change me back into a soldier?"

"Nah," she said. "Just toss you on the junk heap with all my other rejects." Mombi walked over and sat down on her bed. "Now, wizard, what can you do for me? Or should I just make you into a teaspoon? No…, I think a tablespoon, based on your size."

"Please explain to my muddled mind how is your castle so statuesque on the outside and so err… small on the inside?" Diggs waved his arms around. The hut was so small, he almost hit one hand on the far wall.

"In the witching world, image is power." Mombi waved her wand around aimlessly. "Who cares how the inside manifests as long as the outside appears formidable. I want my subjects to think I live in an impenetrable castle. I rarely allow men callers to come inside my fortress, you strong hunk of a wizard man." She batted her eyes at Diggs, and one false eyelash fell off.

Diggs was careful to zig at the same time as the tip of the wand zagged. "I can appreciate that and would love to learn your image-producing techniques. They would come in very handy. So, do your sister witches live similarly?"

"They are not my sisters." Mombi got up, walked over to the kettle, put her wand into her left hand, and stuck her right index finger into the boiling soup. She licked the soup off her finger. "They are just fellow witches. We have divided up Oz. I have the north country. I live in this wonderful home."

Diggs looked around the hut again, scratched his head, and shrugged his shoulders. "Yep, just perfect for you."

Mombi suddenly screamed and waved her finger. "Hot, hot, hot." She waved it in the air and then spit on it. She stopped screaming and continued. "Evanora used her knowledge of magic incantations to conquer the east. She rules over some pipsqueaks called Munchkins, but doesn't call them slaves, just subjects. Theodora lives by herself in the west in a humongous castle. Not as nice as this mansion, but nice. No Winkie slaves, yet, of any sort. That's why she so desperately wants the Magic Cap. The Witch of the West uses potions, powders, and a crystal ball for her magical abilities. She can't even use a wand. Even so, she is almost as powerful as myself."

"Of course." Diggs nodded his head.

"I used up the cap to conquer the Gillikins and drive out Pastoria. Evanora, Theodora and Glinda are dying to get ahold of the cap, but I ain't giving it up. The newest owner of the cap always gets three fresh wishes." Mombi continued, waving her blistered finger in the air. She walked back to her bed, whimpered, and sat down.

"Will you sell the cap to me? I have a great need of it." Diggs walked over, leaned down, and picked up Mombi's grubby hand. Then he shuddered, but still put a kiss on her burnt finger.

"Never," she screamed. "It's mine, mine, mine!" Mombi leapt to her feet, transferred her wand back to her right hand, and pointed it at Diggs. "Nobody steals anything from me."

Diggs put his fingers behind his back and crossed them. "I would never attempt to abscond with anything. I hope to consider you a good friend, not an enemy." He raised his eyebrows, grinned, and winked at her. "I would just like to negotiate a fair trade."

"I doubt, wizard, you have anything I need. As you can see," Mombi pointed at the four corners of the squalid room, "I live in great luxury."

"Of course, of course. How could I improve on perfection?" Diggs shook his head and thought, she truly is "Mombi the Mad."

"But there is a small service you might do for me." Mombi looked up into Diggs' face. "I have great needs."

Diggs began to sweat. "Err, what is that?"

"I am afraid the wizard king Pastoria will again try to regain my kingdom. Never would I give up my lands. I know my Gillikins love me so, but I don't want to take a chance. Bring me the man and his fairy wife. I need some new statues. Or I can always eat them."

"Pastoria's wife died in childbirth. He has a tiny daughter named Ozma."

"Roast baby stew, yum." Mombi licked her lips. "Bring her instead of the dead missus."

Diggs gagged and then wiped his mouth on the back of his hand. He raised his eyebrows. "Why don't you just ask your flying monkeys to get them for you?"

"I already used up my three wishes." Mombi threw up her hands. Her tree branch wand quivered. "But I can still trade it to someone else, someday, like Theodora. The witch of the West can always use it for whatever she wants. Theodora better make me a fair trade, like give me something in exchange that's powerful, to destroy Pastoria. If the trade doesn't give me anything to kill Pastoria, then perhaps I'll use my wand

and transform him into something amusing. The wand can transform anything. Too bad, as I get older, I can only use incantations a couple times a day."

"Your age becomes you. You still are as beautiful as the day is long." Diggs had his crossed fingers behind his back again.

"Ahhhh, I do have that power over a man," cackled Mombi. She smoothed back her hair, stuck out her chest, and wiggled her hips.

"Why don't you just capture or kill him yourself?" Diggs breathed in a vast sigh of relief at his presumed sexual escape. Bad move, he thought, as he began to dry heave from the smell in the hovel.

"I could never leave my fortress. My enemies are always trying to do me in, and my friends even more so. I can't leave my domain." Mombi walked over, reached down, and picked up her one fallen false eyelash from the muddy floor. She looked quizzically at it, put it in her mouth and began chewing.

"I will obtain Pastoria for you. But please, please, promise you'll not hurt them or eat them. Maybe just make him and his child servants? He's a pleasant fellow. If I didn't need the cap so desperately, I would never consider sinking so low. Just give me the Golden Cap and I'll be on my way." Diggs made a walking gesture with his fingers.

"Do you take me for a fool, flying man? Use your own magic to get Pastoria and I will reward you afterward." Mombi shook her head, grimaced, and spit the eyelash onto the floor.

"But beautiful lady, this man Pastoria, or his fairy daughter Ozma might have stronger magic than I do. Do you have anything that I can use? I will make it worth your while."

"I do have the perfect minor powder for this quest. In this cabinet are many magic items I have traded for over the years. I used up my Powder of Life from Dr. Pipt, but have various powders from Theodora." Mombi walked over to the dusty piece of furniture, filled with hundreds of compartments. The cupboard reached almost to the hut's ceiling. "Now let's see, 'P, P, P'. Ah, here we are, 'Powder of Persuasion'. Right between the compartment of the 'Powder of Stone Petrification' and 'Elixir of Putrid'." She bent over, reached into one compartment, and brought the container up to her rheumy eyes. "At least I think this is what that powder is?"

"I hate to contradict you, but you can't alphabetize." Diggs grabbed the small box out of her hand. "Persuasion comes before Petrification, not after."

"Who cares about spelling? I haven't used either powder since I got them from Theodora. I labeled them and threw them into their drawers. This Persuasion should work perfectly." The witch pointed at Diggs' hand. "Be careful. There are only two doses in that container. Don't you want it?"

Diggs raised his top hat, bowed with a sweeping gesture, and straightened up. "Of course beautiful one. What does it do? How can it help me?"

"It will make anyone obeys you completely. Pretty good, heh."

"I do want your 'Powder of Persuasion'. Thank you, fair lady. I will take the powder and be off." Diggs slipped the small box into his front pocket of his greatcoat.

"Now don't get any funny ideas about using that powder to rob me, flying man. When you bring back Pastoria and the brat, then you will earn the Magic Cap. But don't plan on just finding and stealing the cap. You could never get it," she screamed. "I'm too smart for that. I hid the cap where no one could ever find it. And if you try to use Theodora's powder against me, to persuade me to tell you anything, that won't work. The day I traded her for all the powders, I was wise enough to set powerful wards on them so they could never be used against me." She looked up in the air and her voice trailed off, "at least… I think I remembered to do that?"

"You wound me greatly. I would do nothing like that. Now I must be off to pursue this adventure."

"No, don't go. Let me show you this wonderful perfume. I use this elixir frequently. Makes me rather desirable, don't you think?" Mombi took out the Elixir of Putrid from its compartment. She uncorked the potion and dabbed a drop behind each ear, and then poured some liquid directly into her cleavage. "Don't you want to stay for stew? And myself for dessert?" Mombi pulled her dress down to expose her breasts, all the way to her erect, pitch-black nipples. Green warts covered her heaving bosom. She leered at Diggs.

Diggs flinched. "An exceedingly tempting offer, but a knight must pursue, nay, succeed at his quest before he earns any benefits from a fair maiden." He bowed deeply again, then straightened. "I will count the moments 'til I return." Diggs bolted for the door.

Chapter Seventeen

Diggs ran out of the hovel door and was again on a drawbridge before a gigantic castle. "I must find out how she creates such illusions," he mumbled. One purple flying snake hovered over the moat, looked at him, and drooled.

"So, you survived your visit with the witch," said the serpent. "Does that mean Mombi is going to let me eat you now?"

Diggs flinched when he looked at the creature. "Truce. I am doing a very important job for Mombi. I don't think she would be pleased if you ate me." He moved across the drawbridge onto the front lawn. Diggs carefully moved around the glass statues in the path and stepped over the many shards of glass. He yelled over his shoulder, "If you don't behave, she'll probably turn you into a statue as well."

The snake flew away from the moat and followed Diggs. "Bah, do you know how many times I've been transformed since the witch moved into this castle? My natural form was a lion. Then she made me into a giant spider, then a man, then a flea, and now finally a flying snake. I'm getting dizzy with all these changes. She can't make up her mind. I've lived, if you want to call it that, for two hundred and forty-four years." The creature glared, abruptly folded his wings, and dove headfirst back into the moat.

While Diggs walked towards his tethered balloon, he peered around Mombi's garden and yard in amazement. There were more areas of bare lavender dirt than vegetation. He stared at foliage in various shades of purple, vast patches of brambles sprinkled throughout the front yard, flowers the size of his thumbnail, next to seventeen-foot-tall eggplant bushes. One large, ancient tree swayed in the breeze about one hundred feet from his balloon. Its fruit looked extremely peculiar, so Diggs ambled over to investigate. The crooked tree's produce comprised rectangular pieces of metal, varying from unopened buds to rusty, tarnished large carpet, bag-sized ones. The purple bark of the tree flaked. Many rusted open pails, fallen under the tree, radiated a horrible stench. The pails on the branches had no smell coming from them at all.

"Hungry, Gillikin?" said the tree. "My, you don't look like the usual Gillikin. Why are you wearing white and not purple? A coat instead of furs? No matter, help yourself to one of my mature lunchpails. Just make sure you scatter any seeds from them so I can grow anew."

"You are a talking timber?" said Diggs. "What else will I find in this crazy place? And how in the world can it see me, if it doesn't have any eyes? No mouth either?" He reached up and plucked a brightly polished container. "Several of your rusty, tarnished pails looked overripe, Mr. Tree, and your unopened buds are obviously too young to eat." Diggs opened the lunchpail he had picked, and saw a hot dinner staring back at him. Steam carrying wonderful food aromas came out at once. "Roast boar, mashed purple potatoes, reduced purple wine gravy and massive purple grapes for dessert. Looks delicious." Once he closed it, the pail became cool to touch, and the aromas stopped emanating from it. Diggs took the pail with him.

Diggs walked over to the gondola of the balloon and climbed aboard. He added Ozpyrite coal to the glass firebox and stoked the fire. He called to the Gillikin soldiers milling around to hoist the sandbags and drop lines. They lifted the sandbags up and threw them into the balloon basket.

Several tiny voices from the rag nest suddenly yelled out. "Hey, watch where you're throwing those! You almost crushed us."

Diggs moved the sandbags away from the nest. He carefully put the lunch box pail down, but still tipped it over, and it sprang open. As soon as the fragrance from the receptacle released, nine piglets rushed out to investigate. "Soup's on!" they yelled.

Diggs snatched the lunch box back from the horde of swine. "This is my lunch," said Diggs. "Don't be so greedy. I'll share the crumbs with you when I'm finished."

The balloon slowly floated upwards. As it rose, one of the Gillikin guards yelled out, "Great Oz, please take us with you. I don't want to be a glass statue."

"I can't stay, men," said Diggs. "But I'll be back and together we'll overcome this witch." For the third time, Diggs crossed his fingers behind his back.

Diggs used his old hot-air balloon piloting skills to best the wrong direction of the blowing wind and float back to Jinxville. He licked his finger and held it up. Diggs determined that most of the winds continued to blow solely in the northerly direction, probably from off the Deadly Desert. To go south, he side-vented the hot air from the firebox and rotated the balloon. As the envelope spun, the wind pulled the OZ balloon towards the south.

Diggs again added extra coal in order to go high over the mountains. While over the Winkie River, he taunted the River Serpent that something now trapped his cousins in Mombi's moat. The nine piglets kept trying to give him navigational advice, which he steadfastly ignored.

After several days, and with frequent stops at different colored lunch box trees, he arrived back in Jinxville. The crowds poured out of the houses, looked up and began chanting "Oz, Oz."

Diggs maneuvered the balloon, so it hovered over the central square of the village. He threw out all four of the sandbags and drop lines, which were received by the townsfolk and tethered. Diggs patted his greatcoat pocket to make sure his magical possession from Mombi was intact, and climbed over the top slat of the gondola.

The mayor shuffled up to Diggs, carrying two mugs of beer. He handed Diggs one mug, which was already partially empty. The mayor had a large foam mustache. "Great Oz. Here to celebrate my landslide political victory?" he slurred.

An older, very plump woman called out, "Now Horace, be quiet! You know, there was only one vote cast in the election. And once again, it was only yours." She grabbed him by the ear and led him away from Diggs. "Now come to dinner."

Several of the townsfolk crowded around the gondola. They would step up to the railing, look way upwards at Diggs, step back, bow, and continue to look only at the ground. The women would curtsy instead of bow. No one said a word to his face.

Since he towered over the Quadlings, Diggs could pick out individual Jinxians. "I don't see Pastoria the Tinker. Does anyone know where he is?"

The crowd remained mostly mute, though a few groups muttered among themselves. No one stepped forward.

Diggs peered around some more. "What the hell is wrong with you people? Why is no one talking? Oh, there's someone I recognize. Hey, Marvin, do you know where Pastoria is this day? And I command you to tell me why no one will speak to me, except the drunk mayor?"

Marvin trembled and also looked down. "Oh Great Oz, we're all afraid of you. We knew you were a mighty wizard to be able to fly over the Deadly Desert, and we loved to hear tales of your valiant battle against the Chasm Dragon." He looked up. "But it is amazing that you are able to survive Mombi the Mad."

"By the way, I learned to never call her mad." Diggs nodded his head. "But it describes her to a T." Diggs reached down and grabbed Marvin's dingy red shirt. "Do you know where Pastoria is now?"

"I am so sorry, Oz, I do not know." Marvin made a marble shooting motion with his thumb. "There was this Oz-wide marble tournament. Your magic disc gave me great luck and I can't lose. I just got back to Jinxville today."

"Well, has anyone seen him?" Diggs asked the crowd. "I won't hurt anyone, honest."

Dead silence was his answer. Everyone but Marvin's eyes looked everywhere but at Diggs.

"All right, does anyone know where Pastoria lives?" Diggs turned back to his balloon basket, reached down, and pulled out his carpet bag. "Perhaps he is at home tinkering. I must see him and I have a present for him." He patted his pocket again.

Marvin pointed to the central square. "Pastoria lives in the twelfth house past the well. He lives close to me and my parents. You can't miss his house. It's all red."

Diggs sighed, "Of course, it is." He reached into the pocket of his coat and pulled out his change purse. He opened it, looked inside, and plucked out a gold Eagle ten-dollar piece. Diggs shook his head and put it back. Instead, he got a three-cent piece and flipped it to Marvin. "Watch my balloon for me. Don't let anyone steal it. And ask some of your friends to help you load the basket with more coal. I might need to make a quick takeoff."

Diggs strode briskly along a path of red, crushed gravel. After walking past eleven identical rose-colored homes, he arrived at the twelfth. Diggs admired a perfectly manicured front yard surrounded by cardinal-colored grasses, red shrubs, and a central flower garden. Hundreds of roses and carnations were in full bloom. He took a deep breath of the intoxicating fragrances and sighed in contentment. A huge lunchpail tree stood just off to the side of the path.

"Hungry Quadling?" said the tree. "My dinners are first rate." The buds on this tree were open fully, and there were no rusty pails among the leaves or strewn on the ground.

"You trees sure are friendly," said Diggs. "Don't mind if I do. One should never pass up a free meal." He walked over, plucked a brightly untarnished pail, and opened it to look inside. "I wonder what they have in this one? Ah, extremely rare roast beef, boiled red potatoes, redeye gravy and strawberries. Why am I not surprised?"

Diggs put the closed pail into his carpetbag and continued to the front door. He raised his hand to knock when he noticed the door was ajar. Diggs pushed it open, entered the house, and yelled, "Hello?"

A voice from a back room answered, "Come in, come in. We're back here. Have you come in need of my services? Do you need a cobbler, tailor, or tinker?"

Diggs walked through the small house and entered a kitchen. Ozma sat in a highchair, her face covered with red gruel. She banged on the tray of her highchair and splashed up geysers of the cereal. A mostly empty bowl lay tilted on the side of the tray. A chain pulley system ran from a box on the kitchen table connecting the highchair tray to a turned-off stove.

Multiple spoons traveled on the chain, each drudging up gruel from a large pot to deliver it to the vicinity of the baby's mouth. Most of the cereal didn't enter the orifice. The child laughed more than she swallowed. Pastoria read a large textbook and never looked at his daughter.

"Hello Pastoria. How are you?" said Diggs. He stuck out his hand and walked forward carefully, bypassing piles of more gruel on the floor.

Pastoria jerked his head up and leaped to his feet. "Oz. You're back. Was something wrong with the firebox?" He put a metal bookmark down on a page and closed the text. "There is an amazing passage on mechanical, automated sewer systems. It will change our land." He stuck out his hand and shook Diggs' briskly.

"Pastoria, I need you to come with me on an important mission." Diggs continued to hold on to Pastoria's hand. "Can someone watch your daughter while we're gone?"

"What are you saying? I can't leave my work and I won't leave my daughter with anyone." Pastoria tried to yank his hand away from Diggs. He succeeded and stepped back.

Diggs pulled the container of magic powder from the pocket of his greatcoat and tossed half the contents into Pastoria's face. "Sorry, buddy, but I have to do this. I must persuade you to come with me."

Chapter Eighteen

Pastoria immediately froze in place.

Diggs stared at Pastoria. "Are you standing there and thinking about what to do?" He took a step and poked the still figure. "Ouch, he's stone? Damn. Did that crazy Mombi give me the wrong powder?" He closed the lid of the box, over any remaining powder. "Would hate to get that on myself." Diggs looked at the stone statue and shoved the matchbox back into his pocket.

The spell had occurred so quickly that Pastoria did not even look surprised or horrified. The calm expression on his rigid face bothered Diggs. "Well, that certainly didn't work out right. Now what the hell do I do? Real magic sure is dangerous. Did I kill the man? What would Chang do here?"

The toddler screamed. Diggs looked over and saw her pounding on her tray. "Daddy, more!" she yelled.

Diggs rubbed his chin. "What to do, what to do?" He then scratched his head, "No idea, so I better go check on Ozma." He walked nearer to the child. Ozma had pushed her bowl onto the gruel-covered floor. Diggs watched as she picked up a handful of the cereal and threw it at the wall. The little girl laughed as it splattered. She then picked up a second handful and flung it at Diggs. The cereal hit him right in the chest.

"What an arm. You could play baseball for the union troops in the Salisbury Confederate Prison," said Diggs. "But you're not helping things." He looked at the child. "I've really goofed up with your dad. Nothing worked. I planned on using the Powder of Persuasion on Mombi once we got to her hovel and demanded that she let your pa go free. I predicted she forgot to really set any wards against Theodora's powders. She is mad after all. That's why I was careful to use only one-half of the powder. Now what do I do? Kid, are you even listening?"

Ozma blew a big saliva bubble. She then threw some more gruel at Diggs, but missed.

Diggs frowned and watched out for more projectiles. "Little girl, what can I do about your father? I know I'll take him with me and make Mombi use her wand and change him back." Diggs tried to flick the red gruel off his white coat, but just smeared it.

Diggs stared at frozen Pastoria. "Okay, statue, I'm glad that you might be the only skinny Jinxian. You are such a beanpole; you should be easy to carry to the balloon." Diggs grabbed the tinker under one outstretched arm and tried to lift him after placing his left hand in the stone armpit on Pastoria's other side. Diggs heaved, but the stone statue didn't budge. He bent his knees and tried again, to no avail. "I reckon this statue weighs more than ten Jinxians. Well baby, even if I could carry him, or con several young men to carry the statue for me, I doubt the balloon could even lift off." Diggs dropped his hands to his side. "The powder sure made a heavy load." He raised one hand and rubbed his chin. "Think, think! What would Chang do?"

The spoons traveled with the moving chain and then flung just empty air at the child. Ozma howled at being ignored, shoved piles of gruel to the floor, and wiggled the highchair until it rocked back and forth. Diggs walked over to the kitchen table, picked up the huge engineering text, and smashed it down on the kitchen spoon apparatus. The chain ground to a halt.

Diggs looked at Ozma. "Your father, child, was a good tinker and a better person. I wish I never got involved with Mombi. But I thought some magic powders would help me rescue my friend Chang, if he's even still alive. I needed something to trade with the witch. I don't think nine piglets or a saber would interest her. Maybe she would have given me something for the use of my body." Diggs shuddered. "Oh, the sacrifices one makes for friendship."

Diggs ignored the crying child and looked out the back door of the Jinxville' home. He saw a tiny garden shed. A dozen red birds perched on top of the shed. "Maybe there's something in that shed which could help the situation?" A garden surrounded the shed with more vegetables than flowers. Diggs observed red cabbages the size of his gondola, tomatoes larger than his head and rhubarb growing ten feet tall. The only flowers were red narcissus, which appeared to be arguing among themselves.

Diggs heard tiny flower voices debating, "I'm the prettiest in the group."

Another posey stated, "No, I am."

Diggs walked towards the arguing annuals "Hey, you dumb buds, you're all identical, all beautiful." He bent down and plucked one and put it in the buttonhole of his coat.

Tiny screams filled the air. "Monster, murderer!" yelled the flowers.

"I go to that giant compost heap in the sky," said the plucked stem.

"You realize flowers are meant to be shared and enjoyed?" said Diggs. "The dinner pail trees give of themselves." Diggs walked to the shed. He pulled open the small shed door and hammers, screwdrivers, rusty pipes, pulleys, shovels, old shoes, axes, and a kitchen sink fell out.

"What a load of junk! I wonder if there is anything else useful for when I try to save Chang." Diggs put one shovel and axe to the side. He stuck his head inside the doorway of the tiny shed. Startled, Diggs realized he couldn't even see the back wall. "What the hell? How can it be bigger on the inside than the outside?" Diggs stepped back and stared at the birds barely fitting on the shed roof, and he thought he could touch the outside back wall easily. But when he looked back inside, the shed seemed to go on forever. Diggs opened the door fully and went in.

Diggs stepped in and collided with a short mechanical metal man without a head or a right leg. Its rusted, dusty, headless torso barely came up to Diggs' chest. He squeezed behind the figure and noticed a large brass plaque mounted between its shoulder blades. "Prototype given to King Pastoria in honor of his inauguration, by Smith and Tinker." Diggs tried to make out a date stamped on the plaque, but a smudge covered it. The robot man had numerous burn marks on its torso and huge teeth marks on its remaining leg. Diggs touched one of the mechanicals man's arms, and it fell off. "Damn."

Turning, Diggs noticed dozens of spectacles of all shapes and sizes mounted on a wall of wood. Diggs picked one pair off a nail and held it up to his eyes. "What good are these? No magnification, it just makes everything green? Still, I'll use these to protect my eyes when I'm up in the balloon. I'll take them all for any passengers. Boy, I really have to stop talking to myself. I sure miss Chang." He pulled all the pairs off the wall and piled them on top of the equipment he had accumulated.

Looking down, Diggs saw a pile of broken pottery, more shoes, rusty nails, pliers, and torn blueprints. Behind this mountain of debris were two intact pieces of equipment. He walked further into the depths of the shed, going around the pile of junk. The intact pieces, boxlike, whetted his interest and he turned back towards them. "How in the world can I be this far inside this tiny shed? It's getting so dark, I can barely see." Diggs picked up both boxes and carried them outside.

They both looked fairly similar. Both were rectangular with an attached golden horn to one end. But the opposite side from the metal horns differed significantly. One box had a wide, uncovered circular tube end and the other box had an oval aperture with glass over the end. Diggs shook both boxes with no results. Then he peered into the horn, one at a time. Nothing resulted again.

"What in the world are these used for?" Although Diggs had stated this in a normal speaking voice, a booming "WHAT IN THE WORLD" came out of the metal tube. It was so loud, the birds perched on the shed took off in frantic flight.

Diggs held it up and whispered "Hello," with the resulting thunderous "HELLO" coming out of the other end immediately. He whispered "Hello" into the horn of the second box, but nothing happened. Diggs turned the first box over and over, but could not see any power source at all. "No place to put kerosene, whale oil, hydrogen gas, or even boiled water. How does this work? Could this be true magic?" He carefully put the box on the pile with his confiscated equipment.

Diggs again shook the second box, with no result. He pointed the glass at the door of the shed and muttered, "Fire. Maybe it's some kind of gun?" Immediately a ten-foot long gun with flames shooting out of it, materialized in front of the box. Diggs reached for the weapon, but his hand passed right through it. "I'm glad, I didn't burn myself," Diggs muttered. "But I felt no heat at all." When he brought his hand back, the flaming gun remained. Despite the shed door not burning, the smell of smoke filled the air. He could also hear the crackle of flames. Diggs shook the box and the image of the gun, with the flames, shook. "What is this? How does it stop?" Upon uttering this word, the gun faded away.

Diggs now said "Tree." A huge red tree materialized in front of the box as large as the Quadling Redwoods, and the sound of rustling leaves filled the backyard. Again, Diggs's hand passed right through it when he reached for it. When he said, "Stop," it faded away. "Ah, an Illusion Maker, for sight, sound, and smell." He placed this box next to the first one.

Diggs went back into the shed, and walked past the disabled mechanical man guardian. More broken inventions, wires, soles of shoes, ropes, and burlap bags were just beyond the pile of debris. He knelt down and picked up two burlap bags. Once outside, he put his accumulated riches into the two bags.

He carried the two bags and walked back to the house. Ozma was asleep in her highchair, slouched, with drool running down her chin. The stone statue of Pastoria still guarded the child. "Pastoria, how can I bring you to Mombi? You're so heavy. Maybe I can fool her with the illusion maker?" He reached into the bag and pulled out the second box.

"Pastoria," Diggs said. Immediately a ten-foot rigid illusion of Pastoria appeared. "No," he muttered, "that wouldn't fool even crazy Mombi. Stop." The image vanished.

Diggs looked at the sleeping child. "Well, baby, the witch wanted both your father and yourself. But you'll have to do. I must trade for the magic cap, or some powder, in order to save my best friend. But I'll do everything in my power to protect you. We're going for a ride."

Chapter Nineteen

"Now," whispered Diggs. "How do I get you to my balloon without getting the entire village of Jinxville upset with me?" He looked down at the sleeping child. "I have it! It might just work."

Diggs searched through the two stuffed burlap bags and pulled out the Illusion-Maker. While carrying the box, he tiptoed out of the back door, went back to the garden shed, and entered. Diggs headed towards the back of the shed. He again couldn't believe how large it was on the inside, and so extremely dark that he wasn't able to see the debris in the rear of the shed. Diggs lifted the tinker box and commanded, "Fire." A crackling, smoking, ten-foot flame appeared. Using this as a source of illumination, he explored this closest pile of rubble and pulled out an oversized, slightly torn burlap potato sack. Diggs exited the shed, picked up the mechanical man's arm from the ground, and said, "Stop."

He went back to the kitchen and placed some kitchen towels in the bottom of the large burlap bag. He lifted Ozma out of the highchair and swaddled her in more linen. Next to the sleeping baby, he placed the mechanical arm with its fingers sticking out of the opening. Diggs replaced the magic item into the stuffed burlap bag and then picked up the second small bag. "This one only has garden tools, wire, and rope," he whispered to the sleeping child. He rapidly strode back to his balloon. "Please don't wake up, please don't wake up, please don't wake up," he kept repeating.

Upon arriving back at the balloon, Diggs noticed a large pile of Ozpyrite on the floor of the gondola. Marvin and his two friends were trying to teach the nine piglets how to shoot marbles, each shooter being as large as the pigs.

"Boys, you did a fine job on loading the coal and watching my balloon," said Diggs. "Thank you." Diggs slung the second small burlap bag over the railing. "Let me put the rest of this equipment down and give each of you a magic lucky coin." He carefully placed the two remaining bags into the gondola. Once the large sack settled on the floor, a wailing came from within.

"Wah, wah," screamed a muffled voice. "Me hungry and wet. Wah!"

Marvin started to climb into the gondola to look. "What in the world? What's in that bag?"

"Let me out," came a deep voice from the bag. "I'm trapped in here." The bag began to wiggle excessively.

"Do you like it, boys?" said Diggs. "It's part of my new ventriloquism act. I really know great voice throwing, eh?" Diggs pointed down to the largest burlap sack. "Pastoria gave me a mobile mechanical man, which I'll use to make people think it's really alive."

"Well, Great Oz," said Marvin while looking into the basket. "Just to let you know, your mechanical man is leaking yellow oil." He jumped down to the ground.

Diggs climbed into the balloon basket and quickly stoked up the fire. He grabbed the sandbags from his ground crew. The balloon slowly rose. Diggs threw a three-cent piece down to each of the boys and yelled, "They're magical, and should bring you good luck. Don't spend them all in one place."

Once the balloon was elevated enough that anyone on the ground couldn't hear the toddler, Diggs released the captive. "Yikes, you soaked this sack. How is your bladder so large?" He put the bag to the side to dry. Several hours later, Diggs threw some more coal into the firebox. "Well, Ozma, the trip should take about ten days. Try not to drive me loco."

The toddler continued to look up at him and scream. Diggs wrinkled his nose at the aromatic smell of urine, and he decided to jettison the sack and her diaper overboard. He dumped out the farm equipment from the second burlap bag and used his pocketknife to trim it into pieces. He strode over, wrestled the girl down on her back and used one piece as a new diaper. It fell off immediately. Diggs reached into the carpetbag and grabbed some of the dead general's braid cord. Ozma had escaped and was tottering away. He grabbed her, threw back on the cloth that had fallen to the ground, and tied the new burlap diaper on. Ozma howled the entire time.

The burlap ran out quickly, and Diggs regretted discarding the large potato sack. He refused to use the tinker boxes burlap sack, afraid that the mechanical magic boxes could slide through the slats. Diggs located some lunchpail trees and made frequent landings for food. He also looked for anything to use as a diaper for Ozma. During these stops, he let the toddler and piglets gambol in the grass. No one was happy to get back into the gondola.

Until they reached the Winkie River, Diggs had to use the cloth napkins from the inside of each dinner pail for her. Ozma ran through the napkins quickly. The child often crawled or wobbled around the basket without trousers. The piglets complained about the resulting messes. Diggs was extremely careful where he trod. Ozma happily squashed her piles of poop as she chased the pigs.

On the banks of the Winkie River, Diggs discovered a low yellow bush with huge leaves. The foliage was the size of hand towels and roughly the same material. He dropped all four sandbags onto the ground and vented hot air until the balloon settled to the ground. Diggs jumped out, carrying Ozma in under one arm, and gathered dozens of the leaves. He then stored these in the gondola's corner. Ozma helped by trying to rip up two of the leaves, but her small hands did minor damage.

The nine piglets cheered the diaper material discovery since part of their rag nest home had been sacrificed for Ozma's toilet facilities. "It had been a stinky one hundred miles 'til that bush," thought Diggs. He also used several towels to pad the floor of the gondola, making a soft bed for the child.

Diggs again carried the child over the railing and took advantage of the soft towels and the abundant river water to give Ozma a bath. He scooped up the flowing water with a garden shed pail and put the pail directly over an accumulated pile of kindling and firewood. "Getting low on matches," he thought. Diggs lit the kindling and warmed the water.

Diggs stripped Ozma down to her skin and decided he could use a wash as well. He looked at the girl child, blushed, and didn't remove his long johns. Diggs took off his boots, top hat, and outerwear, put Ozma next to the river, and jumped into the water. He came up sputtering. "Damn, that's cold. Oh no, where did she go?" Diggs quickly climbed up the bank and located the child, who was tottering away. He lifted her up, kicking and laughing, and carried her over to the towels and warming water. Diggs dipped a bush towel in the pail and gave Ozma a thorough towel cleaning. He used a dry towel on himself. "There, little girl. We're both nice and clean." He quickly got dressed, lifted Ozma up and flinched as she peed all over him.

Usually, Diggs devoted most of his day to either navigating the balloon or amusing the child. Not that he wanted to pay attention to her, but to prevent her from squeezing through, or climbing over the slats, and falling overboard. "I have to ignore this adorable little one," he thought, "or I might get to attached to her."

"Child, I can't believe I'm selling you to a witch, but I don't know any other way to help my friend. She better not hurt you, or I'll try to see if the petrification powder might work on her after all."

Diggs used ventriloquism to make the machine arm talk, allowed Ozma to chase the piglets, or showed her several pictures from the Illusion Maker. She laughed and squealed when shown illusions of a giant tiger, a flying elephant, and a beautiful fairy princess. Ozma especially loved the roar of the tiger, but didn't like the elephant's odor. Ozma squealed occasionally into the box, but the illusions formed only manifested, from the first person speaking.

Nighttime was worse for Diggs. Between manning the fire box, running after the toddler, and just feeling guilty about what he was doing, by the end of the day, he was utterly exhausted. Five days into the trip, after he carefully tucked Ozma into her towel bed, Diggs collapsed down next to her. He used his carpet bag as a pillow and more towels as linen. Five minutes after settling down, Ozma rolled over and snuggled into Diggs' armpit. He smiled down at her, yawned, closed his eyes, and began snoring.

Diggs and Ozma's beddings were at the opposite end of the gondola from the rebuilt rag nest of the piglets. The little pigs complained that

Diggs' loud snorting kept them up at night. They said that the fifteen feet separating them was still too close.

"Wake up Mister Diggs," screamed the piglet called Slim. He was jumping up and down on Diggs' chest. "Git your caboose up. The young'ins in trouble!"

Diggs slowly opened his eyes and found a piglet staring him right in the face. "Huh, what?"

Slim gestured with his head. "Over there, yonder. She's right near our nest."

"So what," murmured Diggs. He stretched.

"If you'all don't move fast, she's going to fall over the railing. That monkey can sure climb. Dang, if I had me a lariat, I'd have lassoed her."

Diggs eyes flew open, and he jumped up. At the far end of the gondola, Ozma had climbed up and was reaching the top slat on the railing. Diggs ran to the railing in five giant steps and grabbed the toddler just as she reached the top rail. "If they built my OZ gondola any larger, I never would've made it in time," he thought.

"No!" Ozma yelled. "No, me go up." She struggled in his arms.

"Let's go back and see the nice piggy," said Diggs. His breathing and heart rate slowly returned to a more normal level.

As he walked back to the bed area, Diggs again thought about whether he should take the child to Mombi. Was it right to trade his friend's life for a child? "Ozma, I'll try to make sure Mombi doesn't hurt you. And that witch should be able to take better care for you than a stone statue could. I really ruined you and your dad's life. After I save my friend, I'm going to beg Glinda the Good to turn Pastoria back, and then I'll reunite you with him again. Kid, are you even listening?"

Ozma had stopped struggling and fallen fast asleep in his arms. She drooled down the front of his long johns.

Diggs put her down on the towels. He took another piece of long braid out of the carpetbag and formed a loop around her ankle. Diggs tied the other end around his wrist. "I wish I had my friend Patrick's handcuffs. I hope this works."

Diggs begged the piglets to form continuous watches over Ozma. The leader of the lady piglets, Miss Scarlet, organized the shifts. She put two piglets on duty, every four hours round the clock. There were no more attempted escapes.

The balloon arrived at Mombi's home. Upon settling on the ground, Diggs noticed several differences in the structure. Someone replaced the majestic castle with a tiny, rundown hut. : Less guards and more glass statues were observed by him. The huge drawbridge over the moat vanished, and only a small, mostly dried-up stream was present. There was no grass in front of the hut, only lavender rocks, broken tree branches, and dirt. The one lunchpail tree stood surrounded by several moldy pails.

"Why does everything look so different?" yelled Diggs. "I hope Mombi hasn't moved."

The few remaining guards tethered the drop lines to boulders. They just stared at Diggs as he climbed up the slats, carrying Ozma. Their uniforms were even more filthy than at the last visit.

"You come to your doom," said one guard. "Our mistress has been in a terrible mood and is crazier than ever." He frowned at Diggs. "She knows her powers often go through cycles of weakness, and this is one of those times. She has difficulty transforming anything correctly with her wand, and her illusion powers are unsteady. One day there is a castle and a moat, the next a hut and a dried-up stream."

"What is going on?" Diggs put Ozma on one hip, reached back and took out his carpetbag with the other hand.

"These fluctuations occur about every hundred years," said a different guard. "This one is bothering her more than the last two." He turned and whispered to Diggs, "I think she's going through 'The Change'."

"Every hundred years? How long do the people of Oz live?" Diggs and his bundles headed towards the hut. He weaved around many glass statues.

"Ever since Oz became a fairyland, one rarely dies," said the last guard. "Only violent trauma will kill one. People stop aging at whatever age they desire. Mombi only picks twenty-year-old men for her guards. I lived here for over three hundred and fifty years myself. She transformed me seventeen times because of her anger."

"Yes, but her spells are fizzling," said the first guard. "She is running out of help because she breaks the glass statues and she can't turn the statues back into men."

Diggs continued towards the hut, but the guards stayed behind. As he was walking over the dried-up stream, a huge alligator stood on its hind feet and turned to face him. The beast had the head of a man and was wearing a dirty purple fur hat.

Diggs took a step backwards, almost dropping the child. "What are you?"

"Hello wizard," said the creature. "The last time we met, I was a flying snake. Since that time, she has made me a centaur, a giant slug, and now half man, half alligator."

Diggs tried very hard not to laugh. "I wouldn't exactly say you're half man."

"Mombi was trying to change me into another guard. Her magic is really getting erratic." A long tongue came out of the man's mouth and he grinned with a mouthful of huge sharp teeth. One tooth had a decay spot on it.

"My good man, I have just the thing you need. Have you ever heard of a magic toothbrush? No? Well, now you will. It'll save those chompers." Diggs reached down to the ground and picked up a long twig. He dropped his carpetbag and pulled his knife out of the front pocket of his greatcoat. Diggs put squirming Ozma down and put his foot on her back. He whittled the bark off the end of the twig and then flayed the clean end. "Use it twice a day, watch out for splinters." Diggs put the knife back into this pocket, picked up Ozma and the carpetbag.

Diggs walked up to the broken-down door, knocked, and then entered. "Mombi my sweets, I have returned as promised." He dropped his carpet bag and hid the child behind his back.

Mombi sat at a short table. She banged on it with an iron ladle in one hand, and swigged from a purple bottle with the other, swaying with each strike.

"Ouch, ouch," cried the spoon. "Oh, come on. This is giving such a headache, if I had a head?"

"So, you've come back. Couldn't stay away from this body?" Mombi ran the ladle down the front of her dress. She appeared to be in the same clothes she wore weeks ago.

"Please," said the ladle. "I don't want to see anymore. Put out my eye."

"Mombi, I have done my part of the bargain." Diggs smiled mischievously. "I have brought you your captive, as you requested."

The witch looked up at Diggs with a puzzled expression. "I don't see Pastoria. Where is he?"

"Ta da." Diggs pulled the child to be in front of him and held up Ozma with both hands.

"What is that brat doing here?" Mombi squinted her eyes almost shut and tried to focus on the child. "Who the hell is that?"

Ozma began to scream. The girl wiggled so much she almost fell out of Diggs' arms. His knuckles turned white as he gripped her tighter.

"This is Pastoria's daughter Ozma." Diggs could barely hold the girl still. He continued to use both hands to restrain her.

"Where the hell is what'ssss his name, Pastoria?"

"Well, there was a slight problem." Diggs put the child on the floor, straightened up, reached into his pocket, and brought out the container with the Powder of Petrification. He tossed the container onto the table. "Wrong powder. Jinxville now has a new stone statue. I'll trade you his daughter instead." Diggs' voice hesitated, and he mumbled, "if you agree to my terms." His voice became firmer and louder, "I need the three Flying Monkey Cap wishes to save my friend from the Chasm Dragon." He looked down at the toddler. "But I'll only give up the child to you if you promise not to hurt her, ever."

"Hurt her, ha! I'll turn her into a newt." Mombi waved her wand.

Chapter Twenty

Ozma vanished. In the place of the little girl stood a thin, shivering young boy.

Mombi looked with a confused expression on her face at the end of her wand. "Not again." She helplessly waved it back and forth through the air.

"Where am I?" said the lad. "What happened? Who are you?" The boy wore purple, raggedy clothes, which were almost as filthy as Mombi's dress. His pants were frayed at the knees and cuffs, and only came to his shins. He was pale, tiny, with a gaunt face, and looked about with an expression of bewilderment. The lad's lip trembled.

Mombi shook her head. "This is the last time I do a spell when I've been drinking." She pointed the wand at the boy again. The witch violently mumbled an incantation. Nothing happened. "Great. Now I'm stuck with a male brat. I wonder if he'd be good to eat?"

Diggs looked at the boy in astonishment. "Where did Ozma go? What happened to the little girl?"

"Are you my mother and father?" said the boy. He stared at both of them and backed away.

"Yes," slurred Mombi. She impotently swished the wand back and forth again. "Work, damn you."

"Absolutely not," stated Diggs emphatically. He held out both hands out in front of him and made a stay back gesture.

"Please," said the boy. "What's going on? I don't remember my name or where I am. Who am I?" Tears began running down his face.

"What is your name?" muttered Mombi. "Can't be Ozma. Don't want you to remember your past. Something magical? Nooo, something boozy. Yes, I'll call you Drunkard."

"Terrible," said Diggs.

"Inebriated?" Mombi brandished her wand through the air like a conductor leading an orchestra.

Diggs shook his head. "Nope. I don't think you truly know what that means."

"Sloshed?" Mombi put down her wand and took another drink from the bottle.

"Never."

"Tipssssy?" Mombi slurred again.

Diggs put his hand on his chin and stroked it. "That's better, but you're having trouble saying it. Too long. How about Tip?"

"Perfect." Mombi put her head down on the table and began snoring.

"So, are you my mother?" sobbed Tip. "Mom, mama, mema, mommy, where am I? Why can't I remember my name is Tip? Whyyyyy??"

"Quiet lad," said Diggs. "You really don't want to wake her."

The boy stopped crying and looked around the hut. "I'm hungry. For some reason, I crave gruel." He walked over and picked up the iron ladle and went to the cauldron. Tip took a spoonful from the bubbling liquid and then sipped it carefully. He immediately spat the mouthful on the grimy, muddy floor. "That's terrible! What is it?"

Diggs shrugged. "I do not know. But something tells me, Tip, you better develop a taste for that kind of cooking." He walked towards the sleeping witch.

"I feel for you, kid," said the ladle. "I've been making and having to taste that crap for two hundred years. And it's so strong, it's been taking off my varnish."

Startled, Tip dropped the ladle. "What in the world? Who said that?"

Diggs turned around. "Tip I recommend going outside and bringing in some firewood. Also, if you want to eat, there is an immense tree nearby called a lunchpail tree. Pick two ripe pails and bring them in."

"Mister, how can a ladle talk? Now why two pails, mister? I couldn't eat over one and I'm sure Mother eats the stuff from the cauldron." Tip headed for the door before waiting for any answers.

"Please take me with you," cried the ladle. "I can't take the taste of this slop anymore."

"The second pail is for me. I can't eat the garbage in the pot either." Diggs pretended to retch and held his nose. "Boy, work hard and keep a low profile and the witch shouldn't hurt you."

"Mister," said Tip. "What's a witch, and what does low profile mean?"

"She is one. Don't worry about anything else, lad," said Diggs. "Now go." He muttered to himself, "Child sure asks a lot of questions."

Tip looked at Mombi, frowned, and hurried out the door.

The witch was face down on the table and snoring loudly. Purple, putrid smelling drool leaked from her mouth and puddled on the table. Her snores rattled the walls.

Diggs walked over and gently shook Mombi's shoulder. The volume of the snores didn't diminish, and the witch didn't wake. He shook her more aggressively until the witch's peaked hat went flying off. Several purple bugs, three inches long with folded wings, crawled out of her greasy hair and the fur piece raised its head and growled.

"I was asleep," said the cape. "You woke me up." It raised its head higher and snapped at one bug crawling around Mombi's scalp. "When is she going to wash? Oh yeah, witches can't tolerate water."

Diggs kicked Mombi's shins. This elicited a response, and the witch groggily lifted her head. Diggs was about to slap her, but looked at the wand on the table next to the woman and put down his hand.

Diggs stepped back from the table and tried to look innocent. "Are you awake, my dear? I think you drifted off."

Mombi glanced downward, "Huh, what? Why do my legs hurt?" She picked up the bottle and took another swallow. "Where is the boy? I need another statue."

"No, my dear, you need more help." Diggs gently took the bottle away from her now limp fingers. "Look, no firewood, the floor is mildly dusty and your powders and elixirs disorganized. A busy woman like yourself needs servants to do the drudgery of everyday chores." He held the bottle of liquor above her head. "Now, we need to talk about my small payment."

"For what?" Mombi raised her head enough to focus on the bottle, but her eyes were half closed. She snatched feebly at the container.

Diggs pointed out the door. "You now have a new helpful servant. Pastoria will never bother you, and now Ozma won't remember anything, nor challenge you ever. Two enemies gone for the price of one. Just feed him well and don't mistreat him. Maybe after I save Chang, I'll come back and adopt him. At least now I don't have to change her—err—his diapers. For my payment, I would like a draught of the Powder of Life." He put the bottle of booze on the table, just out of her reach.

"Can't do it, tall man. Dr. Pipt, the Crooked Magician, is only in year two of his incantation." Mombi began to inch her fingers closer to the bottle. "The powder takes seven years of constantly stirring four different kettles at the same time. Then it only yields only three doses. It don't come cheap, and I am out." She again tried to reach for the bottle, but Diggs pushed it away from her.

"What in the world did you waste—err—use the powder on?" Diggs picked up and swayed the bottle in front of her to keep her attention. Mombi's head moved back and forth with the movement, like a cobra watching an Indian snake charmer. The fur piece undulated as well.

Mombi grabbed her head with both hands. "I didn't waste the powder, used it to make Felix, my fur cape here, and my talking ladle. Can't remember what I used the last draught on." She scratched her scalp and more bugs jumped off her hair.

"I need something to save my friend Chang or even bring him back to life. I can't abandon him and I don't have enough magic to fight the Chasm Dragon." Diggs bent forward and stared Mombi right in the face. After a whiff of her breath, he pulled his head back.

"I'll only give you something I can't use." Mombi limply waved her hand. "My wand is on the fritz, but I need it to defend myself against my enemies. You can't have my powders or elixirs either. Did you use up all the Powder of Persuasion?"

Diggs frowned, then scowled. "Petrification, not Persuasion." He pointed to the container on the table. "I need something to fight the dragon and save my friend."

"You did uphold your part of the bargain, so I will lend you the Flying Monkey Golden Cap. Hic, hic, just lend it. I used up my three wishes, but it'll be a powerful future trade item. You must bring it back when you use up your three." Mombi rose from the table, turned greener, and sat down again. "But I must warn you. Theodora told me if I don't give the cap to her, she'll kill whoever has it."

Diggs stared right into her eyes. "I'll take that chance."

Chapter Twenty-One

Mombi tottered towards the bottom large drawer of her Powders cabinet. She pulled out the drawer, and hundreds of spiders scurried around. A few purple bottles and containers sat jumbled inside the drawer, on top of a rotten plank of wood. The slab was askew and sat several inches above something below it. "I have carefully hidden the cap in this false bottom."

Diggs reached his hand into the cabinet and barely touched the plank. It immediately fell off, revealing a small dusty golden cap. "Great hiding place." Diggs rolled his eyes. "The magic cap was so cleverly concealed." He tried very hard not to ooze sarcasm.

Mombi grinned at Diggs. Her teeth were either purple and rotten to the gumline or missing entirely. She cackled, "Clever, ain't I?"

Diggs and Mombi bumped heads as they both leaned over at the same time to look into the drawer. "Ouch," Diggs yelled.

"What happened?" Mombi pushed Diggs away from the cabinet and rubbed her temple. Mombi's eyes crossed and then uncrossed. "I need another drink."

Diggs stepped back, reached in, and took up the Golden Cap. "Later, you can drink later. How does the cap work?" he asked as he shoved it in Mombi's face. "I'm going to use it to rescue my friend Chang. The Chasm Dragon will never be able to defeat me…, I hope." Diggs spoke so rapidly, his words ran together.

Mombi grabbed the cap out of his hand. "Remember fool, you summon the Flying Monkeys to do your bidding, only three times." She jammed the cap on her head, dust went flying, and blathered, "You must say the spell exactly."

Mombi stood on her left foot, raised her right hand with the index finger pointed due east. "Um, I can't remember. Damn, what's that spell?"

Diggs grabbed her by the shoulders. "What do you mean, you can't remember? I…", he shook once, "need…" he shook again. Mombi's filthy hair went flying, the cap spun around on the greasy strands, "that… spell."

Mombi blearily looked up at Diggs. She picked her nose and used it to violently scratch her head As soon as she itched, the Golden Cap fell off. Mombi looked down at the cap. "There's the spell. I wrote it down inside so I wouldn't forget."

Mildly embossed along the inside rim of the cap in gold ink were strange words. The script glowed in white, with an inner light of its own.

Mombi picked up the cap and peered inside. "Yep, these are the chants and incantation instructions. Let's see, left foot, right hand and say these words, right foot, left-hand etcetera, etcetera and both feet, both hands. Should work. Remember, both sisters would kill to get it."

Diggs grabbed the cap, read everything, and memorized the entire spell. He stood on his left foot, raised his right hand, pointed east, and said, "Ep-pe, pep-pe, kak-ke. Do I look like a fool?" Diggs switched to his right foot, raised his left hand, and said, "Hil-lo, hol-lo, hel-lo" Now he stood on both feet. "I feel like I should do an exotic dance." He raised both his arms and yelled, "Ziz-zy—"

"No, you idiot, stop! Don't waste it!" screamed Mombi.

"What do you mean? Zuz-zy."

Mombi reached for the cap. "Don't say the incantation out loud. It always summons the monkeys."

Diggs kept both of his arms raised. "All right then, I'll only whisper it. Zik."

"No, you idiot, stop! Spells don't work like that. Spoken is anything out loud!" Mombi stepped back and put her arms over her head.

The door blew open. A tremendous gust of wind stirred up the dust and grit that covered the hovel's floor. Hundreds of flying monkeys blotted the sun seen through the door. The earth shook as the beasts landed. Screeching filled the air. A large monkey clomped into the hut. Four followers rapidly tamped in next. These monkeys were much larger and meaner looking than the first beast through the door. All the creatures bared their teeth at Diggs.

Dozens of outside monkeys tried to push into the hut. The first monkey turned and commanded, "Stop."

The first flying monkey into the room walked up to Diggs. The beast only came up to Diggs' shoulders, but its torso was wider than his. A dusty brown fur covered the monkey's body, with golden fur on its face. Diggs saw a long scar on one side of his face, running from the corner of his eye down to his chin, giving him a crooked, pulled-up grin, and long, sharp yellow incisors. This monkey wore a heavy golden crown and a filthy royal green silk robe. The monkey's wings, which were slowly being folded as he walked forward, were as translucent as a dragonfly's. They didn't appear to be strong enough to transport the beast. "You have used the first of your three wishes. Why have you summoned us?"

Diggs flinched at the inherent ferocity from the beast and wrinkled up his nose at the monkeys' body odor. "But, but, but I was only practicing. I thought it didn't count if I whispered?"

The four followers walked up to just behind their king while folding their huge wings. The king's guards had crossed swords in a scabbard on their backs. These monkeys stared at Diggs and didn't make any sounds, except snarls. They crouched, and it looked like the beasts would rush at Diggs the minute he took a step towards the monkey wearing the crown.

"Well, that was amazing," said Diggs. "I didn't think that would happen. Who or what are you? Are you the Golden Cap, Flying Monkeys?" Diggs looked down at the chief monkey and held out his hand. Then he stared at the guards and took three steps backwards. "Should I bow?"

Mombi peered out from crossed arms over her head. "Of course they're the flying monkeys, stupid."

"I'm King Nikko," said the first monkey. "And these are my imperial guards and followers. We are yours to command two more times only, but we are yours for now." He bowed to Diggs. Most of the others in the hut blew raspberries. The monkeys outside just screeched. "Now what do you require?"

The few Gillikin guards that be seen through the door trembled. One guard tried to bolt into the hut, but a monkey wearing a battered stovepipe hat prevented him. "Mombi, mistress, help us," the guard yelled. A large wet spot spread across the bottom of his furs.

Mombi cackled, "The way my wand ain't working; I can't." She backed up against the powder cabinet.

Diggs looked at the guards and the milling monkeys through the open door. "I love that stovepipe that big monkey is wearing. I prefer wearing a top hat myself. He won't eat that Gilliken guard, will he? Wow, look at all those different headgear. Yep," He stuttered nervously, "hundreds of different hats—panamas, pillboxes, fedoras, stocking caps, derbies, several dented green tiaras, sombreros, and one monkey is even wearing a witch peaked hat. Quite a variety."

Mombi stepped forward and squinted her eyes. "Where's the witch's hat? I've been looking for my other one for two hundred years."

All the monkeys wore filthy green robes, most of which were torn. The tails of the monkeys had squalid lime green ribbons tied around them, with crusted, putrid brown ooze.

Diggs noticed that all the followers and outside monkeys rarely spoke. Mostly, loud growls, screeches, and screams continued to burst forth. Noises from the monkeys' other end were plentiful as well.

Diggs gagged. "Mombi, what's that horrible smell? It's worse than your stew. What was all that on the ribbons, poop?"

Mombi breathed in deeply. "You probably don't want to know."

"What is your first wish?" demanded Nikko.

Diggs held up his hands and stepped towards the king. "But I thought I was only practicing. I wasn't ready with my first wish."

The king's closest guard, a huge monkey, bared its teeth and reached back and drew a sword. The guard's hat, got up off the monkey's head and hissed at Diggs.

"My God," said Diggs. "Is that a live animal, a raccoon?"

The guard held the point of the sword up under Diggs chin. "Step back. Of course, what other kind of coon-skin cap would I wear? You also going to make fun of Matilda's Easter Bonnet, just cause it has dead flowers and bees on it?"

Diggs began to sweat. "Sorry. So you can talk." He backed away from the king slowly.

"Wish now, or we leave," screeched Nikko.

Diggs patted the golden cap. "Let me think. I um, wish you to rescue my friend, Chang."

"We will obey your wish. Now, where is this friend?" said Nikko.

"The last I saw him, he was falling into the Giant Chasm Dragon's ravine," said Diggs with a choked voice.

Nikko glared at Diggs. "Are you sure he's even alive? You used a wish on a hope? He's probably dead and gone. We can't do the impossible."

"Please," said Diggs. "I must find him. I'm still going to go back and question that dragon. Chang has to be alive."

"We will honor any specific wish, but I don't understand the one you're asking for," said Nikko. "The previous monkey king tried to look for Pastoria for centuries and he was known to be alive. Never found that man. Be more specific with your request. Something we could actually accomplish. What else do you want done? Make a reasonable wish NOW."

"Err, can I get back to you in that regard?" Diggs took off the golden cap. He looked at the cap and muttered, "Ziz-zy zuz-zy, zik?"

"I told you not to say the spell out loud and waste it." Mombi grabbed for the golden cap. One guard, wearing a dainty bonnet on her massive head, snarled, and stepped towards the witch. Mombi immediately backed away.

"Summon us when you are ready," said Nikko. "Now do not waste our valuable time. Think before you call for us. Your practice chanting, with a frivolous request, wasted your wish. Remember, we come only two more times." The king unfurled his wings. The other monkeys howled and chased each other around the hut. One threw poop at Mombi. She didn't notice. "Troops, come now, we go back to the jungle," commanded the king.

Nikko walked to the hut door. He became stuck in the opening momentarily because of his huge wings. All of his guards scampered out on all fours, only unfurling wings after they were through the opening.

The monkeys outside, took off, after the king and his guards were in the air. The noise was deafening from the snarls, shrieks, and howls.

Tip came running through the door. "What in the world was that? Where did they all come from? Why were they here?" He carried a small pile of firewood and two lunchpails balanced precariously on top. He dropped the wood in front of the fireplace and the two lunchpails flew off and banged into the black kettle.

"Hey, watch out," said the ladle. "Those pails almost hit my eye."

"Yeah, be more careful," said the Mombi's kettle. "You almost dented me."

"That's right, my kettle. That's what I used the last draught for," mumbled Mombi. "Boy, stoke up the fire and I might keep you after all." She walked back to the table, sat down, and buried her head in her arms.

"Are you sure you're my mother?" Tip threw several pieces of wood on the fire. "Why can't I remember anything before today?" He pointed at Diggs. "Am I to live in this hut? Or do I leave with him? He held out both his hands. "What does my future hold? How come my name is Tip? Where do I sleep? Can I plant a garden? I'd love to grow pumpkins. Can I eat now? I'm starving and I still crave hot cereal? I'm hungry. I need food," he whined.

"Less talking, boy, or I'll reconsider turning you into a statue." Mombi picked up her wand and pointed it at Tip. "Maybe one last try?" The wand fizzled and drooped. "Great."

"Don't hurt the lad," said Diggs. "Or I'll use the cap on you. I'm not sure if I'll miss you or not, son, but at least I won't get peed on again."

"What do you mean peed on?" said Tip. He picked and opened a lunchpail. "Yum! "

Diggs picked up the Golden Cap and put it in a pocket of his greatcoat. "I am satisfied, witchy." He waved goodbye at Tip and Mombi. "I'll try to remember to return your cap when I return." Diggs walked towards the open door. "Now I have an appointment with a dragon."

Chapter Twenty-Two

Diggs picked and loaded several lunch tree pails into the gondola. "There, that should be enough, for you fat little things."

"Not even close," said the piglet leader. "We're always hungry."

Diggs went back to the tree and picked more pails. After harvesting, he patted his front pocket in order to make sure the Golden Flying Monkey Cap was safely in place and climbed into the basket. Diggs went over to his carpetbag, removed his two revolvers, verified their load, kissed them for luck, and put them on top of the bag. Next, he took out his saber and a whetstone. Diggs sharpened the blade by stroking it against the stone. Finally, Diggs stoked the firebox with fresh coal and motioned to the Gillikin guard to throw the tethered sandbags back into the gondola.

In the four corners of the basket, on top of the sandbags, Diggs put the coiled drop lines. "It's lucky those guards are still in shock from the monkeys. They are so befuddled that they haven't begged to come with me. Well, little piglets, we didn't use that much coal during our journey here. We better hope I don't have to stop at Jinxville for another load. I'm not sure how warm my welcome would be once they discover a stone statue of Pastoria or a missing Ozma. I feel terrible about killing that loyal man and enslaving the child. Maybe I could use a magic wish with the monkeys to turn Pastoria back to normal and free Ozma. After I first save Chang."

The wind was blowing steadily north, making the return journey much more difficult, since Diggs wanted to go south. Using his skills as a veteran balloon pilot, he both tacked into the wind and side vented hot air when necessary. "I'm sure glad, little piggies, that this is just hot air I'm using to maneuver. Never want to use hydrogen gas again." Diggs shuddered at the memory of the horrible deaths of his fellow soldiers and the explosion. He zig-zagged steadily south towards the Giant Chasm.

"Well guys, this is a lot of work." Diggs ran back and forth between picking up a piece of coal and throwing it into the firebox. "I wonder if I could teach one of you how to load the firebox with coal. Nah, each of you is the same size as a lump of coal." He ran back to the coal pile and staggered. "All this seesaw motion is making me dizzy."

The piglets didn't comment. They were too busy crowding into one of the open lunchpails and devouring everything inside it. The jostling was worse than the crowds seen on the streets of New York.

Diggs increased his elevation when going over the Winkie Mountains. Upon reaching the apex, the south wind blew harshly against the balloon and gondola. Bits of sands and gravel pelted Diggs and the piglets.

"This dirt actually feels like it is burning us," said the head piglet. The nine piglets stopped eating and ran under the new rag nest.

Diggs tried to shield his half-closed eyes with his hand. "And the sand is getting into my eyes. I can barely see. It burns so much, I wonder if the sand could be from the Deadly Desert?" He pulled his greatcoat up to just below his eyes and over his nose, and clutched it tightly. With a muffled voice, Diggs said, "I feel like Jesse James."

"Make it stop," whined the leader from under the nest. "It's still getting in. It hurts."

Diggs ran to one of the burlap bags and pulled out an oversized pair of green glasses. "There are some goggles for myself and some of these twenty miniature spectacles should fit you." He placed the goggles on and adjusted the silk strap. Diggs reached back into the bag and pulled out nine pairs of small specs.

"Piglet, get your group out here," said Diggs. "Are you the same one I've talked to in the past?"

The head piglet stuck his head out of the nest. "That is correct. Yes, I am the one called Frederick. But you can call me Freddy. Troop, come out everyone."

The tiny pink piglets came out from the nest and allowed the spectacles to be placed. "Troops, this is strange," said Diggs. "You now look brown. In fact, the sky looks green- blue, my carpet bag looks green brown. Everything has a green tinge."

One piglet looked up and said, "Your face looks green. Are you sick? But your wizard clothes are still white?" The piglets scurried back under the nest.

Diggs looked around at all the now green objects. The only thing that wasn't pure green was his white greatcoat, hat, and pants and the "OZ" painted on the balloon's envelope. Why does pure white stay white, he thought?

After cresting the mountain's apex, Diggs released hot air from the envelope and caused the balloon to drop down. At a lower elevation, the burning winds stopped. Diggs removed his goggles, and his color vision slowly returned to normal. "Piglets, take off those crazy spectacles. They might not be good for you."

One of the piglets poked its head from out of the nest. "We like the way they make us look. We're going to leave them on." The rest of them poked their heads out and agreed. They ran back to the lunchpail and continued to make pigs of themselves.

After several hours, Diggs observed the piglets were still eating and their color reverted to pink. The sky again was blue and his carpet bag a dirty brown. He waved to the yellow Winkie River Serpent but didn't stop to banter. The balloon continued south.

After several days, with numerous lunchpail tree stops for food, the balloon progressed south. Finally, the piglets came out of their nest to talk to Diggs. The largest one stood up on his hind feet. "Mr. Diggs, we're all really tired of eating green grub. It's still delicious, but too strange for our little tummies. Why, Fernanda is so upset, she only ate seven times today. She's wasting away."

Diggs bent down to talk to the large piglet. "I would be happy to take the specs off you and store them for the next dusty day." He reached for the spectacles.

Frederick stood up and pointed with his hoof. "Plus Mister Diggs, everything is green except your clothes."

A different piglet complained. "Whal, it never looked like this in Texas. It's too strange for my little brains. Please remove my glasses as well."

Diggs bent down and removed nine pairs of specs. He put them back into a burlap bag and rolled it up tightly. He groaned as he stood up. "My back is killing me."

"Mr. Diggs, everything is still green," said Frederick. "This is terrible. I'm really worried. I hope you can do something about it, after I have a small snack. The green pot roast, lime colored mashed potatoes, and emerald-shaded lemon meringue pie actually don't look half bad. I'll just get used to this."

"I hope your eyes go back to normal, but if not, I'm sure you won't starve little ones," said Diggs. "These specs might make everything permanently green. I guess it didn't affect my vision for good, since I wore them for such a short time."

Diggs had more and more trouble heading south as he got closer and closer to the Great Chasm. The winds off the desert blew the balloon away from his needed direction. Diggs had to side vent hot air frequently to stay on course. "Am I doing the right thing, piggies? Is my friend still alive or am I clutching at straws? I'm going to fight a giant dragon. Am I crazy? I know I'm sure I am petrified."

Finally, the Great Chasm lay before the balloon. Giant flying snakes and other creatures rose from the opening. As they drifted closer, Diggs could see in the hoard of beasts five moth-eaten monkeys that were flying. "Hey piggies! Are these the same monkeys we saw before?" These apes were not brown with golden facial fur, but a dingy gray. All were completely without clothes, but had hats. As the group got nearer, Diggs saw these beasts had many scars and torn areas to their wings.

The group of flying creatures approached the balloon. One of the flying monkeys hovered forward, moving apart from the rest of the beasts. "I'm ex-king Ortho, retired from the Magic Cap Flying Monkey band. Why do you trespass in this domain?"

Diggs observed there were flying alligators, snakes, gigantic bugs, and a floating balloon with one central eye. The balloon ball creature had several tendrils. At the end of each was another small eye. The beast floated and hovered on the north side of the OZ envelope. As it continuously took in huge gulps of air, its main balloon body would blow up to an immense size. It expelled the air in a huge gush, the force of which stopped the drift of the balloon envelope and negated the force of the Deadly Deserts winds. All the creature's eyes would close as the beast blew out its air. At all other times, the orbs stared at Diggs intently.

"Hey flying cannon ball," said Diggs. "Why are you blowing at my envelope?" "That is the creepiest thing that I have ever seen. What in the world is it?" thought Diggs.

The creature didn't say a word. Diggs was sure that several eyes opened wide when he spoke to it, and he thought one of them gave him a wink.

Diggs ducked down under that basket railing and pulled out both of Pastoria's machines from a burlap bag. He had trouble hold them in his sweating, trembling hands. Diggs whispered into the first. "I AM OZ, THE GREAT AND POWERFUL" boomed out from the other end of the box.

All the creatures, except the ball balloon, backpedaled. Ortho flinched. "Yes, wizard, I can see you're mighty. Do you come to parlay with our leader, the Chasm Dragon?"

Diggs stayed below the railing and whispered, "Flame," into the second box. A ten-foot tall fire appeared in midair. Diggs threw his voice and from out of the center of the flame came, "Have the dragon come to me, now. If he still lives after my servant attacked him?"

"I think he will be keen to meet you." Ortho motioned for the other monkeys to fly down. "He told us someone will have to pay with their lives, for his slight scratch."

"Bah," said Diggs. "That was an amusing battle. This one will be to the death."

Chapter Twenty-Three

Most of the creature hoards hovered in the air next to the gondola. Four of the old flying monkeys rocketed down into the chasm, screeching noisily. The giant balloon ball creature continued to take gulps of air and then exhale them against the envelope of the OZ balloon. This constant discharge allowed the envelope to stay in place. The creature's body would start as the same size as Diggs' carpet bag. After gulping in draughts of air, it would blow up to half the size of the balloon's envelope. Then it would exhale and start all over again.

Diggs straightened and reached for his carpetbag. He placed the tinker boxes next to the bag, pulled his dueling revolvers from it, tucked them into his belt, then removed his saber and slid it into his waistband. All these items were too much for his pants, which fell down to his ankles. He yanked them up, uncinched his belt, and refastened it as tight as it went. Diggs agonized about the fact that he now could only latch his belt by using just the first hole in the belt leather. The weight of the items pulled the pants to the top of his hips. "Have to cut down on those lunchpails," he thought. He grabbed the Flying Monkey Cap and jammed it into his coat pocket.

Diggs made sure his top hat was at a rakish angle and pushed back the bottom of his greatcoat, so it exposed the guns in his belt. "I know I look dashing. Hope my quick draw works," he thought. Diggs lifted the two boxes and carried them under one arm. "I'm as ready as I'll ever be," he thought. "I hope I look impressive as I get eaten. How the hell do I fight a giant dragon? I'm scared," Diggs muttered.

From out of the rag nest, burst the nine piglets. They were all wearing their green glasses again. They equipped each of them with sharp splinters of wood. "We'll use our swords to fight to the death." They waved their ineffective weapons over their heads.

"How are they holding the wood with their hooves," thought Diggs?

The creature horde swarmed the gondola. The flying snakes bared fangs and attacked the envelope of the balloon. They bounced off the fabric, causing no harm. The remaining flying monkeys screeched and made faces at the piglets. The rest of the beasts flew at Diggs.

Diggs started to pull the saber out of his belt. Unfortunately, it got stuck, and he began to hop around, tugging at it. The saber sawed at the leather of his belt and his belt parted. His revolvers fell onto the deck of the gondola. His pants plummeted to his knees. Diggs waved his saber at the incoming creatures. "I'm going to go down fighting." He tripped over his bunched-up pants and fell face down on the deck. The two tinker boxes fell down next to him.

Diggs scrambled over and picked one of the tinker boxes. He whispered "Surrender" into the chute. Nothing came out of the other end. He shook it and tried again. There was no result a second time. The hoard hovered and gazed at him. Diggs lifted the box up and peered into it. "Oops, wrong end." He reversed the box and whispered "Surrender."

A booming "SURRENDER" came forth. The beasts retreated.

Diggs stood and pulled up his pants. While holding up his drawers with one hand, he limped over to his carpetbag and opened it. He rummaged through the bag and pulled out his string of trick scarves. Diggs used them to make a make-shift belt and tied it. "Whew, that feels much better."

Diggs picked up his guns from off the deck and put them in his oversized pockets. He put the saber back on top of his carpetbag. "Something like that could hurt someone." He again carried the tinker boxes under his arm.

Diggs turned towards the railing and was face to face with the Chasm Dragon. Diggs jumped. "Yikes. Where did you come from?"

The beast stared at Diggs with one eye. Over the other socket was a giant black patch with a huge ruby in its center. The beast's scales glittered in the sunlight. His one eye peered intently at the wizard. Then the monster grinned at the magician. "Back so soon, wizard? Here to finish this once and for all?"

"Wow," Diggs thought, "that expression of mirth on the dragon's face sure is horrible to look at." Aloud he blustered, "I don't want to have to kill you, dragon." Diggs put down the tinker boxes and pulled out one revolver. His hand trembled. "All I want is my friend back. Where is he? Did you eat him? Is he dead?"

"Bah, put away that peashooter, wizard." The dragon waved its front claw aimlessly. "One usually can't die in Oz. Death occurs only from exceptional injuries or from being eaten. Everything usually heals. Even my eye is sprouting back. Why in two hundred years I'll be as good as new? This was an amusing battle. No harm done."

Diggs dropped to his knees. "No harm?" He now spoke into the first box. "WHERE IS MY FRIEND? TELL ME NOW." The force of the statement from the magic box blew several of the creatures away from the gondola.

"Calm down, wizard. Your skinny friend wouldn't have been enough of a mouthful to make it worth the effort. Now you, on the other hand…" The dragon opened his mouth, showed his teeth, and licked his lips. His teeth were as long as the gondola was tall. The beast sighed. His breath smelled of rotten eggs and brimstone. "Maybe just a little nibble?"

Diggs stood up and pulled out the Golden Flying Monkey Cap. "Where is my friend? I will use this cap to fight you." He took off his top hat and put on the cap. He raised his right hand with a pistol in it. "Damn, what else was there to do?" Diggs scratched his head with the end of the pistol. "Oh, yeah." He stood on his left foot and raised his right hand again. "Ep-pe, pep-pe, kak-ke."

"Stop, you idiot," yelled Ortho, the old flying monkey. "Don't waste the spell."

"Hey, I'm getting the hang of this." Diggs switched to his right foot, raised his left hand and chanted, "Hil-lo, hol-lo, hel-lo."

"Stop, you idiot!" yelled both the old flying monkey and the Giant Dragon. "Don't waste the spell. We're not going to fight you."

Diggs stopped talking immediately. "Huh, what? Why not? Why aren't you going to kill me?"

The dragon glared at Diggs. "I'm not up for a fight. It's about time for a brief nap. Maybe fifty years should do it. Don't summon those screeching beasts. They're so loud, I can't sleep. I'll tell you anything you want."

"Stop," said Ortho. "The dragon said he would kick me out if any of my brethren ever showed up. I don't blame him." The old flying monkey clasped hands and implored Diggs while hovering in front of the balloon. "It's quiet here in the Chasm. I don't want to leave."

Diggs still raised both arms. "Damn, I was just getting into the rhythm." He raised his pistol again with his still trembling hand. "It prepared me to die fighting you. Now where is my friend?"

The dragon reflected pensively. "It was a long fall, but the skinny man stayed on all the way to the bottom of my chasm. Just as I was going to buck him off once and for all, maybe take a small bite or two, he finally fell off. I reached for him, but he disappeared down into a narrow ravine. I looked down at the slit and saw him wiggling and squirming through the narrowest passage. He looked like a snake going down a rabbit hole."

"Chang always was nimble."

"I couldn't fit into that hole and gave up." The dragon looked wistful. "It's probably for the best. If I'd eaten Chinese, I assume I'd been hungry an hour later, anyway."

"And he still might be alive? How do I get to him? Where does the crevasse lead to?" Diggs leaned over the railing of the gondola. "I'll go immediately."

"I live with my followers in the giant chasm. The narrow ravine at the bottom leads to allies of mine," said the dragon. "An underground kingdom. But don't think about going through the ravine. Only my smallest members go down. With that massive stomach, you could never fit through the opening. Plus, your friend really was squirming significantly. Once in a while, after an earth tremor, the opening gets larger for a while, then it closes back up. It was fascinating watching the man contorting through the opening."

Several of the piglets stuck their heads out of the rag nest. "Yes, Ozzy, you've been eating like a pig."

Diggs glared at the dragon "It wouldn't be my first one, but I think it's time for a strict diet. I'll get through that ravine somehow." He turned and looked down at the chubby piglets. "And you, my little friends, are going to join me." Diggs looked again at the dragon. "By the way, how in the world did you recognize him as Chinese?"

"When I was a youngin'," said the dragon. "I went to the country of China to visit my cousin, the Imperial Dragon of Huan Nan Province. We were naughty and ate dozens of what do you call them? Oh yeah, peasants. Your friend looked identical to those people we ate. They were tasty, but the skinny people didn't make a dent in my hunger. I haven't been back there since."

"I can't believe it," said Diggs. "So Oz is a completely different planet?"

"I presume so. It's extremely difficult to travel to. I don't expect you've ever encountered magic before coming to this mystical land?"

Diggs leaned forward. "Have you been to my world often?"

"Well...", said the dragon. "Several times when I was younger. But when I was a teenager, I had a run in with a knight called Sir George. How is that wonderful fighter doing?"

Diggs stared at the beast. "That happened centuries ago. He's dead, if he wasn't a myth."

The dragon pointed to an old scar on his side. "Our fun brouhaha was no myth. I forgot that you Earth people do not live very long."

"So, can I follow Chang through the ravine back to Earth?" said Diggs.

The dragon frowned. "No, wizard. Like I said before, it goes to an underground kingdom, not Earth. I went through a distant portal in the land of Oz."

"This is the closest I've been to my friend in a while. I've got to go through that ravine. I'll figure out something, or die trying."

Chapter Twenty-Four

The dragon only occasionally flapped his wings to remain in front of the stationary balloon. "Beneath my chasm kingdom is the land of the Silver Islands. Although I have never physically visited the lands, through my emissaries I stay up to date with all their news. The Silver Islands is a prosperous area, but undergoes intense turmoil frequently. If your friend landed safely in this land, I hope he survives. He will need to fight and he certainly proved how well he does that with me." The beast pointed at his eyepatch.

"Is there any way to determine if Chang is safely down there?" As Diggs peered over the railing down into the chasm, his top hat wobbled and began to fall off. He lunged farther over the railing to save it.

The dragon exhaled and pushed Diggs and his hat back into the gondola. "I haven't communicated with the Islands in months."

Diggs grimaced at the creature's breath, which smelled of burning horse manure. "Don't you ever floss?"

The dragon laughed. "Last I heard from my emissary, there was another revolution going on. So much wonderful fighting. I wish I could squeeze through that narrow opening. The Islands are huge. There's no way you could ever find Chang again."

Diggs pinched his nose at the odor from the dragon's breath. "Can you please send that emissary? I would appreciate it." He shoved his hat firmly onto his head. "But tell me, dragon, why in the world are you helping me? When we first met, you tried to eat me."

"Yeah," several piglets piped up. "Us too."

"I'm not always hungry, but I just love a good fight." The dragon lazily flapped his wings and picked at his back tooth with one of his claws. "Battling with you and your friend was great fun. I was only sort of kidding about eating you. Why, I consumed a small snack—fourteen oxen, and six horses—just before meeting you both. But the real reason I'm assisting, is, it has been foretold."

Diggs leaned over the railing again. A puzzled expression crossed his face. "What do you mean by that? Are you a fortune teller?"

"Not I, but someone who lives in the Silver Islands is. The seer told of a wizard who would unite the Land of Oz and defeat all the witches."

"I thought Pastoria had done that?"

The dragon flapped his wings once to stay in place. "Yes, but when his magic grew weak, he gave up the throne and vanished. The evil witches took over three of the four countries of OZ. Glinda the Good is young and trying to unite the south, but she has a long way to go."

"So, this magic person foretold someone is coming to overthrow three powerful and evil witches and unite an enchanted country?" Diggs put his hand to his head. "A place which can't exist and I never even heard of? For God's sake, why do you think it's me?"

"Yes, it's you," said the beast. "The seer described a wizard who would arrive in a huge flying machine and called himself OZ. But there's a slight fortune-telling problem. The Silver Island's time moves at a much quicker rate than Oz." The dragon flicked a set of horns and a skull from off his claw, which he had moved from his back molar. He reached in again and pulled out a long piece of intestines. The beast slurped them back in, like a hungry man-eating spaghetti.

"Ew, gross," squeaked a piglet.

"Quiet swine," said Diggs. "This is important."

The dragon had a contented look on his face. "I've lived in Oz, 900 years. During that same time, the Silver Islands have gone through hundreds of emperors and revolutions. Several thousands of years have passed down there. I never get the same emissary twice, they all die of old age. The seer doesn't die. She must of originally slithered down from

Oz. Of course people rarely die in Oz, only because of significant trauma, Silver Islands individuals, not so lucky, they do die there."

Diggs walked over to the rag nest, bent down, began picking up the nine piglets, and put them into his pocket. "Just in case he gets hungry again," he whispered. He looked up at the hoovering beast. "What does that have to do with me?"

"The Silver Island seer is three thousand silver years old," said the dragon. "For three hundred Oz years, she predicted a wizard would come and unite the land. You are somewhat tardy, but here now." The dragon looked at the last piglet going into Diggs' pocket. "I'm feeling a might peckish, just a couple for a small snack?" The beast's long tongue jutted out, and he licked his chops.

Diggs turned to face the dragon. "Let me talk to this seer. Please have someone go down and get her." He looked nervous, "if it wouldn't be an inconvenience for you?"

The dragon pursed his lips, looked down, and gave out a thunderous shrill whistle.

Diggs pounded on the side of his head, then rubbed his ear. "Wow, that was loud. I think I'm deaf. And I thought my tinker box number one was loud. We need to have a bellowing contest someday."

"My follower will be here shortly," said the dragon. The Chasm Dragon turned to face Diggs. "I've summoned my trusted ambassador. As I've said before, never have I gone down into the Silver Islands, can't fit through the ravine."

After several minutes, from the depths of the chasm flew a sinuous hundred-foot-long creature. Difficult to see at first, since it was as dark as the shadowy depths it came out of, and as thin as a ribbon. When it turned sideways, it actually disappeared. The creature twisted in the air and revealed it had hundreds of short wings and even more wiggling legs.

The dragon waved a claw at the beast. "Wizard, I would like to introduce my current ambassador, Maestro, the multi-limbed."

Maestro hovered in midair and stuck out fourteen extremely thin black arms. "Charmed, I'm sure." The creature had two long antennae and multiple bulging eyes.

Diggs flinched away from the outstretched hands. "Why he is nothing more than a flying millipede."

"I, sir," Maestro puffed up his body and sneered. "Am not a simple millipede. But a unique flying millionpede. The only one in all of Oz."

Diggs scratched the back of his head, then shrugged, pointed at several legs, and held his palms upwards. With one hand he pointed to the legs, silently moved his lips, and with his other hand held up fingers. He shook his head. "I never could count that high."

"How can I serve you, oh great dragon?" said Maestro. He folded in half and bowed in midair to the dragon.

"Slither down the convoluted ravine to the Sliver Islands and convince the seer to come up here," said the dragon. "I will make it worth her while." He gestured at the millionpede to go.

"Let us hope she's not taking one of her twenty-year naps," said Maestro. "I would hate to disturb her." It flew down into the chasm.

Diggs had a hopeful expression on his face. "Is the seer good looking? You keep referring to the seer as a female?"

The dragon flew closer and raised an eyebrow. "Ravishing, now, do you have anything to eat while we are waiting? Since we will not battle, I might as well eat. My appetite has increased, I could eat a horse."

"Sounds good to me," came several voices from Diggs' pocket. The piglets jumped out of the greatcoat.

Diggs walked over to the pile of remaining lunchpails. He opened one and placed it on the floor of the gondola. All the piglets scurried over to it, the larger ones jostled the younger ones to the side and the biggest shoved their snouts in. One small piglet climbed over the rest and leaped into the pail itself. The other little swine just jumped on the biggest back's creating a large dog pile. There was only a scant amount of foraging because of the crowd.

As the dragon deeply inhaled the wafting aroma, the gondola and balloon jerked towards the beast each time three feet. "That smells good. Give me one of those."

Over the next hour, Diggs dumped overboard the contents of another and another lunchpail. After each one he reluctantly asked, "Aren't you done yet? There only a few left." One empty receptacle slipped from his hands and the dragon chewed the metal pail itself.

"That one tasted different," said the dragon. "Crunchy, but still tasty."

Diggs threw the empty metal container of the last lunchpail on the floor. "That's it dragon, nothing left."

The dragon flapped his wings and drifted closer. His single eye peered over the railing. "Isn't there still a little something in the piglet's pail?"

Slim stopped eating the remnants of his lunch, backed out of the nearly empty sideways pail, and stood up. "Make one move on this here grub partner and it'll be your last deed ever."

The dragon laughed. Smoke dribbled out of his nostrils. He burped and a small flame shot out. "Whoops, pardon me."

After half a day, some motion developed from the recesses of the chasm. Maestro came out of the shadowy depths and rose to the balloon. He held a silver, shimmering creature. Four of Maestro's long arms loosely cradled the seer. The seer was only one-fifth the length of the emissary, had no distinctive head or tail, both ends looking exactly the same, and a sinuous, silver, segmented torso. The entire length of her body was not ribbon-like Maestro's, but pudgy, with significant slime dripping off every part.

"We have arrived, oh great Selvious," said Maestro to his passenger. He removed two of his arms from her body and waved in the direction of the OZ balloon. "You have floating before you, if you could see him, a wizard, riding in a large round rubbery object."

The seer turned one end, towards the balloon. An elongated, pendulous tongue jutted out from a narrow slit twenty feet and licked the envelope of the balloon. The tongue left a copious slime trail behind, which slowly began to drip down into the basket. "Yes, I detect the presence of a wizard." The tongue then thrust out again and licked Diggs's face. "But this person is a humbug wizard."

Diggs rolled his eyes and lifted his eyebrows. "Oh, yuck, this is the seer? Why does this beast slime everything?" Diggs pulled his top hat more firmly onto his head to protect his cranium from the dripping slime, and then wiped off his face with the back of his hand. He hopped backwards to avoid the mucous raining down from the envelope.

The dragon grinned, exposing his massive teeth. "Magnificent, isn't she?" In mid-air, the beast bowed towards the seer, straightened up and then pointed with one claw. "Maestro was too terse in his introduction of this auspicious personage. May I introduce to you Selvious the Silver Island, All-Seeing, but blind Silver Seer Slug."

Diggs stepped forward and pointed. "This damn worm is the famous seer?"

Chapter Twenty-Five

Diggs continued to wipe furiously at the slime dripping down his face. "Yuck, this stuff looks and feels like castor oil. Thank heavens it doesn't smell as bad." He spit out some of the viscous liquid which splashed into his mouth. "Tastes just as bad. My mom used it for everything." Diggs turned towards the dragon and pointed at the seer. "I can't believe this is your famous Silver Islands Seer? A giant slimy slug? It's bad enough your so-called ambassador is a skinny multi-legged insect. And now I'm supposed to be impressed with this blind 'all-seeing shell-less snail'?" He turned back to the seer and bowed. "Can I share some salt with you, your sluggyness?"

The seer slid into the gondola, nodded at Maestro to release his four arms, and turned towards Diggs. "You are Oscar Zoroaster Phadrig Isaac Norman Henkel Emmanuel Ambrose Diggs, from Selma, Alabama. Husband of no one, father of one daughter, whom you have never seen, let alone met. Con man, poor magician, and worse ventriloquist." The creature bent gracefully at its midsection and elevated itself to be even with Diggs's face. "Did I not 'see' or perhaps forget anything?"

Diggs winced and scowled. "I'm not a bad ventriloquist."

"I would disagree with that," came forth several tiny voices at the same time. One brave piglet lifted its head out from gorging in the lunchpail, glanced at Diggs, bent down, and continued eating. There were now only dregs remaining.

"Current owner of The Flying Monkey Golden Cap," said the seer. "Traitor to Ozma, the rightful ruler of Oz, and someone who didn't even use the right powder on Pastoria." The seer bent forward and came within inches of Diggs' face.

Diggs pulled his body back. "Can I help it if Mombi can't alphabetize correctly? Am I even talking to your correct end?"

"You were a cowardly balloon pilot during your Civil War and an incompetent one before the war." The seer shook its front end at Diggs. Drops of slime flew off and spattered everywhere. "Now you act as a wizard, but you have absolutely no powers. Still, while both impotent and incompetent when it comes to magic in this truly magical realm, you continue to try to use that art while you loyally and bravely search for your only friend, Chang Wang Woe. I've met the man. He was initially lost in the Silver Islands, arrived there thirty years ago, and Woe led a revolt to take over the Islands. He became an emperor, married Tsing Tsing, a beautiful princess, and already has three sons. You will never see him again."

Diggs wrung his hands together. "No, wait, Seer! That's impossible. The whole reason I go on is to find my friend." He turned to look at the Giant Dragon. "Please, your royalness, can't you help me get to the Silver Isles?" The man dropped to his knees and made a begging motion. "I have to find my partner."

"The seer is never wrong," said the dragon. The beast raised its eyebrows. "But we might help you in other ways."

"You will never see Chang Wang Woe again," repeated the seer. "But the future is murky, unlike your past, and you will somehow meet him again. Just don't be mean to scarecrows."

Diggs tilted his head to one side, wrinkled his nose, raised his eyebrows, and wobbled to his feet. "What the hell does that balderdash mean? What do scarecrows have to do with anything? How can I never see him again, but still meet him?"

"You will understand someday. Now, should I continue with your disreputable past?" The seer tried to raise its eyebrows, but it didn't have any. "Perhaps we should talk about your illegitimate daughter, a Dorothy Gale? You will meet her as well."

Diggs put his face back up to the seer. "Okay, you know my sordid past. Perhaps I have a bad press, but doesn't a seer tell the future?" He wrinkled his forehead. "Where's your crystal ball or Tarot cards?"

The Chasm Dragon chuckled. "Wizard, this 'All Seeing Silver Islands Seer' doesn't use those particular predictive items to tell the future."

Diggs turned towards the hovering dragon. "So, what does she or it use?"

"More slime!" the entire group of creatures yelled. "You should DUCK!"

First, the slug spit on Diggs. Then it spit all over the gondola, including the nest, empty lunchpails and the piglets themselves. Before Diggs could even react, the creature's long tongue jutted out and licked up the spittle. The seer's head area turned first pure white, then fiery red, royal blue, dark purple, canary yellow, and finally emerald green. Smoke rose out of the seer's ear hole areas. After several minutes, the head area turned back to silver.

Diggs appeared more interested than disgusted. "Very colorful, but what in the world did it mean? I hoped for all the hues of the rainbow, but saw no indigo or orange. How disappointing."

The monster fondled Diggs again with its tongue, but its head didn't turn any new colors. It sank back and was silent.

"So, slug, what can you tell me about my future?" Diggs pulled out his old handkerchief from his carpetbag and used it to wipe the last of the mucus from his face. He looked down at his drenched greatcoat and sighed.

"Your future is very confusing. First, let me break down the results concerning your huge balloon and companions," said the slug. The seer turned its mouth orifice towards the rest of the gondola, and its tongue extended out again to sweep over the piglets. This time the creature's head turned bright red and stayed that way. Its head then flashed red nine times and finally turned silver at last.

"Help, we're drowning," cried the nine piglets. "Mister Diggs, we didn't sign up for this abuse." The piglets left their eating and crawled into their lair, covered in mucous. They all tried synchronized shaking, then hula dancing, but the slime continued to cover them.

Diggs pulled his scarves from his waist and wiped the floor and tentatively cleaned the firebox. The slime sizzled on the hot structure. "Great, now I'm so fat, my pants don't fall down even without a belt." Within minutes, he swept the floor clean. Diggs and the rag nest, continued to drip slime.

Diggs looked flummoxed. "Oh, yuck! Tell me that was really necessary?" He wiped his face again. "Please don't tell me your prediction voodoo isn't working."

The smoke from the seer's ear orifices slowed down. "Be quiet. I am still processing the information. The only future that is clear is your flying machine. It will take you safely on all your journeys, including your final one. Your little companions' fate is strange. They will continue to be with you for your entire journey, but they will constantly disappear and reappear."

"Well, that doesn't sound good," said Frederick. "It sure confuses me." The head piglet continued to shake. "I want to go back to Alabama. Even with that fat tomcat back home, wandering around the campsite, it's safer than this place. Less to eat however." He headed for an empty, closed lunchpail and tried to open it.

"Your prediction sounds like the crystal ball reader at the circus," said Diggs. "No straight answers and always confusing." Diggs looked down at the piglet. "Well, the slime helped get you guys finally get clean. You all needed a bath."

The seer again rose to Diggs' eye level. "Wizard, your future is interesting. Your flying machine will take you to all parts of Oz. Your enemies will act as friends, and your friends will become enemies. And oh, yes, a final prediction: everyone will try to kill you."

Diggs shrugged. "What else is new?"

Chapter Twenty-Six

Diggs took off his greatcoat and wrung out the sleeves. "So, when will I see, err… not ever see, my best friend again? Seer, this fortune-telling is very confusing."

The slug continued to bend upward at the waist and talked directly to Diggs' face. "Your future is tied closely to the colors I predicted." Words came from somewhere, but no visible mouth was evident. "And the last color, green, is the most important. This is the location where you should start your future."

Diggs bent over slightly and looked the seer right in the… front end? "Is this where I'll meet my friend again? If so, where in this land is 'Emerald Green'? Here in Quadling country, everything is red; and Mombi's area, I think it was Gillikin country, it was purple?"

"The only area in the entire Land of Oz that is green is at the four corners," said the dragon. "I have never been there myself, but several of my followers have." The dragon smiled at the Silver Seer. "She is so sexy. Humph, yes, there used to be a castle, owned by all the kings of Oz. The castle was called the 'Emerald Citadel'. It lay exactly at the intersection of the four Oz countries. Gillikin to the north, is purple, Winkie to the west, yellow, Quadling to the south, red and Munchkin to the east, blue. Nothing else surrounded the citadel and Mombi and the Flying Monkeys destroyed it when Pastoria fled."

Diggs scowled and scrunched up his eyebrows. "Then that's where I'll go." He wrinkled up his forehead, then frowned. "Can anyone draw me a map? I get lost easily. I have to get there."

A tiny voice piped up. "I'll say, it took us ages to get here from Mombi's hut. He would never listen to or ask for directions."

"Quiet, rodents."

The dragon turned in the air and faced the old flying monkeys. "I will help even more." He lifted his arm and pointed with a claw. "Ortho and his companions were part of the band that destroyed the emerald citadel. He was the leader. Afterward, Mombi's next wish was for him to find and snatch the king. When they couldn't capture Pastoria and they didn't even find him, Mombi banished them to my chasm. She thought Ortho was getting 'too old' to lead the band. I took them as a favor to Mombi, but they have been nothing but trouble. I will send them with you to guide you. Then you can keep them."

"Boss, boss! Do we really have to go?" Ortho screeched out these words. His four cohorts only growled.

Diggs dropped his hand and stopped wiping the slime from his face and clothes. He looked down at his soaked clothes and sighed. "Thanks, I guess." Diggs walked over and looked at his fire box. "I'll leave in the morning."

The nine piglets scrambled out of their nest to beseech the seer for more facts about their future. They sat up in a row and put their hooves out in a begging motion.

The seer immediately offered to lick them again. She stated she enjoyed the taste of pork.

"Ahh, help! Protect us!" they squealed. The piglets ran back under their rag nest.

The next morning, Diggs woke up with a sour taste in his mouth. "Oh, my aching head. Who knew an Oz dragon could hold his liquor even better than a Jinxville mayor? And he sure makes true Oz fire water here. That dragon must have one hell of a moonshine still there down in the chasm. White lightning brought me to Oz and this corn liquor, white lightning almost took me out."

Diggs looked down and saw nine staggering piglets. He remembered that they had lapped up any spilled liquid, of which there had been a sizeable amount. "Please, Mister Diggs, put us out of our misery," one squealed. "And Mister Diggs, I hate to say it, but even without my green spectacles, your face looks extremely green."

Diggs started assessing amounts of coal, food stores, and ammunition. He shook his head and then grabbed it with both hands. "Oh crap! I meant to take inventory last night. Way too many glasses of that firewater." Diggs looked at his small pile of coal, an extensive amount of empty lunchpails, and sighed. "We don't have enough Ozpyrite to get lift over the mountains, or lunchpails to survive on." He lifted an empty lunchpail and accidentally dropped it. It clattered loudly against the gondola floor.

Frederick, the piglet leader, had one hoof to his head and one clutching his stomach. "Please don't mention food. And keep the noise down. Do you have any willow bark for this headache? I will never again indulge."

Ortho and the other four flying monkeys flew up to the gondola and hovered. "Good morning, Great Oz. Are we leaving now? Nothing like a little exercise after a fun night of partying. I'll enjoy stretching my wings. On the journey, my troops and I'll look for something stronger to drink. I enjoyed the corn liquor, but it was too weak."

The four companion monkeys just screamed howls and nodded their head in agreement. Diggs put his hands over his ears. Frederick, the piglet, first put his hoofs over his ears and then plastered them quickly over his snout to keep from upchucking.

"Ortho, are there any Ozpyrite mounds between here and the Winkie mountains?" asked Diggs. He motioned for Frederick to go back to his nest. "I know where there are lunchpail trees, but no coal."

The piglet groaned and staggered back into the nest.

"What is Ozpyrite?" Ortho landed with a thud on the railing of the gondola. The entire basket tilted significantly to that side. "Is it good to drink?"

"I can't fly like you beasts," said Diggs. "It's what powers my flying machine." He recounted his pile of coal and shook his head. He muttered, "A few days' worth... not enough."

"Where did you get it before?" said Ortho. The monkey scratched his behind. "Just get more from there."

"They gave it to me in Jinxville. A village, I'm sure I should stay away from. A new stone statue and a missing baby, this might upset people."

Ortho smelled his fingers and smiled. "Huh, what does that mean?" He scratched his head. "Well then, we could just steal some more."

"Sure, a thirty-five-foot-tall balloon with a giant white OZ painted on it wouldn't attract any attention." He carefully shuffled to the other side of the gondola. The basket leveled.

"Is this village of Jinxville, in the same direction as the Winkie Mountains?" Ortho scratched his armpit.

Diggs held his stomach and plopped down on the floor. "Yeah, why?"

"Then load everything we need, but don't take off until night time. The seer didn't say how quickly we had to get to the center of Oz, did she?" Ortho leaped into the air and the gondola tilted slightly to Diggs' side. "I'll come back later with my companions to bed down here, so we can get an early start."

Diggs rolled several times back to the center of the basket. "Great idea. Oh… God. Am I dizzy. I hope I don't throw up. Is everything now level?"

Diggs fell asleep and woke many hours later, with nine piglets staring him in the face. The piglets were all complaining that they were hungry.

"I thought you were all hungover and couldn't eat a thing?" said Diggs. "We have nothing left."

A tiny piglet staggered up to Diggs' ear. "Honey-pie," drawled the little one. "I do declare, I'm feeling a mite better and have a craving for biscuits and gravy. Y'all don't think it'll ruin my figure, do you?"

Several voices piped up. "No, Miss Scarlet, not at all. Get some for us as well."

"You definitely are an Alabama mouse," said Diggs. "Sorry dear, there isn't any food at all. Perhaps the Chasm Dragon has an extra ox or two."

Miss Scarlet scampered back to her nest. "Lord have mercy, I do declare, don't let that beast near us, please, kind sir."

Diggs looked over at the nest. "Don't worry, you're safe." He reached into the pocket of his greatcoat and pulled out his pocket watch. Diggs peered down at it. "We'll take off in three hours." He licked his finger and held it up. "I hope the desert winds come back. Right now, it is dead calm and we would drift nowhere fast."

The next three hours went back by and night fell quickly. Except for loud stomach rumblings from Diggs and the rag nest, all was quiet. There still was no wind, and the balloon hovered exactly in the same place over the chasm. Diggs walked to the carpetbag and removed one of his revolvers. He loaded, then carried the pistol to the railing. He fired the gun into the chasm depths. The echoes from the shot reverberated off the walls of the ravine.

After several minutes, the monster hoard and the Giant Chasm Dragon came flying up. The immense beast stared into the gondola. "Announcing your departure, Oz?"

"We can't go north," said Diggs. "There are no winds coming off the desert and blowing towards that direction at all. I don't have enough extra coal to make hot air to side vent, get moving, and continue in the correct direction." Diggs measured the amount of coal again and frowned. "I'm not sure what to do, except wait 'til wind from the right direction occurs."

The Chasm dragon held up his claw. "I have an idea." He flew to the southern side of the balloon. "I'll blow your envelope with a puff of my breath to get you started." The dragon inhaled, and his massive chest expanded even more. He exhaled and flame roared out.

Diggs dropped to the floor of the gondola. "Fire in the hole!"

Chapter Twenty-Seven

The dragon slammed his lips together, cutting off the flame. "Oops," he muttered through the side of his mouth. "I forgot that might happen."

Diggs' sleeve blossomed with fire. He yanked off his top hat and beat the blaze out. He stood up from the floor of the gondola and glared at the dragon.

The piglets exploded from their burning rag nest, scattering to all corners of the gondola. "Put out our home, put it out," they screamed. Their voices rose higher and higher in pitch. "Put it out."

Ortho and his four cohorts laughed hysterically. They had been sleeping next to the firebox, and the infernos missed them. They stood up and ambled over to the blazing rag nest.

"Please, Misters Monkeys, save our home!" yelled Frederick.

The monkeys milled around and looked confused. Then Ortho pointed at the fire. "Occh, Occh, Occh." His four companions lined up in a single file. Five separate yellow streams shot out. The flames died out.

"A smelly remedy, but effective," said Diggs. He hopped away, making sure no droplets hit his boots.

"You all have to be kidding me partner." Slim hesitantly came out of a corner and stared at the charred rag nest. "Where're we going to sleep now?"

The smell of charred rags and stale urine wafted up into the air. The balloon had not moved an inch. It still stayed in place over the center of the Chasm.

The Giant Dragon grinned and asked, "Should I try again?"

"No, I don't think so." Diggs looked ruefully at the ruined sleeve of his greatcoat. The sleeve was now black, smoldering, and foreshortened. "I don't think my arm could take any more burns." He looked at his reddened extremity. Diggs walked over to his carpetbag and pulled out a nearly empty whiskey bottle. He uncorked it, tipped it up to his lips, drank, and emptied the last of the liquid. "For medicinal reasons only," he muttered to himself.

One of the young piglets was crying as she looked at her home. "Let's tie a rope around the necks of the five flying monkeys, snort, snort, oink, snoick, and have them pull us. That will get us moving. Also, they would stop being such a nuisance."

Diggs put down the bottle and looked startled. "Never heard that unusual crying sound before, snoick?"

"Neither have we," said Frederick. "I think it's a combination of snort and oink. Must be unique to piglets."

Slim came over and put his hoof on the piglet's shoulder. "Now don't you all cry, Miss Scarlet. It was only a place made of rags."

"But it was my home." Tears ran down Miss Scarlet's snout. "I was born a mouse in Alabama, but have lived here in Oz, in this nest, as a piglet most of my life, three entire months. It's all I've known."

Frederick came up to the two other piglets and gave them hugs. "I'm sure Mister Diggs will help us build anew."

Diggs stared up at the motionless, partially deflated balloon envelope. "Piglets, we have bigger problems. We're still becalmed. If we don't get some wind soon, we'll never reach the Emerald Citadel. The fact is, we don't have enough Ozpyrite to make hot air to side vent and push us to the center of Oz. Maybe the dragon could tow us?"

The Chasm dragon reared up and glared. "Never! I am a king. I would never stoop that low. But I have another idea." The beast flew from behind the gondola and faced Diggs. "I will lend you another of my subjects. This person I do want back when you finish with him."

Diggs scowled at the dragon. "Does your subject also breath fire?" He pulled on his ruined coat, his scalded arm sticking out of the shortened sleeve. Diggs shook his arm several times. "Wow, it really smarts. I need to smear some lard on it."

"Mister Diggs," squealed Miss Scarlet. "How could y'all mention that terrible word?"

The five flying monkeys poked at the charred rag nest with their feet. No flames remained. They all jumped up and down when Ortho beamed at them. Ortho pounded his chest. "See. I don't need a Golden Cap to control me. I can figure things out on my own."

"Hey that's a good idea. I could use the Golden Cap to summon the band of flying monkeys to take us to the center of Oz." Diggs walked over to his carpetbag and began rummaging through it. He pulled out his dueling revolvers, saber, several wrinkled paper flowers, and a dozen filthy knotted scarves. "You can use these scarves for your new home. Now where did I put that damn cap? Let's see, Ep-pe, pep-pe or something to that effect."

The dragon bellowed. "Oz, stop and listen." The soaked rag nest blew across the floor of the gondola. Pee dripped everywhere. Diggs looked up and stopped ransacking through his bag. Five of the piglets ran in circles, and the other four cowered behind the firebox. These four quivered and put their hooves over their heads. The five flying monkeys froze and put their paws over their ears.

Diggs pivoted around on his knees and then stood up. "You have my attention." His joints cracked and popped as he got up. "Now, what is your great idea? Some other beast going to tow the balloon?"

"I'm sure you have noticed the balloon ball creature inhaling and exhaling, keeping your flying machine in place." The dragon pointed with one gigantic claw in front of the gondola. "Although the desert winds are mild today, they are still persistent and you would have drifted away from my chasm. I will have a balloon ball creature blow you all the way to the center of Oz."

"Good idea, but this monster barely keeps my balloon in place, let alone moves it." Diggs walked to the railing and looked over it. The small balloon ball creature exhaled at that moment, and Diggs' hat barely wobbled. "Not enough oomph."

The dragon beamed at the balloon ball creature. "I think for a newborn, it is doing a fine job. It's only one hundred years old. Her mother, Esberelda, is still recovering from her arduous labor. She was going to have twins, but she lost one during childbirth. The babies were both inflated, and the boy popped when coming through the birth canal. It devastated Esberelda."

"What in the world are you talking about?" Diggs stared at the dragon and wrinkled his brow. "There are alive balloons? Next you'll tell me they can talk or think."

"Both, but unfortunately, when puffed up, they become overly inflated and are considerably conceited. I will summon Esberelda's spouse. He's large enough to push you easily."

The dragon gave a half roar, half whistle. Most of the piglets again ran in circles and squealed loudly. Miss Scarlet fainted. The five monkeys sat down on the floor of the gondola, folded their wings against their backs, and quivered in place. Diggs pulled out one revolver from his bag, pointed it at the dragon, shook his head, and then sheepishly put it back.

From the depths of the chasm rose another balloon ball creature. Pitch black, and difficult to see, until it opened its ten eyes. The pure white globes, which had no irises at all, glowed against the shadows of the chasm. The creature was only slightly larger than the one puffing mightily at the front of the OZ balloon.

"May I introduce Unolingo, the leader of my balloon ball members." The dragon waved his fore claw at the creature. "His clan has been with me for centuries."

"It won't work. He's puny." Diggs shook his head in disgust. He held both hands up to measure the baby and then compared the size to Unolingo.

"Is that so?" stated Unolingo. He gulped in vast amounts of air. The balloon beast inflated rapidly and soon was twice the size of the OZ balloon envelope.

Diggs stumbled as he stepped backwards to see its entire girth. He looked upward, and his eyes widened. "Wow, please don't pop."

Chapter Twenty-Eight

"So, are you ready for me to huff and puff and blow your flying machine where it should go?" Unolingo demanded all this while expelling no air or deflating.

Diggs thought, "how it was possible? The monster didn't really have a face, but the balloon ball creature looked like it smiled". Diggs peered over the railing. "Where and how does your air come out? Please don't exhale yet."

The beast rotated and exposed a nozzle. "Right here." The spigot was long, thin, and pitch black, with the center portion clenched tightly. "You can tell I'm a male: I have such a big nozzle."

Diggs put his hand over his mouth to keep from laughing. "Of course." He pointed to the north. "Can you blow us all the way to Jinxville, while it's still dark?"

"The 'OZ' shows up nicely in the moonlight," said Unolingo. "I'll aim for that."

The five flying monkeys stood up, stretched their arms and legs, then wiggled their wings and butts, crouched, and prepared to take off.

"Wait, Ortho." Diggs ran over and grabbed onto the head monkey's tail. "Maybe I should just use the Magic Cap to get your ex-band to load up Ozpyrite coal for me. Then we could go directly to the center of Oz."

Ortho growled. "Oz, I insist you let go of my tail." He turned to face Diggs and motioned to his companions to wait. "Wizard, don't be ignorant. You keep forgetting you can only use the cap three times. Use it for major reasons only."

"Well shoot, I already wasted it once." Diggs pushed his top hat backward and put his hand on his forehead. "Why only three times? I just don't understand these things. Isn't it magic?"

"When do I start blowing?" Unolingo took a huge breath and inflated larger. "Your balloon envelope looks like my second cousin Titalango."

"If you're sure we'll make it to Jinxville during nightfall, then start anytime." Diggs saluted Unolingo with his right hand and held on to his top hat with his left. He looked down at his carpetbag and closed it tightly. "Say Ortho, let your four cohorts fly ahead of the balloon, but you stay and tell me about the Magic Golden Cap. Mombi was not very forthcoming. She just said everyone wanted it eventually."

An explosive gust of wind blew from the south. Diggs turned and saw that Unolingo had just exhaled once. The OZ balloon sped up towards Jinxville. The Chasm Dragon waved a claw and yelled, "Be sure to come back and visit again. I love a good fight and I have another eye."

The rest of the chasm creatures dove back into the ravine. Diggs heard one beast yell, "But I never got to eat anyone." Ortho waved his companions on, and the four flying monkeys leaped to the railing on the north side of the gondola. The basket tilted precariously. The monkeys unfurled their six-foot wings and knocked the two end monkeys off the railing perch. These two screamed at their companions, flapped furiously, and flew north. The other two joined them in leading the OZ balloon.

The monkeys' rapidly beating wings created an updraft, and the piglet's new scarf nest went askew. Slim called out, "Hey, I is trying to sleep here, y'all."

Ortho folded his wings and sat down. "I owe you nothing. We will all leave as soon as I direct you to the Emerald Citadel. Why are you bothering me? If it weren't for my obligation and pledge to serve the Chasm Dragon, I wouldn't even be here talking to you."

With no wind coming off the Deadly Desert, Unolingo's gusts steadily pushed the balloon towards the village of Jinxville. Whereas the smell from the desert breezes was void of aromas, Unolingo's breath smelled like a spring day. Each exhalation had a slightly distinct odor. One smelled like rain on fresh grass, and the next flowers opening up their petals to the morning sun. Diggs enjoyed the unique aromas.

A moment later, he wrinkled his nose against a putrid smell. Ortho first grinned, then glared at Diggs. "Flying monkeys have considerable difficulties controlling flatulence from our digestive systems. You could say we are gastronomically expressive. Too much fire water last night, and those Bananabean tree appetizers didn't help either. Now, what information do you desire and why should I supply it to you?"

Diggs held his nose. "Good God, Ortho! Please pass gas somewhere else."

"Or not at all," yelled several tiny voices.

Slim poked his head out from the nest and then advanced tentatively. "Say Mister Monkey, how comes you talk so fine? Almost as good as Mister Diggs' pardner, that tall feller."

Frederick then came out and glared at the ex-king monkey. He motioned Slim to back away. "But you're more mean, threatening to eat us, just like that horrible dragon." Slim headed back into the nest.

Ortho stood up and winked down at the piglet. "When you live with a group of educated masses for hundreds of years, you become cerebrally literate. As a flying monkey, I had many intellectual discussions, ranging from philosophy of free will to true slapstick humor. Pull my finger." He held out his finger. "No? Your loss. Now, I wouldn't call myself a sesquipedalian, but I do like to throw around a large term or two."

Frederick stared at him. "What does sesqua, sesquip, oh hell, what does that big word mean?"

Ortho walked to the railing. "To freely use large terms in speech comfortably. I can understand these tiny piglets don't have the cranial capacity to understand my verbiage, but I had thought him," the monkey pointed at Diggs. Ortho then bowed deeply, and did 'air quotes' with his fingers, "The Great and Powerful Oz could communicate on my level."

Diggs slowly rose up. "Now ape, we are companions, in this endeavor. We talk to each other well enough. Now stay for all our sakes."

"No, I feel more comfortable leaving." Ortho bent his legs and prepared to fly. "I only remain around companions I trust."

"Ortho, stay. Just no more farting." Diggs pulled the Golden Magic Cap from out of his carpetbag. "I command you to tell me what this thing can do, and why do I only get to use it three times? I hoped to use it to rescue my friend or else resurrect him. What the hell can it do for me?"

Ortho sat down again. "Don't make me laugh—you command me. You have no magic like Mombi and no power like the Chasm Dragon. You're lucky my master was in a good mood and not hungry, or he would've destroyed you. But he commanded me to lead, and I will. I'll instruct you, but I don't have to tell you anything about the cap." He looked fearfully at the Magic Cap.

"I need to know exactly how to use the cap to save my friend. I've never had an Aladdin's lamp or a wishing well. This magic stuff is new to me. A short time ago, I was a normal man, a happy carnie, an unhappy soldier, and a successful street performer in New York."

A small voice piped up, "You told us you were a starving conman."

Diggs wrinkled his forehead. He shook his finger at the scarf nest. "Quiet pigs." Diggs shrugged his shoulders. "Now I am supposed to understand how magic works and worse, I'm told that it's foretold that I need to fight evil witches and unite this entire land." He stared down at his boots. "This frightens me. Before I was a nobody, now I'm supposed to be a king?"

Ortho bounced up. "Before I was a king, now I am a servant. How do you think I like it? Figure the cap out by yourself."

Diggs held up his hands, palms up. "The brains of my operation, gone. How the hell can I do it without Chang? Impossible, I don't have the knowledge! All my life, all I had to do was take care of just myself. Now the seer tells me I have to take care of an entire land. I don't know if I can honestly do it. The only difference between me and all the Oz people is I'm somewhat taller."

"And fatter," squeaked several voices.

Ortho rolled his eyes, growled, and bared his teeth. "You just need to know you have two more wishes. You don't need to know anything else about the history of the cap, it's a long and shameful story."

Diggs now interlocked his fingers and begged. He held the cap with just two fingers. "Then please tell me about the cap so my last two wishes will work to my advantage."

Six more of the piglets came out of the scarf nest and sat up at attention. "We also want to hear."

Frederick looked back at the nest. "Hey, where are Slim and Miss Scarlet?" The scarves vibrated and then moved up and down.

One of the younger piglets blushed. "They had something important to discuss. They don't want to be disturbed."

Ortho sighed and looked Diggs right in the eyes. "The cap is ancient and controls the clan three times for each owner."

Diggs turned the magic item around in his hands and squeezed the hat open and closed. A voice projected from the depths of the cap. "Please Mister Monkey, why only three wishes?"

Ortho grimaced. "You are pathetic. Very well. Decades ago, the flying monkeys dunked a powerful wizard three times in a river. Three times in the river somehow equaled enslavement for three services forevermore. By the way, your lips moved."

Diggs smiled. "Any knowledge is helpful. Please continue."

Ortho waved cavalierly. "The wizard got married to a powerful sorceress, built the Emerald Citadel, had a child who was Pastoria the First, the end. I'm done. Satisfied? Now, got any food?"

"Now come on, there has to be important details?" Diggs leaned over and picked up a lunchpail. He opened it and showed Ortho it was empty.

The monkey jumped up, snatched it out of Diggs' hand, and threw it at the man's head. The pail just missed, and it flew over the back of the gondola. Ortho sat back down.

Diggs flinched. "Hey, stop that! I'm glad your aim isn't as good as Ozma's."

Unolingo stopped puffing and yelled, "Hey, that almost hit me. Do you want me to pop?"

The balloon slowed significantly. The four monkeys soon outdistanced the gondola.

Ortho jumped up and cupped his hands around his mouth. "Come back, men! We're losing you."

The monkeys looked around and screeched. One of them did a backflip when he stopped.

Ortho waved and motioned them to stop. "Idiots," he murmured under his breath. He then sat back down.

Unolingo began to exhale again, and the balloon moved north. When it got near the four companion monkeys, they led the way.

Ortho looked bored, then grinned. He scratched his rear and held his finger up and pointed it at Diggs. "Any more stupid question? Just remember that we always obey the three wishes, no matter how incompetent the owner of the cap is at the time."

Diggs backed away. "Monkey, what is wrong with you? Quit acting like an animal. What about that Nikko? He refused to look for Chang, with my first wish." Diggs gulped. "The clan didn't even try."

Ortho spit on the floor. "Bah, that rookie. For a Mombi wish, I spent a century looking for Pastoria. Yeah, Nikko should've tried. The monkeys probably wouldn't have found him in the Silver Islands, but the cap commands you to always attempt the wish. You must have not stated it correctly. The Chasm Dragon says the Silver Island time moves at a much faster rate than ours. By now, your friend is a century older and probably dead. Give up."

"Never! The seer says I'll meet, err… not meet him. Oh crap, I'm so confused. But I'll keep trying."

Ortho raised one eyebrow. "Maybe you're not so selfish and worthless after all. May I leave your royal presence now?" He stood up, gave a halfhearted bow, and prepared to fly.

"Not yet." Diggs turned the cap over in his hands and peered at the inscription. Then he looked up at Ortho. "We'll talk more later."

The balloon drifted over Jinxville. Although it was the dead of night, the full moon streamed light down onto the balloon. Diggs kept at twenty-five feet, in order to diminish the chance of being seen.

"Unolingo, take a break. We want to stay in one place for now." Diggs released one sandbag, and drop rope to stabilize the OZ balloon. He sent the monkeys and empty burlap sacks down to pilfer Ozpyrite coal. Hours later, after many trips, there was a large pile of coal near the firebox.

"Oz, there is a stone statue in front of town hall," said Ortho. "It must be heavy cause there are drag marks leading up to it."

"That's not good." Diggs wiped his brow.

"And during our last trip, we stole these small beer kegs. We found them near the mayor's house and figured we could make better use of them than the Jinxians. Something for us to drink." Ortho placed one in front of Diggs.

On each keg was Ozma's picture. Printed under the picture was, 'Have you seen this girl?'

Chapter Twenty-Nine

Diggs pulled up the one sandbag, attached to the drop rope. "I think we better leave immediately. They will not consider the Great Oz so great if the villagers somehow link a new stone statue and a missing child to me. Someday, I'll come back, get some real magic, change Pastoria back, and free Ozma—I mean Tip. I'm pretty sure my friend Chang is worth all this effort, but boy, the situation is getting complicated."

Diggs signaled to Unolingo to take in breaths. The balloon ball creature inhaled, rapidly went from carpet bag size to twice the size of the envelope in just a couple of minutes, exhaled, and the OZ balloon moved north.

The five monkeys bent their knees, preparing to take off. Diggs again grabbed only Ortho, by his shoulder this time. "I have some more questions. Let your companions fly ahead and guide us to the Emerald Citadel. Have them take off one at a time this go around, so the gondola doesn't tip so much."

"You know there is nothing but rubble there now?" Ortho motioned to his four cohorts to fly. A big smile crossed his face. His chest swelled up with pride and he gushed, "We really destroyed the castle! There are mostly green stones, but nothing else."

Diggs jammed his top hat down onto his forehead, saving it from the force of Unolingo's breath and the updraft of the monkey's wings. "What did it look like?"

Ortho put both hands palms upward. "It looked like a big square thing. I'm only a monkey. A smart one, but I live in a chasm, before that, the jungle."

Diggs walked over to his carpetbag and pulled out the Illusion Maker. "I have an idea." He held the box up to his mouth and said, "original Emerald Citadel."

Floating above the gondola was a ten foot tall castle with majestic turrets, a towering central one, and high walls throughout. Inside the illusion, hundreds of voices rang out, heard in joyous singing, and wonderful cooking aromas wafted out. Embedded in the castle walls surrounding the keep were thousands of glistening green stones.

"Indubitably. That's the place." Ortho scratched his armpit.

Diggs peered at the structure intently. "Are those real emeralds?"

Ortho plopped down and opened a beer keg. He took a large swig. The monkey squinted his eyes, half smiled, and slowly held the container out to Diggs. "How the hell should I know? They weren't good to eat. To us they were just rocks."

Diggs reached for the beer, but dropped his hand when the monkey growled at him and withdrew the keg. The beast winked, grinned, and handed the container to him a second time. Diggs took a drink and returned it to Ortho. He wiped his mouth and asked, "they built The Emerald Citadel out of emeralds?"

Ortho took another huge swig. "The band was slaves to those magic people. They weren't stupid like someone else I know and used their first wish of the Golden Magic Cap to make the Flying Monkeys obtain building blocks. It's told the clan went all over Oz to collect marble and granite, and everyone built that castle in one month. I bet those magic wizards helped with real magic." Ortho looked at Diggs. "Not like you. My ancestors must have had some fun cause they caused much mischief while constructing. You never saw so much 'flying' monkey poop. Literally." Ortho grinned at this statement. His huge yellow canines bared.

Diggs screwed up his face. "Not a pleasant picture."

Frederick and three other piglets crept out from under the firebox. "Got any popcorn? I love to nibble, even when it's green, when I am listening to a story. And can we have some of the beer?"

Ortho screeched at the piglets and lifted the beer out of their reach. He slowly stood up. "The architecture pleased the two lovebird magic people, but they hated the grey granite color." Ortho taunted the piglets by holding the keg just above their heads.

The four piglets leaped up to try to obtain the keg. "Dash it all. Piss off, monkey," said Frederick.

"I already did," said Ortho. He bounced the keg up and down to tease them. "The pair used sorceress magic to turn the entire building into pure white marble. They wanted the building to be a unique color: white. That's also why all royal magic users are the only people allowed to wear white. The more white worn, the more powerful you appear. White means you are good, black, evil. Nothing can make the colors ever change to any other."

Diggs looked confused. "But Glinda only had a white tiara, red clothes. And she gave me an all-white outfit."

"Glinda is one of our younger witches." Ortho paced back and forth while guzzling. "She's only four hundred years old. She likes to buck tradition. I think when she matures, she'll wear more white. As for your attire, even though you are a humbug, monkeys are not the only people who love a good joke. Glinda is famous for her sense of humor and she knew you were totally powerless." He looked at Diggs with a wide grin that showed all his long teeth, then Ortho stuck out his tongue. "You're wearing white clothes should get you in lots of trouble."

Diggs looked at the castle once more and said, "So, that's why the vixen wanted me to wear white. Unfortunately, that makes sense." He smiled at the illusionary Emerald Citadel. "That palace sure was beautiful." Diggs picked up the tinker box and held it up to his mouth, "Stop."

The OZ balloon drifted past Jinxville and started over a forest. Diggs looked down and noticed that nestled amongst the many different red trees were lunchpail trees. Diggs yelled to Unolingo to stop exhaling. He wanted to moor here temporarily.

"Ortho, get your crew to fly down with sandbags and tie the drop ropes to some trees." Diggs bent down and picked up one sandbag, straining and using both arms. He quickly closed his eyes and scrunched up his face. "Ow." He dropped the bag and rubbed his back. "Must be my lumbago."

Frederick looked up at Diggs. "No, all that beer, and getting no exercise boss."

Ortho screeched, and his cohorts flew back. He gestured at the bags. "Boys, take one each and tie it to a tree. We will be here for a while." The companions grunted, easily picked up a bag with one paw, and flew off.

"Why do you talk so articulately to me and grunt and screech to them?" Diggs continued to rub his back. He gestured at the four flying monkeys. "I thought everyone and everything in Oz could speak the same language."

Ortho picked up the last sandbag with his foot. He looked at Diggs, sighed, and shook his head. "They can speak fluent Ozian, they just choose not to. They wish to monkey around with their speech." He jumped over the side of the gondola, unfurled his wings, and headed for the ground.

The basket rocked back and forth like a ship on huge waves. Diggs staggered towards the center of the gondola.

The balloon drifted slightly 'til tethered. Now they were over a central meadow. Seen by the light of the full moon were giant Black-Eyed Susans. These flowers stood as tall as the short trees. Flitting from flower to flower were hundreds of buzzing creatures. One flower stalk was suddenly pushed down, and the insects followed the central bud to the ground.

Diggs ran to the railing and stared downward. Something pushed another flower stalk over. "It can't be an Ozquake? Too localized? I don't see what's doing it?"

Diggs yelled down to the flying monkeys to pull the balloon to the ground. They pulled, and the gondola settled quickly. When it was just a foot above the meadow, Diggs climbed up the slats and leaped down. "I'll start looking for lunch box trees." Diggs flinched and looked up quizzically. "Wait, what's that?"

A flicker of flame burst out near the stalks, followed by a small squeak. Diggs ran back to his basket. "Ortho, I'm going to get my fire sticks to protect me. Something is pushing over the flowers and maybe the same thing is breathing fire. Could be another dragon?"

Diggs climbed back in, took his revolvers out of this carpet bag, and muttered, "I'll be positive they're loaded this time." He gently shook the guns and heard the bullet rolling around in the chamber. Diggs frowned. "Boy, it sounds loose. I hope I loaded it correctly?" He shrugged his shoulders, shoved the pistols into his belt, and came back out of the gondola.

Ortho pointed at another giant flower being pushed over. Diggs heard an intense buzzing sound near the collapsed flower and saw a small flame. The buzzing sound stopped, replaced with a crunching, smacking sound.

Diggs motioned to the five monkeys to come with him, and he tentatively crept over to investigate. A blue rectangular creature chewed up red and yellow striped bees. The animal had a square head, rectangular body, four skinny limbs, and a short box-like tail. The beast looked up at Diggs and his companions, and tiny flames came out of his eyes.

Diggs pulled his revolvers out of his pants and shakily pointed them at the creature. "Don't come any closer! I am an expert at using these. What manner of beast are you?"

The creature gave a rectangular grin, showing many small boxlike teeth. "Hello, care to join me in my honeybee lunch? They are quite delicious, especially if lightly roasted first."

Diggs pulled back the hammer on the guns. "Helps to cock it, first. You didn't answer; what are you? Are you magic? Are you alive?"

The creature stopped chewing and looked pensive. "Do I think I'm alive? No one's ever asked me that before." It put a rectangular limb up to its head and looked thoughtful. "I do need to breathe and eat." The beast waved at Diggs. "Of course. I've never run into anyone else in this forest to ask that question. I am called a Woozy."

"What is a Woozy?" Diggs carefully uncocked the pistols and shoved them back into his belt.

"I am."

"Are there many of you?"

"I'm the only Woozy I've ever met. I used to live in Munchkin country, but one day I got lost trying to go back to my cave. I walked for a long time." The beast looked up in the air and frowned. "Ended up here. Good honey bees to eat, at least." The creature trotted over to another Black-Eyed Susan and pushed it down. "Sorry, I'm still hungry. Care to join me? There's plenty for everyone."

Diggs looked around nervously. "Are there any dangerous animals in this forest? I'm only making a brief stop to get lunchpails. Then I'm off again."

"Yes, many horrible beasts, even lions, and tigers and bears." The Woozy began crunching again.

"Then I'll skip the insects and hurry to collect my pails." Diggs turned to go. "But just for curiosity, creature: you're so small, and have tiny teeth. How do you defend yourself against creatures of the night?"

"I have very tough skin and a huge, horrible growl." The Woozy stopped eating and looked up. "It can deafen creatures for miles when used."

Diggs walked back to the Woozy. "I could use a companion with a power like that. I'll cover my ears and you show your growl. I have a magic tinker box that makes loud noises. The combination would be unstoppable."

The Woozy shook his head in refusal. "I'm afraid I would hurt you, it's so powerful."

"Please try." Diggs motioned to the monkeys to cover their ears. "Monkeys, do you know anything about this beast?"

Ortho looked down at the Woozy. "Even during my extensive travels, I never came across such a creature. He must be truly unique. We should let him run free."

Diggs put up his hands over his ears. "I'm going to have to go up against evil witches, and I need lots of weapons to defeat them. I'll keep him around with lots of honeybees."

Ortho glared at Diggs. "So going to make that Woozy a slave, like you do your piglets?"

Diggs looked startled and then glared at Ortho. "Never. The piglets are my friends. I never would do that, I'm strongly against slavery." He made sure the monkeys had their paws tightly over their ears. "Please, Mr. Woozy. Let her rip, show us your deafening roar."

Chapter Thirty

"All right, but don't say I didn't warn you." The Woozy took a deep breath, opened its mouth, and a chirping of a tiny cricket squeak came out.

Diggs raised his eyebrows and nodded. He didn't take his hands off his ears. "Please go ahead, I'm ready anytime for your thunderous roar."

The Woozy looked up at Diggs. "But I roared. Are you deafened permanently?"

The five monkeys looked puzzled and then screeched in laughter. They jumped up and down.

Diggs removed his hands from his ears. "I think I detected a puny pipsqueak." He chuckled. "Well, you tried."

"Next to my ears, it always sounded thunderous. Sorry." The Woozy went back to eating.

"Is everyone in Oz crazy?" Diggs turned and started looking for lunchpail trees. The four cohort monkeys came with him.

"I want to stay and hear some more thunderous roars," Ortho howled.

"Do you need me to come with you to protect you?" said the Woozy. He stopped munching bees. One partially crushed form hung out of the corner of his mouth.

Diggs took off his top hat, bowed, straightened, and then grinned. "I think we can survive without your magnificent help. But thank you anyway."

Just past the giant sunflowers were lunchpail trees. Diggs noticed that even the most mature ones were the same height as the flowers. "I wonder if the immature ones have baby formula and gruel in the pails? I could get several pails for Ozma. Whoops, not needed anymore. I doubt Tip would enjoy pablum." Diggs plucked several ripe pails and asked the monkeys to help carry them. "Don't open them now. I do not know how, but they will stay fresh and hot as long as they are unopened. Why just last month, I had one that contained delicious churned strawberry ice cream and the darn stuff didn't melt 'til I opened the pail. I had the box, in the basket for a week after picking. I had to keep the piglets away from the pails. They nosed around the pile every day."

The monkeys rose slightly in the air. Diggs gave each monkey several pails to carry. They looked confused. Ortho returned and instructed them to carry one in each hand, foot, and one for their tail. Thus encumbered, they flew across to the OZ balloon. After four trips, Diggs said they had enough. He walked to the gondola and climbed aboard. The piglets were already nosing through the pile of containers, trying to open one.

"Finally," said Frederick. "Food. Why, we haven't eaten in hours! It seems like years." He stood on his hind limbs and made a begging motion with his hooves. "We're starving." The other piglets nodded their heads in agreement.

"Men, I mean monkeys," said Diggs. "Go back and get one more ripe load, each. I'm not sure I considered the piglets' voracious appetites."

The monkeys flew off and came back an hour later. They looked very sheepish, and Diggs noticed that several of the lunchpail containers were significantly dented. He sighed, "I trust the Woozy is still all right?"

Ortho grinned. "That creature has one tough head. It was an amusing brawl. He sure is happy here. I'm glad you didn't carry him off to slave for you, like we have to."

"Ortho," said Diggs. "I repeat, I don't believe in slavery. Once you direct me to the Emerald Citadel, you and your companions are free to return to the chasm. Why, if I can, I'll use my last wish in the Flying

Monkey Cap to give the entire band their permanent freedom, if I haven't used the wishes up."

Ortho looked respectfully at Diggs. "Maybe I misjudged you, wizard? Should I load the rest of these pails?"

Diggs wrinkled his brow, then nodded. "I hope they're still edible."

After the monkeys hoisted the four drop ropes and attached sandbags, Diggs added more Ozpyrite coal. The balloon rose quickly. He motioned to Unolingo to exhale. As they drifted north, Diggs waved to the Woozy, who didn't look up. The beast continued to flame, crunch, and swallow loudly.

Diggs shooed the four flying monkeys off the gondola. He asked Ortho to stay and continue his tale. "So, Ortho, if the Emerald Citadel was all white, why is it called 'emerald' and why did the seer tell me that is the green area I must go to?"

"The love birds lived in the Citadel happily for years," said Ortho. "They had several children. Their first born, now known as Pastoria the 'Incompetent' was defective. For some reason, he inherited few magic powers."

Diggs nodded his head. "Sounds like the Pastoria, I met. He was a nice guy, but now something happened to him and he's a stone statue." Diggs' head tilted forward, his eyebrows arched outwards, and his mouth drooped. Diggs slowly straightened up, shrugged his shoulders, and looked off into the distance. "I wish things could have been different."

Ortho jumped up. "That's Pastoria the eighth. That's the one I looked for years. He had almost no magic, and he is the one who finally lost the citadel."

"Yeah," said Diggs. "That's the one. But what's with the green color?"

"So," continued Ortho. "The parents felt obligated to entrust the crown to Pastoria, but felt embarrassed to call him a wizard king. And since he wasn't a wizard, he couldn't live in a white castle. First his mother tried to infuse him with magical powers, but that totally failed. His dad gave him a few magic powders and potions, but Pastoria never truly was a wizard. He was more of a humbug."

"I can relate. Sometimes you can make mistakes with powders and potions."

Ortho's fingers inched towards one of the several lunchpails. He raised his eyebrows.

Diggs nodded. "Go ahead."

Ortho took one from the top and popped it open. "Ozdolpho and Gayelette decided the color of the white marble had to change. Throughout Oz, there were common stones, and they wanted something non-white, but unique on the walls."

Frederick wandered over to Ortho. "Hey monkey, any popcorn in that pail? My fellow piglets and I need something to go with the beer."

"Help yourself, pigs," said Ortho.

All nine of the piglets rushed towards the lunchpail.

Ortho screeched. "If you take anything but popcorn, I'll eat you. Now where was I? Oh yeah, the rulers felt gold from Winkie country, rubies from Quadlings, amethysts from Gillikin, and sapphires from Munchkin country surrounded them. They could find everywhere all these common stones in their singular countries, the rulers wanted something different."

"Make sense," said Diggs. "But how did they arrive at green?"

Ortho brushed off piglets that were climbing up his legs. "The four countries of the Land of Oz come together in only one spot. This area, when excavated for the white citadel, contained thousands of green stones called emeralds. These junk stones existed nowhere else in the land. Since they were unique, the rulers used these worthless stones to adorn the white citadel. Now it was called the 'Emerald Citadel.' Over the generations, they passed the crown on and many Pastorias ruled for hundreds of years."

Diggs shook his head. "Gold, rubies, amethysts, sapphires, and emeralds worthless. I must be in heaven," he thought. Aloud, he added, "Why was the citadel destroyed?"

Ortho used one hand to reach into the lunchpail and pull out morsels to eat. Between bites, he used his hand to occasionally scratch his butt and then smelled his fingers.

Diggs gagged.

"At that time, there were two good witches and two evil," said Ortho. "Each witch lived in a separate country of Oz, but didn't really rule them. The evil witches' power grew. A minor evil witch called Mombi stole the

Golden Magic Cap and controlled the flying monkeys. First, she destroyed the Good Witch of the North. Latesha the Wise was ancient and her power was waning. Mombi didn't even have to use her first wish from the cap to destroy the good witch. An evil witch from the South attacked Glinda the Good, but lost. Rumor is the Giant Chasm Dragon aligned with Glinda, and that's why she won."

"That makes sense," said Diggs. "She wouldn't really fight the dragon with me. Of course, I never got around to asking her."

"Hey boss," gasped Unolingo. "Can I take a break? I'm out of breath."

Diggs lifted his arm and motioned to the ball balloon creature to stop puffing. He didn't take his eyes off of Ortho's smelly hand, afraid the monkey might touch him.

"Mombi and the two other evil witches," said Ortho. "Evanora and Theodora decided to destroy Pastoria the eighth and rule all of Oz. Mombi summoned my clan and would bloviate daily about how she would be a better ruler."

Frederick chomped on popcorn "What in the world does that word, bloviate, mean?"

Diggs wrinkled his brow. "I have to agree, I don't know that term either."

"In plain Ozian," said Ortho. "It means rant or speak pompously."

Diggs nodded. "That's Mombi for you."

The balloon rotated in lazy circles. Unolingo, in a deflated state, drifted into the gondola, settled to the floor, closed its central eye, and began to saw logs. Each snore was a loud wheeze with an occasional huge gulp of air. The beast scooted several feet backwards with each exhalation and came back to the original spot with each inhalation.

"Wow," said Diggs. "That's very strange to see. I wonder if he'll pop if he snores too much?" He scratched his head.

Ortho stared at the balloon ball beast also and nodded. "With Mombi's first wish for my clan, and the help of the other two witches, they leveled the Emerald Citadel. While they were celebrating their victory, Pastoria and his wife escaped. A loyal servant pretended to be the king, and the witches tortured him for days. Just before dying, the man reluctantly admitted to the hoax. Mombi was furious and used her second wish to have myself and four loyal comrades try to track him down. She used her third wish to have the rest of my clan enslave the Gillikin people."

"Those poor people," said Diggs. "Her soldiers looked miserable."

Ortho shrugged. "Evanora, the Wicked Witch of the East, said her great beauty would win over the Munchkins, plus she didn't believe in slavery. Theodora, the one from the West, wants the Golden Cap to help enslave all Winkies. The evil witches united with each other to destroy Pastoria, but afterwards, even though sisters, the women have battled ever since. Evanora and Theodora are fighting a Civil War."

Diggs stared. "Sounds familiar."

Chapter Thirty-One

"Now Mr. Monkey, hold your story," said Frederick. "I need more popcorn. You know Mister Oz, all the food in the lunch box trees is always green, but this the first time I have ever seen green popcorn. My eyes still never see normal colors."

"Our eyes see green also," said several tiny voices. "But no matter, we're hungry, so get more for us to nibble on as well."

The head piglet waddled over to the pile of lunchpails and nosed open the closest one. "Nuts, it's only nuts, in here as the appetizer, no popcorn. Yikes! Pork chops with spicy pepper jelly. You wouldn't make us become cannibals, Mister Diggs, would you?"

"Find a different pail, Frederick," said Diggs, a bit frustrated. "I'm busy." He sat back against his carpet bag and swiveled toward Ortho.

Frederick nosed open a second one, a third, a fourth pail. "The appetizer in this one is just nuts, this one, more nuts, finally, yeah, popcorn." The piglet pushed over the other opened lunchpails. They clattered and fell all over the floor of the gondola. "Start your story, monkey, I'm listening." The piglet brought the mound of popcorn over to the firebox area and settled down. He didn't share it with his companions, still in their nest.

"Frederick," said Diggs, "I've told you several times, that as soon as you open those pails, hot food gets cold and cold items get warm. Don't be so lazy and waste the items." Diggs uncurled from his sitting position, complained about his aching joints, and walked over to the pile of receptacles. He grabbed a handful of nuts from one pail and downed them. Then he took a pork chop from another. "They smell wonderful, just a little snack." Diggs lifted the chop to his mouth and took a big bite. Juices ran down his chin. With his other hand, he snapped the lids closed on the four opened pails and put them to the side. While chomping, he put the unopened ones in a neat stack again. Once finished with his pre-lunch, he walked to the railing. He tossed the bone over the side and watched it fall. "We're going over the Quadling mountains. Next stop Winkie country."

"We still have quite a way to traverse," said Ortho. "I could get there much quicker."

Diggs walked back to Ortho. "Yes, but I've never learned how to fly. Not much lift with these stubby arms." He flapped his arms in Ortho's face and then sat down on top of his carpetbag. "The gondola floor is too hard. I'm going to pick some towel leaves, pad my sitting area, and use them for something other than diapers."

"What do you mean, diapers?" said Ortho. "What in the world did you need them for?"

Diggs shook his head. "It's a long story. And speaking of stories, please continue your tale. Why are you not the leader of your clan anymore? And why are all five of you living in the chasm?"

Ortho frowned. "Mombi's first wish was successful. My clan, of which I was the king, destroyed the Emerald Citadel in just four days. Of course, Mombi used her wand, Theodora used her potions and powers, and Evanora spoke incantations. Pastoria's weak magic did nothing to stop us, and his wife was not powerful enough with just fairy magic. Glinda the Good just hid in her southern country. Mombi had already destroyed Latesha of the North and the northern country was in chaos."

"I thought Mombi ruled Gillikin country?" said Diggs.

Ortho slid over to Frederick and tried to steal some popcorn. The leader piglet placed his chubby body between his haul and the monkey's probing fingers.

Ortho sighed and moved back. "Only, with the help of the second Golden Cap Wish. At the time of the fall of the Emerald Citadel, it was a land of savagery and pandemonium."

Frederick was so astonished he missed his mouth due to concentrating on the tale "Wow!" The rest of the piglets came out and sat in a row. They were so fascinated with the story, they didn't notice that Frederick was hogging the popcorn.

Diggs wiggled around on the carpetbag, trying to get more comfortable. "How did you and the rest of the monkeys destroy the Citadel?" He stretched his back again. "Damn lumbago! My joints are killing me."

Ortho screeched and laughed, then stretched with his joints popping. "Poor young human. Try being five hundred years old. Now to continue, Mombi transformed some of the Citadel guards into peacocks. Then Theodora used a potion she stole called 'True Form' on the walls. The reinforced marble turned into blocks of sandstone and crumbly granite. Evanora muttered some magic words. The walls, and gates, shrunk, started falling, and the horde pulled down the rest. My clan and I chased every soldier, peasant, and working people out of the Citadel. It was great fun."

"Boss man," said Slim. "Down yonder looks like we've crested the mountain and that there is a wide river below. Ball balloon man stopped blowing. He looks right confused."

"Tell Unolingo," said Ortho, "to follow the river. This is the major portion of the Winkie River. One of its branches, just a little further ahead, will take us right to the ruins of the Emerald Citadel."

Diggs stood, turned, and waved to the ball balloon creature. "Hey Unolingo, stop and take a break." He turned towards Ortho. "I don't think he's paying attention? Maybe I should use my old semaphore flags?" Under his breath, he asked Ortho, "Let's get something for him to eat. What do those kinds of beasts eat? Hydrogen gas or maybe just hot air?" Diggs walked over to the group of piglets. "All right fellows, let's re-open those four lunchpails and eat our dinner."

Ortho rubbed his stomach. "I'm hungry. But how the hell should I know what that gas ball eats?"

Diggs motioned to the Unolingo to come aboard. He turned back to the monkey. "Now, Ortho, didn't you live near him for centuries?"

Ortho shook his head. "The Great Chasm earned its name. It was massive. I rarely saw the balloon creatures and never consorted with its kind."

Unolingo deflated and came aboard. "I'm not sure you will need me much longer. There is some wind picking up, and the wizard should be able to fly his contraption. It will be much slower than if I provide my expert help, but doable."

"Please stay a while longer," said Diggs. "You never know when the winds could change. Are you hungry?" Diggs picked up a lunchpail and held it out to the creature. He popped it open. "This sure smells great. Can you tell? Do you even have a nose?"

"I feed on the air itself," said Unolingo. "Hot fumes are more nourishing than cold, but any suffice. I never tried hydrogen gas. I'm sorry I missed out." He let out one more gush of air, blew off Diggs' hat, and closed his central air nozzle. "I'll just rest if you don't need me. Maybe I'll just close my eyes for a minute, but I won't sleep. I'm here for you. You can count on me to be always on call and alert. I tended to my hunger needs previously. We really only eat once a month." He deflated slowly, completely, and then settled into a wrinkled heap at the back of the gondola. Unolingo closed his central eye and immediately snored loudly.

The balloon creature deflated to the size of Diggs' carpet bag. Diggs walked over to it and looked down. "Great lookout! Always alert?"

The OZ balloon continued to drift northward, but its velocity slowed significantly. Diggs put down the lunchpail and walked to the railing. In the river below, a large serpentine head lifted high out of the river. Diggs estimated the creature was about one half the length of the gondola.

"I see you survived your journeys," yelled the snake. "Where did you go?" The serpent lifted its head as high as possible and stuck out its tongue. The head was bright yellow, but its tongue was purple. "Nope. Still can't reach the bottom of this flying contraption. Come lower. I want to see if I could pull you down."

Diggs shuddered and scooted back from the railing. "No, thanks Mr. Serpent. We're just passing through."

Ortho stood up and peered over the railing. "Yipes," he screeched "I hate snakes." He blew a raspberry at the creature. "We need to follow the river, I hope that slimy thing doesn't follow us." Ortho shielded his eyes and yelled, "Fritz, Horatio, Brutus, and Oglethorpe, don't fly too low or that water serpent will grab you."

"I'm sure," said Diggs, "that if I side vent, I can follow the tributary of the river, right to our target. You continue your story, Ortho. I'll eat the rest of this pail and tend to the hot air nozzle."

Ortho walked back to the pails. "I need some food now. I'm glad you got Winkie lunchpail tree meals. They often have bananas." He flipped open six pails until he found a bunch and sat down with them. While talking through a mouthful of the fruit, the monkey continued, "Mombi easily captured the false king and tortured him. Evanora tried to use her feminine wiles to get him to talk, but he held out for a full week. It took Theodora's Powder of Persuasion to get the genuine answers. Ozians are very loyal."

Diggs spoke through his full mouth of food. "Shoot, that would have been so much easier than what I had to do. But then, Jinxville wouldn't have had such a great stone statue in front of the mayor's house. Too bad though, he was a nice guy, smart as well. I feel really guilty about the entire situation."

Ortho ignored him and tossed two banana peels over the railing. "Mombi was furious and transformed the man into an inanimate iron ladle. She muttered something about not being done with the man yet. She used another wish and sent myself and my four bodyguards to find the real Pastoria and his wife. We searched for one hundred years but never could find them. I determined later that there was a fairy aura cast by Lorelei, his wife. When we reported back to Mombi, my group found she had used her third wish and had an upstart named Nikko and the rest of monkeys, conquer, and then enslave the Gillikins."

Diggs nodded his head. "Met the gentleman. Kind of pushy."

"At first, I tried to take back my throne, in direct combat, but I was old and Nikko easily defeated me. Mombi was going to turn me and my friends into statues, but she had already used up her wand transformations for the week."

Diggs held up both his hands with his fingers in the air, put his thumbs together, and stared at Ortho through the opening. He smiled. "You'd have made a nice glass statue."

"Instead, she banished us and told us to fly over the Deadly Desert and leave Oz. We headed south and as we came over the Chasm that housed the Giant Dragon, he came up. After a brief brawl which we lost, the dragon said he loved the fight, needed more followers, and invited us to stay."

Diggs looked up from eating yellow squash, applesauce, and fish. "So maybe Chang is one of his followers?" He smiled. "Delicious, smoked catfish with turmeric."

"Don't you listen," said Ortho. "The Silver Slug Seer is never wrong, confusing, but never wrong.

"Couldn't really hear her very well. Too much slime in my ears."

"She says he is in the Silver Islands and you will never see him again."

Diggs shook his head emphatically. "No, she said I would never see him again, but I would see him again, at the place of green? Also, something about scarecrows?"

"So, that's why we are heading to that area?" said Ortho. "Are you going to use your second wish to rebuild the Emerald Citadel?"

Diggs struggled to stand up, threw out his arm, and pointed farther to the north. "Why stop with such a small plan, and build just a citadel." He bent forward, raised up his other hand and spread his arms wide. "With everyone's help, I'm going to build an entire Emerald City!"

Chapter Thirty-Two

The wind from the south picked up briskly, causing the balloon to float due north. Even with side venting of the hot air, Diggs couldn't get the OZ balloon to go northeast, as he required.

"No, no!" shouted Ortho. "We're going the wrong way." The monkey screeched, jumped up and down, unfurled and furled his wings. The gondola bounced from his weight.

All the piglets appeared and stared at the ex-king with wide eyes and trembling snouts. "Is there something wrong?" Frederick inquired. "Are we doomed? Maybe we should eat something if the end is near."

Beneath the gondola, the Winkie River tributary branched off, heading to the Northeast. The OZ balloon continued to follow the main channel of the river, going straight north. The foliage, stones, and rare cow were now all a shade of purple.

"We're not in Winkie country anymore!" screamed Diggs. He continued to side vent air fruitlessly and then added even more coal. "We have to turn. I don't want to be entertained by Mombi again. She might want her cap back early." Diggs shuddered. "Or even worse, my body. Wake up, Unolingo."

"My cohorts left," said Ortho. "They followed the tributary and haven't looked back at all. Those fools. We must turn soon. Hey balloony, wake up."

Diggs licked his finger and held it up. "The due north wind from the Deadly Desert suddenly picked up." He shook his head and frowned. "I sure wish we had Glinda's wand to blow us where we want to go."

Ortho ambled over to the ball balloon creature and shook it. Unolingo didn't stir. The monkey then kicked the ball-beast. His paw sunk into the rubbery skin of Unolingo and bounced back. The creature still didn't open his central eye, or even lift its eye tendrils.

Diggs stood up and walked over to the ball balloon creature. "This always worked on my snoring tent mates back in Alabama." He bent over and squeezed shut the creature's nozzle. The wheezing sound from Unolingo's nozzle abruptly stopped. "Of course I was positive where the air came out, when someone had a nose and mouth." The balloon portion didn't rise and lower anymore. The creature shuddered and rose slightly. Diggs let go of the nozzle.

The ball balloon creature opened its central gigantic eye. "Huh, what? I wasn't sleeping, just closed my eye for a moment. I was alert, on watch." A tiny amount of drool came out of its nozzle. "What do you want?" All of his minor eyes flew open.

"Unolingo, sir," said Diggs. "You'll have to get to work again. We're off course, heading almost due north, and we want to go northeast. If you look below, we're following the Winkie Main channel." He pointed to the south. "We want to follow the tiny tributary that branched off about two miles back."

Ortho walked to the railing and pointed down. "Now we're following the Gillikin River Main Channel. These Oz folks are very territorial and name everything after the country it's in. They named the Winkie Mountains the 'Winkie Mountains' on their north slope and the same mountains are the 'Quadling Range' on the south."

Unolingo floated up and went to the front of the OZ balloon. He inhaled rapidly and expanded to his normal massive size. Upon exhaling, the envelope first came to a standstill and then drifted south.

Two and one-half miles later, Diggs pointed downwards. "Here's where we turn." He pulled out his semaphore flags and signaled to Unolingo.

Unolingo took in a huge breath but didn't exhale. "Why the hell are you waving those colored clothes?"

Diggs put down the flags. "Sorry, I forgot we hadn't worked out any signal system. I was trying to tell you need to blow on the west side of the gondola. I'll side vent and if we both work at it, we'll be at the Emerald Citadel in no time."

In the distance, four tiny specs appeared coming towards the OZ balloon. Twenty minutes later, the monkey companions stopped in front of the balloon. "Where did you go?" said Horatio. "We were flying along, following the old route, and suddenly you vanished. We were worried a witch got you."

"Dang, you are suurrrre... stupid," said Slim. "Y'all should've looked around once in a while. Or at least could've grunted at us when y'all went straight or something."

"Slight navigation error," said Diggs. "No problem. We just lost a little time and ruined Unolingo's second nap. All you fellows come aboard if you need to rest."

"They'd rather stretch their wings," said Ortho. "I'm going to join them. I have nothing more to say to you. Also, I'll work off these bananas." He burped.

"Go ahead," said Diggs. "Just don't go too far, and get out of sight. I'll feed the piglets and have a little more food myself." He patted his large belly. "I have to work hard to maintain my trim figure."

The OZ balloon followed the small branch of the Winkie River for the next day and one half. The balloon was propelled forward by Unolingo. The five monkeys only came aboard to eat and sleep during the trip. The monkeys jettisoned a prodigious amount of banana skins over the side.

Diggs also threw gnawed meat bones and fruit skins over the side. "Those monkeys sure make a mess!" He carefully saved the cleaned out lunchpails and put them in a pile. "Save the empties, piglets. We'll plant these strange seeds near our future emerald city and grow some lunch trees ourselves. Since these are from a Winkie tree, I wonder if the meals will stay yellowish, or will they take on a new green tinge?"

The balloon drifted over an extensive lake, the culmination of the Winkie River tributary. Brightly colored tents, comprising dozens of red ones, slightly fewer blue and yellow ones, and a rare purple, nestled across the area. Yellow bunched tents dotted the farmland and pasture.

The red tents were close to the lake, the blue ones were at the base of a large hill, and the rare purple ones were at the edge of a dense forest.

Hundreds of people milled around smaller tents in the clearing. Diggs couldn't hear any yelling, talking, or singing coming from the crowds. It was eerily quiet.

Despite being elevated, Diggs could smell baked goods, barbecued meat, and fresh fruit aromas coming from the tables in front of the tents. Diggs took out his spyglass and observed the milling customers interacting with people manning the tents. The crowd would go up to a table and point to an item. A tent owner would either shake their head "no," put a thumb's up to agree or appear to barter by holding up a couple of fingers. The red tents had many fish on the tables, the purple had large carcasses of something and he could not tell what was in the yellow and blue areas. He couldn't hear any talking or shouting of any words at all being exchanged.

Diggs aimed the balloon for the central clearing. "This is it! The Emerald Citadel. Balloon ball, sir. Stop breathing."

Unolingo quit exhaling. Diggs stopped putting coal in the firebox, vented out the hot air, and the balloon descended. It surprised him when a thunderous shout, "Oz," rose from the crowd.

Diggs ran to the gondola railing and looked over the side. As the balloon came down, he saw people of red, blue, yellow, and purple costumes jumping up and down and all yelling, "Oz!"

He noticed that every time they yelled "Oz," if their neighbor next to them wore different colored clothes, they would look quizzically at each other. Then they would shake their heads, shrug shoulders, turn away, and totally ignore the other person. They repeated this over and over.

Diggs walked back, and with the help of the monkeys, threw the four sandbags over the railing. The crowd pulled on the drop ropes, and the balloon soon settled to the ground. Diggs vaulted over the railing. The crowd yelled, "Great Oz, you finally have come!" Again there were quizzical looks among people standing next to each other, if they were not from the same colored country. The crowds all ran up to him and prostrated themselves on the ground. After getting up from the grass, one purple-dressed man and three women, one clad in blue, one in red, and one in yellow, hesitantly came up to him.

The red-dressed woman pushed to the front of the small group and said, "I welcome you to this small Quadling village, oh Great Oz. I am their mayor." She bowed again.

The yellow costumed woman now moved forward and said, "I welcome you to this small Winkie hamlet, oh Great Oz. I am their mayor." She bowed again.

The purple man started forward. Diggs cut him off. "Yeah, yeah, you're going to welcome me to your village and tell me you are their mayor. But why are you welcoming me individually? Why aren't you talking amongst yourselves and just appointing a central spokesman?"

"I'm sorry, oh great leader," said the man in purple. "I only speak Gillikin, I don't speak Winkie or Quadling, and I have no idea what the others said." He tried to throw himself down.

Diggs stopped the man from falling to the ground. "What the hell? You're all speaking the same tongue. I understand each of you perfectly."

A blue-clothed, tiny woman stepped forward. "We are not as multilingual as you, oh great liege. I heard you just now in fluent Munchkin and I assume these villagers heard you in their native tongues." She shrugged her shoulders. "I don't know."

"You all are crazy," said Diggs. "I was speaking plain Ozian! Everyone can talk to each other."

Ortho landed and came up to Diggs. "This is the Emerald Citadel area. The ruins are up there on the hill. Do you need me anymore?" He sniffed. "I wish to return where I am appreciated."

The village folk stared at the monkey and backed away quickly.

Diggs put his arm on Ortho's shoulder. "Please don't leave yet, I'll have need of your band during the rebuilding process."

The red dressed lady said, "Do you now control the flying monkeys, Great Oz? Vicious creatures. What was the beast saying? I do not speak animal, I only converse in Quadling."

"Now hold on," said Diggs. "These tents and this village have been here for hundreds of years. Huddled together, strictly by color. This determines 'which' country you belong to. And after all this time, no one talked between the different countries? Plus, all the animals I have encountered spoke as well as I do. So, you all must understand each other?"

"Brilliantly explained oh great one, but untrue." said the lady in blue. "These other villagers are not as articulate as my fellow Munchkins. Your fluent Munchkin is flawless. I be sorry the other mayor didn't understand ye." She curtsied this time.

"Perfect Gillikin," said the man dressed in purple.

"Perfect Winkie, no accent at all," said the woman in yellow.

"Perfect swine, but a little hard to understand," teased tiny voices from the gondola. "Ha!"

"Perfect———," started the remaining woman.

"Stop," commanded Diggs. "You're giving me a headache." He climbed back over the railing into the gondola. Diggs strode over to the carpetbag and pulled out his saber and a tinker box. After checking he had the correct box he carried them back to the group.

"Now then," said Diggs. "With the power that is invested in me." He climbed up onto the railing of the gondola. Diggs wobbled, and then regained his balance. He waved the saber over his head and held the box up to his lips. "ABRACADABRA! FROM NOW ON, YOU ALL SPEAK AND UNDERSTAND THE SAME DAMN LANGUAGE!"

Chapter Thirty-Three

"Amazing, oh Great Oz," said the lady clothed all in red. "I can understand everyone jabbering in the entire crowd, even the muttering monkeys."

"I can understand, the Quadling woman," said a female draped only in blue. "It's a miracle."

"No, it's magic," yelled the Gillikin man. "Oz is truly a great and powerful wizard." He bowed deeply again. So did the entire crowd.

Diggs held out his hands. "Now everyone can communicate." He pointed to the crowd. "Please send a representative to each of the four countries of Oz." Diggs gestured grandly. "Let it be known that there is now a magical universal Ozian language!"

"We will do your command, Oh Great One," they all yelled at the same time. Several runners from each respective country took off at once.

Diggs hopped off the railing, put down the tinker box, and held up the saber. "Let's get to business." He pointed the blade at the group. "Are you the representatives of your respective areas? And who's in charge of the central area? I assume it is a market? Whatever they're selling, it sure smells wonderful."

"Welcome, oh Great Oz," said a lady wearing an elegant crimson outfit, "to the village of Smithersonville. I am mayor Lothicia. This is a village at the very northern tip of Quadling country." She curtsied to Diggs and then stepped back.

A short man attired in dirty purple furs hesitantly stepped forward. "And the same welcome, from the hamlet of Munch. I am mayor Bort. This is probably the smallest and definitely the farthest southern village in Gillikin country." He stumbled, stepped back, and bowed.

"Welcome," said a doll sized woman, "from the burg of Roundstone. I am councilwoman Martha. This is the farthest western village in Munchkin country." She curtsied, twirled around, causing her blue skirt to flare out, did a quick jig, and walked back two steps.

The last woman started to speak when Diggs cut her off. "All right, I know, you're the representative of a village of the farthest eastern portion of Winkie country." He wrinkled his brow. "But I thought this was the Emerald Citadel, not a bunch of small villages."

"That is true," said Lothicia. "Our respective villages have been here for hundreds of years. First, we supplied and serviced the kings or queens who resided in the Emerald Citadel. Then, after the witch and monkeys destroyed the Citadel, we just kept living here and traded among ourselves. We could only barter since we couldn't speak each other's language."

Diggs took a step back as he inhaled a strong fishy smell coming from the woman's hands and clothes. "Not the brightest group of candles in the candelabra," he muttered to himself.

"Many years ago, Mombi swooped down and enslaved most of Munch," said Bort. "She could only conquer us with the help of those horrible flying monkeys." He spat at Ortho's feet. "Mombi and the monkey clan carried most of the villagers off. A few households hid in the mud of the lake or deep in the forest and thus escaped. That is why there are so few purple Gillikin tents. But we still serve an important niche in the area, we are mighty hunters of beasts of the forest." Bort was wearing torn, filthy purple furs, and carried an old blunt spear. His greasy hair and crumb-filled beard were down to his chest. He showed wide gaps of missing teeth

"I didn't introduce myself," said the last woman. "I am Wanaderella and our village is, of course, from Winkie country, Winkieburg." Wanaderella's smile was as glowing as her golden colored clothes. She had a wonderful smell of fresh baked bread emanating from her and Diggs stepped closer and inhaled deeply.

Ortho pushed past Wanaderella and glared at Bort. He growled, "Listen, Bort. I was not part of the band who helped Mombi subdue all the Gillikins." He puffed up his torso and clenched a paw. "My four companions and I are prisoners, err… guests of the Chasm Dragon, doing a service for the Wiz, and haven't seen Mombi for centuries."

Bort dropped his spear. He bent down, picked it up, and shakily pointed it at Ortho. He dropped it again and ducked behind Wanaderella's skirts.

Lothicia stepped forward again. "Are you here to defeat the evil witches and rule all of Oz, great one? That would indeed be joyous news. You have already made our lives easier. Uniting the land would just be wonderful." From the front pocket on her red apron, a pink kitten popped up its head and purred.

Diggs stepped up to Lothicia. "Red Quadling tents are the largest portion in this area, but this village is quite a distance from Glinda the Good. If you are so worried about wicked witches, then why don't you all live near the good witch?"

"She is too young," said Lothicia. "Merely four hundred years old." She stroked the cat while speaking.

"Just a baby," said another man, who pushed forward. This Quadling's body odor reeked even harsher of fish fumes. He had a large, fat kitten draped around his neck.

"Glinda is indeed good and caring," said Lothicia, "But she is in the infancy of her magical arts. Her spells occasionally misfire and often wear off. In another hundred years of practice, she will be ready to take on the evil witches. Until then we need a wizard to protect us. You are indeed welcome."

"Can we get ye food and drink, Oh Great One?" said Martha. This woman dressed in blue was so tiny, Diggs had to stare down significantly to look into her eyes, since she only came up to his knee. A full-figured woman, but on the diminutive side, wearing a revealing low-cut dress.

"You can't be as old as the rest of these villagers?" said Diggs. "You are so petite." He bent way down and picked up one of her hands. "And you are so comely."

Martha blushed to the roots of her blue hair. "You flatter me, oh Great Oz. My laugh lines and wrinkles are older than most of the people in these villages. As my clan says, a kind word broke no one's mouth. Now, no more false flattery. Would you like some sustenance, a place to rest, or a tour of our villages?"

Diggs smiled. "I am rather full from partaking, of lunch box trees pails. I would love a tour of the nests of villages. Please do me the honor of being my guide."

Diggs climbed back into the gondola and opened the firebox door. He closed off the vent, so no more hot air came out. Next, he uncovered the piglet's scarf nest. "Would you guys like to look around with me?"

"Whall, I cain't palaver for everyone," said Slim, "but I reckon I'd love to go."

"All of us," squeaked the rest of the piglets.

Diggs pulled out his greatcoat from the carpetbag. "Well, it's hot, but I need the extra pockets." He slipped the coat on. "Great. I'm sweating already." Diggs bent over and swooped up handfuls of piglets. He dumped them into one of his front pockets.

"Don't crowd me boys," yelped Miss Scarlet. "A lady needs her space." She squealed and then giggled. "Okay, who goosed me, and how? We all have hooves."

"First stop," said Martha. "Our central open-air market. Please follow me." She turned and led the way.

Diggs slid his saber into his belt. He picked up both revolvers, made sure they were loaded, and stuck them in the other front pocket of his coat. Finally, he put back tinker box number one and slipped number two into the pocket next to the revolvers.

The entire group walked into the open-air market. The crowds parted immediately for the royal assemblage. Diggs walked up and examined each colored tent and table intently. The Gillikin table featured different barbequed beasts, gutted, and quartered. Most of the beasts were four legged, but Diggs noticed one that had eight. There were several pelts available for barter, including a fur from a nine-foot-long purple bear, with the glaring head still attached. Diggs couldn't be sure, but he thought the eyes followed him around the table.

The Quadling fishmongers were processing many fish at various tables. Most of the massive fish were still flopping, opening, and closing their mouths. The smaller fish were already decapitated. All the scales of every fish were multicolored. One of the larger ones opened its mouth and screamed, "Help me! I can't breathe."

Miss Scarlet popped her head up. "Poor fishy!"

Abraham stuck up next to her. "Yum, that's the largest herring I ever saw. I wonder if they make Gefilte fish here?"

Diggs gently pushed the two back down. "Quiet guys, they might want to use you all for miniature pork chops."

A Winkie woman carrying a huge basket walked up to one of the fish merchants. She pointed to one of the huge fish and then pulled back the cloth covering the items in her basket. The woman now held up five fingers and showed the Quadling her line of baked goods.

The woman dressed in yellow giggled and said, "I forgot we can now understand each other. It will make it so much easier to trade. I would like that giant sturgeon and will give you five muffins in exchange."

The Quadling man shook his head. "No, that is a rare catch. I would need twenty muffins and a dozen donuts for that prize fish."

"Ten and two."

"Ten and two will only get you smelt."

"Done. You, sir drive a hard bargain." The Winkie woman piled the baked goods onto the table and scooped up her fish dinner.

The Winkies had mounds of baked goods, flours, unprocessed wheat, and bushels of corn for sale. All their goods were the brightest yellow or gold color imaginable. The baked goods gave off a fresh, yeast-like odor that made Diggs' mouth water.

They piled the Munchkin table high with jumbles of different vegetables and bowls of fruit. They made some fruits and vegetables into jellies and jams, stewed or just in their native state. All the fruits and even the vegetables were a shade of blue.

Diggs picked up a giant eggplant. "When I floated over this area, I saw the obvious source of the fish, forest lands to hunt the beasts and the farmlands for the wheat goods. But where do the Munchkins get so many different blue vegetables and fruits?"

Martha pointed to the surrounding countryside. "Just outside Roundstone is a grove of vegetable and fruit trees. We blessed us to have a bountiful harvest of blueberries, plums, bluebell apples, blue corn, and many others. Productive the trees they are, and picked they enjoy regularly. They just wish the harvesters didn't have such icy fingers."

Diggs put down the vegetable and picked up a plum. He took a bite. "Yum. So, these trees talk also? I enjoy communicating with lunchpail trees." The juices ran down Diggs' face.

Martha laughed at the mess. "Talk, the trees do. We could understand the trees of Oz, but nothing else outside of our native tongues. Before you taught us the foreign languages, we had to use sign language to barter and trade. Easy, it be now."

"I'm glad I could help. I have accomplished the first part of what the seer predicted. Now I will do the next part she told me to do and then wait for my friend Chang to arrive."

"Where will you wait? Which village are you coming to live in?"

"Not exactly one," replied Diggs. "Starting tomorrow, all the separate villagers are going to be considered citizens of my new Emerald City."

Chapter Thirty-Four

"Now," said Diggs. "What else is there to see?" He peered at the rubble up on the hill. "Is the Citadel worth touring?"

Ortho shook his head. "It is worth seeing only if you enjoy piles of granite blocks with weeds growing over them." He puffed out his chest. "We did a wonderful job of destroying the castle." The monkey hung his head and frowned. "I wish I did as good a job finding that Pastoria. If I had, then Mombi wouldn't have banished me."

"All right," said Diggs. "I guess we'll tour the four villages. Martha, if you could lead on to your village of um, Roundstone was it called?"

"As you command, oh Great One, but let someone else go first," said Martha. "My village folk have a special surprise for you and it be not finished yet."

"Oh, please, oh Great Oz, let's go to Smithersonville," said Lothicia. "It's the largest village and the most important." She stepped forward and tugged on his hand.

"That is wrong," said Bort. "We're the best. The smallest, but the most important."

"Quit arguing," said Diggs. "I command you. From this moment on, you are all Emerald Citizenizians, err… Citizienii, err… Citizens. In fact, continue with your respective former occupations, but everyone's costumes have to change. No more red, blue, yellow, or purple dress.

Everyone should wear green." He pointed to the ruin on the hill. "Yes, everyone in my Emerald City should always green."

"All right me Boyo," said Martha. "But I do have one question. Where do we get green cloth to change our garb?"

"Yeah," said Bort. "I never have killed a green-colored beast. And since fur is the only clothing us Gillikins wear, I need to find a green creature."

"Great Oz, perhaps you could use your magic powers and transform all of our clothes to green?" said Lothicia. "I'm sure it would be something you could easily do."

"Yes, that would be the easiest," said Diggs. "Let me ponder that and get back to you all soon."

"It's settled, oh Great One, we'll go first to Smithersonville," said Lothicia. "We've established our little Quadling village nearest to the Quadling Lake and have supplied the other villagers with fish and freshwater."

"Winkie Lake," interjected Wanaderella. "It's in Winkie country."

"Gillikin," started Bort.

"Stop," said Diggs. "All this petty bickering is ridiculous. I have named the entire area Emerald City, so the lake will be the Emerald City Lake. Now Lothicia, continue with your tour."

The group walked towards Smithersonville, a small red village nestled around the lake. In front of every house, was a dock with a tiny fishing boat moored. The grouping of houses appeared much smaller than Jinxville. There was no central well, Bar or Town Hall building. All the houses and yards were shades of red and were extremely well kept up. Many moored, dilapidated boats were falling apart. Trawlers with holes in the planking, ripped sails on sailboats, half-sunk skiffs, staved in rowboats, peeling paint on paddle boats, and even warped surfboards.

The group hugged the lake's shoreline until the placid lake formed a small inlet. Strewn along a sandy beach at the mouth of the inlet, was many tables where the Quadlings processed fish products. There were baskets containing gutted fish carcasses, piles of heads and mounds of entrails. The smells coming from the area were not pleasant like the ocean, but more like something hundreds of cats would enjoy. Weaving around the legs of the tables and the fish merchants were dozens of felines, meowing, crying, howling, and complaining about how hungry they were.

"We bartered the fish bodies in the main market square," said Lothicia. "We trade all the guts to the Winkies for their grain crops and to the Munchkins for the fruit and vegetable trees, while the heads go to these precious pink pussycats, who keep any vermin away from Smithersonville. These adorable creatures are a significant source of companionship, but the only trouble is the cats are always hungry."

"I know several others who can relate to that," said Diggs.

A pink head lifted out of Diggs' pockets. The piglet looked around and ducked back inside. "My ears didn't deceive me, Mister Diggs. I heard what that lady was talking about. Please don't let those ferocious beasts get at us."

Diggs patted the pocket gently. "Don't worry, little one. No one is going to eat you."

"The lake's water supplies us with fourteen types of fish," said Lothicia. "We even harvest two types of octopi and four types of kelp. The only trouble, no one likes to work too hard at fishing. If the lake didn't constantly magically regenerate its bounty, we would have nothing to trade. The fish are easy to catch."

"I'll have to find a way to motivate everyone better," said Diggs. "My Emerald City residents will have to eat."

"Can't you just use your magic wand and feed everyone?" said Lothicia.

"Err, hum… of course," said Diggs. "But I don't want everyone to get lazy. Now, let's go back down to the lake."

A trawler was just pulling in as the tour walked down to the waters. Its flue belched black smoke. The boat leaned severely to one side and settled deep in the waters.

Lothicia waved at two men standing on the tiny boat. "Ahoy, Captains Quakerman! How was your catch?"

The two captains were identical images of each other. Standing six-foot, four, thin as rails, with red beards down to their knees and auburn hair to the small of their backs. They both had eye patches over their right eye. The two men bent down at the same time and scooped up a huge pure white fish, which they tossed up on the shore. It barely made it to the edge.

The fish flopped around at Diggs' feet. The creature opened and closed its mouth and gills. "Mommy, I sure wish I didn't go after that bait."

"Aaaarrrrrrrgggghhhh, a terrible haul again," said one captain. "I don't even know why we go out."

"Aye, I'm ready to give up," said the other. He put his hand on his abdomen. "Plus, I get sea sick on this little lake."

"Oh Great Oz, may I introduce to you Captains Quall and Quint Quakerman," said Lothicia. "Ex-pirates and some of the worst fishermen you've ever met."

The two men pulled up to the dock and turned off the motor. After a final belch of smoke, the engine died. The captains jumped over the railing and landed on the beach. They walked up to Diggs.

"Where in the world could you be pirates?" said Diggs. "I have seen no large bodies of water or merchant ships anywhere in Oz."

"Yep," said Quall, or maybe Quint. "Terrible buccaneers. We weren't too successful. That's why we retired. The trouble is, we're not any better as fishermen than we were as pirates." He bent over, and his beard dropped into the water. The captain used his foot to push the fish back into the water slowly. "Oh hell, fishy. Just go free. These Ozwhalefish are rare."

"Brother, you're too kindhearted," said the other captain. He pushed greasy hair off of his forehead. "But to tell you the truth, I was just about to do the same thing myself."

Diggs pulled off his top hat and wrinkled his forehead. "Why did you return such an enormous fish to the lake?"

"Arrr, that be just a baby," said one of the brothers. "You should see a big one."

Diggs stared into the water. "That was a baby? It was huge! What do you mean it was rare?"

"They infrequently found these beasts in Oz," said the other brother. "The gigantic adults love to travel to different worlds via magic. There they love to capsize ships and swallow sailors. This baby said his family was real important. His Mommy once ate someone famous named Jonah and his Dad battled someone named err… Ahab? Dangerous creatures. I'm glad we got rid of it."

Captain Quakerman reached over and grabbed his twin around the shoulders and grinned. "I think it's time we embarked on our next career. The seventh one will be a charm."

"Just as long as we don't try duck hunting again," said the second brother. "Having only one musket between us and the fact we couldn't hit the broad side of a barn made things difficult."

"Do you gentlemen still own the musket?" said Diggs.

"Yes," said the first captain. "Fairly dusty, but I'm sure it's around here somewhere."

"Then I now have made you both the Royal Guard of the Emerald City," said Diggs. "With all the strange beasts and evil witches throughout the land, I need bodyguards. Report to me with your gun, up on the hill, bright and early."

Both men lifted their eye patches and stared with both eyes at Diggs. "You are really offering us a job?"

"Yes," said Diggs. "Royal Guard and my personal bodyguards. See me very early tomorrow."

"Aye, wizard," said one of the captains. "We'll be there bright and early. Noonish Okay? We have to get our beauty sleep in."

Diggs shrugged. "I can see going on Oz time is going to be a problem."

Chapter Thirty-Five

"Begora, where to now, oh Great Oz?" Martha said, while tugging on his knee.

"I know Ozians are on the smaller side," said Diggs. "But why are you Munchkins so incredibly tiny? And why do you sound like my Irish cop friend?"

Martha smiled up at him. "Later, later Oh Great One, all will be explained."

Diggs smiled back. "All right, so shall we peruse the blue village now?"

"I doubt your surprise be ready yet, let's go to one of the other sites."

Both Bort and Wanaderella spoke at the same time. "It's our turn…"

Diggs turned to the woman dressed in glowing yellow, bent down, and held out his arm. "Ladies first."

The group left Smithersonville, turned left, and headed for Winkieburg. Bort trailed in the rear, complaining the entire time. "It's not fair, Gillikins are always last," he muttered under his breath. "Just because Wanaderella gots big boobs."

Diggs slowed down as they cut across through the central market. "The smells are wonderful. Maybe just one little bite to tide me over for the long walk."

Three heads poked up out of his pocket. "We're all starving," said Frederick. "My group hasn't eaten in a whole hour. And even more of the piglets would be complaining if they weren't asleep in here."

"Hey Oz, see if they have any corn pone or biscuits," said Slim.

"No, I declare, I want some beignets, although they do ruin my figure," said Miss Scarlet.

Wanaderella stared at the piglets. "What in the world, is that in your pocket, oh Great Oz?"

Diggs waved his hand toward his pocket. "I would like to introduce my piglet friends to you. The rarest creatures in any world. I found them when I was at a wizard convention on the island of Madagascar, which is on the world I come from, Earth."

"Aye, all the inhabitants of Munchkin country, we be well acquainted with areas of Earth," said Martha.

Diggs' eyes widened. "What, what? How do you know of Earth?"

Martha grinned up at the wizard. "Later, later. 'Tis grand to be curious, but wait, all will be told. Now before ye be more knackered, you look so tired, let's carry on."

Diggs stared down at the wee woman. "There goes that Irish speech again. Do all Munchkins speak like you? What gives?"

"Speak like this, we do. But more importantly, what's up with those delightful pigmy piggys?"

"They keep me from getting bored, as they are wonderful conversationalists. But the only trouble is they often disappear on me." Diggs picked up Slim and Miss Scarlet and pushed them together. He opened up his hands and showed no piglets remaining.

Martha smiled politely. "'Tis utterly amazing."

Bort's mouth fell open. "Wow. Where did they go?"

"This is so romantic, and cozy," came a tiny voice from Diggs' greatcoat sleeve.

Diggs looked down at the sleeve of his greatcoat. "Don't pay any attention to the voice in my sleeve." He bent down and whispered, "Quiet, or I'll make you into pork chops."

The group entered the yellow village of Winkieburg. The houses were in a U shape, facing huge farm fields. Just before the farms was a central village square with a well in the center. The square was empty of inhabitants.

Planted in the fields were rows of corn and wheat. Although enormous heads of produce appeared on every plant, the stalks in the fields stood only one foot tall. But the corn ears and the wheat heads each loomed at least three feet.

"How in the world do the stalks support the weight of the ears?" said Diggs. "Even in Nebraska, I never saw such yields as you're getting."

Wanaderella cavalierly waved her hand. "Special magic fertilizer."

A Winkie man rode on a horse-drawn cart, weeding the fields. Diggs stared as he noticed that the equipment was floating between the rows. "That's the largest horse I ever saw, pulling the plow."

"Look again, oh Great One," said Wanaderella. "That's the source of the fertilizer."

A yellow dragon, the size of a bull elephant, drew the cart. An occasional beat of its long wings was keeping itself, the farmer, and thrasher aloft. Covering the dragon were long, luxurious feathers, not scales. The beast would frequently turn around and appeared to be complaining to the driver.

Diggs pointed with a trembling finger. "That beast is absolutely huge. Larger than the one elephant I've seen once in my traveling circus. Are the creatures also fire-breathing? Is Oz overrun with these beasts?"

"We use the front-end product to heat our houses in the winter," said Wanaderella. "And the rear end, merchandises as fertilizer. In our main Winkie bakeries, the dragons are used to keep the ovens warm. Oh look, here comes the noon delivery of baked goods now."

Flying in from the west was a line of six dragons pulling carts. They all landed in the central square. Thin veils of steam trickled out of their nostrils. When the last beast landed, a Winkie came out of the house closest to the center square, reached up, and pulled on a long cord. There came a piercing whistle, and dozens of people garbed in yellow came streaming out of the houses and began unloading the carts. The dragons ignored the activity, and instead reached into packs that were strung around their necks, with delicate front claws, and pulled out slender reed-like stems. At the same time, each beast breathed out fire, inhaled on the reeds, and blew out smoke. All the dragons exclaimed simultaneously, "Ahhhh."

Wanaderella frowned. "Nasty habit, but we can't get them to stop smoking Ozlocoweed. They say it helps them fly."

The uncovered carts gave off the baking aroma of ginger and turmeric. Dozens of biscuits, muffins, rolls, and donuts were unloaded. Children, tinier versions of the already short people unloading, would often, run up and filch baked goods. They seemed to concentrate on the donuts' boxes.

Diggs wandered over and grabbed a donut as well. He took a bite. Thick cream oozed out and ran down his chin, and the confectionary coated his lips with powdered sugar. Some of the sugar drifted down onto his greatcoat. Diggs started to brush it off, but instead, wet his finger, scooped it up, and smiled. "Color blends with my wizard clothes, so who cares? Now, where are the baked goods coming from? Don't you make them here? These donuts are amazing."

"Most Winkies are farmers or bakers," said Wanaderella. "Here in Winkieburg we concentrate on farming. We sell our wheat, corn, and yellow squash to the bakers and cooks in central Winkie country. There are huge bakeries in those cities. They use the raw materials and turn out these wonderful baked goods and trade them all over Oz. Plus we have the finest muffin, croissants, tart, and wheat bread bushes in all of Oz. The donuts have to be filled after being picked. We had it easy, bartering in the central market with Gillikins, Quadlings and Munchkins. Now that we can communicate with our fellow Emerald City citizens in the future, it will be easier yet."

The last Winkies in the unloading assembly line reached in the bottom of the carts and picked up smaller containers with steam coming off of them. The people juggled the boxes and screamed, "Hot, hot, hot!"

"What are they unloading now?" said Diggs. "Such an unusual aroma, it doesn't smell like spices used for baking. If my nose doesn't deceive me, it smells like mustard and curry powder."

Wanaderella giggled. "That crazy chef must be in charge and cooking today. Sheik Abu Dorina is from the middle eastern part of the country is making his famous scorpion peppers, curry laden pot pies. They're not real popular. They burn everyone's mouth off. The dragons love them, though. Would you like to try one?"

Diggs grimaced. "No, thank you. I want to continue to keep my taste buds. But speaking of dragons, where do all these beasts come from?"

"I'm surprised you would ask that, oh Great Oz," said Wanaderella. "They all came from your world, Earth."

Diggs squeezed his donut. The rest of the cream exploded from the center, and hit Bort right in the chest. "What?"

Chapter Thirty-Six

Wanaderella batted her eyes, smiled, and gestured broadly with both arms. "Silly! The Land of Oz is only isolated from nearby lands, physically. The Deadly Desert surrounds us and cuts us off from neighboring countries. Magically, we are a separate world, but intricately connected to your planet Earth." She motioned to a lad, to pick up another donut. Wanaderella took the pastry from the child and handed it to the wizard.

Diggs seized the new donut from her, but didn't bring it to his mouth. He pointed it at Wanaderella. "Please continue."

Bort wiped the cream from Diggs' squeezed donut off the front of his fur. He looked at his messy fingers, put his digits into his mouth, licked and swallowed. "Good."

Wanaderella stared at Bort, grimaced, and sighed. "Now, the dragons like to tell tales of evolving from beasts called dinosaurs. When they came over early to Oz, they kept their feathers and were peace-loving creatures. If they stayed on Earth longer, and came later, they evolved differently. Those later dragons developed a love of battling and grew scales instead of feathers. The Giant Chasm Dragon enjoys relating how his great-great-grandfather used to fight with metal men on Earth, called 'knights.'"

Diggs swung his new donut back and forth, gesturing with it at each key point in her dialogue. Every time he waved the pastry, more cream came out the end. Bort followed the stream of pastry filling, mouth opening and snapping, like a trained seal leaping in the air after a fish.

Wanaderella just frowned at the Gillikin. "That's why the Giant Dragon loves to joust anyone who enters his territory, but never really kills them, just threatens to eat them. He says he only met one real knight."

"Wait, what are you saying," asked Diggs. "There are magical ways to come to Oz? And the Chasm Dragon was never really dangerous? I lost my best friend, Chang, for nothing?"

Wanaderella patted Diggs on his chest. "I am so sorry to hear of the loss of your friend. We thought you both had come through a portal. After all, no one had heard of anyone coming via a portal for hundreds of years. We rejoiced when we heard a mighty wizard had finally arrived!"

Diggs pointed the donut at Wanaderella. "I must find a portal to go home again. Where are they?"

"I can't comment on these magical portals. I do not know where you would find them?"

"I will send out a royal decree and have everyone search for them."

Wanaderella wrinkled her brow. "Like I said, no one has come through or even seen one for centuries. Our dragon friends came a long time ago and settled in Winkie country. They love the golden sunshine and they are multiplying like mice."

"Hey," yelled a voice from Diggs' greatcoat pocket. "I resent that remark."

Diggs shook his head. "So, the seer told me I would see my friend again, although in a novel form. She was quite confusing and extremely slimy. Couldn't understand half of what she predicted. But if Chang is alive and finds his way to the 'green' area, we now have a way back home. I just have to find one of these magic dragon portals."

"We do not want you to leave," said Wanaderella. "Also, the magic portals are extremely difficult to find." She held her hands palms upwards and shrugged her shoulders.

"If you're done being impressed," said Bort. "The next town on the tour will really amaze you, Munch. My village is small, but the most important one in the grouping." He tugged on Diggs' sleeve. "Right this way." Bort pointed with his blunted spear.

"I hate to interject," said Diggs. "But perhaps we should go see Martha's village next. The mystery concerning her size and language intrigues me."

Bort pouted. "No fair."

Martha shook her head. "Prepared a major event for you. 'Tis not ready yet, I predict."

Diggs gestured at the Gillikin. "All right, Bort. Lead on."

A dense forest grew to the north of the ruins on a tall hill. Nestled in front of the woods was a small grouping of purple huts. As the entourage came closer, Diggs saw the huts were actually canvas tents. In front of the 'houses' stood drying racks with many pelts and furs of various sizes. Next to the racks were huge fire pits, with smoke billowing out of them. Men, women, and even children, all dressed in torn purple furs, were busy roasting huge carcasses of meat in the embers of the pits. The cooks were turning the roasts with charred bloody spears.

"Best meat in all of Oz," said Bort. He pointed to a far pit with his spear. "That beast I killed yesterday with this very spear. It was a larbor, err… larberos, larborisss, err, tough battle."

"Laborious?" suggested the Wizard. Diggs coughed and waved his hand briskly in front of his eyes. "Why is there so much smoke? Why don't you just cook them, not carbonize them?"

"You have to really roast them to get all the poison out of the meat so it's able to be eaten." Bort put two filthy fingers in his mouth and gave a piercing whistle. "I'm calling my hunting partner for you to meet."

From out of one of the tents came a woman leading a large, furry, sinuous creature on a leash. The lady had a head of black hair cascading to the ground. In her other hand, she carried a gleaming short sword, and was dressed in fur from neck to ankles, with heavy boots. The woman came up to Diggs and Bort and stopped.

Diggs reached down to shake her hand but hesitated, since both of hers were occupied. "Madame, I hear you are an expert hunter."

"Nah," said Bort. "That's just my sister, Brenda Beeezelman. Best butcher in all of Munch. This is my hunting partner, Spot."

The furry creature stood up from all fours and held out its paw. It stood eye level with Diggs and towered over everyone else in the touring group. It was thin, had slick brown fur and a narrow tail. With one paw, it raised up, from off his eyes, oversized, tinted spectacles.

"What manner of beast are you good, err... sir?" said Diggs. He hesitantly took up the other paw and shook it.

"Sebastian Percival Oberon Tiberius at your service," said the creature. He whispered, "Bort cannot remember my entire name, so I just let him call me Spot. I am, man-wearing-wizard white, a giant weasel."

"A weasel? Why don't Gillikins just use dogs?" Diggs let go of the paw, saw his hand was muddy, and wiped it on the back of his trousers.

"Never heard of that animal," said Spot. "Are you sure they exist? Besides, only weasels are used to hunt basilisks. We are immune to their poisonous bite, and our trendy specs help us avoid their paralyzing gaze."

Diggs shook his head. "Now a basilisk is a creature that really doesn't exist. Just an exaggeration."

"If so, then what is roasting on that fire?" Spot pointed to the smokiest fire pit. He reached up and unclasped the leash and collar from around his neck. "Here Bort, Brenda made this for you."

"Are you done with me, wizard man?" said Brenda. "Then I have to go pluck the feathers off a cockatrice and cook it. Now Bort, put on the collar, Spot is tired of you getting lost in the forest during each hunt. By the way, hunters, Brave Brandon is going to look for a manticore tomorrow. You are both invited if you're not too chicken."

"Bort," said Spot. "It takes real cunning to kill a manticore. Let's stick to easier beasts."

"Aw shucks, partner," said Bort. "You never let me have any fun."

"A cockatrice, a basilisk, a manticore?" said Diggs. "Impossible. Those are mythological beasts. Next you will tell me ancient Earth creatures like the wooly mammoth or giant sloth are found in Oz."

Both Spot and Bort pointed to three of the drying racks. On them was a massive, brown, shaggy pelt that overflowed all three and still spilled significantly onto the ground. They next pointed to a central tent which had a roof composed of a different giant fur.

"But," sputtered Diggs. "Those creatures are extinct?"

Bort wiped the spittle off his face. His hand left streaks of clear areas in the midst of dirt, soot, and grim. He shook his head. "Naw, they live all over the forests of Gillikin country and don't stink at all."

Diggs laughed. "How is it possible that dragons live in Winkie country and mythological or extinct beasts live in Gillikin country?"

"The Land of Oz is truly a magical place," said Spot. "All these creatures existed in Oz and used to visit your world until they had to escape because humans persecuted them or the weather got too cold."

Diggs stared at the weasel in amazement. "Another portal from this land of Oz to my planet? Sounds like a significantly easier way to go home then by exploding balloon."

"Indubitably," said Spot. "But not always open and difficult to locate. Of course, the beasts used them for centuries. These include giants, cyclops, harpies, and gigantic bees found in Winkie country, numerous different dinosaurs in Gillikin country, and the weird race of people in Munchkin country."

Bort sniffed the air and drooled, "Hungry, oh Great Oz? Care for some brontosaurus stew? It's very fresh."

"This is just preposterous," said Diggs. He threw both hands, palms up, into the air.

Spot stared right into Diggs' eyes. "By the way, the rumor going round is that after you build a central city here, you are going to conquer and unite the rest of Oz."

Diggs backed up. "No, I was told that I will meet my long-lost friend in a green area. So, I decided to build the Emerald City." He sighed and shook his head. "I'm not a fighter."

"I'm not sure you could avoid it," said Spot. "All the evil witches will not stand for anyone coming in and taking over any of their territories. You will have to fight all of them or quickly make alliances."

Diggs shuddered. "An alliance with Mombi, yuck! But I don't think she will give me any problems. I sorely regret it, but I already did her a huge favor."

Spot sniffed the air. "The smoke is shifting, we should move before basilisk roasted poisonous fumes overcome your group. : Evanora, the witch of the East, is mostly a non-violent person, plus her troops are just Munchkins. Theodora, of the West, is another story. She commands legions of creatures. And a word of advice, never try to confront her troops if you hear howling, or during a full moon."

Diggs stared at the weasel. "You can't mean that included in her armamentarium are werewolves?"

Chapter Thirty-Seven

"I really don't want to fight anyone," said Diggs. "After I build the 'green' area, I hope Chang, in whatever form he's in, will find me. Although, with my mighty wizard powers, I'm sure the evil witches will be no match for me." Diggs fingers cramped as he crossed them behind his back again.

"There are only a few homes remaining in Munch," said Bort. "Mombi flew in on her broom and with the help of the flying monkeys enslaved most of Gillikin country, this village included. The few of us who escaped did so because we were hunting in the dense forest. I really miss my fourteen brothers and six sisters." A tear ran down his face, clearing another small line on his dusty face.

"Mombi's powers appeared weaker the last time I confronted her," said Diggs.

Bort lifted his broken spear and shook it threateningly. "So, will you help us overthrow her? I will be happy to fight at your side."

Diggs cleared his throat. "Er, humph, of course, of course. But first we have a lot of building to do. Is there anything else to see in Munch?"

Spot laughed. "No, you hit the chief points."

"Then, oh Great Oz, we should move on," said Martha. "It is time for my Munchkins' special program." She turned and whispered out the side of her mouth, "'tis wise that you didn't partake in the brontosaurus stew——terrible gamey taste."

The group skirted the edge of the purple forest and headed east. The village of Roundstone consisted of rows of tiny, neat blue houses with blue lawns, and various fruits and vegetable trees planted around the village. But as opposed to the empty central squares in the other villages, in Roundstone's middle, was a large group of extremely short men, dressed entirely in green.

The dozens of men all stood as short as Martha, about the height of Diggs' knee. Besides their green outfits, they all wore tall green hats and green and white striped stockings. Every one of them had scraggly reddish-green beards, and many had corn cob pipes tucked into the corners of their lips. Perhaps because of their height or their immature beards, they all looked about seventeen years old. The men huddled around a large black kettle and several toted musical instruments.

"Great Oz," said Martha. "Present to ye, the Roundstone Old Folks Home Ensemble, may we. They will play a song, sing, and dance for you, to welcome you to Roundstone village."

"Old folks?" said Diggs. "They all look extremely young. And what in the world are those unusual instruments? I recognize the routine ones, fiddles, miniature harps and is that some type of banjo, but those others?"

The instrument wielders formed a line and the ones without, stepped forward. The non-musicians took their lit pipes out of their mouths and placed them in their pockets. From out of the houses streamed a dozen blue clad women, who joined the first line of men. Martha excused herself and joined the line with the women.

"A one, a two," yelled one man in the back row. The man was carrying an instrument which looked surprisingly similar to an octopus. "For you, Oz, we play poems and songs with pipes and drums. A thousand welcomes when anyone comes… That's the Irish for you. As we like to say, 'May you be in heaven a full half hour before the devil knows you're dead'."

"What?" said Diggs. "What do you mean, the Irish?"

Everyone not holding an instrument broke into a Gaelic song and began dancing a jig. The dancers started with their arms completely at their sides. As the tempo changed, they changed to skipping, and then changed again into whirling reels, with their arms thrown over their heads. The performance went on for a full hour.

Diggs scratched his nose and smiled. "So much energy they have," he whispered to his pockets. "I assume you piglets are as hungry as I am right now."

Frederick poked his head out of one pocket. "We're all starving. No food in over an hour! You should hear all the growling tummies!"

At the conclusion of the concert, Diggs, the piglets, the representatives, and the rest of Roundstone village burst into applause. The entire ensemble bowed deeply, and the octopus player drained saliva out of a spit valve of his instrument. The remaining musicians began to pack up their equipment in cases that were stashed behind the kettle.

"I want to shake the ensemble's hands and look at those strange musical instruments," said Diggs. "I now see a guitar in the back row. Played some fiddle myself, when I was younger. But there are a lot of things I don't recognize."

Martha came over, her face dripping sweat. "Enjoy it, did ye? We practiced and performed for our village often, but never for Smithersonville, Munch, or Winkieburg. Before your spell, they wouldn't have understood our Munchkin language."

Diggs held up his hand. "Now wait, was it Munchkin or Irish? Your words sounded like something my Irish cop friend, Patrick, would have said? And where did all these strange musical instruments come from?" Diggs walked past the kettle and then halted. "What the hell?"

The black kettle came up to Diggs' waist. He bent over, drooling slightly, and with a trembling hand reached inside. Diggs pulled out a handful of yellow coins. "Is this what I think it is?"

"Aye, 'tis a pot of gold," said Martha. "Worthless in Oz but in Roundstone, we always say, 'May your pockets always hold a coin or two.' So we like to have some ready when we come to your Earth. I so hoped you enjoyed the concert and dancing."

Diggs muttered to himself, "I can't resist." He peered over his shoulder as he slipped some coins into his front pocket. "Loved the concert, but please tell me what those unusual musical instruments were that they were playing?" He pointed at the empty cases. Diggs continued to covertly slip more gold into his pocket.

"Let's get the conductor to tell us their names," said Martha. She waved at a short man, dressed all in green, who carried a baton. The man bounded over to them and bowed.

"Enjoy the concert and singing, did ye, Oh Oz?" said the conductor. The man stood as tall as Martha, barely to Diggs' knee. His eyes twinkled with merriment, and he smiled constantly. The words that came out of his mouth were musical.

"Great Oz, may I introduce to you my husband, Shamus McDoodles," said Martha. "Married unhappily these last 360 years. But as my pa said, 'Better be quarreling than lonesome'." She smiled as she quoted her father.

"Now Martha," said Shamus. "It 'tis not so bad, I be saying. May the hinges of our friendship never grow rusty." He leered broadly and winked at her. "And ye know how to oil me fence post."

Martha giggled. "Now, Shamus, Oz wants all the names of all of our unique instruments. Especially the octopus one."

"Aye, Oz, you have a keen eye. These beauties came over from the old country, 900 years ago. The one you are referring to is an Uilleann pipe. Only three of them in all of Munchkin country. Very difficult to master, and Murphy is excellent on the beast. Let me call him over."

The man who came over to the group looked similar to Shamus. He carried a miniature instrument which looked somewhat like an octopus, with fewer legs. "Me pipes inflate with this here bellows. I wear them strapped to me waist and I don't have to blow into the pipes at all. It lets me sing with me wonderful voice."

"Ach, the sound of ye singing could curdle milk," said Shamus while laughing. "If we let any of our blue cows near ye."

Murphy swung the metal pipe end at Shamus's head. Diggs noted that Murphy deliberately missed striking the conductor.

"I be the only Uilleann pipe player in the land who can play while standing," said Murphy. "It be because of my great strength. Me muscles have developed from hoisting so many mugs of beer."

"Aye, I be always parched myself," said Shamus. "Great Oz. We also serenaded you with tea accordions, different flutes and whistles, a bandore and several small harps."

"Which instrument is the bandore?" said Diggs. "I'm not familiar with that term."

Shamus pointed at the instrument being put into its case. "In your country, you might have called it a banjo."

Diggs clandestinely reached for one more handful from the kettle. "Err... why is there a huge container of gold just sitting out in the open?"

"As you know, gold is worthless in Oz," said Martha. "You people think highly of it in your home. Every hundred years or so, we like to visit your world and bring some trinkets along."

"You Munchkins have visited my Earth?" said Diggs. "How come no one has ever reported such short people? At least, none that I ever heard of?"

Martha reached for Shamus' hand. "Only the men visit. We women folk have more important matters at home and hearth to take care of. We never leave the village, just let the men roam."

Shamus reached into his pocket with his other hand and took out his still lit pipe. "Aye, I myself visited two hundred years ago. One tall folk almost caught me. Lost me favorite green hat escaping. "

Diggs pointed to all the men. "I'm honored you've heard that everyone is going to be citizens of my Emerald City and have already found green clothes."

"Sorry I am, oh Oz," said Shamus. "'Tis not in your honor we wear green. That color's been the garb of all leprechauns for years."

"This is just impossible," sputtered Diggs.

Chapter Thirty-Eight

"Ach, we love to travel, 'tis loads of fun," said Shamus. "Every couple of hundred years, our village goes to Earth for a month. Latesha, the Good Witch of the North, before Mombi destroyed her, loved to go with us." He took a deep draw on his pipe and blew out a perfect shamrock shaped smoke ring. "Did ye ever hear of witches in your world? Where do ye think they came from? I really want to go back to the old country, but not sure if any of the witches will send us agin'. Mombi never leaves her castle. Perhaps you, oh Great Oz, will work some magic and send us off?"

Diggs stared down at the little man. "Ah…" He paused in mid-sentence. "Maybe I could use my second magic cap wish to take have those monkeys take everyone, back to Earth?"

Shamus blew out a banana shaped smoke ring. "Nay, those magic beasts cain not exist outside of our lands."

" I wish there was a simple way to get home. This is getting to be too much to handle. So do disappearing villages, mythical creatures, witches, and even leprechauns, all come from Oz?"

"Aye," said Shamus and Martha both. They smiled and looked at each other. In concert they said, "Oz be a magical land, full of wonder."

"I'm sure the old country wants to see our village and pot of gold again," said Shamus. "Hopefully, we'll be leaving agin' in seventy years. If ye can't take us, we just have to figure out how to get there." He blew out another smoke ring, a perfect coin shape with Diggs' face on one side, the word 'Oz' on the other. "Do ye want to come along?"

Diggs slapped his hand to his forehead. "My head hurts. Several months ago, I was transporting wounded soldiers, getting shot at by Rebs, and eating the worst food of my life. Today I'm talking to leprechauns, having spells cast on me by witches, and eating gourmet food from lunchpail trees. This is still hard to understand and can't be real." He shivered despite the heat.

Shamus put his hand on his hip and glared. "What do ye mean, real? We be as undeniable as the nose on my face." He puffed on his pipe and blew out smoke, showing an angry leprechaun with an enormous nose.

Diggs shook his head. "No one on Earth ever catches a leprechaun. You're just rumors when there is mischief. Only stories about the 'wee men'."

Shamus waved his pipe back and forth. "We like to have a little fun. Ye do not see the women folk, they just stay in the village, singing, dancing, cooking, and drinking ale and our Irish mint tea."

Martha boxed his ears. She then wagged her finger at her husband. "Ye make it sound like we women folk do nothing important in Oz or on Earth. Why, if it weren't for us you never would have food, clean clothes, or have anyone save you when caught by the big folks? Shamus McDoodles, ye be sleeping on the couch again tonight."

Her husband hung his head, looked back up, and gave her a hangdog look. "Now sweetums, ye know I was only fooling. We men only get in trouble when in Ireland. We never cause mischief in Oz."

Martha grinned, showing deep dimples. "That is a false tale." She wagged her finger at him. "Why it just be yesterday, I had to drag you home from the pub after a drunken brawl with Will O'Reilly."

Shamus looked defiantly at his wife. "Ach, the man said he should be head conductor. Anyway, I was winning."

Diggs smiled. "It sounds like you manage to get in trouble while you're here in Oz."

The other small men dressed in green, packed up the rest of the instruments and left. From out of one of the houses on the square, came an old man dressed in blue. For a Munchkin, he was huge, as tall as Diggs. His beard was blue tinged and full of bits of shiny metal, his clothes tattered and filthy. But he was wearing pristine, large eye-glasses that sparkled in the sunlight. The spectacles kept sliding down his nose.

"I'm glad that noise has finished," said the tall Munchkin. "I couldn't hear myself think." He walked up to Diggs and stuck out his hand. "Ku-Klip is the name, tin smithing is my game."

Diggs grabbed the hand, looked down at it, and tentatively gave it one pump. He then lifted it up and looked at the calloused ridges on all fingers with grimy dirt under each bitten down nail. "Huh, what did you say? I'm confused? Who are you?"

Martha disengaged, the two men's hands. "Oz, may I introduce to you Ku-Klip, our Roundstone resident oddball and builder."

"Master tinsmith, at your service," bragged Ku-Klip. "I can build anything, even once re-built a man who had managed to cut himself into pieces."

Diggs gave the man a hesitant smile. "So you can help build my palace and Emerald City?"

"I would be happy to! It'll be the best tin castle in all of Oz!"

Diggs stepped back and looked at the man. "Use tin, never!" He threw up his hands. "We must make it of marble, granite, and emeralds. Not, that cheap metal."

Ku-Klip glared at the wizard and shook his head. "Sorry, tin is the only substance I deal with. And it's amazing to use! Why, if I had any idea where that tin man I built years ago was today, I'd show you."

"Thanks anyway, builder," said Diggs. "But why does this small town of Roundstone have its own resident tinsmith? There can't be that much call for business?"

Ku-Klip looked over his shoulder. "I'm hiding from Evanora, the witch of the East. She's not happy with me for tinafying together her servant's suitor after the witch made his axe chop him up. Best work I ever did."

Diggs stared at Ku-Klip. "What in the world are you talking about?"

"Long story," said the tinsmith. "I'll tell you another time, wiz." He turned and looked down at Shamus. "Conductor, I'm leaving this town. Too noisy!" He reached up and pulled tin ear plugs out of his ears. "I'm going back to my forest. I'll send for all my manufacturing tools later." He walked away.

Martha looked nervous. "Great Oz, Ku-Klip was our only artisan in all of Roundstone. I doubt if any of the other countries' villages have any builders to help you construct your city. We might have to send out word throughout the Land of Oz to get you some help?"

Diggs rubbed his chin, pondering Martha's question. "I don't want to wait that long. I know!" He patted his head and almost knocked off his top hat. "I'll use my second wish from the magic cap." He gestured to the crowd and pointed. "Everyone, back to my balloon."

One piglet raised its head from his pocket. "Is it time for lunch?"

Several inhabitants of Roundstone followed the group towards the OZ balloon. Shamus yelled to his band to bring out their instruments, so they could have a parade. Even Ku-Klip came back to investigate what was the excitement. The cacophony brought out more residents of Smithersonville, Munch, and Winkieburg. The two Quadling captains had found the rifle, and they took turns shooting it into the air. The crowd grew to several hundred by the time it arrived at the OZ balloon.

In front of the gondola, Ortho and his companions were snoozing on the ground. The noise of the parade woke them up. They stretched and screeched at the people.

The nine piglets crawled out of Diggs' pocket. They scampered under the railing of the gondola and then climbed up the slats.

Diggs climbed over the railing and dropped into the gondola. He bent down and rummaged through his carpet bag. Diggs pulled something out of the bag and stuffed it into his front pocket. He turned back to face the crowd and loudly cleared his throat.

All the inhabitants of the future Emerald City crowded around the gondola. Diggs' two Quadling bodyguards struck a regal pose in front of the balloon and stood at attention. However, a few minutes later, the two men quarreled and began tussling over who got to hold the one antiquated rifle. Ortho and his four companions jumped up and down with excitement. The nine piglets lined up on the railing of the gondola and watched Diggs intently.

Diggs put one hand into his shirt and raised his other one. He put one foot on the bottom slat of the railing and raised himself up. He boomed, "my fellow Ozians! With the help of my powerful magic and the Flying

Monkeys, I will build the Emerald City in just a week." He puffed out his chest.

The nine piglets let out a cheer.

Diggs pulled the Golden Flying Monkey cap out of his pocket and placed it on his head. He muttered to the piglets, "I feel like I'm Lincoln giving that there Gettysburg Address."

"Who?" asked Miss Scarlet. "Is it good to eat?"

Diggs hopped off the railing and reached down into his carpetbag. He pulled out tinker box number one, held it up to his mouth, but shook his head and put the magic item back into the bag.

Slim stared at Diggs. "Dang good idear, oh Great Oz, not to use that damn thing. The last time, it purt-near ruined my eardrums."

"I thought it might have more showmanship, if I only used my natural booming voice," said Diggs. "But it might be too much to use the magic box. I'll just have to project." He stood on his left foot, raised his right hand, and said, "Ep-pe, pep-pe, kak-ke." Diggs switched to his right foot, raised his left hand, "Hil-lo, hol-lo, hel-lo." Now he stood on both feet, "Now I'll bring it home. Just like I'm back performing in the circus. Ladies and gentlemen, in the center ring. Now Diggs, stop your fantasizing." He raised both his arms and yelled, "Zoz-zy, zaz-zy, zonk." Nothing happened.

Chapter Thirty-Nine

Diggs threw up his hands. "What the hell? Why isn't it working?" He pulled the hat off his head, wheeled around, and peered anywhere for any of the flying monkeys. Diggs started to throw it to the ground but instead held it out to Ortho and whimpered.

Ortho frowned, and then sighed. "You might want to refresh your memory of the correct words." The monkey pointed into the magic cap. "You botched up the spell."

Diggs whined. "Did not."

"Did so," yelled Ortho. "Read the inscription to yourself again."

Diggs held the hat up to almost touching his face, squinted his eyes, and moved his lips. "Damn. You're right."

Diggs jammed the cap back onto his head. He stood on his left foot, raised his right hand, and said, "Ep-pe, pep-pe, kak-ke." He switched to his right foot, raised his left hand, "Hil-lo, hol-lo, hel-lo." Now he stood on both feet, "I won't goof this up again." Diggs raised both his arms and only whispered, "Ziz-zy, zuz-zy, zik?"

The horde of arriving monkeys blotted out the sun. The king landed first, just in front of the gondola. Then his royal bodyguards arrived. As Nikko folded his wings, he walked up to Diggs. The ground thudded as the remaining hundreds of monkeys delicately came down.

"We are here to answer your second wish," said King Nikko. He turned and glared at his screeching troops. "Quiet! I can't hear myself think." Nikko turned back to face Diggs. "What do you desire? Wish carefully. You only get one more after this one."

"I command you and your troops to build an Emerald City, right there," said Diggs. With a grand and sweeping gesture, he pointed to the hill and surrounding countryside.

"Give me a break," said Nikko. "We're just fucking monkeys, not architects. We're good at tearing down things, but building? Do you have blueprints or even emeraldprints?"

Ku-Klip hesitantly stepped forward. "If you changed your mind about it being all tin? I could whip you up some plans in no time."

Diggs held up his empty hands. "I can't draw up any plans. Wait, I know! How about a large-scale model?"

"That would work," said Nikko. "Where is it?" The monkey scratched his groin. One body guard stepped forward, picked fleas off of the king, and then popped each insect into the monarch's mouth. A crunching sound filled the air.

Diggs made a stay motion to the king. "Wait right here. Ortho, fly into my gondola and get me my carpetbag."

Nikko stopped chewing. "Yes, go lapdog Ortho. Running errands is all you're good for anymore."

Ortho bared his teeth and hissed at Nikko. He turned, unfurled his wings, and flew into the OZ gondola. In just a short time, he returned, carrying Diggs' carpet bag. Ortho dropped it at Diggs' feet, then stuck out his tongue and gave Nikko a raspberry.

Diggs rummaged through the bag and pulled out tinker box number two. He looked up in the air and thought for a full half hour.

The monkeys howled and screeched. Several of them threw feces at the Munchkins hats and hooted with each direct hit.

Diggs grimaced at the beasts and then spoke quietly into one end of the magic box for about fifteen minutes.

The monkeys began wrestling with each other. Shamus challenged a smaller male to a fall, and the beast defeated him in seconds.

Immediately, a ten-foot model appeared. Everyone stared, and all horseplay stopped.

The model showed the four villages surrounded by a high green wall with only one central gate. A green brick road led up to the gate. The wall displayed banners with 'OZ' in white letters every twenty feet. At the four corners of the walled city were watch towers.

Each house, in every outlying village, was of the same green color. Roadways connected the separate towns, and each municipality had innumerable parks, fountains, and majestic green gardens scattered throughout. The fountain gave off a lime scented water, which sprayed forth and tinkled merrily while changing to a different shade of green every minute.

The roads inside the city, and connecting the villages, were of crushed emeralds. Placed throughout each garden were statues of Diggs, wearing white wizard clothes. In the center of the model, rose a huge palace with four towers. The top of the major section of the palace was flat and had a label, 'BalloonaPad Site.' Painted on the ground of the landing site, was a huge 'OZ'.

Surrounding the palace were smaller buildings, labeled with signs such as Police Station, Accounting Office, Visitors Bureau, Lunchpail Tree Restaurant, and several Bars. The entire model structure glowed with a green hue and gave off a welcoming smell, like freshly baked mint cookies.

"Wait until you see the details on the inside of the palace," said Diggs. "What do you think, Nikko? Maybe a few more statues of me?" He carefully put the Illusion Maker on the ground. Diggs pointed to the top of the hill where the ruins were still located. "Use the material from the 'Emerald Citadel' to start the palace. We should make the walls out of granite."

Ku-Klip raised his hand "Ah."

"No, tinsmith," said Diggs. "No part of the city can be out of tin. Now Nikko, part of your troop should mine the marble and granite." He beamed with excitement. "Part will build the exterior of the city and the rest the interior. Be sure to build a strong wall for protection. It must fully enclose all my future inhabitants. We'll use the lake to irrigate the gardens and trees. The fountains are only for decoration. Nikko, I need the entire city built in one week."

The king chortled. "Ain't going to happen."

Shamus danced an excited jig and blew out a miniature Emerald City smoke ring from his pipe. "What do ye want us Munchkins to do?"

"The leprechauns will find emeralds," said Diggs. "We'll need plenty for adornment of the roads and to put on the walls of the palace."

"Are you done with our services, Oz?" said Ortho. "My followers and I got you here and we wish to go home. I'm having trouble breathing from the stench of these new arrivals. When I ran the clan, we were never so unruly or unkempt."

Diggs shook his head. "Not yet, Ortho. I really need your help. You and your companions will be in charge of running errands and communication. I might need to talk to the Chasm Dragon or the Silver Seer, to see if I have any questions about if I am going about this correctly and how I'll be reunited with my friend Chang again." He sighed, "I really miss that idiot."

Nikko stuck out his tongue at the old king. "Yes, Ortho, you just run errands. You're good at that. Are you sure you can find the chasm again? You never did find Pastoria."

Ortho furled his wings, bared his teeth, snarled, and threw himself at Nikko. Nikko's bodyguards leapt in front of the king and seized Ortho before he touched the monarch.

The bodyguards shook Ortho 'til his teeth rattled. "Shall we kill him, sire?" The four of them had no difficulty containing the elderly ex-king.

Diggs quickly reached down and picked up from his carpetbag, his tinker box, number one. He lifted it up and whispered into it. Immediately, the words, "STOP YOU FOOLS!" bellowed out.

All the monkeys looked over at Diggs. They all shuddered and cringed. Nikko's guards released Ortho, but one gave him one final shake. Ortho glared at the bodyguards. The ten-foot model of the Emerald City faded away.

Diggs dropped tinker box number one and looked disgusted. He stared down at the now turned off Illusion Maker and scratched his head. Diggs then took off his top hat, threw it down, and stomped on it. "Oh shit! All that planning and thinking. I forgot 'Stop' turns off the illusion. Well, back to the drawing board."

Chapter Forty

Diggs picked up the Illusion Maker and shook it. "Damn, hair trigger mechanism," he grumbled. "Now, this thing will only respond to the first person talking. So you all will not interfere with my images, but please keep me from saying s-t-o-p. By the way, is there a time limit on a wish?"

"We will serve you as long as it takes to build the Emerald City," said Nikko. "But of course we don't have a model anymore."

"When I was king, we honored all wishes, no matter the time involved," said Ortho. "Mombi's third wish was to find Pastoria. My companions and I searched for two hundred years. We flew everywhere in Oz, but couldn't find him. When I came back to Mombi's castle to tell her I would keep looking, this upstart had stolen my throne."

"All real Flying Monkeys will honor any wish," said Nikko. "And we'll not fail like someone else I know."

Both monkeys bared teeth and hissed at each other. They advanced, furled, and unfurled their wings, beat on their chests, and danced around each other.

Diggs stepped forward and put his arms between the monkeys. "Boys, boys, calm down. Too much work ahead of us for there to be fighting." He put the Illusion Maker up to his mouth and whispered into it continuously for one hour.

All four of Nikko's companions continued to glare at Ortho, to make sure he didn't make any threatening moves towards their king.

Shamus turned back to his monkey foe again. "We still have some time, two out of three falls?"

The monkey just scratched.

Finally, a similar model appeared before everyone. This time, however, all the buildings splayed open so one could study the interior. In the Emerald City, all the village houses had the typical chairs, beds, and cooking areas. The buildings surrounding the palace showed desks, chairs, and tables. The police station had a formidable-looking jail and all the bars had long counters with tall chairs under it. So detailed was the model that there were even spigot beer taps and tiny emerald bottles behind the counters on the 'Bar'.

The lunchpail restaurant had a myriad of transplanted trees surrounding it. Inside the building were many tables, chairs, and a long counter with emerald colored sawdust on the floor. The kitchen had a roaring fireplace, with nothing cooking in it. From the fireplace, billowed smoke.

The interior of the palace was magnificent. Multiple levels with several bedrooms scattered throughout. Overstuffed furniture was in the master bedroom, and the bed looked like it could fit two. A massive throne loomed in a large room with no other furniture. In every room, were tall, burning tapers.

All the furniture, fixtures, even booze bottles, and other accoutrements were green.

"I hope this is detailed enough for your clan," said Diggs. "I'm especially proud of the interior details. Why the inside looks so comfortable, I might even stay after my friend Chang finds his way here. Yep, that's me, the Wizard of Oz, the Great and Powerful." He reached for his nonexistent suspenders to strut. "Use the granite and marble from the destroyed Emerald Citadel to start the building."

"The ruin will not have enough material to build an entire city," said Nikko. "Where do we get the rest of the granite and marble? And also, what about the insides? I doubt you want your bed to be made of stone?"

Ku-Klip stepped forward and raised his finger. "Ah, tin?"

"While I searched, for Pastoria," said Ortho. "I flew over granite quarries in the far eastern edge of Munchkin country, near the Deadly Desert. The stone is a blue-gray color. In the mountainous region of northern Quadling country, I can find a pinkish marble. So there is plenty of stone, but this won't make a green Emerald City?"

"Um, err, let me take care of that later," blustered Diggs. "This could be a big problem," he muttered to himself. "Nikko, here's how we'll get everything inside. Send part of your clan throughout Oz and tell the people there is now a new wizard tax. I shall collect it as pieces of furniture. We should be able to get enough pieces in no time."

"Are you sure you could find the stone, Ortho?" said Nikko. "Or are the rocks rattling around in your head the only ones you can easily find?"

Ortho pointed at Nikko's chest. "Do you want my help or not, youngster? Should we make the wizard wait months as you search fruitlessly?"

"Don't make me do a magic spell," threatened Diggs, while he had his fingers again crossed behind his back. "You will go look for the stone together. Ortho, I also want one of your companions to go with the group that collects the furniture tax. I want nice soft pieces. The last part of your clan, Nikko, can begin building with materials from the ruins immediately. I think we should start the palace first. It'll give my subjects something to look up to. Now fly monkeys, fly."

■ ■ ■

The outside walls of the palace took three weeks to build. One third of the flying monkeys used granite and marble from the ruins of the Emerald Citadel. Ku-Klip waited to leave and kept giving his two cents worth of advice. After the tin-smith butted in for the eighth time and recommended that one use tin instead of marble for the tenth time, Diggs lost his patience.

"Ku-Klip, either go back to your home in Munchkin country or just quit giving advice," said Diggs. "You're interfering with the flying monkeys and not helping."

"But tin would work so well for supporting walls," said Ku-Klip. He unrolled a dozen blue-prints to show his architectural points.

Diggs swept the plans off a short table onto the ground. "For the twentieth time, no! If you want to help, build a home for my piglets. They're tired of living in a urine-soaked nest."

Diggs stayed with an alternating village each week. While staying in Munch, he actually became fond of brontosaurus stew. He was once invited, to go on a manticore hunt by Brave Brandon, but Spot convinced him it was too dangerous. Spot didn't have to try very hard to talk him out of going.

Diggs' week in Smithersonville was very enjoyable. The Quadlings were excellent cooks and were masters at fish dishes. He stayed with his new tall royal guard twins and was pleased to finally sleep in a bed that was actually long enough for him. The large bed pleased Diggs, since most of the Quadlings only came up to his waist.

At the end of a pleasant week, Diggs packed his carpetbag and walked to Roundstone. He was looking forward to bantering with Martha, but he still had some questions to ask the Munchkins. The height difference continued to perplex Diggs. Whereas most inhabitants of Smithersonville, Munch, and Winkieburg were short and somewhat stout, the citizens of Roundstone varied significantly. Male leprechauns and their wives barely came up to his knee, but Ku-Klip and many other Munchkins were as tall or taller than Diggs.

Diggs walked up to Martha and Shamus's front door. He dropped his bag and knocked. Martha opened the door immediately. Shamus stood next to her.

Martha stepped forward and hugged his knee. "Welcome, oh Great Oz, welcome."

Diggs reached down and patted her on the head. "Looking forward to staying with you."

Ku-Klip came running up to Diggs. "Wiz, oh wiz, I have some great tin ideas for the piglet's castle." The tin-smith tapped him on the shoulder and tried to get Diggs to turn around.

Diggs reluctantly turned and looked Ku-Klip right in the eye. He then looked down at Martha. "It is most strange, that except for a few standouts," Diggs jabbed his finger into the tin-smith's chest, "the majority of Oz inhabitants are short. Why are Munchkins so varied?"

"It 'tis an interesting story, wizard," said Martha. "Years ago, all Munchkins were the same as the rest of Ozians. A good, but mischievous witch named Circe ruled us."

"Wait," said Diggs. "There was a Greek mythology witch named Circe."

Ku-Klip hurried away. "Boring! I have important work to do."

"That be her," said Shamus. "When she tired of causing trouble here in Oz, she went to Earth and built up her reputation there. I think she was the one who turned the lot of us into wee folk and transported Roundstone to Earth every hundred years. Finally, she just stayed on Earth."

"But—" sputtered Diggs.

"Then our next witch fell in love with some explorer from your world, who found his way to Oz," said Martha. "He was a tall man, so she transformed herself, and a lot of Munchkins, as house servants, into your man size and we've been different sizes since."

"Now I'm really confused," said Diggs. He looked down at the two Munchkins. "I wasn't the first person to travel to Oz? When did this take place and who was he?"

"Oh, a few years ago," said Shamus. "His name, his name? I ken remember? The witch named Morgan Le Fay."

Martha smiled happily and licked her lips. "That handsome man was Henry Hudson. Cute..." She looked up at the sky and sighed. "Why I'd have sat on his lap anytime, if you get me meaning." She poked Diggs in the knee with her elbow. "He stayed in Oz for many a year and then one day, poof, he and Le Fay just vanished. We be stuck with Evanora ever since. Evil she be, but not as wicked as her terrible sister or that Mombi."

"I read about Henry Hudson, the explorer who vanished," said Diggs. "And everyone knows about the fictitious witches Circe and Morgan Le Fay. Are you saying that all were related to Oz?"

"The same as dragons, ogres, cyclops, manticores, and non-extinct mammoths," said Shamus. "They all started out or ended up here in Oz. For a while, we worried we were going to be overrun with Earthians. But thank the heavens, no one for the past three hundred years."

"And great wizard, I hope you're the last," said Martha. "Now this week, Oz, ye stay with us. Shamus can sleep on the couch and you will share my bed."

Diggs smiled and shrugged his shoulders while looking down at the diminutive woman. "It is an intriguing offer, but anatomically impossible. I'd squash you."

Chapter Forty-One

On the last day of his week in the Munchkin village, Diggs stood outside his host's home smoking a miniature corn-cob pipe. "I sure miss my chewing tobacco."

Shamus hurried up to Diggs. "Great Oz, the leprechaun's chores be going well. We have found loads of emeralds for Emerald City's walls and roads. But the Gnome King refuses to allow us to dig for any more jewels, and we've run out. The internal green roads will end right at the main gate. What material should the monkeys use for any path leading up to the Emerald City?"

Diggs looked down at the man and raised one finger. He pulled it down, lifted it again, and scratched his head. Diggs again started to point at the gate, brought it down, and sighed. "Wait, I do have an idea." He walked back to the Illusion Maker, "now add a road going up to the main gate."

A large green brick road materialized, leading to the main gate of the model. The road was wide at the gate, but dwindled to nothingness about ten feet from the rest of the model.

"Ye, that be a road," said Shamus. "But we canna get any more emeralds for it. We need to make the bricks out of something else. Something common."

Diggs pulled some leprechaun gold coins out of an inside pocket. "That's it, something common. Have the monkeys use gold." He shook his head. "I can't believe I'm suggesting this." The man held the gold up to his heart and a tear came out of his eye. Diggs bent over the Illusion Maker again and muttered into the box. The green road turned yellow and immediately past the main gate split into four branches. One went north to Gillikin country, one east to Munchkin country, one west to Winkie country and one south to Quadling country. But they all joined up at the main gate, leading into the Emerald City, and all, were yellow brick.

Diggs packed up his belongings and headed to Smithersonville. He stretched and moaned. The beds at Shamus and Martha's home were so damn small.

Frederick and the rest of the piglets ran up to him. "Master," said the piglet leader. "We need a break from Ku-Klip. All he talks about is tin, tin, tin. Boring." The other eight piglets nodded their heads in agreement.

"Don't you like your new miniature castle home?" said Diggs. "I'm going to Smithersonville for a week. You all can come along."

"The house is bodacious, don't think I ever want to go back to Texas," said Slim. "And all the Winkie gals keep bringing us wonderful grub. But they all keep saying how beautiful yaller the food is, but it ain't. It's dadburn green."

Diggs reached down and put Slim in his pocket. "Piglet, I told you those magic spectacles have changed your color vision permanently. You'll have to live in a green world."

The remaining piglets squealed, "pick us up". Diggs divided the group and put half into each of the front pockets of his greatcoat. "I'm heading to Smithersonville, don't jump out of my pocket and fall into the lake. Can piglets swim?"

Abraham poked his head out of the pocket. "Oy vey. People say when a pig flies, now you want us to swim also? Just kidding, Oz. Practicing my stand-up routine."

Diggs grimaced, "Piglet, don't give up your day job."

Diggs finished walking to Smithersonville with various piglets, popping their heads out and giving various comments. He was pleased it was a quick journey, and he didn't have to put up with so many complaints.

Lothicia came out of her house and up to Diggs. "You would honor my husband and I if you would stay with us this week." The Quadling wore a red sundress with two huge front pockets. On her head was a colorful bonnet and draped around her neck was a pink kitten. From each pocket poked up another kitten. All three cats lifted their heads up and sniffed.

"Meow," said one kitten. "What's that wonderful smell? It's better than fish or stewed wooly mammoth." The feline licked its lips and purred.

Miss Scarlett raised her head out of Diggs' pocket, trembled, and cried. "Ah declare, Mister Oz, protect us from those horrible beasts. I'm sure the monsters want to devour us. They frighten me so. Why my body is all aquiver."

"Why I never," stated Lothicia. "My pink kittens would never do anything so naughty."

Slim popped up. "I'll protect you Miss Scarlet. I reckon if I had a shooting iron, I could make those ruffians dance."

"I knew there was a reason I was allergic to felines," said Diggs. "Don't worry, Slim and Miss Scarlet, no one or nothing is going to hurt you. If anything happened, those pink cats would have to face my wrath."

Slim squinted at the cats. "They're dadburn green, Mister Oz, not pink. Ain't they ripe?"

"Again, it's the effect those glasses had on your eyes, Slim," said Diggs. "Everything here in Smithersonville really is red. So cats, do we have a truce, or do I have to sic my attack piglets on you."

"We were only funning," said the kitten on Lothicia's shoulder. "The three of us will be glad to show the piglets around. And you, Lothicia, have our feline word of honor, that there will be no snacking on piglet chops."

Frederick stuck his head out of Diggs' pocket. "Oz, we will go look around with the cats. For some reason, I trust them."

Abraham popped up. "Say, kitties, are any of you Jewish?"

The lead cat asked, "What's that? Is it good to eat?"

All the piglets crawled out of Diggs' huge two pockets. The three kittens leaped down and all the animals sauntered off into the depths of Smithersonville village. "Say boy-chick cat," asked Abraham. "Does anyone here have any herring?"

Lothicia reached up and grabbed Diggs by his coat. "Please, Great Oz, honor us by staying at my home. I'm considered the best cook in Smithersonville."

"Thank you, my dear," said Diggs. "But my back is still killing me from the small beds in Roundstone. I should have taken Ku-Klip up on his offer of a full-sized tin bed. It couldn't have been any more uncomfortable. I'm going to invite myself back to the home of the Quakerman twins. Not only can they work at being my royal guards, but they have a large enough bed for me to get a good night's sleep."

Diggs bent way over, smiled paternally at her, and kissed Lothicia on the cheek. He whistled and walked towards the lakefront. Diggs turned and looked up at the hill. He smiled. "We have nearly completed the outside walls of the palace," Diggs murmured.

It's only week four, he thought, and soon I'll have a place to live. Although, I have to admit, rooming with my future subjects proves interesting. Have to continue to do little things to make them think I'm a powerful wizard. And what do I do when those damn witches show up?

Diggs arrived at the lakefront and turned to the left. He soon came to the home of the Quakerman twins. Diggs looked up at the sun, then down, and saw the position of where his shadow lay. It must be about two in the afternoon, he thought. He pulled out his pocket watch and confirmed it. "The boys are probably still in bed," he muttered to himself.

A tall head popped out of the house's window. "Ahoy, Oz!" yelled one twin. "What brings you here this early?" A tall red nightcap, with its tip hanging out of the window and almost touching the ground, adorned the head sticking out. The cap's tip was just slightly shorter than the man's red beard.

A second head materialized. "Brother, the shame! You're not completely dressed!" The first twin pulled his head back into the window and came out a moment later. Now he wore an eyepatch over his left eye. The second twin wore an identical patch, but no nightcap.

"I was hoping to bunk again with you gentlemen," said Diggs. "Most of the other beds in the Quadling village are just too small and you can continue practicing being my royal guards. Never know when the witches will show up."

"We'd love to have you, Oz," said one twin. "Just need to get rid of a few things."

Both twins pulled their heads back in and immediately loud voices clamored. A confused look spread across Diggs' face. The argument appeared to come from the rear of the twin's house, so he headed that way. His concern turned into a smile as Diggs saw five scantily clad women exit from the back door.

"I see why you're awake so early," said Diggs.

"Err, they are just our housekeepers," said one twin.

"Right…" replied Diggs.

Chapter Forty-Two

Diggs had a gigantic smile on his face. "I would like to bunk with you both for the next couple of weeks, if it wouldn't put you out? I hope I didn't chase out your companions permanently?"

"Nah, they're just some friends," said Quall. "They'll be back again."

"Yah," said Quint. "We're popular with the Quadling ladies. They love our large, err… feet."

His brother winked and poked him in the side.

During the next three weeks, construction on the palace's exterior crept ahead at a snail's pace. The interior development was nonexistent. Between Diggs lack of engineering knowledge, absolutely no help from the villagers around the new city and either boredom or pure mischievousness on the behalf of the flying monkeys, little got done.

"No, no, no, Nikko," said Diggs. "Your band can't put the outside walls together with stone, mortar and poop."

"I'm sorry, Oz," said Nikko. "They're not used to doing the same chore day after day. I will talk to them, again."

"Shipment coming in," yelled a voice.

From the direction of the setting sun, came a bevy of four dragons towing huge carts. They landed, wisps of smoke leaked out of their nostrils, and immediately the beasts complained. "Untie me," said the lead creature. "It's past time for my smoke break."

Five monkeys and four Ozians rushed up and unleashed the dragons. Then the group began to unload the carts.

"Looks like another load of furniture," said a short man from Winkieburg. "Some tiny blue beds from Munchkin country, red chairs from the Quadling area, and yellow bathtubs from my neck of the woods. Nothing again from Gillikin country, don't they have furniture up there? Some of the lots a might small, but the rest look comfortable."

"They look fine for a Winkie," said Diggs. "But everything is just too small for myself. Oh, just put it in storage 'til I sort everything out."

"Pretty color on the chairs," said a woman from Smithersonville. "Not real green, though. And you haven't gotten us ladies' green cloth yet, oh Great Oz."

"I'm working on it," said Diggs. "I'm building an entire city here. Give me a break."

The next day bloomed with several Quadling men talking about taking the day off to drink. Several Munchkin men wanted to dance instead of work, and all the Gillikins wanted to hunt. The flying monkeys stood around, scratched, and screeched.

"No, work first, rest later," said Diggs. He reached up to pull out some hair, but stopped when he remembered how little he had left.

From the direction of the rising sun, came a new procession. Three flying objects and a huge rambling man. As everything came closer, Diggs saw that the flying things were carpets belching black smoke. On two of the rugs were blue garbed men, and the third piled high with equipment of sorts. The slowly walking fellow easily kept up with the flying carpets and it appeared to be a ten-foot-tall metal man. The carpets hovered over the partially constructed palace walls and then settled in for a four-corner point landing. Dust flew into the air.

"Are you the Wizard?" asked the first Munchkin man. He reached over and pushed a switch in the middle of the flying carpet. The rug gave out one more belch of smoke, rose two inches, and then settled to the ground. The man wore traditional blue Munchkin garb, with a mis-buttoned shirt, sagging pantaloons revealing blue polka dot boxers, and a poorly tied bow tie. On the top of his head sat the largest pair of eyeglasses Diggs had ever seen.

"Yes," said Diggs. "I'm OZ, who are you and what the hell is that?" He stared at the two men and then pointed at the mechanical metal man.

"I'm Rodolpho," said the first man. He pointed to the second carpet. "And that's Alfonzo. We're interns from the firm of Tinkers and Evers. Our masters said we're worthless, but we know how brilliant we are in engineering. We wanted to see the Emerald Citadel project."

"It is the Emerald City, city not citadel," said Diggs. "How in the world did you hear about this?"

"News travels fast in Oz," said Alfonzo. "Especially when a hoard of noisy monkeys are mining granite next door to one of our work sites."

Diggs walked over to the first carpet. "But why are you here?"

"We've been summer engineering interning, with the firm for two hundred years," said Rodolpho. "But all I do is get them coffee."

"And all I do is stoke up the flying carpet's boiler every day," said Alfonzo. "And then vacuum the rugs every night."

"So, we sort of borrowed some equipment," said Rodolpho. "Checked out three rugs, stole Herbert, and here we are. We came here to see if there was anything we could do to help with the project."

"But how can interns help?" said Diggs. "And what is this huge metal thing? Who is Herbert?"

Alfonzo held up a T-Square and pointed with it. "We're engineer interns from the finest firm in the land of Oz. We want to help you build the Emerald Citad, err… City." He turned and pointed at the metal man. "That's Herbert. We're experts, here to help build. Now, where are your blueprints?"

Rodolpho bent over and yelled at his partner. "No idiot, this is for the Emerald City. Therefore, they must be greenprints. Alfonzo, where did I put my glasses? The metal man is our fifteenth generation of Tinkers and Evan's, mechanical man. He can do any heavy lifting for your new city."

"Is that similar to the metal man you gave the old king, Pastoria?" said Diggs. "Ortho, fly over to the gondola and bring me the large burlap sack. I want to show these men some history."

The old monkey flew off and returned in just a few minutes. "I think this is the sack that has more in it than potatoes."

Diggs reached in and pulled out the rusty mechanical arm. "This was part of a metal man with an ancient plaque attached to it."

"Amazing," cried Rodolpho. "I think that is part of the original, prototype man. Over six hundred years old. What else is in that sack?"

Diggs next pulled out the Illusion Maker. "This is what I used to create a model of the future city. I was afraid the Illusion Maker might wear out, so I put it back in the sack to give it a rest. I'll show you the exact replica tomorrow again." Diggs held the tinker box up to his mouth. "Fire." A ten-foot crackling, smoky flame appeared.

"Wow," said Alfonzo. "An antique Illusion Maker, it looks second or third generation. The bosses are now in their thirty-third generation. The newest box projects images that are realistically 3-D, moves, communicates, and responds with you, and then becomes alive after a simple spell is spoken. We could have brought several more up-to-date ones, if we knew how primitive the facilities were here."

Finally, Diggs took out the last tinker box. He held it up and Rodolpho stared at it.

"I have never seen one of those, except in the Tinker Museum," said Rodolfo. "The display label on it is Loud Voice Box. Totally worthless, except to scare small children."

"I'm looking forward to you two and Herbert helping to build our city," said Diggs. "There will be lots of heavy work for the mechanical man to do."

"He will be helpful," said Alfonzo. "And Tinkers and Evans build them to last. Guaranteed for a thousand years."

"Wonderful," said Diggs. He smiled, walked over, and patted Herbert on the back.

The metal man's arm fell off.

Chapter Forty-three

Immigrants began to arrive from all parts of the Land of Oz. Masons, accountants, carpenters, administrators, fabric designers, seamstresses, and even a master gardener poured into the city. The only country poorly represented was Gillikin country. The populous of the outlying villages swelled from approximately four hundred inhabitants to over a thousand.

Diggs lectured to a small group of Ozians and some flying monkeys in front of his almost constructed palace. He spread his arms wide. "Now that the palace is getting completed, we need to build many more homes inside the walls of the city." Diggs took off his top hat and pointed with it. "Make sure that they arranged the houses around the huge central garden and town square. Have the administrative buildings off to the side of the square. I want lots of places for my people to sit and enjoy themselves. Build a giant fountain and swan pond in the garden. I want lots of restaurants and bars." He put his hat back on his head and picked up some emeraldprints.

The Ozians cheered, the monkeys hooted, and everyone dispersed, except one. A very round woman dressed in red minced up to Diggs, sniffed, and said, "Master Oz, I need a moment of your time. The situation just will not do."

"Excuse me, madame," said Diggs. "Who in the world are you? What are you talking about?" Diggs looked down from the enormous pile of papers he was going over, to the rotund woman. She's as wide as she is tall, he thought.

"I am Madame Fritchecka Titterman. Don't let this hideous green leprechaun hat I'm wearing fool you, I am as Quadling as they come. The hat is in honor of the new Emerald City. Sir, I'm the foremost garden designer and landscape architect in all of Oz. Why Glinda the Good herself, had me design her magnificent rose garden at her palace. I decided to plan your Emerald City garden and it will be spectacular. But everyone says, you want green flowers, especially roses. Where do you expect me to find those?"

"By gosh," thought Diggs. "My new garden designer looks just like a ripe tomato." He replied, "Madam, we will find them."

Transplanted from all parts of Oz were hundreds of lunchpail trees. Even more empty pail seeds, were placed. Diggs proclaimed that all inhabitants of the city could have a variety of meals every day. The dragon and Flying Monkey poop made the trees grow like wildfire, and the mature trees produced hundreds of lunchpails. The central garden was as spectacular as Madame Titterman said it would be. There were thousands of perennials planted and staged, so hundreds were constantly in bloom. None of the flowers were green.

The masons, carpenters, Herbert, and seamstresses sped up the completion of the Emerald City significantly. Unfortunately, the accountants, administrators, the two engineer interns and the mischievous Flying Monkey band slowed everything down severely. The construction did progress.

A high wall with only one central gate enclosed the city. Rodolpho stared at the central entrance. "Oz, we need a drawbridge and a moat."

Diggs sighed. "We're not having a moat, and with no moat, we don't need a drawbridge."

"Then at least a barbican above the central tower and a portcullis on the gate," said Rodolpho. "Those would be so amazing."

Diggs scratched his head. "Look I'm not an engineer. I don't speak your language. What is a barbican or a portcullis?"

"A barbican is a double tower above our gate or drawbridge. The drawbridge that you won't let me have." Rodolpho pouted.

"And a portcullis?"

"A heavy grating that can be lowered down grooves on each side of a gateway to block it. It will help keep invaders out."

Diggs shook his head. "I doubt our enemies will knock at our front door." He trembled. "When they attack, and I'm sure those witches will come someday, they will probably come by broomstick or flying chariot. Those structures won't keep them out. No to both."

The leprechauns found a few more emeralds and then pried up the inner cities' road way of gems. They embedded these jewels everywhere on the outside walls, making it a true Emerald City.

The palace had four tall towers, one at each corner. Flying high over each tower was a representative colored banner from each one of the countries of Oz. They erected a tall pole at the highest point in the center of the palace, and a flag with the four different colored countries with a green city emblem in the middle flew daily.

During the first year, in order to prove he was a benevolent ruler, Diggs came out on the palace's balcony and made his first decree. Years prior, he had learned from a fellow con man some tricks of rhetoric. Using long sentences, the rhythms would put the audience into a mild hypnotic trance. This would make everyone more susceptible to his message.

Diggs raised his arms. "My fellow Emerald Citizens, I stand before you a humble wizard, nay, a humble man, who wishes only the best for all of you. My first proclamation as your new ruler is that all money is banned and everyone in the city can ask for and receive any commodity they wish. Happiness and prosperity is the new order of the day."

Diggs turned to Ortho and said under his breath. "They don't realize that for the past hundreds of years, everything already was on the barter system and little money in Oz has circulated."

The inhabitants of Emerald City loved the "new" system, and the word spread rapidly throughout the land. A few Ozians became lazy and didn't contribute to the economy, but most grew bored and happily continued to work at their previous occupations. The entire land quickly became more united under the barter system.

During that year, something continuously pulled away Diggs from his supervisory duties, from trying to prove to his subjects that he was a great wizard. He pulled the poor nine tiny piglets out of his sleeve and made to appear, and disappear repeatedly. When the two interns were elsewhere, Diggs used the Illusion Maker and his adequate ventriloquism skills to fool the Emerald City inhabitants. However, people were becoming suspicious that he was a humbug and he mostly stayed hidden in the growing palace. The piglets always ruined the 'magic' by talking inside his coat sleeve, and even Bort often noticed his lips were moving during ventriloquism shows.

During the second year, most rooms in the palace, local homes, and all city buildings became furnished with adequate, although small, furniture. Diggs proclaimed he abolished the Furniture Tax. The people of Oz loved the powerful ruler. There still was no word from the witches.

Diggs knew he was a better ruler than a wizard. He knew during his third year that he would have to con the Ozians and even the evil witches into believing that he knew real magic. Diggs sent out a proclamation that anyone in Oz could come and benefit from his powerful spells, but by appointment only. He would see one person weekly with a problem. Diggs specialized in his 'elixir of confidence', 'amulets of good luck', and 'thinking cap of intelligence'.

"Now Winfred," said the wizard. "You're worried that no one likes you and you can't get a good job. Drink my 'elixir of confidence'."

The slouched over, disheveled, Munchkin man drank the green lake water. "Did it work?" The young man frowned, showing rotten teeth, and wouldn't even look Diggs in the eye.

"Work." proclaimed Diggs, while he grabbed the man's shoulders and pulled him more upright. "Why, you just radiate confidence. Now stand up straight, push out your chest, put on a new clean outfit, see a dentist, and go meet some girls. Tell them, in the future, the wizard will have to rescue all Munchkin women from this handsome, confident man."

Winfred straightened fully, threw out his chest, brushed back his greasy hair, strutted, beamed, looked right into Diggs' eye, and exclaimed. "Yes, I feel it worked. Thank you Great Oz, thank you wizard! I'm going to tell everyone how powerful you are."

Diggs smiled and waved him out of the throne room. His held breath exploded out. "Whew, that man's breath! And I can't believe how rotten those teeth are."

Quint Quakerman knocked and entered the throne room. "Wiz, those five-leaf clover good luck charms are giving me and my brother problems. Two of the leaves keep falling off."

"I have to use a better glue," muttered Diggs under his breath. He stared at the Quadling. "Aren't they still giving you good luck?"

"Oh, they're working fine," said Quint. "My brother, and I had dates with four ladies each, every night this week. One from each country." He scratched his head. "At least I think the Gillikins were women. They had longer beards than we have, great tits though."

Diggs stared incredulously at the man. "You and your brother sleep with four women at a time and every night during the week?"

Quint shrugged his shoulders. "Yeah, no big deal. By the way, Bort is worried the 'thinking cap' you gave him is not working. He is still having trouble remembering which end of the arrow attaches to the bowstring."

"Isn't he more successful hunting?" said Diggs. "The cap should be making him more wise."

Quint nodded. "Yep, he finally figured how to hunt bunny rabbits without getting hurt. I think Spot gave him some pointers?"

By the end of the third year, it petrified Diggs that he had heard nothing of the wicked witches. He assumed Mombi was just always drunk and overworking Tip, but it still concerned him about the lack of response from the other two.

The group of five exiled flying monkeys had changed their minds and decided to live in the Emerald City. Diggs took advantage of their presence and sent them to the different areas of Oz to act as scouts and his representatives.

One monkey reported back that in the East, the wicked witch was oppressing her subjects. The Munchkins didn't consider themselves slaves, but they weren't happy. In the West, the witch had enslaved all the non-Winkie citizens and used them to build her a massive castle. The Winkie human population had risen up once to oppose the evil one, but she beat them back. In the South, Glinda was gaining magic power, but was becoming an isolationist. Her subjects said she rarely left her castle. All she did was try to improve her magic abilities and read from her 'Book of Records'. It frustrated her that many of her earlier spells were wearing off and were not effective anymore. One monkey also visited the Giant

Chasm Dragon, who told the messenger that the dragon craved another good fight. Diggs could call the dragon at any time.

Nikko and the rest of the band of Flying Monkeys left after completion of the city. As they flew off, Nikko yelled, "Remember Oz, you have one wish left." They left a ton of monkey manure behind.

"Diggs," said Ortho while scratching his rear. "The situation in the west is becoming dangerous. I had lunch with Monroe, the leader of the witches' flying wolf band, an old friend. He said the witch barely beat back the human citizens of Winkie country. She wants the magic Flying Monkey Cap to enslave all the Winkies. Theodora will come for it."

"I still have one wish left," said Diggs. "It'll do her no-good 'til I use it up."

"Not true," said Ortho. "Whoever holds the cap, controls the monkeys, whether or not the wishes are exhausted."

"Damn." Diggs scrunched up his face. "Then I better make sure she doesn't find the cap."

Ortho started to unfurl his wings. "You better do more than hide the cap. I'm sure she'll come for it someday. With or without her army." He flew out the window.

Diggs pried himself out of his undersized Quadling bedroom chair and began pacing. He decided they needed an Emerald City standing army to defend the walls and palace. Diggs rang for his Imperial Guards. After only an hour and one half, Quint and Quall sauntered up, both chewing on huge roasted turkey legs.

"You flmmpf, flmmpf, flfff," said Quint through a mouthful of food. He swallowed. "Paged us, sire?"

"Hey," said Quall. He pointed his breakfast at this brother. "I'm on call today. I should have answered."

"I am," said Quint.

"No, me."

"Stop!" yelled Diggs. "You two bicker more than the hens in a chicken coop. I need the opinion of both of you, anyway. We need an army as soon as possible. You two will be my generals."

"Can't do it, Great One," said Quint. "I have a terrible pirate injury, lost an eye, can't fight." He pointed to his intact face, which was without his usual eyepatch. "Damn, forgot my patch again."

"Same as I," said Quall. This brother was wearing a patch over his left eye. "Also, can't stand the sight of blood, especially my own."

From out of the tin house in the room's corner, crept one of the tiny piglets. The swine was dressed in full armor and helmet and had a sword strapped on its back. The piglet stood up. "We'll be your army."

Eight more piglets and twenty kittens came out, all dressed identically. "We're all ready to make those varmints dance," said a different one. "Sure wish I had me a shootin' iron instead of these pig stickers."

"Slim, I assume," said Diggs. "Why are you and those cats dressed like that? And where did you get those weapons?"

"Whal," drawled Slim. "Before Ku-Klip went back to his forest, he made us this here tin armor and weapons. The kittens of Smithersonville agreed to join us. Besides, they said, there was no risk to them. They say they have nine lives. Ku-Klip also made a slew of tin trumpets. We could use them as warning signal devices."

"Great idea," said Quint. "My brother could go up on the walls and blow one. He's full of hot air."

"Very funny," said Quall. "Yeah we'll do signals like, one blast by land, two blasts by lake."

Diggs nodded his head. "A fine idea. But I feel we need something a little more complex. We could base it on the semaphore flags that I have in my gondola. Or maybe use the code invented by Mister Samuel Morse."

"Hey, Wiz," said Quint. "You know this code thing-a ma-jig thing?"

Diggs shrugged his shoulders. "No, it wasn't around that long before I came to Oz. I know a little of it and we can change it. I'll work out the details later, maybe two short blasts, one long for invasion. Three short, two longs for city fire. And so on. We could have one person from each country stand on the parapet watch towers, right next to their country banners. We just have to make sure they know the codes by heart."

"We can try to blow the horns," said Frederick. "But I'm not sure we could see over the railings."

"Thanks for the offer, little ones," said Diggs. "You just stay indoors in case of attack or foul weather. You and the kittens are a little tiny for a standing army."

"You still need someone to fight," said Quint. He motioned to his brother, and both started tip-toeing towards the door.

Diggs waved to the twins. "Wait men. One of you go, find what's-his-name from Munch village. You know, the hunter? I'll ask him a question. The other twin, find Ortho and tell him to come here for a mission in the North. We'll find some fighters up there."

Quall turned back. "What fighters? Mombi would never give up her guards."

"Not them or the glass statues," said Diggs. "We'll recruit manticore hunters from the forest. They must be really fierce?" He looked off in the distance, sighed, and crossed his fingers.

Chapter Forty-Four

Quall brought Bort and Spot quickly to Diggs' chambers. Ortho returned to the window as well. The wizard walked up to the hunters. "Where can we find the fiercest manticore hunters in the Gillikin country?"

"No idea," said Bort. "I try to avoid dangerous places like that."

"Coward," said Spot. "Without a doubt, you'll find them in the Gugu Forest, in the Northernmost portion of Gillikin country, and home of most ferocious beasts in Oz. There are manticores, lions, tigers, bears, giant leopards, Kalidahs and worse of all, invisible giant bears."

Bort began trembling. "No Spot, don't even talk about Kalidahs! And I think invisible giant bears don't exist in Oz anymore."

Diggs turned to talk only to Spot. He raised his eyebrows. "What is a Kalidah? How can bears be invisible?"

Spot shuddered. "Kalidahs are huge, monstrous, and fierce beasts. They have bodies like bears, heads like tigers, with claws and fangs so long and sharp that they could rip anything in two."

"And you found these in Gugu Forest?" said Diggs.

Bort began whimpering. Spot patted Bort on the head, then stroked his cheek. The weasel looked Bort in the eyes. "There, there, they won't ever get you. The Kalidahs are so territorial that they rarely leave the forest. They are so fierce that when two come together, no matter if even one is a male and one a female, one usually dies. I do not know how they ever have sex and reproduce."

"And these invisible bears, are they extinct?" said Diggs.

Spot continued, stroking Bort's cheek. "No, they now live in the Valley of Voe. Centuries ago, one of the Rainbow fairies took what made them invisible, dama fruit, and transplanted it out of Oz. Too bad, the fruit was delicious, but it probably saved a lot of Gillikin lives, because all the bears left, following the scent of the fruit."

Diggs muttered to himself, "This place gets weirder and weirder. The Gugu Forest still has enough fierce beasts that there might be hunters in it?"

Spot shook his head. "Actually, the beasts wiped out all of them, but one. The strongest and fiercest of all hunters."

Diggs turned toward his monkey companion. "Ortho, I want that man to be the general and leader of my armies."

Bort winced. "You'll never find that person if you are looking for a powerful man."

"Why in the world not?" said Diggs.

Bort hung his head and then looked up. "Cause the mightiest and fiercest hunter in all the Gugu Forest is my mommy."

Diggs dispatched Ortho, and the monkey flew out the window. Bort bolted for the door, whimpering. The piglets and kittens tittered and went back into their tin castle.

"I can't face that woman," cried Bort over his shoulder as he was leaving. "She thinks I'm such a failure."

■ ■ ■

Ortho returned in four days. He was even more dusty than usual and had extremely red-rimmed eyes.

"Man, can that woman drink," said Ortho. "I thought I could hold my liquor. She drank me under the tree stump and apologized that her batch of Ozshine was weaker than usual."

"When is she coming?" said Diggs.

"Well, that is a slight problem. On the day I left, I was not only super hung over and couldn't remember my name, but she still hadn't given me a straight answer."

Diggs painfully extracted himself from another miniature Munchkin bedroom chair. "Then I want you to go back and get an answer from her."

Ortho trotted for an open window. "I will not go back. My liver wouldn't take it."

Diggs shook his head and sat in the chair again. "Naw, this damn seat is so small, the floor is more comfortable." He had just settled down on the floor, when out of the tin castle marched a parade of piglets and kittens.

"Hup, two, three, four," cadenced Frederick, the head piglet. "Tiny bubbles in my beer!"

"Tiny bubbles in my beer!" replied the rest of the troops.

"Makes me happy," yelled Frederick. "And full of cheer. Sound off, one, two."

"Three, four!" they all whooped. The entire company did an abrupt right face.

"Company," commanded Frederick, "Halt!" The group stopped in perfect unison. "First Lieutenant Slim, inspect the troops."

"Yes sir, Captain," yelled Slim. "Private Benno, your shoes ain't shined."

"We're not wearing shoes, Captain," said Benno. "We have trotter hooves, Sirrrr…" The piglet shook his head and shrugged. "You idiot," he muttered under his breath.

Diggs burst out laughing.

"Oh, right," said Slim. "Now Master Sergeant Tom of our Kitten Korps, why are your men out of uniform?"

The twenty kittens were outfitted identically to the piglets. They all wore tin armor and helmet scabbards on their backs and crossed swords in them. But the cats were all wearing green spectacles. Ten of the felines wore perfectly fitting specs, ten others wore a mismatch of ill-fitting or oversized goggles.

The sergeant stepped forward and saluted. "Begging your pardon sir, but it confused my troops when you kept saying, 'don't attack 'til you see the green of their eyes.' We thought the green spectacles would help us out. We've only had them on for three days."

"Remove them immediately," yelled Slim. "They aren't part of our Oz battledress!"

Tom stood straight and saluted again. "Kitten Korps, attention! Present paws and remove your spectacles." He pulled off his goggles easily. "Damn sir, everything is still green."

"Doesn't surprise me," said Frederick. "We also all wore the green specs for three days and even now only see green, and that was years ago. Now Communications Specialist Abraham, report."

The piglet pulled out a long parchment from a fanny-pack. Abraham read, "We have determined the coded warning blasts. There will be three shifts of scouts for each tower. They will know by heart the different signals for attack on the city, witch coming, hail storm, tornado, earthquake, city wide fire, and attack by killer bunnies. Bort from Munch insisted on that last one. But Oy Vey, those two Imperial Guard twins, can't remember any of the signal blasts at all. I'm not sure they should guard the city at the main gate."

Diggs slowly stood up from the floor. "My royal guardsmen are loyal, just a few cards short of a full deck. How are the scouts doing?"

Abraham shook his head. "The scouts are the worst trumpet players I've ever heard. I still think we should have had Ku-Klip make us ram's horns—shofars—instead." He twisted the report into a long tube, with a curved end, and pretended to blow into it. "Those are really easy to sound blasts, short or long."

From the directions of the north tower came two long blasts, a squeal, and then two short blasts. Then repeated two more times, but without the squeal.

Abraham's ears perked up. "Great, that coded signal is not in our repertoire. What does it mean?"

Everyone in the room rushed to the window facing North. Flying towards the city was a person on the back of a huge black beast with a human head. Four identical creatures were flying next to the first, each one attached by a leash which appeared to be a dense chain.

The group flew up to the main gate, and the rider addressed the Imperial Guard, who manned the entrance bellowed, "Is this the Emerald City?"

Diggs stared down at the five beasts. They all had the head of a human, the body of a lion, and an enormous tail of venomous scorpion. The heads were arguing with the person riding on the central beast and among each other. While they were yelling, Diggs could see triple rows of teeth in their huge maws. Vast amounts of drool dripped from their mouths.

Diggs saw Quint wave the group through. "My courageous guard," he said to the room. "Quick, everyone hurry to the throne room." Diggs turned and went back into the room.

The wizard sat on his throne and heard booming footsteps trudging up to the fourth floor. Entering the room was a short, purple dressed person. A long purple beard and pigtails touched the floor. Diggs thought there were breasts under the newcomer's fur tunic. The woman carried a double-headed axe that was as tall as she was wide. On her waist was a huge broadsword, and on her chest was a bandolier containing a dozen daggers and two huge pistols.

"I am Oz," said Diggs. "I assume I have the pleasure of addressing Bort's mother?"

"So my idiot son is here," bellowed the woman. "Your flying monkey didn't mention that, just that there might be a dangerous fight. I am Ursula, the Unfearful. I brought five of my pets and some toys to help." She raised her axe, brandished it, and then sang at the top of her lungs, "Death is life! One should die as they have lived!"

The nine piglets squealed and ran out of the room.

Diggs flinched at the sight of the axe. "Welcome? So you'll help fight the witches?"

Ursula pulled out one pistol and discharged it into the ceiling. She continued to sing, "The brave man shall fight and win, though dull his blade may be."

Diggs stared at her and scratched his head. "What the hell does that mean, and why are you singing?"

"You asked me to come to the Emerald City to fight," screamed Ursula. "My tame manticores should be helpful. Better to die with honor than live with shame."

The manticores and kittens jumped up and down with excitement. Diggs grimaced and frowned. He looked at the bullet hole in his ceiling. "I hope there will not be any dying, so you'll protect me? I'm not sure I can rely enough on my fighting piglets."

"Those cowards?" stated Tom Kitten. "That's a joke, Great uniforms tho. Hey wiz, anyone knows what we should do with all these green glasses?"

Ursula spread her arms wide and pointed out the window. "Why is this tiny place called the Emerald City? Except for a few emeralds embedded on the outside walls, it's not as green as those spectacles on the felines?"

"Of course, I now know how to remedy it!" exclaimed Diggs. "I hereby make an edict. Everyone entering or even viewing the city must wear a pair of my magic green glasses for three days."

"That which has a poor beginning is likely to have a bad ending," Ursula stated.

Diggs grabbed one pair of glasses from a kitten. "No, it will work! We'll rotate the specs among the populous until all the inhabitants have worn them long enough. Also, I'll have Quint or Quall stationed at the main gate with spectacles. Anyone entering must comment on the color that they see the buildings are. If they say anything but green, they must have glasses placed before entering. After three days, everyone will see green."

Chapter Forty-Five

Several weeks later, Diggs turned to a supplicant, yawned, and handed her one of his 'magic items'. "Now remember, young subject, luck is how you make it."

A teenage Winkie girl looked down at her new five leaf 'good luck' clover, smiled, and curtsied. "Oh, thank you Great Oz, thank you."

Diggs got up from his throne and headed for his bedroom. As soon as he entered, he saw Rodolpho sitting on the floor in front of a pile of nuts and bolts. There was a dense, dark cloud of smoke coming out of a very familiar looking rectangular box.

Rodolpho threw his hands up in despair. "I know I can fix this. And then I'll make it work as well as one of our new ones."

A minor explosion came out of the recess of the box and pieces of metal flew all over the room. One metal fragment knocked off Rodolpho's blue hat and a second one hit him right in his safety green goggles.

Trembling, Rodolpho looked down at the wreckage of the machine. "I'm sure glad Oz is making everyone wear some kind of green glasses. They sure saved my bacon." He looked over at the tin castle in the corner. "Bad expression. Sorry, piglets."

"What the hell is going on, Rodolpho?" yelled Diggs. "You ruined one of my tinker boxes!"

Rodolpho looked up and cringed. "I'm so sorry OZ, Please don't turn me into a frog. I thought I could turn your Illusion Maker into a more modern model and I made a slight miscalculation."

Diggs bent over and picked up some rubble. "Slight miscalculation? It's destroyed! Get out!"

The junior engineer leaped up and started running out of the room. "I'll make it up to you somehow. I promise." He left the door open behind him.

The warning horn gave one short and three long blasts. "Now what the hell does that mean?" thought Diggs. "The signal is not a storm, fire, or flood?" He rubbed his chin and tried to remember what that exact warning was he set up. "Termites maybe?" He ran up the stairs to one of his towers and looked out.

From the East, in the distance, came a tiny figure. As the person flew closer, Diggs thought it was a woman, but the character remained small. The approaching body waved and shouted something unintelligible at Diggs, who was standing on the high walls, of the palace.

"What did you say?" yelled Diggs. He thought about running to his carpetbag and getting his spyglass, but figured the person would land soon enough. He weaved down the stairs, went through his throne room, and finally retreated to his bedroom. "I'll just be under my bed," Diggs yelled to the room as he slammed the door.

Suddenly, Quint Quakerman pulled open the door and burst into the room. "Master Oz, sorry for bothering you, but we're being invaded. No, not an invasion if it's just one person. What is the Invasion signal....? I seem to remember, that warning would be three shorts and one long. So what do you call it when one person only is coming? I know, we're being boarded."

Through the open bedroom window, entered a tiny woman on a broomstick. She rode the broom sidesaddle. The female wore a stunning navy-blue gown, which fell all the way to her feet. But the dress was slit so high on each side that it hung open enough that it exposed her legs, feet, and even hip bones. "Was she wearing blue panties or not?" murmured Diggs. On her head she wore a tall peaked blue hat, with a black band, and around her neck, nestled into her cleavage, was a small glowing blue stone. The woman had long black hair, a large bust, and a flawless, bronzed complexion. She looked about the same size as a small rag doll.

Quint took one look at the probable witch and bolted for the door. "I'll just let myself out." He opened the door, ran through, and left it open.

"Truce, wizard," said the woman. "I've come for peace, not war. My name is Evanora Nessarose Thropp and I'm the witch of the East." She swung her leg off her broom, displaying a lot of shapely gam. Evanora carefully held onto the broom with one hand. She looked down at her mode of transportation. "In case I have to make a quick getaway."

"Evanora?" said Diggs. "The Evil Witch of the East, the enslaver of the Munchkins, the oppressor of leprechauns, the sinister sister of the Wicked Witch of the West?"

The woman waved her hand in the air and sniffed. "All bad press. I'm really a very nice person. Besides, she's only my half-sister. Different fathers. I would be happy if it were, different mothers also, if possible. It's my sister, Theodora Elphaba who believes in slavery." She whispered to Diggs, "By the way, never call her Elphaba. It means 'greeny' and she hates it. Everyone teased her with that name as we grew up." Evanora looked thoughtful. "I think that's what turned her evil."

Diggs wrinkled his forehead and shrugged. "I'll remember that."

Evanora smiled. "Munchkins are just my subjects, not slaves." She raised an eyebrow. "I'm not evil." Evanora leered, "Just wicked."

Diggs bent way over and peered into Evanora's face. "What brings you to the Emerald City?" He also took a quick glance down the cleavage of her gown.

Evanora stared up at Diggs. "I have come to meet the new wizard who has rebuilt the Emerald Citadel. My subjects are tame enough now, I can leave them behind and not fear rebellion."

Diggs shook his head. "It's now the Emerald City. A symbol of the new united Land of Oz.

Evanora put her broom onto the floor next to her. She then reached into a tattered large purse that was slung around her shoulder and pulled out a petite chain with a glowing jewel on the end. The jewel was the size and color of a pea. "I have a small present for you, as a token to be worn around your neck, to symbolize that I stand for peace."

Diggs took a step backwards. "How can I be sure I can trust you? Maybe it will harm me?" He squinted his eyes and peered at the pea. "And not to be ungrateful. But it's so small, it would never fit. Guess, I could use it as a watch fob?"

Evanora put her hand over her heart. "I would never be dishonest and fool you." She muttered a few words and waved her hands over the chain. It grew ten times in size and became so heavy she could barely hold it. "Now bend down."

Diggs hesitated, then stepped forward and leaned over. "All right, but what is it?"

Evanora slipped the chain with the tiny pea sized jewel on the end over his head. She said the same spell and waved her hands over the jewel and it grew in size ten times. It now was a huge, glowing emerald. Dozens of identical smaller emeralds that didn't glow composed the chain. "Only one amulet of a specific purpose can exist at the same time, and this is one of my favorites. The 'Amulet of Unsurpassable Charisma.' Your subjects will now adore you. As a witch, I of course am immune to its magic." Evanora began to sweat and fanned herself with her hand. "Just be sure to not remove it. The spell wears off immediately." She now wiped sweat off her forehead. "My, my, my, I don't know my own power. This must be one of my better amulets? Why are you suddenly so infatuating?"

Diggs gloated. "I have that way, on most women. Let me pay you back for the wonderful gift and offer you a drink." He mimicked lifting up a glass and drinking. "We can toast to a long friendship."

Evanora gestured with her hand in the air, pushing the proposed drink away. "Unless your offer is a homemade witches' brew, I have to refuse. Witches don't do well with most liquids."

Diggs smiled. "I've had that reaction, to some myself."

Evanora now waved her hand. "Let me conjure up some of my favorite witches' brew."

"I have a better idea." Diggs reached down and grabbed the waving hand. He bent over and raised the hand to his lips. First, he blew fiery breath on the back of it and then laid on a deep kiss. "It is such a shame you are so tiny. I could really show my appreciation."

Evanora smiled, muttered a long incantation, and grew immediately to Diggs' eye level. She shivered. "So extremely appealing." Her gown, hat, shoulder bag, and womanly figure grew in proportion to her height. She muttered the same words, waved her hands over her broom, bent over, and picked up her enlarged vehicle. "Let me stick this under the bed."

"Won't fit. Most of the blasted furniture in my palace is too damn small."

Evanora stared down at the diminutive bed and small end table next to it. She turned and peered around the room at miniature chairs and piled up pillows and linens on the floor. She pointed to the bedding. "I bet that's where you've been sleeping?"

"Yep," said Diggs. "Our tin smith offered to make me a tin bed, but I turned him down. He made me a normal sized throne, but uncomfortable! I can't get used to sitting on the bare metal. My subjects sent me tons of furniture for the palace, but it ranges from half size to really tiny. The bed is ridiculous."

"I can remedy that," said Evanora. She spoke the same spell and began twirling around in a circle. Evanora waved her hands as she spun. She spun faster and faster. All the furniture in the room glowed and grew to Diggs' size. The witch continued to whirl. "Now all the furniture in your entire palace is your size. "Whoa, I'm so dizzy!" The witch stopped twirling and waved her hands only at the bed. It now grew ten times in size. "If we're going to party, I like to have an adequate sized playground." She then looked through the open door at the huge tin throne. The witch pointed her finger, spoke a different spell, and massive, ornate cushions popped up like mushrooms in a rainstorm. "I can't have you sprain your butt when ruling."

Diggs stared at the witch. "You are so powerful, but even more beautiful."

"Yes, my amulet is of Ultimate Beauty," said Evanora. "But perhaps this form is not to your liking?" She snapped her fingers, and she was now only as tall as Glinda the Good. Bright red hair, very pale skin, and an average body. "Or this?" The witch smiled and snapped again. Standing before Diggs was a tiny Asian woman wearing a silken beaded dragon sheath dress. She had black hair cascading to her knees and a diminutive waist and bust.

"I love the original," said Diggs. "Please return to your original form."

The witch nodded and snapped her fingers. "As you command, you charmer, you." Standing again before Diggs was Evanora in her now original, but taller form.

Diggs scooped the witch up, walked over to the door, and closed it by pushing with Evanora's foot. He then carried her over to the bed. The man nuzzled her neck as he walked. Her scent was of newly opened violets, kissed by a spring rain. Diggs gently laid her down on the bed and began to remove her clothes. He traced every inch of her skin with his tongue as he slowly peeled down her dress.

With one hand, Evanora reached up and pulled off her shoulder bag. With her other hand, she flung down her broom. "More, more," she cried. "It's been so long. But whatever you do, don't remove my amulet, or my shoes." On her feet were magnificent silver shoes. She playfully stretched out her legs. "They help me look taller."

Diggs whistled. "Interesting," he muttered, "Witches don't wear long johns or britches under their gowns."

The rest of her naked body had truly grown large in proportion to her height. Her breasts were massive, with creamy skin and large black erect nipples. Tattooed on Evanora's left hip, in blue ornate cursive writing, was 'You say Wicked like it's a bad thing'. On her right hip was, 'Merlin was here,' and directly over her mons area was a 'blue arrow' pointing down.

Diggs tore off his clothes. "Should I leave this on?" He pointed at the amulet.

Evanora emphatically nodded her head.

Diggs balled up his clothes and threw them all on the floor. Evanora looked over at Diggs' package, frowned, and wrinkled up her forehead. "Adequate, but I know a way we could have even more fun." Evanora spoke a similar incantation, and waved her hands, very close to his erection. Diggs grew another three inches in length and gained a full inch in girth.

"I am Oz, the Great and Powerful," bragged Diggs. "But if we had your sister's Powder of Petrification, I could last all night."

Chapter Forty-Six

The next morning, a pounding on Diggs' bedroom door woke him up. He attempted to swing his legs out of bed, but rumpled sheets wrapped around them. Evanora lay naked next to him, snoring. Diggs looked down at her and smiled. He wrinkled his forehead, pondered, nodded, and muttered, "I wonder?" The wizard reached towards her neck and began to lift her amulet off, but stopped when the door knocking became more frantic. Diggs pulled the sheet over the sleeping witch.

"Just wait!" Diggs yelled. "I'm coming." He freed his legs from the clinging sheets and crawled to the edge of his new bed. The mattress was so large it took him a full minute to get to the doorway side. Having to crawl over a battlefield of strewn pillows, kicked off blankets, and street clothes slowed down his process.

Diggs swung his legs off the edge of the bed and walked to his closet. He grabbed an off-white robe with a blazing pure white 'OZ the GREAT' on the back. Diggs threw it on. The pounding on the door increased in intensity even more.

Diggs cracked open the door, and standing there were Ortho and his four companion apes. Ortho was just about to kick at the door with his foot as the door opened. The associates were standing in a line and bouncing up and down.

"Wiz, we have a problem," said Ortho. "Brutus," he pointed to the smallest of the four monkeys standing next to him, "barely got out of

Winkie country alive. He was representing you there. The wicked Witch, with the help of her non-human allies, mounted a counterattack against the Winkie human citizens. The people could barely fight her off. There was an enormous loss of life on both sides. But under the yellow flag of truce, Theodora came to talk to them. If they surrendered, she would let them live. However, she stated, they would become her slaves."

"It sounds like the Winkies are outstanding fighters," said Diggs. "Wonder if some of them would like to join my army?"

Brutus went up and down on his tip-toes. He barely stood as tall as the other three ape's, chests. "During the parlay, the Winkies asserted they would rather die than become slaves. The people said they knew the wizard would save them. Theodora then laughed at the Winkies and screamed that the wizard didn't have as much power as she did. But she wouldn't take any chances and would someday come and destroy you." The ape pointed his finger and shook it in Diggs' face. "The witch said you would be too much of a coward to face her, and if you did, you'd die."

Diggs began sweating, swayed, staggered over to a chair, and collapsed down into it. "I, of course, will protect my subjects. It's just that I'm so busy right now," he blustered. "Maybe in a couple of weeks. Did the woman say when she was coming to kill me?" His voice cracked. Diggs wiped his brow with a trembling hand.

From the bed came soft snores. A silver shoe and a lot of naked shapely leg poked out from under a sheet and then got pulled back in.

"Soon, the Wicked Witch is coming soon," said Brutus. "And she said she isn't leaving 'til she gets the Golden Cap. Bah, you are nothing but a coward! I am ashamed of you. How can you not help your subjects?" He growled and shook his head. "Your people trust and believe in you." Brutus threw up his hands. "I'm going to the Chasm Dragon to see if he will help the Winkies."

"Stop, Brutus! Don't go," said Ortho. "The wizard is doing the best he can. We have to stay and support him."

Brutus stepped into the bedroom and began unfurling his wings. "You stay and help this loser. Oz, the Great and Powerful, ha. You are acting more like the Small and Insignificant." He took a running start, finished unfurling his wings, and flew out the open window.

"Please leave, everyone," said Diggs. He put his head in his hands. "I must think. And close the door behind you."

Moments after the door was gently pulled shut, a frantic pounding on it began. The knocking was even more frenzied than before.

Diggs looked toward the door. "Ortho, can't you leave a man alone?" He moaned and rocked in the chair, side to side. "Oh, damn it." Diggs got up and yanked open the door.

In the doorway was Alphonso. His fist was coming forward to knock again, and it struck Diggs in the chest. "Let me in! It's an emergency!"

Diggs rubbed his chest and winced. "What's the damn emergency? Couldn't it wait until the morning?"

Alphonso shook his hand and then rubbed it on his shirt. "That really hurt! No, it couldn't, Great One. Besides, its already noon."

"Get on with it," said Diggs. "Have a lot of reasons to get back to bed, and I don't mean sleep."

Alphonso reached into a briefcase and pulled out a sheet of parchment. "This note, this note! I doubt you can read it, it's written in old Munchkin."

Diggs signed and muttered under his breath. "I told them over and over, it's all one language?" Forcibly, he said, "Just read the damn thing out loud quickly. Now."

Alphonso held the note right up to his face. "Forgot my glasses. Let's see."

Diggs pointed to the specs sitting on his head. "Son, they're right there."

Alphonso pulled the spectacles into place. "I'm sorry I broke the wizard's Illusion Maker. I now leave to go to make amends. Signed Rodolpho Fastbottom."

"So, we have one less incompetent intern engineer," said Diggs. "We completed The Emerald City months ago."

"The problem is, he absconded with all three of the flying carpets, lots of our equipment, and he tried to take Herbert."

Diggs gave a puzzled look. "Not good, but what do you mean he tried?"

Alphonso shrugged his shoulders. "It looked like Rod had commanded the metal man to get up on a carpet. My Herbert must have stumbled off the carpet, hit the ground and one of his arms and both legs fell off."

Diggs laughed. "Can you fix your indestructible metal man?"

"Of course! Herbert is under full Tinker and Evans warranty."

Diggs waved the intern away. "Go do it and be sure to close the door on your way out." Diggs turned, licked his lips, dropped the robe to the floor, and skipped back to bed.

A gentle knocking came from the bottom of the door. Hesitant at first and then picking up slightly in intensity.

"Good God!" whined Diggs. "Am I never going to get back to bed?" He picked up his robe and walked back to the door. While dragging it on, Diggs opened the door.

The leprechaun couple, stood in the doorway. Shamus's eyes bulged out at the sight of Diggs naked front. The tiny man carefully didn't look higher, than mid-thigh. Shamus slowly took his corn-cob pipe out of his mouth and blew out a smoke ring that curled into a question mark. "What!"

His wife Martha wasn't so careful with her line of sight. "Wow!"

Diggs finished closing and cinching his robe. "Now, what is it? I'm occupied!"

"We had an appointment," said Shamus. "My wife, and I made it a month ago."

Diggs began to close the door. "Come back tomorrow. I'm busy."

Shamus put his boot in the opening. "Please, sire, you were the one who suggested we meet. I won't take up much of yer time. It's very important."

Diggs pulled open the door and noticed that Shamus had not moved his foot. "Make it quick."

"Aye sire, we be having a problem getting enough green cloth for all the Emerald City citizens. We leprechauns got our green cloth from Ireland years ago."

"Everyone in the city will get my magic green goggles," said Diggs. "That will take care of this problem. Now go."

From the area of the massive bed came a seductive voice calling, "Oscar, where are you? Come back to bed and play."

Shamus stared at the figure rising in the bed. He took another puff on his pipe and blew out another question mark.

Evanora sat up with the sheet falling to her waist. The witch waved to the tiny couple. She straightened her back, stuck out her nude bosom and made it heave. "Oh, it's some of my wee subjects." The witch made no attempt at covering up her unclothed state. "You can join us if you wish."

"Bah," spat Shamus. "We will never give in, evil one. You call us subjects, but we be slaves witch. Be careful, Oz, if you lie with this creature. She be dangerous. I'm sure sooner or later she'll give you the 'Mitten'." He took another smoke puff and blew out a pair of mittens enclosed in a circle, and a line through the pair.

Diggs stared down at both the small couple and the smoke rings. "What in the world does that mean?"

"Give the 'Mitten,'" said Martha. "Means when a lady simply discards one." She pointed at the witch, then wagged her finger at her, and both ran away from the doorway.

Diggs again closed the door and turned back. Before taking two steps, a booming, frantic knocking occurred. The wooden door jumped with each knock.

"Inconceivable!" yelled Diggs. "What now?"

Diggs yanked open the door. Standing there was one of the Quakerman twins and Ursula the Gillikin. She had yanked the Quadling way over. The royal guard was still in his night clothes, but the dwarf was in full battle armor. Ursula had the man by his ear. They both, were wearing green goggles, the twin's specs were covering his eye and the eye patch both.

"I came to make rounds and this Imperial Guardsman was still asleep at noon," said Ursula. "There was no one at the main gate and people were pouring through. Only a few were wearing your mandatory green spectacles. Patrolling the north wall were my manticores, but the only patrol on the west wall, were pigs and kittens. Now, one, your spectacle system ain't working and two, if we get attacked in any direction but from the north, we're doomed."

Diggs looked at the twin. "Why aren't you at the main gate? People must wear those green glasses for three days. And not over, a seeing eye that has an eye patch over it."

"It's too hard," whined the Quakerman. "We only have a few glasses and more inba… inhabit… settlers are coming every day. I have no idea if someone has worn the goggles for the three required days or not. By the way, Wiz, I'm going to wear these greenies for six days. I switch my eye patch from side to side and I don't want to hurt either eye."

"Are you Quint or Quall?"

"I be Quint." He whimpered, "My ear is sore." He tried to look imploringly at Ursula, but she just pinched his ear firmer.

"Quint, we're going to set up a password," said Diggs. "Whenever you or your brother passes a citizen in the city, ask them for the password."

"What do you mean? What's a password?"

"I'm getting there. And whichever of you two are manning the main gate, don't let anyone through it until you ask them the password. If anyone in the city, or coming through the gate doesn't give the correct word, hand them a pair of green glasses. No one can enter the city without wearing green spectacles for three days."

"What will the password be?" said Quint.

Diggs smiled. "I'll make it simple, even for you. The password is 'Green'." He turned his back on the couple. "Close the door behind you. I'm going to be occupied. Tell my subjects, I'm giving my all for them." Diggs began scurrying back to the bed, to the waiting witch. "If I don't survive, tell my piglets to remember me."

Chapter Forty-Seven

Months passed. Every citizen in the Emerald City wore the green spectacles for the prescribed three days. Everyone but Diggs and Evanora. They rarely left his bedroom, except to eat, or when he pretended to rule and sat on his throne. Most of the green glasses now resided in the burlap potato sack Diggs had initially brought from Pastoria's house.

One day, suddenly, the sound of a trumpet sounded in the air. Three shorts, one long blast. The royal guards stationed at the main gate scratched their heads and looked puzzled. "Do you remember what that means?" said one of the Quakerman twins.

"Don't rush me, it'll come to me," said the other. The twin cupped his ear and turned in the signal's direction. He looked way up at the wary watch Winkie in the West tower.

The warning repeated once, twice, thrice! There was less and less time between blasts.

"Oh yeah," said Quall Quakerman. "It means we're being attacked." He nodded his head.

"Yes, brother," said Quint Quakerman. "I do believe you are right."

"Attacked!" said both brothers, at the same time. "We have to close the main gate and warn the wizard."

By this time, hordes of inhabitants from the outlying villages were streaming towards the main gate of the Emerald City. Gillikins and their hunting animals carried bows and arrows and guns from gun trees. Quadlings streamed in carrying harpoons, gaffs, and kittens. Winkies carried pails of boiling oil, long sharp knives, and heavy frying pans. The Munchkins and leprechauns danced into the city, carrying nothing as weapons, but wearing their heaviest boots for stomping.

"I be the faster runner, so I'll go tell the wizard," said Quall.

"I be stronger, so I'll close the gate," said Quint.

"Actually, I'm stronger," said Quall.

"You're not!"

"Am so. Wait, we're wasting time," said Quall. "Now, I'll run."

"I'll close the gate after everyone enters," said Quint. "Of course, after they tells me the password."

"Do you have our gun?" said Quall. "And the green goggles, if they fail the password?"

"Yeah, now run," said Quint. "Here be the potato sack." He nudged the bulging potato sack with his foot. Quint next reached down and lifted his gun, peered down the muzzle and shook it. "Are you loaded or not?"

A group of purple fur dressed people and creatures came to the gate. Quint held up his hand. "Password?" He hesitantly stared at the weasels and backed away.

The entire Gillikin deployment, including the hunting animals, all said "Green" at the same time. They also pointed at the Emerald City walls while speaking. Quint let them by.

Quint didn't recognize the next group of Quadlings. "Password?"

"Huh, what?" said the person in the front. "We arrived yesterday from Mercerville. We were told to go into the green city if there was a warning signal? Is this the right place? Go to the Emerald City? Sure looks gray to me."

Quint reached down and grabbed a handful of green spectacles from the burlap bag. There were many sizes, even small ones. "Wear these for three days. Don't take them off even when you sleep. You could hurt your eyes. Now enter."

The saying of the password or the handing out of green glasses continued until the last person came through the gates. Quint put down his rifle and pulled the immense door of the gate closed. The tip of his green beard got stuck, and he yanked it free. "Ouch," he yelled as he lost several hairs. "I sure would love to know how my lovely red whiskers turned this ugly green months ago. It must've been the doing of our wizard," he muttered.

■ ■ ■

The last repeated signal died away. Diggs wrinkled his forehead, shook his head, and rummaged through his pockets for his list of what the sounds meant. He pulled out the parchment and studied it. "Oh yes, my signal for a witch attack. Yikes!" Diggs leaped off his throne, dropped the list to the ground, and ran to a window. He saw that the attack was coming from the west. The wizard ran into his bedroom and grabbed his telescope. He turned and ran up a flight of stairs to the west tower.

Diggs put the scope to his eye and saw a woman, followed by three flying wolves. Dressed in yellow, the woman wore a tall hat with a black band around it, and was carrying a large shoulder bag. "At least she isn't carrying a wand," Diggs thought. The flying wolves were constantly snarling, were the size of mastiffs and had long, pointed yellow teeth and glowing eyes. They were slobbering profusely.

Diggs pulled down his spyglass. "Hah, hah, who's in charge here. Who sounded the alarm?"

Trembling before the wizard were four Winkie men, one woman, all the nine piglets and the Kitten Korp. The woman stepped forward. "I'm in charge. Petrous sounded the alarm."

Pete beamed and strutted. "I have great eyesight. Saw them coming from a long way off, I did."

"It looks like the witch of the west is coming," said Diggs. "We have to make a stand here. I'll just remain in the back."

Diggs organized his fighters quickly. He put the Winkies first, then the Kitten Korps, and finally his piglets. The telescope shook as he lifted it up. "I'll supervise from back here. Damn, no saber, err... wand."

The witch and the three wolves landed and advanced to the tower party. "I am Theodora Cackle. I'm called the Wicked Witch of the West and I'm proud to say I earned that title. I need to speak to the man who calls himself the Wizard of Oz."

One of the Winkies walked back through the grouping, grabbed an arm, and pulled Diggs forward.

Diggs raised a trembling hand. "Err… I'm the wizard." He turned to the Winkie, "Damn it, don't shove."

Theodora looked up at him. "Hah, it's you little man? Oh well, I've come for the Golden Cap of the Flying Monkeys. Give it to me immediately and I might let you live."

"What do you mean little?" said Diggs. The witch only came up to his waist.

The witch started groping into her shoulder bag. "I'm referring to your powers. Now, give me the cap."

Diggs pointed at the watch tower group. "Never. It's hidden well, and my citizens will fight you to the death to protect it."

"Stupid move, wizard," said Theodora. She turned to the wolves. "Attack."

The Winkie woman bent down and picked up a massive cast iron frying pan. She whirled and smacked the lead wolf in the head. The wolf collapsed immediately. The other two wolves snarled, but hesitated.

"Everyone, protect your wizard," cried Diggs. He ducked behind the group.

Theodora shook her head and pulled out a handful of small containers and two small bottles from the bag. The witch peered down at the labels and threw back everything but one container.

The Winkie woman advanced, swinging her frying pan left and right like a long ball baseball hitter. All the wolves retreated, but the unconscious wolf on the ground didn't move.

Theodora opened the remaining container and took out a pinch. She threw it on the Winkie woman, who immediately petrified, still holding her pan upright.

"Yikes," screamed Pete. "Poor Lizella, she always was braver than smart. Sorry, Wiz, we have to run. We probably have some bread in the oven." Petrous yelled over his shoulder, "Men, come with me." The Winkie men bolted.

The Kitten Korp, and the nine piglets said, "We'll protect you, sire." They all advanced on the wolves.

Diggs moved behind the tiny creatures. "Advance men, don't fire until you see the whites of their eyes."

Slim pulled out his custom-tree made six-gun. The trigger guard was large enough for his hoof to fit. "OK boss, but all their eyes are green." He fired at the witch and the bullet bounced off.

"Idiot," said Theodora. "You think I wouldn't prepare? My 'Elixir of Repelling' works every time."

The kittens pulled swords and moved ahead to confront the wolves. "Surrender wolves," yelled Tom, the leader. "We outnumber you twenty to two."

"Yeah, but since Bernie, is down for the count," said one wolf. "That makes ten for each of us." He pounced and swallowed Tom kitten, whole. "Wow, that sword really smarted going down. I can't imagine how it's going to feel going out the other end."

The two wolves leaped upon the remaining nineteen kittens. Blood and fur flew. Slim backed up and shot his last five bullets at the wolves. He missed every time. Diggs stood there trembling and slowly backed up. The witch just laughed.

Diggs whimpered, "No, no, nooooo!" He staggered around in a circle.

The last kitten slithered down the lead wolf's throat. The beast burped. "Now for some pork."

Diggs screamed. "Men, I don't have my saber on me and I can't defend you. Retreat!" He turned and ran for the tower stairwell. The piglets followed.

"I'm too full to follow," one wolf whined. "We'll take a brief nap and come down later."

Diggs scampered down the stairs, and the pigs followed. The piglets ran into their tin castle. Diggs ran to his carpetbag when interrupted by a voice.

"Oscar, dear," came a sleepy question. "What's going on?"

Diggs looked at the bed. "Your sister's arrived. Get over here."

Evanora threw back the top sheet and crawled across the mattress. While on her hands and knees, she occasionally reached up and wiped sleep sand out of her eyes. The witch was wearing a new, extremely wrinkled blue dress, her silver shoes, and the amulet. "I got up for some breakfast, dressed, and then took a quick nap instead." She finally crawled off the bed and walked over to Diggs.

Through the window flew Theodora. She landed in front of them, got off her broom, and looked at Diggs. "You are not a wizard," cackled Theodora. "You are not even much of a man. If I had Mombi's wand, I'd turn you into your correct form, a weasel or perhaps a mouse."

"I'm happy to report that Mombi's wand is probably on the fritz," said Diggs with a quivering voice. He ducked behind Evanora.

"And you, my so-called sister," said Theodora. "Siding with this nothing, of a person. How could you?"

"Yes sister, I am on his side," said Evanora. "He loves me and sees my true inner beauty. He might not be a great wizard, but he is a good man. Oscar is uniting Oz fairly and isn't trying to make slaves like you."

"All the Winkies will be mine!" screamed Theodora. "I'm going to unite Oz, my way. Slavery is the way of the future of this land. Once I destroy this humbug, I'll be on my way. Now Evanora, stand with me or fall with him."

"Now ladies, said Diggs. "Can't we come to a mutual understanding?" He crouched down behind Evanora.

"I stand by my brave Oscar's side," said Evanora. "Stand up dear," she said out of the side of her mouth, down to Diggs. She looked up and stared defiantly at Theodora.

"Wizard," said Theodora. "I can't decide which of my powders or elixirs to conquer you with. Perhaps I'll use the last of my 'Powder of Petrification' and turn you into a stone statue. Yes, I still will, but it might be more fun first to use my 'Powder of True Form' and turn you into what you really are. I predict you're a snake or skunk. Then I'll petrify you and have a nice desk ornament. Of course, I'm not sure if I should waste my True Form on you. It's my rarest powder, made from ten ground up cyclops eyes." The witch cackled. "Those boys sure weren't happy with me afterwards. But it's worth wasting. I can't wait to see what you'll turn into!"

Theodora reached into her heavy shoulder bag. She pulled out three containers, peered down at her hand, and dropped two of them back. Theodora slid open the box cover, cocked her arm, and then tossed the powder at Diggs.

Diggs sprang up and pushed Evanora into the shower of the powder. The beautiful witch screamed and changed. First she shrank from being almost as tall as Diggs, to a height barely coming up to his knee. Her voluptuous figure contracted to an emaciated stick. No breasts at all were visible. Evanora's perfectly smooth, bronzed skin turned a sickly green and out popped warts all over her face, with more skin growths populating the back of both hands. She stooped over and grew a large hunchback. Stringy, greasy, black hair hung to the ground. She reeked of skunk cabbage that was left for too long in the scorching sun. Even her elegant blue gown changed into a short, ragged, filthy black sheath. On her now-shriveled legs were still the beautiful silver shoes. Evanora could barely stand on her deformed legs. Around her neck, she wore a pea shaped lump of coal.

"How could you?" screamed Evanora, in a shrill voice. "You've destroyed my Amulet of Ultimate Beauty." She spoke an incantation and waved her hands at Theodora. Evanora shouted bizarre words in a voice that was a cross between a shrieking tom cat mating and the trumpeting of a charging bull elephant.

Theodora looked at her sister with a frown on her face. "You are powerful, sister. I'll not want to test spells with you at this time. I'll return later to destroy this man." She slung a leg over her broom and quickly flew off out the window of the bedroom.

Evanora clasped her hands to her face and hid behind them. "Oh, what a world, what a world!"

"It's not so bad, honey," gagged Diggs. "You're still beautiful to me." He closed his eyes when he spoke to her. "I need your magic against your sister." Diggs whimpered, gagged again, and backed away from the witch.

"Beautiful," said Evanora. "You can't even look at me. It's all your fault! She meant the powder for you. You… you pushed me into the powder's path, you coward. I would have protected you. You fool! I hate you and will never see you again. You'll pay for this." Evanora shoved Diggs as hard as she could. He barely moved. She limped over to the bed and reached under it. The witch pulled out her broom with difficulty. It was huge in her hands. She waved her hands over the broom, and it shrunk down to a diminutive size. Evanora glanced at Diggs' groin, started to incant, but burst out crying blue tears instead. "It's not worth it."

Diggs placed his hands protectively over his groin. "But dearest, don't go."

While wobbling with some difficulty, Evanora put her leg over her broom. "As soon as I make another Ultimate Beauty Amulet, I'll return to kill you, unless Theodora does it before me. I can't live, looking like this again." She elevated on her broom and flew towards a window. As Evanora sailed out, she snarled over her shoulder, "Besides being a coward, you were a lousy lover."

Diggs hung his head. "Great, now I have two witches to contend with. This is a fine kettle of fish. How do I get out of this pickle with my skin intact?"

Chapter Forty-Eight

All nine piglets crawled out of the tin castle. The leader stood on its hind feet and faced Diggs. "Wonderful, Great Mister Oz," said Frederick. "Now there are two evil witches on your tail, so to speak."

"That one witch sure gave you the glove," said Miss Scarlet.

"Da what?" said Slim.

Miss Scarlet blushed a deeper pink than usual. "I meant the Mitten."

"Oy vey," said Abraham. "All our kitten friends are dead. Now what do we do?"

Three other piglets wailed and cried that all their kitten friends died. Tears ran down the snouts.

"I can't believe I missed hitting dem dag-nabit wolves," said Slim. "I should have saved our friends. Darn hard to aim with hooves. Sure wish I had my paws back."

"Troops, I know when to retreat." said Diggs. "I think it's time to consider leaving this land. It's too hot for us to stay. I thought Evanora was my friend, but now she's my enemy. We'll go back over the desert sands or somehow find one of those magic portals."

"Captain," said Benno. "Do you think it's time to abandon ship? What about waiting for your skinny, tall friend with the long pigtail?"

Diggs started throwing things into his carpetbag. "It pains me to leave Chang, but I have to be alive to wait for him. Piglets, pack up your things. As soon as we inflate the balloon, we're leaving."

Diggs left the carpetbag and ran up the central stairs to the Ozballooniport. The completely deflated envelope lay collapsed on the ground. He attached the opening of the envelope to the stack of the firebox, being careful not to twist or kink the skirt. He loaded up the firebox with Ozpyrite coal and patted his pockets for a match. There were none, in any pocket. Diggs held out his hands and yelled, "Ignite, Inflamo, Fire." Nothing happened. "Didn't think it would work for a humbug, but it was worth a try," he muttered into the air.

Diggs returned to his room, bent over his carpetbag, and rummaged through it for his tin of matches. "Damn, I can't find any."

The piglets were nowhere to be found. Diggs heard rustling noises coming from the tin castle.

Diggs heard a loud thud behind him. He turned and a horse with a long twisted horn in the middle of its forehead was furling its wings. The wizard spun and jumped to his feet. "Who the hell are you? What the hell are you?"

"Where's Theodora and my fellow soldiers?" said the equine. "Am I late to all the fun again? I couldn't help that the yellow clover near your city looked so enticing. I just had to have a little nibble." The equine belched. "Okay, maybe more than a little nibble. Well, no big loss. Wizard man, prepare to die."

"What, why?" said Diggs. "What do you want with me?" Diggs began backing up until he tripped over his carpet bag and landed on his rear.

"No offense," said the animal. "I'm here to kill you."

Diggs inched his hand into his open carpetbag, and the first thing located was his saber. "But why? What have I ever done to you?"

The horse lowered her head, her razor-sharp horn aimed right at Diggs' face. "The three wolves and I work for our Mistress Theodora. We always do what she tells us, if we want to keep on breathing. And she told us to kill you. You're still alive and Theodora's not here, so I have to finish the job."

Diggs slowly stood up, saber in his right hand. With his left hand, he lifted his amulet off his chest and presented it to the beast. "You don't want to kill me. I'm extremely charming."

"Sorry, wizard," said the equine. "I'm a unicorn, and only young virgins can completely charm us. You're certainly not young and from the smell in this room, you ain't no virgin." The unicorn lunged.

Diggs parried and then did a straight lunge repost. The unicorn easily stopped this counter attack. The wizard stuck downwards with the blade of the saber, but the unicorn swung her horn upwards. She blocked the saber and her horn tip flipped the amulet and chain off his neck. The magic item flew across the room, hit the wall, and the chain broke in two.

"Yikes," screamed Diggs. He waved his saber back and forth. "Help! Help! Anybody! I'm being killed!"

The unicorn lunged again, and its horn went through Diggs' left shoulder. Blood spurted and saturated his white shirt. As the beast pulled back, Diggs dropped his saber and grabbed the horn with his right hand near the unicorn's forehead. He didn't let go, and the beast began dragging him around the room. Blood streaked the floor.

"Damn," cried Diggs. "Stupid charm amulet doesn't work and Glinda the Good's protection kiss must have worn off. I thought this magic stuff was reliable."

The unicorn shook its head, trying to free the horn.

Diggs' cries for help got weaker as he lost more and more blood. Diggs lost his grip on the horn. The unicorn stepped back and pulled its now saturated horn out through Diggs' shoulder. The wizard fell to the floor into a puddle of his own blood.

The animal shrieked, snorted, stamped its foreleg, and then pawed the ground. She advanced towards Diggs, lying on the ground.

Suddenly from out of the tin castle exploded the nine piglets in full armor. One piglet raised a miniature tin ram's horn and let loose a blast. Two piglets went to each of the unicorn's hoofs and cut at them with their small swords. This made the beast dance around, as she avoided some swords by kicking out with her hind hooves. Benno and Slim went crashing against the wall. Abraham kept blasting on the horn. The beast ignored the bleeding Diggs.

The bedroom door crashed open. In poured many leprechaun men, Munchkin women, Gillikins of some sex or the other and Winkie women. The leprechauns began stomping on the unicorn's feet; the Gillikins hit her with spears, and the Munchkin and Winkie woman went over to tend to Diggs' wound. Attacking, the creature lowered its horn and swept it sideways. Abraham and several leprechauns crashed into the wall. Abraham staggered upright and continued blasting on the horn.

The unicorn bellowed, "I can't deal with you little elves. I leave." She unfurled her wings, turned, and flew out the window.

The crowd in the room cheered. "We won, for the wizard!"

Diggs moaned. "It hurts. I can't raise my arm." Blood saturated his shirt and stained his greatcoat. His face turned pale, and he started sweating.

"We must stop the bleeding," said a tiny woman dressed in blue knelt next to him. "Does anyone have any cobwebs on them?"

"No," said a rotund lady dressed in a wrinkled yellow dress. Her smiling face had streaks of white all over it. "But I always carry a bag of flour with me for baking. This will have to do." From out of her apron pocket, she lifted the bag. She pushed open the greatcoat from off Diggs' shoulder and enlarged the rip in his shirt. The woman poured flour directly into the wound.

The Munchkin lady lifted up her dress, blushed, and tore a large strip of cloth from her petticoat. She folded it and then shoved it directly into the wound.

Diggs' bleeding slowed. "Damn, that hurts! Thank you for saving me, citizens."

The Winkie woman put the bag of the remaining flour into Diggs' right front pocket. "In case you start bleeding again, sire. We would do anything for you. Flour is an old home remedy. Our Winkie men are always cutting their fingers when cooking, and flour usually slows any bleeding down. I had a bag handy cause I was in the middle of making pies."

The signal began anew from a tower, three shorts blasts and one long.

Diggs struggled to stand. "We're being attacked again." He stumbled over to his carpetbag. Diggs reached in and took out a pistol. He transferred it to his left hand. "Not sure what good it'll do, since I can't raise my arm, but we'll see." Diggs reached in and took out the other gun with his usable right arm. "Nah, this is stupid." He put them back. "I'll get them later."

"Oz!" yelled one leprechaun. "You're hurt. You can't go out there." The small green man walked over to the broken amulet chain. "Oz, let me fix this quickly. Is it some kind of protection spell? You might need it. Don't go outside."

Diggs looked down at his limp, swinging left arm. "I have to. A witch is coming for my head. And I'm not sure which witch it is." He half smiled and looked over at the piglets. "I sure wish I'd been carrying matches."

Chapter Forty-Nine

Diggs walked to the window, looked out, and heard the signal again. "Attack must be coming from the north," he muttered. "The North tower scout is always off key when blasting a warning."

Diggs almost had to crawl up the stairs, needing the support of several citizens to help him. One follower carried up his full carpetbag. "I have to see what's happening. Damn, my arm is killing me!"

Death and destruction greeted Diggs when he got to the top of the tower. There were three dead giant beasts with slit throats lying in a pool of their own blood. Acrid smoke wafted through the air, carrying the sickly sweet smell of blood, but also roasted flesh. Diggs gagged. "Reminds me of the hospital tent in Franklin," he thought.

Bodies of friend and foe littered the walls of the tower. Ursula stood at the ramparts, with a huge two-handed battle axe in her right hand. Her left arm ended a few inches below the shoulder. She had cinched a rope around the bloody stump. Ursula was smoking a massive cigar.

"Ursula!" screamed Diggs. "Go below for medical attention!" He stared in horror at the large amounts of blood dripping from her upper arm and off her axe.

Ursula quickly turned around. "Hello Oz. About time, you showed up. Nah, this minor scratch? It was lucky my fellow hunter Bernard could get a tourniquet on it, before he lost his head." She pointed to a short body, dressed in bloody purple fur, with a missing cranium. "I always fight while smoking my battle cigar. Makes me concentrate better, not having to smell the spilled guts of my enemies. This time it came in handy to cauterize my wound. Only hurt a little."

"What… What happened?" said Diggs.

A boulder whizzed by just missing Ursula's head. It crashed into the far tower wall. The thud reverberated. Diggs shook his head when he saw it was a solid gold nugget.

"Three hill giants came with Kalidahs on leashes," said Ursula. "My troops could kill one of the large folk with arrows before they could batter us severely with boulders. The second giant picked up their pets and threw them over the walls. One of the beasts got me and took off my arm." She looked wistfully at the stump. "I dispatched it with my axe. The other Kalidah killed most of my troops and two of my Manticores 'til my last Manti stabbed it. We killed one more giant with arrows, but the last one keeps peeking over the wall, and mostly just throws things."

More Oz troops entered the tower, including Diggs' Imperial Guard, Quint and Quall Quakerman, and several Winkie women. The twins ran up to Diggs.

"There you are, Oz," said Quint. "We've been looking all over for you."

Quall turned towards his brother. "Yeah, but mostly you were hiding under beds."

"Men," said Diggs. "I'm having trouble standing up. Quint, you open my carpet bag and get out my two pistols. Quall you get out my tinker Boom Box and Flying Monkey Cap. Put the cap in my pocket and just hold the box up to my lips."

Diggs staggered to the wall and looked down. Two giants lay on the ground, with a multitude of arrows sticking out of them, like large pin cushions. The last giant, dressed in ragged furs, stared right at Diggs.

Diggs turned around and gestured to Quall with his good arm. The Quadling put the Boom Box up to his lips. Diggs whispered into it and, 'I AM OZ, THE GREAT AND POWERFUL! SURRENDER OR DIE' came booming out.

A massive amethyst followed by a gold nugget came crashing into the tower. Then a snarling Kalidah came flying over the wall.

"I guess he ain't surrendering," yelled Ursula. She raised her axe over her head.

With two quick swipes, the Kalidah opened the belly of a Winkie woman and took off the head of a Manticore. A Winkie woman stared incredulously at her guts falling to the ground, and then she joined them. The remaining Manticore raised its scorpion tail and plunged it through the Kalidah's chest. The beast screamed and the Winkie woman whimpered. Both gurgled and died.

"Damn," said Ursula. "Nothing left for me."

"Quint," said Diggs. "Put one pistol into each of my hands." He grasped the guns and staggered back to the walls. Diggs was at eye level with the giant's head. He raised his right arm and fired his pistol. "Damn, I missed. His head is bigger than the envelope of my balloon, and I missed? I can't lift my left arm. Quint, raise my arm and aim the gun. Quall, come over here and reload my other pistol. Quickly, men!"

Quint lifted Diggs' left arm with a quivering hand. Diggs fired and hit the giant in the eye. The monster collapsed in a heap.

Quint jumped up and down. "We've won, we've won!"

Ursula pointed with the stump of her arm, towards the west. "I'm not so sure. Look"

Two moving black clouds covered the setting sun. The front shadow was comprised of dozens of individual shapes, constantly moving like ants covering dropped food. The second shape appeared to be one enormous dark cloud. As the shadows came closer, one tiny shape continued to cackle and scream.

Diggs could barely hold himself up. "What in the world are they?"

"The third wave attack is from the witch," said Ursula. "I thought she'd try an air attack, and those are her minions. I planned on this and had the reserves on call." She reached into her right boot and pulled out a whistle. The dwarf puffed out her cheeks and blew into the small fife. No sound came out at all. Ursula repeated the maneuver two more times.

Diggs collapsed to the floor and crawled to his carpetbag. He tossed his right pistol into the bag and limply dropped his left gun. Diggs reached into the bag and pulled out his spyglass. "Quall, put bullets into my guns while I look at what's coming towards us."

Quint screamed, "Don't bother with that scope, boss. They're almost here!" He ran over and tugged Diggs to his feet.

The men turned and saw hordes of creatures coming at the tower. "I think it's time that I called out my reserves," said Diggs. He reached into his front pocket and pulled out the magic Golden Flying Monkey Cap. He shook his head and his top hat went flying off. Diggs plopped the magic cap on his head. "Quint, get on my left side."

Quint ran over to Diggs' injured left arm. "Why boss? Um, I think dis one is your left?"

Diggs stood on his left foot, raised his right hand, and said, "Ep-pe, pep-pe, kak-ke." He switched to his right foot. "Damn, I can't raise my left hand. Quint, lift it up for me, now."

Quint grabbed Diggs' left arm and raised it to the sky. "What is you doing?"

Diggs winced. "Ouch, not so rough, with the arm. Hil-lo, hol-lo, hel-lo. Quint, keep holding up my arm." Now he stood on both feet, raised his right arm himself, and yelled, "Ziz-zy, zuz-zy, zik. You can let my arm go now, Quint."

Behind Diggs a huge breeze swirled, rattling the fallen weapons. A second gust of wind brought the sound of buzzing. Multiple thuds occurred behind Diggs, and the continuous gale force of air almost blew his cap off. Diggs turned and faced hundreds of flying monkeys. Four landed on the tower, the rest hovered in the sky.

The monkey king stepped forward and bowed. "What is your last wish, oh Great Oz? Are you going to set us free, like Ozians promised for the last four hundred years?"

Diggs swung his right arm to include all the monkeys. "My last command, err... wish, is that your clan protects me from the witch and her followers. Oh, protect the Emerald City people also, if possible."

Behind Diggs, a loud cackle resounded. He turned. "Shit, Theodora's here. Quint, raise my left arm so I can shoot her."

"You don't have a pistol, boss," said Quint. He moved next to Diggs.

Quall finished loading the dueling pistols and straightened. He tried to shove both guns into Diggs' right hand, but the wizard dropped them both.

Theodora pulled something out of her shoulder bag. "Flying Monkeys, eh? I have something here that'll take care of both you, wizard, and their king." The witch opened the container and threw the entire contents at them.

Chapter Fifty

Quint pushed Diggs to the side and the wizard fell to the ground. A yellow powder coated the royal guardian, most of it getting tangled in his long beard. The Quadling turned to stone, frozen in place, his arms held out in front of him.

"Damn," yelled the witch. "That's the last of my Petrification Powder. I'll have to go and make some more, or get something else."

"Monkeys attack!" commanded Nikko. "Kill the witch."

Diggs slowly stood up from a tumbled heap on the floor of the tower. "Oh my God, Quint, are you okay? Speak to me. What happened? Someone help him!"

Quall stood up from beside the carpet bag. He turned and looked at the statue that was his twin. Quall then bent over and picked up both guns. The Quadling lifted them, aimed at the witch, and pulled the triggers. Both bullets didn't even come close to hitting her. He continued pulling the triggers on the empty pistols while screaming, "You killed my brother." Quall threw the guns at the witch. He missed, with those as well.

The witch looked at Diggs. "I'll be back, wizard. I need that cap." Theodora reached into her front pocket of her dress and scooped a handful of powder.

Quall jumped towards Theodora.

The witch tossed the powder on herself. She vanished.

Quall came down on empty air and landed with a bump. "Where'd she go?"

Diggs ran over to the statue of Quint. "Is this the same as what happened to Pastoria? Shit, it is. Why did Quint push me out of the way? He couldn't have known the powder would kill. Could he? Why, oh why, did he do it? That stupid amulet of mine influenced him. He had to be on my side."

Quall slowly got up and walked over to Diggs with tears in his eyes. "No, Great Oz, you're not wearing the amulet. Any of your subjects would have done it. You're our ruler, our wizard, and everyone's friend."

Ursula walked over to Diggs and Nikko. The bleeding of her arm stump had slowed down to just a trickle. "Just cause the witch vanished, we're not safe yet. Theodora's air corps is just about to arrive. We're in for a proper fight. That giant cloud, is just one creature. The Imperial Roc of Oz. It was last seen flying away from Oz. I guess it came back and brought friends. Nasty wyverns, harpies, and even a cockatrice. Behind this first wave is something I never encountered before, but there sure are a lot of them. I hope our reserves get here soon."

Diggs staggered to the edge of the tower. "There is a sockdolager."

Nikko rambled up to the wizard. "We don't have enough flying troops to attack. And what kind of creature is a sockdolager?"

"It means, any large one."

From the east came a small group of flying creatures. They landed on the tower next to Diggs and Nikko. There was Ortho with three of his compatriots, six yellow Winkie dragons and five flying… dinosaurs?

Ortho walked up to Diggs and bowed. "Great Oz. We are here to fight on your behalf. I insisted Brutus see if the Chasm Dragon would come assist you before going west."

The largest of the yellow dragons landed next to Ursula. "We're here, as you requested. Now we expect time and one half benefits while we're here. Satisfactory?"

The first of the flying dinosaurs also flew up to Ursula. "Hi, I, Petey, love to help out. Nothing ever going on in my life. What for me to do?"

Ursula looked disgusted. "How about less talking, more fighting? You guys attack those monsters."

Ortho directed his three companions to go after the harpies. Nikko screamed at his group to approach and neutralize the Roc. All the yellow dragons joined the monkeys, but the Roc simply reached out with its talon, grabbed, and then ate three of the feathered dragons. The giant bird next seized one of the Flying Monkeys, and put its lifeless body in its beak, chewed once and spit it out. The dozens of Flying Monkeys continued to attack the giant Roc. But like gnats around an eagle, they were annoying, but did little harm. The last of the yellow dragons backed away. Now the Roc stopped trying to eat the monkeys. The gigantic bird burped, looked bored, and just flew away.

Ortho's two companions fared poorly against the harpies. The half-human and half-bird creatures raked one of the old monkeys across the throat, and Fritz plummeted to the ground. The troop of Flying Monkeys came to help and attacked the dozen harpies. Five monkeys killed two harpies immediately by ganging up on them and snapping their necks. Several female monkeys taunted two of the other harpies. "Nyah, nyah, nyah, you're ugly and you would never fit in." The harpies burst into tears and fled. The remaining Ortho companions and the other Flying Monkeys teamed up and dispatched any surviving harpies.

The three surviving yellow dragons approached the one cockatrice. The Winkie dragon leader called out, "You're fighting for the wrong side. Just because you have a head of a rooster, don't act so bird-brained. You're one of us, a two-legged dragon. Plus, we're going to get paid for this battle. I doubt that witch is giving you more than chicken feed." The cockatrice's eyes crossed, looked confused, nodded its head, and stopped battling.

The wyvern dive bombed towards the group comprising Diggs, Ortho, and Nikko. Nikko's gold crown made the dragon beast drool. The bipedal dragon flipped in midair and came at the monkey king, leading with its arrow-shaped tail. "I'm going to take that wonderful gold off your dead body, add it to my hoard, and then I'll stab that wizard."

Diggs screamed, "I need my pistols!"

Ortho calmly stepped in front of Nikko and watched as the wyvern's tail pierced his chest. Ortho reached down and tore the wyvern's head off its body. He pulled the tail from out of his sternum, blood gushing, and turned towards Nikko. "I give up my life gladly, you are my king." He staggered towards Diggs. "And you are everyone's ruler." Ortho closed his eyes, gasped, fell down, and died.

Nikko and Diggs both howled to the heavens. The monkey king looked down at the bloody body of Ortho. "Stubborn, but loyal to the end." Nikko turned to Diggs. "We fulfilled your last wish. My band has lost too many monkeys." He gestured to Ortho's surviving three companions. "You are now part of the troop again. You earned a place. Take Ortho's body for a decorated burial. We go now."

Diggs also looked down at Ortho's body. "How can I live after losing another compatriot? What could I've done to protect you better? Goodbye, my loyal friend." Tears ran down his face. He turned to Nikko. "But what if the witch comes back? What about that approaching vast cloud of buzzing creatures?"

"Your wishes are finished. Not our problems now," said Nikko. "We fly!" The monkeys and Ortho's corpse went towards the east.

Ursula rushed up to Diggs. "I recognized some of that last cloud. Stymphalian birds. We're doomed. And I still don't know what is making up the larger part of the cloud."

Diggs reached up to his head and pulled off the Flying Monkey Golden Cap. He turned it over once in his hand and stared fondly at it. "Ziz-zy, zuz-zy, zik. Real magic, and I can't use any more wishes. Sigh, we're going to die." Diggs looked at Ursula. "What the hell are Stymphalian birds?"

"You don't want to know," said Ursula. "But I'll give you a hint: they eat everything and are always hungry."

Shamus came bounding up the stairs with an emerald chain in his hands. "Oz, Oz, begora. I have fixed your magic thing."

Quall jumped in front of Diggs and held out his hand. "Halt! Who goes there?"

Diggs pushed Quall to the side. "Quiet, you idiot. It's just Shamus. What do you have?"

"Your amulet, sire," said Shamus. "Maybe you can charm your enemies?"

"Nah," said Ursula. "The birds will probably just eat it." She looked up into the sky. "I remember what the buzzing part of the cloud is. Giant honey bees from the wheat fields of Winkie country. They definitely look riled up. We're doomed."

Diggs bent down and let Shamus put the Amulet of Unsurpassable Charisma over his neck. He straightened up. "Team, here's the plan. My arm is useless, so I'm going to go down to my room and hide under my bed. Everyone else run down to the central area and have all the Emerald Citizens pull ripe lunchpail containers off the trees. Open them in the central garden, near all the flowers and roses. Then clear out. The birds will go to the pails, the bees to the flowers. Too bad the Woozy isn't around to feast on honeybees."

"Brilliant," yelled the crowd. "What the hell is a Woozy?"

Diggs smiled. He began trudging down the stairs.

Diggs entered his bedroom, walked over, and plopped down onto a chair. Several piglets poked their heads out of the tiny tin castle in the corner.

Frederick looked around and wrinkled his snout. "Is it safe to come out yet, wiz? It sure was noisy outside."

Diggs took a deep breath. "What the hell have you guys been eating? It suddenly really smells in here." He got out of the chair and walked to the window. "Wow, it's terrible in this corner."

"Honest, boss man," drawled Slim. "None of us et in at least an hour. I reckon' we're close to starving to death. Boy, it smells like cabbage."

"Actually, exactly similar to skunk cabbage," said Diggs. "I've smelled that odor before?"

From the corner came a disembodied voice, "You're not as dumb as I thought, Oz. I forgot my Invisibility Elixir only covers up my physical presence, not my aroma. I'm here to kill you and take the magic cap."

Diggs reached into his front pocket and pulled out the bag of flour. He lifted it to his mouth and tore off the tie. Diggs threw the entire bag at the area the voice was coming from.

A short, yellow-white flour-covered figure appeared. Diggs visualized jigsaw pieces of white flour next to invisible parts of the witch's body. A fragmentary hand dipped into an incomplete handbag. A yellow bottle came out the bag and something lifted it to a partially flour covered face. A gulping sound occurred, and green replaced the clear parts of the witch.

"Curses! I look terrible covered in flour," said Theodora. "You're clever again, wizard, but it won't save you, you charming man. I have to kill you, or do I? What is going on? Damn, my sister's amulets."

Diggs looked down at his amulet. "Wow, so this is what real magic acts like. With Evanora, I thought she loved me just for my good looks. Begone witch, and never return."

"Oz, I'll return with a powder which will overcome your amulet, and kill you," said the witch. "But I'll make you a deal. Give me the magic cap and I'll leave, never to return."

Diggs stepped back and thought for a minute. He finally handed the Golden Flying Monkey Cap to Theodora with a trembling hand. The man sighed. "Deal. I don't really trust you, but I don't have a choice. I know I'm making a huge mistake. Please, please, promise me you won't use it to hurt anyone." Oscar Diggs shook his head and frowned. "I certainly don't feel like a wizard or wonderful anymore."

Epilogue

For weeks afterwards, Diggs shut himself into his bedroom and refused to see any citizens. He even installed a cot in his throne room, behind a curtain, for the rare times he left his solitary nest. Diggs didn't hold his weekly cons of giving fake magic presents to individuals. He had the piglets tin castle moved from his room. Diggs only allowed Quall access, and that was just to bring his lunchpail meals.

"Great Oz," said Quall. "You have to come out sometime. Your subjects miss you. I know it upset you about the death of Ortho, my brother, and other Emerald Citizens, but you have to overcome it."

"Declare this edict, Quall," said Diggs. "Nobody gets in to see the wizard. Not nobody, not nohow."

Quall put down a lunchpail. "All right, boss. By the way, Rodolpho the engineer brought back an up-to-date Illusion Maker. The image will talk to you and even move. Unfortunately, the idiot can't remember the spell to make the illusion come to life. Too bad."

Diggs waved his hand lethargically. "Just put it in my throne room, behind the curtain, next to the throne."

Several days later, Quall rushed in. "Oz, the Giant Chasm Dragon, is here with hordes of his followers. He wants to know if there's anything still to fight and if not, anything to eat?"

Diggs wore the same clothes as the last time Quall had entered. His aroma was not pleasant. His sparse hair was unkempt and a beard had started. "Tell him he missed out on a great battle. His loss, ask them to leave. Politely, of course. They can eat whatever they wish, first."

A week later, a signal horn blasted. Diggs dove under his bed and trembled. Quall knocked at the door, opened it, and entered. "Guard!" yelled Diggs. "Is that the signal that the witches are attacking?"

Quall looked under the bed. "No, sire, you can come out. That was the signal for a tornado. Somewhere in Munchkin country, I believe."

Four months of solitude later, Diggs now at least was bathing regularly, combed his hair, and cut off his beard. He even occasionally tried some sleight of hand with his piglets. He still only saw Quall. Diggs wiggled and felt his tin throne still didn't have enough cushion on it. He wondered how Ozma, err... Tip, was doing? Did Tip ever have to eat that horrible concoction?

Quall, the guardian with the green whiskers, pounded into the throne room. "Oh Great Oz, you have visitors. The biggest lion you have ever seen, a living man made of tin, a tall girl in a blue and white dress, wearing silver shoes. She says she is from a place called Kansas and her name is Dorothy Gale. And the strangest of all, a living straw scarecrow who claims he knows you, and you still owe him two dollars?"

Diggs jumped off his throne and smiled. "Chang, my friend, finally!"

The End

About the Author

Scott B. Blanke is a retired Mayo Clinic surgeon. He is a member of the La Crosse Area Writers Guild and the Mississippi Valley Writers Guild and is a group leader. His interest in *The Wizard of Oz* began as a child and now, as an adult, he read the stories to his children and reads to his grandchildren. His personal collection of *Oz* titles numbers in the hundreds and he is a member of several *Wizard of Oz* clubs.

Scott lives in La Crosse, Wisconsin with his author wife. Scott enjoys gardening, specializing in exotic garlic, and amateur photography.

Note from the Author

Word-of-mouth is crucial for any author to succeed. If you enjoyed *Oscar Diggs, The Wizard of Oz*, please leave a review online—anywhere you are able. Even if it's just a sentence or two. It would make all the difference and would be very much appreciated.

    Thanks!
    Scott B. Blanke

We hope you enjoyed reading this title from:

www.blackrosewriting.com

Subscribe to our mailing list – *The Rosevine* – and receive **FREE** books, daily deals, and stay current with news about upcoming releases and our hottest authors.
Scan the QR code below to sign up.

Already a subscriber? Please accept a sincere thank you for being a fan of Black Rose Writing authors.

View other Black Rose Writing titles at www.blackrosewriting.com/books and use promo code **PRINT** to receive a **20% discount** when purchasing.

Made in United States
North Haven, CT
27 December 2021